LAST EXIT FOR THE LOST

This special edition is limited to **1,500** signed copies.

Last Exit for the Lost

Last Exit for the Lost

Tim Lebbon

CEMETERY DANCE PUBLICATIONS

Baltimore
❖ 2010 ❖

Copyright © 2010 by Tim Lebbon

The following selections were previously published: "Black" in Dark Terrors 6, 2002; "Body" in Dark Arts, 2006; "Casting Longer Shadows" in Jason & Molly/Horror Express, 2005; "A Ripple in the Veil" in Poe's Progeny, 2005; "Forever" in Mammoth Book Of Sorcerers Tales, 2004; "Hell Came Down" in The Darker Side, 2002; "In Perpetuity" in Night Visions 11, 2004; "Kissing at Shadows" in Cemetery Dance #36, 2001; "Last Exit for the Lost" in Phantoms Of Venice, 2001; "Life Rained Off" in Prism: Bfs Magazine, 2003; "Making Sense" in Cemetery Dance #44, 2003; "Old Light" in Mammoth Book Of New Jules Verne Stories, 2005; "Pay the Ghost" in October Dreams, 2000; "Skins" in Exorcising Angels, 2003; "The Cutting" in Mama's Baby, Papa's Maybe, 1999; "The Horror of the Many Faces" in Shadows Over Baker Street, 2003; and "The Stuff of the Stars, Leaking" in Children Of Cthulhu, 2002.

All rights reserved. No part of this book may be reproduced in any form or by any electronic or mechanical means, including information storage and retrieval systems, without permission in writing from the publisher, except by a reviewer who may quote brief passages in a review.

Cemetery Dance Publications
132-B Industry Lane, Unit #7
Forest Hill, MD 21050
http://www.cemeterydance.com

The character and events in this book are fictitious.
Any similarity to real persons, living or dead,
is coincidental and not intended by the author.

First Limited Edition Printing

ISBN-13: 978-1-58767-170-8
ISBN-10: 1-58767-170-0

Cover Artwork © 2010 by Edward Miller
Interior Design by Kathryn Freeman

For Mum, with love.

Acknowledgements:

With thanks to all the editors, without whom many of these stories would not exist: David Sutton, Lewis Davies & Arthur Smith, Richard Chizmar & Bob Morrish (several times over), John Pelan (ditto), Stephen Jones, Benjamin Adams, Vicky Cook, Paul Miller, Michael Reaves, Bill Sheehan, Jason Williams & Molly, Gary Fry, Mike Ashley & Eric Brown. And finally, a big thanks to Joe for such a kind introduction.

Table of Contents

Introduction by Joe Lansdale
9

Last Exit for the Lost
13

The Cutting
37

Pay the Ghost
47

Kissing at Shadows
77

Hell Came Down
91

Black
111

The Stuff of the Stars, Leaking
147

Life Rained Off
165

Skins
169

The Horror of the Many Faces
189

Making Sense
219

In Perpetuity
237

Casting Longer Shadows
335

A Ripple in the Veil
359

Forever
373
Old Light
409
Body
431
The Evolutionary
459
Nothing Heavenly
489

Introduction
by Joe Lansdale

Horror, as of late, seems to be making a comeback, and there are a number of writers working feverishly in the field, many of them inspired by the glory years of the eighties when horror was as popular as sex without condoms. It should be noted that these glory years also contained a large number of less than glorious works, and that this is the reason horror finally got sick and died a slow, withering death for a few years, but like all famous monsters, HORROR has made a comeback. Blood has been mixed into its ashes, and it has risen. Maybe not to its full height, but indeed, it has risen, and it shambles forth. And the blood that stirred and solidified its ashes is the blood of new writers. As well as that of some old pros. But the field of late seems to be rich in new wordsmiths. Some of these writers are quite good; a large majority of them are slingers of hash, or as we used to call them, ham and eggers.

Joe Lansdale

They write responsibly enough, and for those readers whose main needs in reading horror is the horror itself, which for me, in short time becomes little more than the same parlor trick gone stale, as one is easily able to see the bloody rabbit in the hat, but for those aforementioned readers who look for nothing more than who can be the grossest, they are successful enough.

I should pause here to suggest that gross is not an evil tool, but when it's the only tool, it becomes annoying. When you have a serious job to do as a writer, it's best if you have more in your tool box than a large hammer and a monkey wrench.

Some writers have larger, fuller, tool boxes.

Writers poised for greatness. Writers like Tim Lebbon.

I would even say that Tim has already dipped his toe in the pool of greatness, and the ripples have begun. The reason for this is simple. Tim Lebbon can actually write.

He doesn't just know horror fiction, he knows fiction. He doesn't just know blood and guts, though he is not afraid of that, he knows what makes one care about what happens in a story, what makes the horrors truly horrible. And it really isn't just a guy chasing someone with a chainsaw.

Tim's work is stylish and feverish, and its influences come from close and afar. He knows the field, but he doesn't just live for the field of horror. He's a man that can write anything, and I think in many cases an argument could be made that many of his stories are not horror stories at all. This is not to say, my God, at least he's not writing horror. I don't mean that at all.

I am a great fan of horror and see it as a valid form of literature, as valid as any others. I have certainly tried to put

Introduction

my brand on it, as have many writers. I'm merely suggesting that in some cases, Tim seems to be mining quite a different territory, and the horror label should not be his only label.

The stories contained in this collection, like Tim's previous stories, all have an echo and a texture that are the ingredients of not only the greatest horror fiction, but of great fiction of any kind. Symbols. I'm not talking about that high school crap where the teacher looks in the back of her text book with the special red notes and tells you that "the rose represents beauty, and how it must fade," etc.

I mean there is more in the scene than the scene. He appears to write simply, but the words have a careful texture and they build like a craftsman building a chain mail suit of armor. The horrors have meaning. They are about the weaknesses and the strengths of human beings. They give us a chance to visit not only our waking nightmares, but our hopes, sometimes with the petals falling off, sometimes in full bloom. It is all represented in Tim Lebbon's fiction.

To put it more simply, Tim really knows what it is to be human.

Okay, you say, who the hell doesn't? Well, from the actions of many, I would say that a large majority of our "damned human race" as Twain put it, fails to know what it is to be human. But failure or success, it takes a rare and wonderful talent to be able to express humanity in all its forms, to make it real through the magic of language.

Thank goodness Lebbon can do that. His kind are rare and should be appreciated with the same marveling eye that observes by microscope the intricacies of the snow flake.

Joe Lansdale

Read these stories. Be aware. You are entering the realm of one fine and wonderful and magical and damned great writer.

Ladies and Gentleman.

One of the best.

Tim Lebbon.

Tim. Top hat and cane, buddy. And take it away.

Last Exit for the Lost

I've never been to Venice, but since the parcels arrived I've realised that I belong there.

I have seen that wondrous city through the eyes of a woman, a man and a disturbed young boy, and each vision filters out one element of the place in favour of another, sheds different lights on differing aspects, highlights one building and drives another far into the background. In short, I have lived a life there three times over. Three memories make for a greater whole, I thought, they combine to give me a more real picture than I would have even standing there myself, looking out over St Mark's Square, listening to the string quartet serenading the rich tourists and feeling the breeze as a flock of pigeons takes off nearby.

But then yesterday I found the final packages, from Janine, and I realised with a jolt that throughout the preceding three days I had never actually *felt* anything about the city. I'd seen, tasted, heard and sensed, but nothing had changed inside. Slowly, over the past twenty-four hours, I've come to recognise the humbling fact that I've not experienced any deep emotion about anywhere—or anyone—for the past twenty years.

Since the last time I saw my daughter Janine, in fact.

Until yesterday I had no idea where in the world she was.

―⁂―

The first package was delivered to my next door neighbour while I was out.

Keyse rang my doorbell an hour after I'd arrived home from the pub. I stood from my sofa, stared out through the blinds and wondered what the miserable old fuck wanted. We never socialised and only existed comfortably as neighbours because it was easier to do so than to fall out. But I hated his haggard stoop and his bald head, almost as if they were intentional attributes chosen by him to make himself appear more wretched.

I put down my fresh can of beer and answered the door. "Evening Peter," I said, trying not to breathe in too deeply. From the smell I guessed that Keyse hadn't bathed for weeks.

"O'Dwyer," he said. He always used my last name. It made me feel like I was in school again. "Had this." He handed me a heavy, square package, about eighteen inches to a side, wrapped in thick brown paper and secured extravagantly with what looked like a roll of glossy brown tape.

"Thanks," I said as he walked away. *Ignorant shit*, I thought, but I was glad to be rid of him so easily. It could

Last Exit for the Lost

have been worse, I knew. I could have had a neighbour who would stand there expecting me to open it in front of him, shed my secrets for him to see and comment upon. Open this package. This mystery package.

I never had anything through the post other than bills, circulars and the occasional magazine I subscribed to in a vain attempt to lighten my grey life. Certainly not a parcel, a present from person or persons unknown.

And certainly, *definitely,* never from Italy.

I walked back into the living room and propped it up on the settee, picking up my can and draining it in one swig. There were more in the kitchen and I went to fetch one, glancing back at the package, staring into the fridge for a few seconds as I thought about just who or where it could have come from. The name and address on the front were correct, there was no mistaken identity, although the post code was absent. A commercial venture? A useless 'gift' that I should pay for within fourteen days, or return? Something that someone had ordered with my credit card number? I could think of nothing else. I had no idea what it was, or whom it was from.

It shames me to say that Janine never once crossed my mind. Well, she never did anymore. As far as I was concerned I was childless again.

So I did the only thing I could do and opened the parcel.

It took almost half an hour to snip off all the packaging, cut the strings tying a dry cloth around whatever the mystery was inside, and all the while my patience held. I'm usually dreadfully impatient, I have no time or inclination to waste time on anything other than exactly what I wanted to be doing. Ironic, now, thinking back on what this used to mean.

Tim Lebbon

Sitting in this grey, dank, dark room, wishing my life away so that it would be evening again, time to drink, time to pass out in front of foreign TV programmes about prostitution and porn, superficial 'documentary' attempts to lather our screens with barely-concealed filth.

That was me back then. Opening that first packet, I realise now, I'd begun to change already, even though I had yet to see what it contained.

It was a painting. An original, an oil of a young boy standing against a plain, pocked masonry background, the canvas rough-edged where it had obviously been sawn out from some bigger picture. I did not recognise the boy, nor the place. There was nothing to indicate where it could be, nothing but that dead-flesh coloured wall.

The boy was dark-skinned, tall, thin and handsome, with watery eyes, black hair and big hands. He stared out from the picture with a wan, melancholic expression, and I wondered just how long he'd stood that way for the artist, and whether the painter had used artistic licence to get the effect he'd achieved. Surely no boy this young could have been that sad. He looked as if he was seeking something on my side of the picture.

I tipped my head back to take another drink from the can.

It was hours later when I saw the painting again, rising up above me where I lay on the floor at the foot of the settee. Hours, because I was living it.

For a time I was in that painting.

For a while, I'm sure, I was that mysterious Italian boy.

Last Exit for the Lost

There's nothing here for tourists. The water is black and it looks oily, thick, and when he throws a stone in it seems to be swallowed up without causing ripples. The sun never touches this thin canal between buildings, and the only time it's disturbed is when one of the locals punts by on their tatty old float.

So he sits by the water and throws another stone. He's brought them specially. There are none lying around, all the paths are swept by the old women looking for something to do during the hot afternoons. He chose these from a fountain in one of the myriad hidden courtyards scattered across the island, they were slippery with moss but that was fine, that was okay. Each of his sins is a slippery thing, and as he lobs the stone through the shadow and into the dark water, he imagines each one being a sin swallowed and drowned forever. Here was the time he'd taken Julio's lunchbox at school, opened it and spread snot in the boy's sandwiches. Splash...one sin less. Here, his guilt at the first time he'd masturbated, and the thousand times since. He throws the stone harder because it deserves to make a bigger splash. The water swallows it with a thick *glop*. A minor theft, a broken vase, a lie, his sins follow each other into the canal until his pockets are empty, and even though he can still remember a few awkward times from the past few months...well, if only it would work for real.

If only it would work. Because the final sins are huge.

He's sweating from the running and the fear and the panic, and as he stands and walks into the sun it seems to dry his perspiration, melt away those terrible things. A colourfully-attired American couple bump into him and ask him something in English, and for some reason he does not understand them. The words are clear and recognisable, but his brain will not combine them and dredge meaning from memory. They may as well be talking Chinese.

The tall, thin American man says something else, shakes his head and storms away, talking loudly and dragging his wife after him.

The boy laughs at the receding tourists and darts across the square, waving his hands as he runs through a panicked flock of pigeons, wondering whether they'll shit on him. His parents told him of the power of sin and the divine gift of redemption and eventual forgiveness, but he does not believe in God. It is his secret, of course, he goes to church and says mass and takes communion, but like most secrets—and he has many, most of them secret even from himself—it eats at him. It guides his way through Venice, steers him along this alley and that, over canals, through courtyards, searching for a way to assuage his unshed guilt. Seeking the largest stone to throw into the deepest canal. But he thinks that no stone is big enough, and there's no water deep enough to help him now.

Ironically, he does not wish to die corrupted. He has to find another way. If only he had some friends, but people don't like him because he's strange. Unique, his mother used to tell him. His poor mother…

And then he slips on a shadow and falls onto his side. The breath is knocked from him and he rolls into another narrow, quiet canal, so similar to the one that has just swallowed his sins.

It's an accident.

Last Exit for the Lost

Nothing intentional here, no death wish, no easy, cynical way out.

The water is not dirty, not really. Just still. Untouched by the sun and allowed to gather filth on its surface. It's the sort of place he prefers, hidden from tourists and seen only as a passing place for locals.

He surfaces, screams echo back to him and him alone, and then something pulls him under. It's nothing physical, nor animal, but as the boy sucks in a lungful of water he thinks maybe the stones are pulling him down. Maybe the combined weight of his sins are exerting some awful gravity on his body, hauling him through the water to the muddy bed where they lie amongst old cans, watches, dirt, rotten timber, food wrappers and perhaps a corpse or two waiting for nothing.

It is only after his heart stops and everything goes dark that sensation leaves him alone.

And then one final sin shouts him into eternity: *suicide... suicide...*

After surfacing from this strange vision—I was wet and for a moment I panicked, before realising it was sweat soaking my clothes—I did the only thing I could with this mysterious gift: I hung it on the wall. Two eye-hooks in the back of the thick canvas and a piece of picture wire strung between them, it looked very fine between the tall bookcases in my living room. The boy stared at me as I straightened him, his dark fluid eyes never leaving mine, but I was not uncomfortable. I could almost see myself.

The picture looked totally at home on my wall. I didn't know where it had come from, who had sent it or why, but it could have been with me forever. I kept walking by and glancing at it, and I became sure that if I were to move it slightly to one side there would be a patch of cleaner, more vivid paint beneath it.

A day after it had gone up, I could not recall what the living room looked like without it.

I ate my normal lunch the next day: a plate of cheese and biscuits, washed down with a bottle of cheap red wine. I knew good wine, or I had once. It no longer interested me. It was the end result I sought now, not the means it took to get there. A three pound bottle of wine had the same intoxicating effect as one costing ten pounds. I sat in the usual chair and looked at the usual view—a wall of books with thin strips of wall peering between bookcases, each strip marked at head-height with a painting. I wondered whether there'd been a painting before where the new one now hung, and for the life of me I could not recall.

Another swig of wine, and then I started on a second bottle.

I'd known these books once. I'd read them and studied them and taught them, tried to write my own treatise. I'd been an academic, I'd had friends and followers and…and family. But I shunned all that for enjoyment. I'd rather sit and drink a bottle of Scotch than explore the writings of dead people. *What do you want?* my wife had screamed at me. *What do you want?* I'd thought it a foolish question then, still did now, but at least time gave me some sort of an idea of what she'd actually meant. There was much more import in that statement than a blank, blind plea for an explanation.

Last Exit for the Lost

There was despair and fear and dread and pity and sadness. All I could hear was my wife interrupting my life, while inside my fear of intellect distilled the failures awaiting me.

Janine had cried when we argued.

The boy in the picture blinked. I paused with my wineglass halfway to my lips, tongue staining red as I bit my lip. He stared at me from a distance, so beguiling and unknown, and yet in his eyes I was sure I could see myself reflected. They seemed wetter than before.

I leaped up, spilling the plate to the floor and knocking over the half-empty second bottle of cheap Spanish red. As I neared the picture I was sure the boy's mouth twisted itself out of a sneer, but my glasses were not perfectly level on my face, my left eye was slightly blurred…and pictures don't move.

"Who sent you?" I whispered. I thought of the strange vision from yesterday, the alien memory that had implanted itself in my mind, replete with sights and sounds and smells. I'd been trying not to think about it too much. The wine helped. But the boy…the Italian boy staring at me from a place I had never been, giving me part of his life with just a glance…he was most sobering.

"Fuck off," I said, deciding to go for a walk. I needed something stronger than wine.

—⚉—

It was only five minutes to the off licence. I left the overgrown front garden of my detached house, noting that there were another three full bin-bags just inside the gate. Someone had been tipping their rubbish. They thought I wouldn't care, and they were right. It was only deep inside where my old, responsible self was held prisoner that I felt infuriated.

The woman behind the counter avoided my eyes as she wrapped my bottle of whiskey. She'd chatted the first few times I used the place, but then when I began spending more and more money there she'd effectively broken off contact, far more embarrassed by my affliction than I ever was. I fully expected her to refuse to serve me one day, but that time never came, for which I was glad. She had seemed pleasant enough. It would be awful to have to shout and rage at her, lessen her in public. And I would. I knew that. And she did too.

I left with the bottle and decided to return straight home. I didn't want to go there, I needed a seat in the park for the afternoon, watch young lovers strolling hand in hand blissfully unaware of the shit their life would become, because in a way that comforted me. In a way, I thought everyone deserved it. But something drew me back to my dank, stinking house, where the wallpaper was so rotten it slid from the walls.

And I think I knew before turning the corner into my garden what I would find there.

The package leaned against the front door. My name and address were written in the same hand as before, although it seemed more hurried, less particular. It was the same shape and size. I carried it in, propped it against my fireplace, opened the whiskey and sat in my tatty armchair.

I wondered what would be released, were I to open it.

The Scotch went quickly. My eyelids drooped. The boy watched me from the wall, he'd always been there, and

Last Exit for the Lost

occasionally I thought I heard someone talking Italian from a room in my house I'd never been in. I didn't understand Italian but I could hear the words anyway. *Sorry, papa. Sorry, papa. There was a shout and a smash, and it hurt, and I didn't mean...Sorry, papa.* And perhaps even then I was not the same man I'd been two days before.

Instead of falling into a drunken slumber I hauled myself from the chair and picked up the package. It took me a long time to strip the wrappings, and by the time I'd finished I could hardly remember starting. The whiskey bottle seemed to have emptied itself and I felt worse than ever. Then I turned the painting around.

The man was around middle-age, but he had the eyes of a geriatric. Tall, sombre, big hands, his trousers slightly too short and the sleeves on his jacket hitched to reveal his skinny wrists. He was dressed in black and white, a tatty old suit, incongruous against the sun-bleached crumbling wall that provided the background. The same background as the boy staring down at me from between my bookcases.

The new canvas was sawn as well, rough along both edges...and there was something slightly wrong. I looked closer, the picture wavering in and out of focus as the alcohol worked its way through my veins. It made the man swim, as if viewed from just beneath the surface of rippling water. There was a smudge on the canvas to the man's right, a splash of something dark against the masonry wall. Perhaps it was the shadow of whoever or whatever had been cut away.

I closed my eyes and breathed in deeply, trying to pull myself back from drunken oblivion, and when I opened my eyes again I was somewhere else.

Somewhere a long, long way away.

Tim Lebbon

He sees the blood and the body and she's still moving, she has to be, *surely*, because if she's still the consequences are too awful to contemplate. He cannot move for a while because it is something he has feared for so long. His son, most-loved and oft-feared, always had this potential within him. There was nothing wrong with him, that's what the doctors told them, nothing actually *wrong*, he was just anti-social and unbalanced and sometimes the violence came to the fore before anything else, a lashing out of tongue or hand which would be regretted so much by all of them later on.

They had lived with it because there was no other option, but he has always feared his son. His wife, however…she loves him without reservation.

He moves, steps into the tall-ceilinged room, and a breeze sends the drapes shifting at the balcony doors. Below the balconies someone laughs as they pass by in the street, a foreign laugh because it does not acknowledge the melancholia of this place. From somewhere further away a shout rises between buildings, and it is distorted so that it's impossible to tell whether it holds fear or wonder, or both.

He wishes such distortions were possible in here. The sun has picked out something wet lying by his wife's head.

The drapes blow again, gusting in as if ghosts are seeking entry from outside. They rarely had the doors open because the balcony was too unstable to stand upon, but today his wife must have been warm, his son seemingly calm. Perhaps the lure of cool air outweighed the certainty of a tourist's uncaring, unknowing laughter.

Last Exit for the Lost

Something wet and dark, and not just next to her head but beneath it as well, leaking out from her skull. Blood.

He keeps moving but his legs are becoming weak. They are determined not to let him reach his wife but he fights them, stumbling across the sun-drenched floor just inside the open doors, feeling the cool gush of air and the hot kiss of the sun upon his face and arms. He staggers and slips to his knees next to her, crying and mumbling something even he cannot understand. She is a good woman and he is a good man, that's what hurts the most; they're good people and there's no excuse for any of this, no rhyme or reason. They could have been well-off once, but they forwent that in favour of looking after their son, who was already exhibiting his extraordinariness even in those early days. The fits of terrible temper, the shouting, the abuse, they were all negated by one of his lovely smiles or the sight of him dancing as he sang one of his own songs for them, skipping along beside the canals, dropping stone after stone from the bridges, telling them he was trying to hit the same place every time so that the ripples did not overlap. And that's how they spent their lives, trying not to let the ripples of his uniqueness overlap and cause interference. They tried to live with it instead of against it.

She's facing away from him. The blood is tacky and dry, a paste more than a fluid, and he's glad her expression is hidden from view. He will never see her again.

And then he hears the crying.

Something touches his neck. He flinches away, thinking it's a spider or a fly, but one of the drapes settles on his shoulder and then flows back to the window as the breeze passes.

"Sorry, Papa," the voice says, and then he knows who is crying. The idea that he's heard this very phrase before, in the same context and for the same reason, comes and goes. "Sorry Papa, there was a shout…" His son says more but he does not hear, he's too involved in trying not to stare at his beautiful wife's ruined head. He can guess what happened…a row, a shouting match, not at all unusual…his wife losing her temper, maybe even lashing out, and then falling…the corner of their marble table especially sharp that day…

"What have you done?" he manages to croak, looking around to see where the boy is hiding. He finds him curled beneath the table, knees drawn up and hands by his face, perhaps thinking he can return to the foetus he once was, back to a time when, perhaps, he was normal.

His son tells him but it is all too much.

"Where's Janine?"

His son tells him that too, but it makes no sense.

After a minute, or an hour, or a day, he stands and leaves the room. He will return to his wife but there is something he must do, just a small matter to take care of before he holds her in his arms again. In the bathroom he empties the pills into his hand and swallows them with mouthfuls of water. Sleeping tablets, headache pills, old bottles half-empty from the back of the cupboard, their uses unknown, whatever afflictions they were prescribed to treat long-since defeated, or lived with. He stares into the mirror, frowns and leans in closer. He does not know those eyes. They are the eyes of a man living in a world where his beautiful wife is dead, and he refuses to make their acquaintance.

By the time he returns to that draughty room he is already dying.

Last Exit for the Lost

He lies down and takes her in his arms. After a while his son runs away.

I woke up crying. It was a long time since I'd shed tears and it shocked me, but there was no way I could stop them. My mind was muddled as I surfaced from sleep, filled with images from dreams mixed in with things that may have been more than dreams. I stood unsteadily, reaching out for the wall as I stumbled, and my hand brushed the sawn canvas of the boy. I looked at him through the distortion of tears. "Killer," I said, but it felt all wrong. "You poor boy." Even that felt false. In the end I turned and reached for the portrait of the father, wiping tears from my eyes with one hand while I held him up in the other.

He'd been a good man. He'd never done anything bad, never put himself before his family, and now he was dead. How unfair, I thought, how terrible that he had to take his own life…

And then I wondered just how I knew all this, and I dropped the picture and ran from the room. I didn't quite make the toilet before I vomited, and for the last few steps puke ran down my front and onto the carpet. It had the rank rich smell of alcohol. It was mainly fluid because I hadn't eaten at all that day, and in the pan it stilled until I thought I could see my reflection in there, blue skies above my head instead of the grey bathroom ceiling, the water deep and oily, the smell of baking bread and diesel wafting along the alleyway.

"What is this?" I managed before I was sick again.

I thought someone touched the back of my neck with a cool hand, but it was only sweat pooling there.

Later, when I was cleaned up and dressed, I made myself something to eat. I was changed even more by then. I actually thought about what I desired instead of simply throwing a packet in the microwave, discarding Indian, Chinese and Italian in favour of a simple shepherd's pie with an additional plate of roast potatoes to accompany it. I was hungrier than I'd felt in a long, long time. As I listened to the microwave humming and the plate turning, I thought of a small boy crying in a kitchen as his father slowly cooled before him.

And I wondered how the people in these paintings—and in my mind—had known Janine.

There was another bag of rubbish languishing against my front fence. There were seven of them there now, I knew I should move them, but at least none of them had split. The dustman was due the next day. I didn't know it, but by then I would have dragged them into the house and opened them myself.

And I would be crying again.

I went for a walk. It was not often I left the house with any specific aim in mind other than to buy food or, more often, another bottle of mind-numbing drink. That day, however, I knew that there were things to see, memories to hunt down, and if I was too far gone to actually re-live them, at least their passing would be mourned at last. I was not totally changed—not yet—but I was as different from the man I'd been the day before as…well, as different as I now

Last Exit for the Lost

am to *anyone*. Some things change a person so much that they can barely even recognise themselves.

It has taken a long time for me to accept four people staring at me from the mirror.

I walked through my history. It had been an age since my past had concerned me, and reliving it now—most of the memories were vague reflections of true events, hidden by time and worn by my jaded outlook—was a frightening experience. I passed my old primary school first, remembering the time I told a girl I loved her beneath the demountable building when I was barely five years old. I wondered where she was now, what she was doing at that exact instant, if she was even still alive. I would never know. I had told her I loved her and I would never know where she lived or when she died. These things are hidden from us, more so than the path of our own futures, information stolen as routes part and fate whisks us away into the chaos of life. The present is always beaten by the future.

Next, a whistle-stop tour of my teens, houses where I had lost my virginity, got drunk, experienced my first taste of drugs, fought with a best friend, cried, laughed and generally raged at the future, believing as all teenagers do that it could never harm me. I knew differently, of course, but the memories were sweet for a time. The father in me smiled sadly and the teenager frowned, wondering just what he had missed out on. I wanted to tell him *nothing, the place you lived was a kind of Heaven*, but considering what I had seen I thought that would be insensitive. Instead I walked, and looked, and realised as the sun dropped into the smog that each place I passed took up a chronological order in my memories. It was as if the streets and parks of my home town were laid out for me that day, twisted back onto and into themselves so that my eight-hour walk made sense.

It did. It made good sense. By the time I turned for home my face hurt from smiling; not because I had done so much, but because my muscles were unused to the expression. I saw for the first time how trees in the park swayed in subtle dances too intricate to ever be copied by humans. I noticed sparrows darting in and out of gardens, children playing complex games of chase and catch on the football field, my neighbours averting their eyes and turning away if they saw me. It did not make me angry; I deserved it. And although I had never felt either, I viewed all these things with a father's total love for his family, and a young boy's confusion at the internal turmoil he lived with.

When I arrived home past eight o'clock, exhausted and invigorated at the same time, I was not surprised to see a third parcel on my doorstep and several more bags in my overgrown front garden.

I stooped, groaned as I picked up the package and something inside me whispered *together again*.

I was pulling off the wrapping as I opened the front door.

She walks through the city and thinks about her life, and each place she passes calls up a memory.

She sits and looks out over the water for a long time, watching the tourist boats bob here and there, listening to the distant echo of their guides crackling through bad speakers, smiling sadly at couples seeking romance aboard gondolas.

Last Exit for the Lost

They are her lifeline—she works in the Café Roma, serving meals and taking tips and trying to ignore the occasional slap or tickle—and yet she greatly resents the tourists' freedom, so much so that she often wishes they would find somewhere else to go. They pay her wage but, ironically, they keep her trapped here, unable to travel even if their son had been able. They come from everywhere and she lives nowhere, seeing the same things day in, day out. Scenic trips along the Grand Canal, shopping in the Rialto food markets, winding alleys, bridges leading somewhere new…all lose their allure after thirty-five years. She walks the streets and the byways without a second glance for things the tourists had come thousands of miles to see, and it sometimes amuses her how surprised they all seem to be at her indifference.

And yet she does not feel sorry for herself. She is past that, it came earlier in life when their son came along, grew up, showed himself to be what he is: a boy with problems, problems beyond solving. She resents it sometimes because she cannot understand why this happened to them, but feeling sorry for herself would be one large step towards giving in. That is something she can never do, no matter what. Giving in would be to admit defeat. She owes her darling son much, much more than that.

She walks back through the squares and courtyards, passing in and out of the tourist areas like the shadow of a cloud across the city. She hears all the voices and languages, and thinks of all the places she will never go. Britain, that's somewhere she so craves to see. Green fields; London; tea and scones. Janine says it is a bad place, but her life there was not good. Terrible how trauma can taint beauty so.

She aims back to their flat, passing through several dilapidated courtyards and responding to the few greetings thrown her way. Back here the smells are more pungent and the sounds further away, as if Venice itself has avoided giving this place the tourist make-over. She pauses for a moment outside her front door—she does this often, breathing in, calming herself and wondering just how things are going to be today—and then walks inside.

For a while, the day is good. She opens the balcony doors to let in some fresh air. She smiles at her son and tells him she loves him. He does not smile back.

Instead he screams at her. He's in one of his agitated moods, angry for no reason, aggressive and violent and resentful of things he cannot name, so she walks quickly into the living room. He's standing at the window. He threatens to throw himself out.

She darts for the boy…

—⚉—

I woke up. I knew what day that was, what time, and somehow I opened my eyes and escaped sleep before I could see those terrible events.

The husband and the boy stared at me from the wall. Their expressions were as grim as ever, but their eyes seemed lighter. I glanced at the window to see if the moon was shining through, perhaps casting a strange silvery glint on the paintings. But no, it was dark outside, and the moon was hidden by clouds. I looked down and saw the painting of the mother in my lap. I must have been gripping it for hours while I slept, because my knuckles were locked white and

Last Exit for the Lost

my thumbs pressed down into the canvas. I had to sit there for several minutes before my hands would unclench, all the while looking into the painted woman's eyes, feeling as if I was looking into my own.

When I finally managed to wake my tingling legs and stand, I leaned the painting against the coffee table. A piece of folded paper slipped from behind the backing. It was off-white and thick, good paper, meant to last a long time.

I opened it. I didn't know what to expect and yet, somewhere inside, voices were already whispering her name. They had heavy accents, these voices, but I heard them clearly enough. They were coming from inside my mind, after all.

Janine.

It had all happened so quickly. Three days before, I was a contented drunk, successfully hidden from my own intellect behind a defensive wall of apathy, alcohol and antagonism. Now I was…someone else. Someone with an interest in the mirror and the strangers I saw there. A man with a past again, even though it was still confused and tangled by my decades of inattention. This sheet of paper would change things yet again.

I glanced from the window at the pile of bags in my front garden, and looked at the letter.

The words took me away, but not as the dreams had seemed to. They transported me because I wanted them to, they lifted me and gave me back what I had once been by their simple associations…and also because I knew who they were from before I started reading. My thumbs were pressed where hers had touched. This paper had particles of her skin on it, pieces of her, my daughter Janine. Tears hit the paper and smudged the ink as I read, but I kept well ahead of them.

Hello Daddy. I guess you know by now that this painting has been a suicide note. I don't know what you've been doing these past 20 years, but unlike you, I care. *That's why you were the person I knew had to receive this painting, cut into three, separated just as its subjects have been. And with those separate parts, a bit of who they represent, because this family was more a family to me than you ever were. They took me in and cared for me when I ran here from Britain, and for a while there was a lot of happiness in their house. But then I was forced to acknowledge something that I had known for a long time: bad things happen to good people. Their heartache was awful. The day it all ended was something of a release.*

I had painted them only the week before.

Afterwards, I wanted to send them away to somewhere they'd always dreamed of going. And I wanted to talk to you one last time before I go too. I've sent you the nearest thing to a family I've ever had. I hope you treat them well.

The bags in the garden are full of Janine's possessions.

I'm savouring them. The first bag I emptied and searched through had some clothes, a pile of old paperback books and photographs from a life I have never known. I will take time to reacquaint myself with my daughter before I look through the rest of the bags. I need to take it easy. I don't know what I'm going to find in there.

Last Exit for the Lost

I hung the paintings together on the wall and found that they fit almost perfectly. There's one portion missing: a piece sawn off next to the father. I have a feeling I may find it in one of Janine's bags, a self-portrait where she imagined herself to be most at peace. And although I look forward to seeing her again, I'm still a little nervous about her joining her adopted family here with me.

Soon…

Because they found me, Janine, just like you intended. *You* found me. And contrary to what you may think, I care too.

I am a family again.

The Cutting

When I was thirteen years old, I discovered the value of life.

I was curled up into a ball on the settee, a much-thumbed book of ghost stories propped open on my knees. The monsters and ghouls barely held me entranced any more, now that I knew they were not real. But their tortured souls and pathetic wails possessed a pleasing nostalgia, which I was still too young to identify or appreciate.

The knock at the door stirred me from some eldritch basement. I dropped the book with a start, jumped up and leapt into the hallway, almost colliding with my Granddad.

"Great lout!" he exclaimed, but his lips twitched into a smile as I beat him to the front door. The frame had swollen in the damp. It squealed as I hauled on the handle. A shadow fell in, sprawling across the hall carpet like a drunk. Outside, darkening our step with his immense bulk, stood a man. He had a head the size of a pumpkin, arms like bags of cricket balls and a paunch that already seemed to be trespassing.

"Jack Jenkins, I'm after," he roared. I cringed and took several hasty steps back, bumping against my Granddad where he stood behind me.

A strange silence settled over the scene; stranger still, because I had been expecting a loud exchange. Granddad had a booming voice, but Mum said it was there to drown out bad memories. I'd never really understood that. I couldn't come to terms with how shouting could cover your thoughts, though I was often berated for trying it myself.

The stillness was almost complete, intensified by the lonely intrusion of everyday sounds. The click of the hall clock. The steady *drip, drip* of rainwater falling from the broken porch gutter.

There was silence, true, but above me a whole conversation was held in one glance.

"Henry," Granddad said, his voice unreadable.

"Jack." The man reached over my shoulder, and I sensed my Grandfather clasping the hand in his own. Then came the frantic rustle of clothing as they shook. Weirdness vanished, and smiles lit up the scene.

"Davey, this is Henry Jones, my old Sergeant Major." Granddad beamed down at me as I moved aside. I'd only ever seen this look on his face when he uncovered a series of books he'd read as a boy, or when he reminisced about building dens in the hayloft or chasing geese around his Mother's garden. It was an appreciation of old times, which I could never really share with him. It made me want to leave him alone with his old Sergeant.

"From the war?" I asked.

The Cutting

"Well, yes, son," Henry laughed, "from the war." His face was made of clay, changing expression from grim to hearty without passing any intervening stage. "Your Grandfather not talked about me, then?"

Another awkward silence. Granddad never spoke about the war. Mum said that was why he was so excited when other memories came to him, because it meant he'd found something else other than his time in the camp to tell them about. I'd always wondered whether these other things would ever run out, and force my Grandfather into an eternal muteness.

"Don't really mention it, much," Granddad said. Henry nodded, shrugged, still looking at me, as though he had been expecting as much.

"Davey, run into the kitchen and rustle us up a pot of tea, won't you son? I'm sure Henry fancies some tea. Tea, Henry?"

Henry nodded and smiled, clapping his hand on Granddad's shoulder, exuding a natural sense of authority. Granddad led him through the door into the front room. He switched off the television mid-way through a football match, an act virtually unheard of. The huge mass of Henry Jones lumbered into the room and the door swung shut behind him, as if repulsed by his bulk.

I stood there for a moment. I suddenly felt excluded, cold, frozen in time. Grumbling fragments of conversation drifted through the door, losing their meaning in the wood but still holding their tone. It was one that I could not identify. Words and phrases sprang at me from the story I had been reading—*surreptitious...insubstantial footfalls on the wet floor...the painful memories of times long since fled*—but none of them really seemed to suit the occasion. Or maybe I just didn't want them to.

I was sorely tempted to press my ear to the door. But my parents had brought me up to respect my elders and their privacy, so I went straight into the kitchen. Still, the disturbing sounds reverberated in my mind, refusing to lose themselves, conjuring terrible images.

I put the kettle on the stove and went about preparing what I thought would be a suitable afternoon tea. My Mother was usually here to do it, but today she had gone into town to buy some beef for our upcoming celebration. My Dad was forty in three days' time. I put tea in the pot. One spoonful each, one for the pot, which I thought invariably went to make a horrible brew, but adults seemed to live by the rule. I found some cakes in the cupboard, only fairy cakes from the local school fayre the previous weekend, but still fresh and attractively decorated.

The kettle mumbled away on the stove. I sat on the kitchen stool, flicking my fingers together, rocking slowly as I tried desperately to remember the big man's name. Much as I took pride in an above average intelligence for my age, my powers of observation and short-term memory left much to be desired. Always had my head stuck in a book, so Mum said. Mind elsewhere. Wandering.

Granddad had seemed strange. Animated, more so than his usual plastic, stern self. And there was something else, a reaction that I could identify from my reading that afternoon. He had been in awe. As though the man he was looking at on our doorstep—the man whose name I was still struggling to recall—was a ghost.

The Cutting

Images from my ghost book haunted me. Strangers on the doorstep. Old men with wizened heads. Cruel ghosts with no form, but plenty of anger.

The kettle began to whistle and I almost fell from the stool. I waited until the water was bubbling, then poured it into the pot, blowing steam away so that I could see the leaves stirring and tumbling in the water. I could read no future in their frantic motion.

The door burst open. For the second time that minute I jumped, scalding myself with splashes of spilled water. I yelped and rubbed at my arm, fighting back tears.

"Sorry, son," Granddad said. He ruffled my hair again as he passed by. Unbelievable! I loved receiving affection from him, but the occasions were rare. Today, twice in a row!

"Is your Sergeant Major comfortable? I found him some cake."

"Good lad. Yes, he's fine. He won't be staying long, though. Just come for something." My Granddad stood in the pantry doorway, staring in, as though vaguely uncertain of what he was looking for. From behind, standing like he was, he looked years younger.

"What?" I asked. A tin lid clattered to the floor and rolled from behind the door. I poured milk into two mugs, the tea soon after. The sugar was in a bowl in the living room. Granddad cursed quietly under his breath.

"Son?" he said.

I turned around. He had opened the holiday savings tin. We were going to Cornwall for a week in the summer, all of us, to travel around the coast and visit the old fishing villages. Most of the time we were going to camp, but for the first and last nights, my parents were saving to put us up in posh hotels. It didn't really bother me, camping was great fun as far as I was concerned, and hotels were an unnecessary luxury.

And now, Granddad had the money from the tin rolled into a clump in his hand, like a dead origami bird.

"Son," he said again, "I have to ask you a favour." He shrugged. He seemed bashful. He smiled uncertainly and trod from foot to foot, like a child in front of their headmaster. "Well, two actually. The first is that you don't tell your Mum or Dad about this. Not about Sergeant Major Jones, nor this." He waved the wad of money at me. "It'll be replaced, and they never need to know about Henry. We'll not see him again, I reckon."

"The tea's ready," I said. "You all right, Granddad?" He nodded, and he was telling the truth. He was fine. I could see it in his stance, a sort of tension preceding the realisation of an old ambition. As though he'd been waiting for this day his whole life.

"The other favour...could I borrow your savings? I need another twenty pounds, and I just don't have it on me." There was something different in his voice, something alien. I realise now that this was the moment when he spoke to me as an adult for the first time.

My Granddad, asking to borrow some money from me! I almost couldn't answer, such was the shock, but then something nasty wormed its way into my thoughts. Nasty, and worrying. Like why did he suddenly need this money? What were he and Sergeant Major Jones after?

"Why, Granddad?"

He jerked back slightly, as though he had not expected me to ask. For a moment so brief that I may even have been

The Cutting

mistaken, he looked as though he was going to tell me off. Then, a rueful smile pressed his lips together and he nodded his head.

"I'll tell you this once, son," he said. "But it's like...a secret. And a wound; it hurts! And it may be strange to you. Difficult to understand. And I'll probably never mention it again." He suddenly looked pale, but it was a greyness beyond terror. It was more like a memory of death.

I sat down slowly on the stool, forgetting the tea, forgetting the big stranger, who may or may not be a ghost, sitting patiently in our living room. He was waiting for his refreshments and the bundle of notes in my Grandad's hand, but for a while it was as if he had never arrived. It was just my Granddad and me. I realised quickly that I didn't want to hear what Granddad had to say. I imagined that it would cloud the way I looked at him for the rest of my life.

I was right. It did. But at the time, when I was a scared boy with ghost stories still reverberating in my head, I could never guess in what way.

Granddad leant against the kitchen units and stared at the bundle of money in his hand.

"When the Japanese had me," he said, "on the railway of death, I was in a labour camp with Henry Jones. We were cutting the railway into a mountain. Literally moving the mountain by hand. There were over a thousand of us when we started." He did not look at me, just kept his eyes on the money. He did not tell me how many of them were left by the time liberation came.

"The camp guards were a mixture of Korean and Japanese. They were cruel, sometimes for fun, sometimes because there was hardly enough food and water for them, let alone us. They did terrible things, son. I hope you never have to see anything like that, or live through it. And you don't have to know. But they were terrible things." His voice cracked, but his expression held no tears. It displayed a mixture of anger and what I could only identify as pride. I sometimes saw the same expression when he watched me playing rugby for the school. I was painfully bad, and usually did more damage than good to the team effort. But Granddad told me that trying was the most important thing.

"One time," he continued, "we'd been at the cutting for ten hours, non-stop. They'd only given us one drink. We were passing out, dehydrated. The heat there. Awful.

"But there wasn't enough water. So I asked Henry if I could have some of his. I said I'd pay him two hundred pounds when we got back to Wales, if he'd only give me half a cup full. He smiled at me. I remember that, because I think it was the only smile I saw that day. But he agreed, and he took me up on the offer, and he gave me the water."

I could barely speak. The tea was growing cold, and my Granddad's knuckles were white bones around the money.

"Now, he's here to collect the IOU I gave him," he said, smiling at last.

"Two hundred pounds?" I said, aghast. "For a cup of water?"

Granddad shook his head. "It isn't for the water, son," he said. "It never was. Henry was as certain as any of us that we were never coming home." He went back to the living room.

I never did take the tea in to them. The stale cakes ended up in the bin. When Henry Jones left soon after, he glanced down the corridor at me. I saw something on his face which

The Cutting

looked almost impossible on such a huge, rugged man—the diamond glint of tears. He smiled briefly, and I thought he was embarrassed at crying. It showed how much I had to learn about being grown up.

Granddad never mentioned that afternoon again. For a while after Sergeant Major Jones had paid us a visit, I wanted to talk about it. I wanted to ask him whether he thought a ghost had visited him from the past. Now, years later, I think he would have smiled and said nothing. But even at the time I knew it was something to do with honour, and I kept my word.

As a man proud of the promises he himself had made, I think Granddad appreciated that immensely.

Pay the Ghost

Lee lost his daughter on Hallowe'en. He didn't mislay her, or leave her behind in a car park, or walk down a different aisle in a shopping centre...he lost her. One second she was there by his side, beautiful little Moll, sauntering along with a child's exaggerated gait. The next, gone. Vanished.

Taken from him forever.

Nobody saw anything. The police appealed for witnesses, distributed posters, asked a local schoolgirl to walk with Lee in a reconstruction, trying to jar memories from those in the area at the time. To no avail. They received over five hundred calls from members of the public, all of which led nowhere. For one terrible, soul destroying day, they questioned Lee. They even found one of Moll's shoes a mile from the scene, but it offered no significant clues. There was no blood staining it. This did not comfort Lee at all.

He knew how these things usually worked out. *We're treating this as a missing person inquiry*, the police said at every press conference, but in his heart Lee knew where Moll was now. Dead in a ditch. Raped. Murdered. Some fucker had taken his little girl and killed her, and they didn't even have the humanity to give an anonymous tip to tell the police where her body was buried. That would end one facet of his suffering at least.

The criminal psychologists said that this gave the kidnapper (they still used that term, never *murderer*) a sense of power.

Fucker.

Yes, Lee knew how this would end. And his wife Kate had known too. That's why she had left him eight months after the kidnapping. She…actually…blamed…him. *You should have been holding her hand, you shouldn't have let her go, there are people out there, sick people, and now one of them has…*

As if every father expected his daughter to be stolen away at every minute of the day. As if he really could have done something to prevent it.

He'd been left a hollow man.

It had happened on Hallowe'en. He remembered not because of the hype and the commercial vultures destroying the occasion, nor the reputation it held for supernatural events, and witches, demons and lost souls being abroad. He recalled it purely because of Moll's request earlier on that fateful day. *Daddy, can we pay the ghost?*

He'd never even bothered to ask her what she meant. And now, almost a year later, things were just as bad as ever.

Daddy, can we pay the ghost?

He remembered the words but not the voice that spoke them. He could conjure Moll's face from memory although

Pay the Ghost

sometimes, like now, he had to sit and stare at a photograph to remember every dimple, crease and curve of her expression. She was only six years old when she vanished. And he could not remember her voice.

Lee took another sip of tea. It was cold, but his hot drinks usually were by the time he came to finish them. He spent so long inside his own head that time just slipped away, and he hardly noticed the minutes, hours and days ticking off the months of his life. Someone screamed at him from the television and he glanced over the lip of the cup. Witches frolicked beneath a dead tree, leaping up to swing from skeletal branches, cackling and laughing when their noses fell off or their black wigs slipped to reveal the girlish hair beneath. A shadow crossed the screen and then there were more things in the picture, a collage of grotesque monsters, leaping and rolling and tickling and growling. The inevitable caption covered the fun, saying where and how the costumes could be bought or hired.

It was two days until Hallowe'en, a two-day countdown to the anniversary of Moll's disappearance. Lee couldn't help wondering where her body was resting, what state it was in. He started to cry but the tears acted as magnifiers, etching terrible images in his mind's eye even as he threw down the photo, tried to forget her face because he did not want to see it as he was seeing it now.

"Let me forget!" he pleaded. He did not believe in God—how could he?—but he had to talk to someone. He bent forward and picked up the photo. It was ragged from his own sweat and grease; he had held it close every day for a year. "Moll…"

Tim Lebbon

There was a loud knocking at the front door. Lee looked up and his heart stuttered, but only for a second or two. It took a lot to scare him now. He stood slowly from his armchair and left the darkened sanctuary of his living room.

At the door, something remarkable happened. He felt space moving outwards from him, horizons expanding and an invisible weight lifting away from his shoulders and head. Something touched him: a thought, a feeling, a shred of optimism. It was such an alien sensation that he did not recognise it at first, but when he opened the front door it flooded through him, buoying his spirits and telling him that, somehow, everything was going to be all right.

Strange thoughts…because the thing on the doorstep shocked him rigid. "Let me in," it whispered.

Lee could not speak.

"Let me in!" It shoved past him, glancing over its shoulder as if something worse might be following.

It was human, but other than that it bore little resemblance to anyone Lee had ever seen or imagined. It was dreadfully thin, an echo of Belsen still walking, with flesh so wasted that the skin was shiny and stretched where bones pressed out. And the skin itself was a freakish colour, an orangey hue clinging to it like juice-stains and shimmering in the changing light. It staggered instead of walked, jerking its head with a birdlike movement, scanning its surroundings.

"You have to care," it said. "You *have* to."

"Care?" Lee was still standing by the front door, unable to move, trying to understand what was happening. The flush of euphoria still echoed at the extremes of his senses, even confronted with this horror. It felt all wrong.

Pay the Ghost

"You have to, you must," the thing muttered, scratching at its scalp, ragged nails scoring vivid red lines. "You used to care, you do now, you will again, you must."

"Care?" Lee said again, louder.

The thing stood in the corridor outside the kitchen. It turned and stared at Lee, and at last he knew who it was. Impossible, but he knew all the same. "Care about Moll!" it said.

"Kate…"

"I've been looking," the ruined thing that was Kate said, "I've never given up, all I've been doing is searching. Not living, just searching, four months without pause. Do you know what that can do to a heart, a soul? Can you see?"

"Oh Kate, what's happened…?" Lee moved at last. He walked to Kate with his arms held out, yet desperate not to touch her. She had blamed him and he had hated her for that, but whatever had happened to her since then—

—what could have happened to make her like this? Her hair had mostly gone, the flesh all but sloughed from her bones, leaving her little more than a leathery sack. The orange hue was sickness, starvation, waste.

And then, in the wan light leaking from the living room, he saw her eyes. And they were grotesque in the shrunken face, because they were full of hope.

—⁂—

"I don't know what he is," Kate said. She was talking of the man whom she claimed had Moll. Already, Lee was confused.

He busied himself making her a cup of tea, stealing covert glances at this thing that had been his wife. Never exactly beautiful, Kate had always been striking in her own way, her greenish eyes and bright auburn hair always turning heads. Now, she would turn heads for all the wrong reasons.

"He's not a man. Well…maybe he is, but he doesn't act like one. I don't think he eats." She grabbed Lee's arm as he set a cup on the table beside her. "What sort of a man doesn't eat, Lee?"

"When did *you* last eat?" he asked gingerly, trying to keep the look of disgust from his face. She stank. Sweat, urine, faeces, the stench of the road, the aroma of dispossession. And her breath was full of death.

"I can't recall."

"Kate—"

"I don't blame you anymore, Lee," she said, her voice surprisingly strong.

"But you're sure you've found her? You know exactly where she is?"

Kate nodded.

"Have you been to the police?" Lee could not contain the excitement in his voice, and that sense of euphoria he'd felt when the first knock landed on the door rose once more. Maybe it was an omen, advance knowledge that his year of hell was over, that Moll would be back soon.

She looked up and her eyes burned. "Finding her did this to me. All the effort, the time…do you think I want to leave it up to them?"

"We can't do anything—"

"There are others, as well."

Lee frowned. "Kidnappers?"

Pay the Ghost

"Children. He has a house full of them, must have been taking them for a long time. I couldn't see properly, I didn't get close enough…but there's something wrong with them…" Her shoulders shook and her head lowered, trailing wisps of hair into her tea. Lee thought she was crying, but no tears fell. It was doubtful her body could spare the moisture. "I think maybe he's a ghost."

Can we pay the ghost?

"Moll?" he said. "What's wrong with Moll?" The absurdity of this whole scene washed over him, and for a moment Lee wondered whether he was imagining it. He had not touched a drop of alcohol since Kate left him, yet ironically his own reality had been more prone to hallucination since then than ever before. And now here he was talking about his daughter—Moll, whom he'd thought of as dead for almost a year—in the present tense.

She may be alive, he thought. Kate might be right. She's mad, and ill, and she looks diseased…but she might also be telling the truth.

"I didn't get close enough to see properly," she said. "Lee, I'm so tired. I want all this over with."

"So do I. If you're right, it can be. It will be." He should call the police, he knew. Let them handle this, raid wherever it was Kate was talking about. "Will you take me there?" he asked instead.

His wife nodded. He could almost hear the muscles in her neck straining with the effort. "Soon."

"When Moll was taken…on that day…she said something to me before she went. I've never told you before. It just sounded so odd."

Kate's eyes snapped open, bright pearls in her orange sandy face.

"She said, 'Daddy, can we pay the ghost?'"

"What can that mean?" she croaked.

"I don't know. Maybe the man you saw was following us that day, pretending to be a beggar, and Moll thought the same as you…that he was something strange. And maybe she wanted to give him some money. You know what she was like, always concerned." He closed his eyes. "And perhaps that's how he took her. Appealed to her better nature…"

Kate shook her head. "I can't remember. Isn't that strange? I can't recall anything about Moll at all."

Lee set about making her some food, his mind in utter turmoil. He'd spent a year in the darkest places he could imagine, a landscape of despair and depression where only an occasional rise lifted him above the black clouds, however briefly. Now he had been snagged and boosted right into the sunlight. Given hope. If what Kate said were true and Moll was still alive, perhaps he had a future after all.

Kate ate minutely and slept, and there was nothing Lee could do to keep her awake. It was dark outside, midnight having rolled by while he cooked, and he could hear occasional shouts and infrequent explosions as kids fired premature fireworks into the frosty night.

He had lost his daughter when she was dressed as a witch—black sack cape, cardboard pointy hat, old broom—and the little pockets of her jeans were already bulging with sweets and loose change. *Trick or treat* had been the chant that night.

Daddy, can we pay the ghost? she had said.

Pay the Ghost

Whether or not some ghost or madman had extracted a strange payment, Lee was sure of one thing. He would have payback. Soon.

—⁂—

Lee no longer worked. He'd quit his job soon after Moll's disappearance and never managed to hold down another. Some sympathy work had come his way for a while, but with his mind constantly distracted, his performance suffered. Soon even sympathy was not enough to buy him employment, and people forgot. That was one of the most terrible, unbearable factors of all…people forgot. Their eyes claimed otherwise—not many people could meet his stare nowadays—but inside, for them, it was old news. *You're the guy who lost his daughter. Tragic. Now, let's move on.*

For Lee, every morning he woke felt like the first day without Moll.

That day before Hallowe'en was different. He took the same route along the canal and into town as he used most days, usually just to clear the cobwebs and try to take his mind elsewhere. Sometimes he would stand next to the canal, open his mouth and exhale, ready to jump in and sink. He'd never been stupid enough. He'd never been brave. On this occasion, however, not everything existed to haunt him. He saw a mother walking with her child and hoped he would do that again with Moll. The dirty waters held no allure for him anymore, in fact he found the idea of harming himself repulsive. How could he leave Moll without a daddy? Her mother was close to death, so what sort of a parent would he be if he killed himself? A bad sort. A waste.

Tim Lebbon

And another way this walk differed from all the others... he had a destination. His walk held purpose, a purpose he had never believed existed any more. He was going to find his little girl. That morning Kate had given him directions. She had been wandering for months looking for Moll, and at last she had stumbled onto a hideaway, a place on the very edge of town where strange noises and sights convinced her that something was amiss. It was a bus journey, and then a twenty minute walk past a condemned housing estate on one side, and a huge deserted business park on the other. The place, Kate said, was somewhere it should never be.

She would not tell him what the noises and sights were, and she pointedly refused to return with him. She obviously knew that, with even the slightest possibility that Moll was there, Lee would go anyway.

Almost two hours after leaving home, Lee arrived at the housing estate. At least half of the houses were boarded up and several were burned out, looking ready to tumble into ash at the slightest provocation. Those not closed up looked equally dilapidated. Windows were cracked and smashed, front doors held the sledgehammer scars of forced entries, brickwork bore the strange hieroglyphics of graffiti, combinations of mis-spelled words and crude pictures forming a distinct language of degradation and apathy and hate. Some houses were vandalised more than others, their occupants staring through dirty windows with the glassy gazes of the newly-dead. Perhaps, Lee thought, because they knew that *they* would be soon.

He skirted the estate, heading around towards the deserted business park. If he kept just outside, he thought, maybe he could stay apart from the desperate people who lived here, even try to pretend he was not like them at all. A group of men stood smoking against a wall, following him with blank, bland eyes. A woman pushed a pram up and down kerbs, never slowing, never seeming to notice how much its frame was bouncing and shaking. Her expression remained the same even when her child started to scream. Lee wanted to go to her, point out what she was doing, but that would mean crossing the line and entering the estate.

They could watch him from in there, gazes loaded with whatever accusations he chose to read into them, but he was still out here. Just passing by.

A group of kids—some no more than two or three years old—ran from an alleyway, across a patch of oil-spotted grass and back between two houses. Their cries echoed back at Lee, screams and shouts and something in between. *Why couldn't you take them?* he thought, hating the way his mind was working. *Why take Moll, why not them?*

Moll had always come to him when she was hurt or confused and he had let her down. *I never gave up hope*, Kate had told him that morning, yet he had never even *had* any hope. Dead in a ditch, he had thought. How he despised himself for that. How he despised himself for so much.

On his right, a deserted petrol station. The pumps were long since gone, the shop a shattered remnant of what it had once been. Even the graffiti had been smashed down.

To the left of the petrol station, a path leads across to the business park, Kate had said.

Lee found the path, leading behind a retaining wall and across an area of heavy undergrowth. As he started along the trail, he wondered what Kate had seen and heard.

Keep going until you reach the burned out car on your left.

And there it was, an old Escort resting on grotesquely melted and reset tyres, its exposed metal skeleton half rusted away.

Pass the car, aim for the big hanger-like building...it was a furniture warehouse, now it only houses bats and cats and drop-outs.

Lee eased himself past the car's sharp edges, brushing aside the heavy arms of spiked bushes as he looked for the warehouse. He'd gone a hundred paces before he saw a hint of white to his right. He moved that way for a while and mounted a small rise from where he could see the old warehouse, white paint stripped and covered with a decade of bird shit.

Look to your left, towards the electricity pylon. You'll see the house. Quite old and grand, as if it was there way before the estate and the business park. I expect it was. Way before.

Lee could see no house.

Someone screamed, high pitched and angry. It could have been a fox, he thought, as a shiver played with his spine. Just a fox crying out, but it was daylight and it sounded like a kid, so much like a little girl crying bitterly for the father who had deserted her, never really believing that he would come to rescue her after so long. Something dashed in front of him, rustling one bush and disappearing behind another.

He froze, heart thumping. He could not bear the thought of coming to grief now, not so near to seeing Moll once more.

Pay the Ghost

Definitely no house. He stood on tiptoes and scanned across towards the pylon, sweeping his gaze left as far as the roofs of the housing estate, and right again all the way to the hulking form of the warehouse. No roof above the bushes, no walls standing proud, nothing to indicate that there had ever been an old house here at all. He went over Kate's directions in his mind, closed his eyes for just a second before the scream erupted again.

It could be Moll. Now, so near, it could be Moll.

Lee ran into the bushes, aiming roughly towards the pylon. In places it looked as though a path snaked between the small trees, but then it would vanish and the only signs of humanity were heaps of refuse here and there, old tyres, stacks of newspapers soaked into congealed masses. The scream came again from his right, and he changed direction to find it. Undergrowth whipped at his body and face. He felt a sudden coolness on his cheek and realised he had been cut, the blood bathing his skin, his flesh open to the day. He tasted the blood as he ran, and the scream came from behind him.

He spun around and tried to orient himself. The pylon was behind him now, and try as he might he could not see the warehouse. It should be to his left, but even though he strained and hauled on the branches of a small tree, he could not lift himself high enough to see it. Either he had passed the house or he had not yet gone far enough to find it. He started towards the pylon once more.

Something cracked to his left, a heavy foot snapping a dead twig. Then the same sound came from his right, and again behind him, and he ran blindly through the bushes and shrubs, eyes half closed against the clutching branches, face stinging as they struck at him again, opening new cuts. Blood dripped from his chin and he wondered if it was the land bleeding him, drawing blood because it needed a strange sustenance of its own—

The first he knew of the ditch was when he stumbled into it. He closed his eyes and tried to tuck in his limbs, but he struck the stump of a dead tree and went spinning and flailing. The breath was knocked from him as he hit bottom, landing in something soft yet sharp, like butter laced with glass.

He opened his eyes and instantly regretted it. In those first few seconds he wished so much that could not be unwished later, no matter how hard he tried: he wished that Kate had never come to him; that she had not mentioned Moll; that they had found his daughter's body a year ago instead of leaving him in limbo, only to be plucked up and given hope and then faced with this…this…

Carnage. It was a word he had heard used many times but he never truly understood its meaning. And now here it was. A human carnage, a waste-ground of ruined parts. Some bits he could identify, even though most of the skin had been burnt away and the flesh melted into horrifically sculpted shapes. Here and there a smear of fat held the impressions of the heavy raindrops that had cooled this burning pit. A skull sat atop a pile of bones, hair gone, eyeballs shrivelled beans in their sockets. Lee touched it and the bone crumbled under the featherweight of his fingertips. Other bones powdered as he scrambled to his feet, giving up a fine dust, a rich stink and a gritty feel at the back of his throat.

All of the bones were small.

He tried to scream but he had lost his voice.

Pay the Ghost

He was covered. He had slithered into the trench on a sheen of burned bodies, their fats and juices lubricating his way. Beneath his feet the ground squelched. The air was thick with the stink of the pit. A greasy smoke still hung around the pale roots of the plants lining its edges, and sick warmth radiated from the bare earth walls.

Lee tried to scream again but the indrawn breath scraped at his throat. He gagged, leaned over and puked, closing his eyes so that he did not see what his vomit was mixing with around his feet.

Moll!

Lee forced himself to look around, the guilt of the past year providing the stimulus. Was she here? Was his daughter here, killed and burned, or perhaps burned alive? There was no way he could tell, nothing to distinguish one body from another, let alone identify them.

Small bones.

He found his voice at last and screamed, and it seemed to Lee—as he scrabbled at the slick ditch walls, staggered through the undergrowth, heading in any direction away from the pit—that his scream was echoed all around by others. They could have been his own terrified shouts bouncing back at him, but they sounded out of time, higher pitched, like a mocking impersonation of children by someone who had never had them.

Eventually he found his way back to the road, pushing his way through a hedge not far from the old petrol station. He ran past the estate, meeting the stares of its inhabitants. They could not frighten him any more. *Look after your children*, he wanted to scream at them, *keep them inside, there's a monster and I don't know its name*! But he could not catch his breath, and he was sure that they would ignore him anyway.

Back into town, a bus trip where he was the centre of disgusted attention—his clothes stank, he had rusty brown stains on his face, the blood both his own and that of others—and then he arrived home.

It was late afternoon. By now Lee's senses had calmed down to merely panicked, and he could smell and feel what he had found. He so wished that Kate had told him about the pit.

"Moll!" she screeched as he opened the front door. She came at him, a haggard shadow skimming along the hall wall.

He caught her by the shoulders. "No Moll," he said, "and no house."

Her manic eyes widened even more, dwarfing her shrunken face. She touched his cheeks and looked at his clothes, sniffed. "But you found the burning pit? The way back to the other place? They've used it already, they must have tested it, oh God, not Moll—"

"I have to shower," he said very precisely. "We have to tell the police." He moved her gently to one side and closed the front door, but on the second stair he sank to his knees and began to weep. Tears came, real tears, for the first time in months. He had previously thought he had cried himself dry, and that a desert bitterness was all that could replace his grief.

"Did you see or hear anything else?" Kate asked.

"Screams."

"Moll, do you think?"

Pay the Ghost

Lee shrugged. The tears stung the cuts on his cheeks and forehead and chin. "I don't know. I can't remember the sound of her voice."

―⚒―

Lee sat with a cup of cold tea in front of him. Kate was trying to prepare food, but her ragged breathing and constant groans told him that she would be at the point of collapse very soon. He did not care. He stared at the fresh scratches on his hands and listened to his wife slowly dying nearby, but all he could see was the pit coated with charred and melted remains. The bones…they had been so small…

"She's there!" Kate said. "I tell you, she's there in the house. He hasn't burned her yet, I know it."

"There is no house—"

"I'll take you, we'll go there and see. Tomorrow. We'll go tomorrow."

"Tomorrow…" Lee trailed off. Tomorrow was Hallowe'en, a year to the day since Moll had been lost.

"Maybe only I can find it." She spoke slowly now, easing herself into the chair next to Lee and touching his arm with stick fingers.

Lee shook his head. "Have to call the police. So many bodies…"

"You haven't yet."

He could say nothing. She was right. He should have called them but he could not. Not while there was the remotest chance that Kate was right, that only she could find the house. Maybe he had not been looking hard enough, maybe he had not believed that Moll could still be here in this world with them, not suffering somewhere in the next. Perhaps all it took was faith.

"Tomorrow..." Lee said, resting his head on his arms. He closed his eyes and Moll popped into his mind instantaneously, her wild laugh when he was tickling her, the frown she had copied from him. Then he imagined her shouting and tried to hear her voice, but it was still lost to him. Tears squeezed from his closed eyes. He felt Kate wiping them from his cheek.

—m—

Daddy, can we pay the ghost?

Lee snapped awake but the voice had gone already, fled with the dregs of his dreams. His neck and back ached, his arms had gone to sleep and flopped onto his lap like the limbs of a corpse. It was morning.

"Kate!"

He heard her approach along the corridor...and when she arrived in the kitchen he could not help but let out a gasp. His wife looked even worse than she had yesterday, if that were possible. Her skin, previously a subtle orange from malnutrition and exposure to the elements, was now a rusty gold. It clung to her protruding bones like Clingfilm. The remainder of her hair had fallen out. She had lost several more teeth during the night.

"I haven't slept," she said, "in six weeks."

So much had changed. So much had been distorted and knocked out of joint over the past year. But for a few brief seconds in Lee's memory it was just him and Kate again, young lovers, dreamers, selfish in their love but knowing they had all to give when the time came. And the time had come and gone, been stolen away. Events ruled, not emotions.

"Oh Kate," he said, "I loved you so much."

"We had better go and find Moll." Each word was an effort.

"I'll carry you," he said.

Kate shook her head. "People will stop us. I know what I look like. Wait until later, and they'll think…" She sobbed dryly, rubbing her big eyes with one gnarled hand. "They'll think I'm dressed for Hallowe'en."

"I can't wait—"

"We have to."

Lee looked desperately at the clock, saw that it was late morning already and resigned himself to a long few hours.

Outside, it had started to rain.

—ɯ—

They did not talk much that afternoon. Lee was preparing in his own way, though he found it difficult to concentrate on anything other than Moll. Her smile, her walk, her laughing mouth, but not her voice. He had lost that and no amount of hope could recover it. Only the real thing…the real voice… would make it live for him again.

Darkness fell. By five o'clock the witches, ghosts and demons of the neighbourhood were abroad, knocking on doors and laughing and running and singing and screaming.

Lee led Kate out along the street, forcing a smile for passers-by as they stared at her, their eyes widening in admiration at the effort she had put into the haggard-old-witch routine. The world around him felt as alien as ever, as far removed as it had been on the first day that Moll went missing. The people he saw meant no more to him than pictures in a book.

They reached the estate and walked around to the old petrol station. They were both soaked to the skin and the rain never let up for one instant. Kate wheezed and moaned and coughed, and every now and then they had to stop for her to sit down, her knees popping and bones grinding each other where joints were worn away. But she never once complained. She had been looking for a long time—*Do you know what that can do to a heart, a soul? Can you see?*—and now that the end was in sight she was drawing on unknown veins of energy and determination.

The estate presented an eerie scene. Lights flickered in many of the houses, even those boarded up or gutted by fire, but the streets were virtually deserted. An occasional shadow flitted from one alley to the next, but there were no children trick or treating, no gangs of kids throwing eggs at windows or splashing cars with flour and water, no drunken teenagers using this particular night as an excuse to cause even more chaos and ruin and pain to those around them. It was almost totally silent. Lee tried to convince himself that the shimmering lights in most of the houses were from television screens, but he was sure that they were candles.

"Here," Kate said as they walked alongside the petrol station. It was dark behind the retaining wall, but she moved unerringly, hardly needing light to find her way. Lee wondered just how many times she had come this way, before she realised that she would need his help to go the final step.

Pay the Ghost

She's mad, he thought suddenly, *driven insane by our loss, she's leading me on a wild goose chase...*

But there was the pit. And Moll's words in the voice he could not hear: *Daddy, can we pay the ghost?*

"Here," Kate said again, turning, twisting left and right between trees and bushes, past the gutted car. "Here...and around here..." He followed because she knew where she was going, and he was lost already. If she left him now—or collapsed and died—it would take him hours to get out of here.

"Can you see him?" Kate asked quietly.

"Who?" It was very dark; he could make out only the vague outlines of trees and bushes around them.

"Him. The one from the house. He's with us."

Lee shuddered, reached out and rested a hand on Kate's shoulder, an involuntary need for contact. Then he looked around. "I can't see," he whispered. He tried to believe it was the rain making him cold.

"To the left."

She spoke without turning her head, but Lee had to look. There were bush-shadows hulking against the sky, something taller that must have been a tree, pattering with falling raindrops...nothing else.

"Nothing!" he hissed.

"What are you?" Kate suddenly shouted.

Lee jumped. Something small scurried through the bushes with a startled squeal.

"A revenant," a voice said from the night. "A guide, but not for you." It moved as it spoke, as if its owner were circling them, but that was not possible. They were surrounded by trees and bushes, none of which were being disturbed other than by the rains. In fact the voice was so quiet that Lee thought he may well have imagined it, a chance combination of raindrops and expectation and rustling leaves forming sense from usual chaos.

"One that you paid...handsomely."

"Oh my God!" Lee hissed.

"Just keep going," Kate said, "he's spoken to me before."

"What did he say?"

He felt her shoulder stiffen beneath his hand, then she moved on and he was forced to follow. "Kate?"

"All sorts of things," she responded, not answering him at all.

"Oh Daddy," it whined in imitation of a little girl's voice, "can we pay the ghost, Daddy?"

"What have you done—"

"Ignore it!" Kate said sharply. "It's trying to bait you, make you lose yourself. I know the way, but however hard you hold onto me you'll never get there if you let it distract you."

"How do you know all this?"

She whispered, so quietly that Lee may have misheard her in the rain. "Been trying to find this place for a long time."

They continued on through the dark, and now Lee had a real sense that there was something there with them, walking in the same direction but unconcerned at trees or branches, or unseen holes ready to snap their ankles. And sometimes the voice came from the dark, so quiet and blended with the rain that it seemed little more than memory.

Pay the Ghost

"Such a sweet girl," it whispered, "tasty and whole." A flurry of something leaving a tree to their left. "And her voice, so grown-up when she screams for those who deserted her." The haunting bark of a fox in the distance, or perhaps not a fox at all. "Ahhh yes…her poor voice."

Lee did his best to ignore what was said. He wondered if Kate could hear the same words, or whether her torments were personal to her. He kept one hand on her shoulder and the other in his jacket pocket, curved around the haft of the kitchen knife, the only weapon he had thought to bring.

Kate stopped suddenly. The house seemed to have appeared from nowhere. At the same instant as Lee saw it silhouetted against the clouds, the voice vanished back into the hiss of rain.

"This wasn't here yesterday."

"It's always been here."

"What about the pit? Where's the pit?"

"You really want to see that place again? I bypassed it. Brought us here, not there."

Lee let go of Kate and went to a window, trying in vain to see inside. "No lights on. Deserted."

"Don't you ever sit in the dark?" she rasped. Then her shadow slid to the ground as if the earth itself were consuming her, and a terrible rattle came from her throat.

Lee ran to his wife and picked her up, shocked at how light she was. He held her slumped across both arms. In the darkness her features were hidden from him. There was a glint in her half-open eyes…but she could easily have been dead.

He heard a noise through the downpour, a whisper as of water gently flowing between rocks. He held his breath and stood very still, glancing over his shoulder at the house as he did so. Its dark windows looked back. A hanging gutter gave it an expression of bored irony. He noticed for the first time that it had only windows, no doors, as if once inside there was no escape.

The noise increased in volume. It came from back in the bushes, perhaps the way they had just come, perhaps not. Lee was too disorientated to decide for sure.

"Kate!" he whispered, shaking his wife very gently. She groaned but did not wake.

He could stay here until morning, wet and tired and frightened, while Moll perhaps sat inside this strange house. He could try to find his way back to the road. Or he could investigate the noise…the noise that was louder than ever and which, he was certain, was composed of individual voices mumbling and whispering to each other, or to themselves.

He stared at the house. No, it was deserted. Whatever Kate had said about sitting in the dark, this house was empty. He could feel the building itself watching him, but no one from inside. And besides: no doors. That was freakish. He did not want to stay here on his own.

He slung Kate over his left shoulder and set off through the rain. His right hand closed around the knife handle and slipped it from his jacket. As he walked the rain lessened and the moon peered from between storm clouds. It was as he stared at the ground to avoid holes or dips that he became aware that he was following a large trail of footprints. Most of them were very small.

Through the bushes, closing in on the sound, Kate murmuring and twitching on his shoulder, the knife singing

Pay the Ghost

as the occasional raindrops hit it…Lee realised at last where he was going.

From the shelter of a clump of trees he saw the people, dozens of them, standing and staring down into the pit. They were the inhabitants of the estate, some shifting from foot to foot, others simply standing and staring. They all seemed to be on their own. He followed their gaze and could not help uttering a terrified gasp.

The pit was full of children.

Some were sitting, others standing. There must have been twenty toddlers and teens in there, crying and hugging, sometimes staring blankly at the earth wall or the sky far above them.

"Kate!" Lee said, shaking his wife, letting her slip unceremoniously to the ground. He held the knife before him, shaking now, trying to realise the consequence of all this, struggling to piece together what was happening. His wife stirred in the mud.

"Come to pay the ghost?" a voice said in his ear. He spun around but there was no one there, only shadows. When he looked back towards the pit everything had changed. They were all looking at him. Even the children.

Even Moll.

"Oh my God!" he gasped, stumbling from the cover of bushes and into the faint moonlight. Nobody moved to stop him, and he ran to the edge of the pit, staring down at his daughter where she stood with her back against the earth wall. She looked up at him but did not smile. She did not seem to recognise him.

"You bastards!" he shouted, brandishing the knife, sweeping it in slow, clumsy arcs to keep the people at bay.

They had closed around him while he was looking at Moll. To get out now...to reach Kate and freedom...he would have to fight his way through them. "What have you done to her? What are you doing?" He was screaming and crying at the same time, strengthened by rage and weakened by a terrible sense of hopelessness, born of the realisation that she had been here all along. He had given her up on the day she disappeared, yet a year later, here she was.

He held out his hand to Moll. "Come on, darling. Come on. Daddy's here, I've come to take you home." He kept glancing back, but none of the silent people seemed ready to attack him. They simply stood and watched, eyes wide, shifting slightly as if impatient for something to happen.

The air stank of petrol. There were hay bales and dead ferns in the pit with the children. One of the kids seemed to have no legs, another shivered on the ground, bald and emaciated...and Lee was certain that in the shadows, even more dreadful mutilations hid themselves away.

"Leave her," a voice said.

Lee looked around but none of the people seemed to have spoken. He waved the knife at them.

"Leave her alone," the voice said again, "you've lost her."

"That's my daughter in there!" he screamed, and a shape manifested itself before him. It came from the darkness and formed a shadow, and when its eyes and mouth opened they reflected no moonlight.

"Not for a long while now," it said.

Children whimpered behind and below him. Somewhere a flame popped into being, and an excited ripple passed through those gathered there. The final drops of rain hissed as they hit the naked flame.

Lee's anger burst out. He slashed at the figure, lunging and stabbing and slicing with the kitchen knife. Even as he did so a sense of unreality grabbed him, the realisation that he was actually trying to kill someone...and this was aggravated when the knife found nothing but air.

The shape shifted, came towards Lee and actually seemed to touch him, a coolness far more deep-felt that mere temperature, a black, engulfing cold that touched his lungs and heart and spine with its gossamer fingers. "You can leave...now."

"Me," Kate said from behind the assembled people. "Me, use me. Please." The watchers stepped aside to let her pass. She slithered through the mud, pushing with her feet and pulling with her hands, unable to stand but finding motion like the reptile cast out from the garden.

"Kate, Moll's here, Moll's in the pit!"

"Put me in," she said, "please, me instead."

"You're not a child," the voice breathed. "A child's flesh burns better."

"I found you," Kate shouted, her strength surprising Lee. "That must count for something."

"Determination and love," the shadow whispered. "And...well, you've been due to us for some time now."

"Please," Lee pleaded, tears blurring his image of the moonlit night and the shadow that hovered there before him. "My daughter...please."

"Your wife..."

"Yes, yes!" Kate gasped, squirming forward once more, touching Lee once on the ankle before tumbling into the pit.

She cried out as she struck the bottom, the tears continuing as Moll knelt gingerly beside her. "Honey," Kate said. But her daughter stood and turned away.

The shadow laughed, a horrid sound. "Take your child that has forgotten you."

"You have to let these kids go…" The futility of what he was asking for struck Lee then. He was talking to a ghost. He was outnumbered. He should have gone to the police, although he was certain they would have never found this place. There was something odd about it, something removed from the norm…the trees and bushes seemed unconcerned that there was a ghost in their midst, one with human consorts.

"There will be a fire," the shadow said. "If you would avoid the flames, take her now."

One of the silent watchers kicked over a barrel of petrol and let it run into the trench. The children stirred, Kate began to pray.

"Moll," Lee said, holding out his hand, never once taking his eyes from the shadow shifting before him. Kate must have boosted her from the trench, using whatever final reserves of energy she could find to save her daughter and doom herself. Moll's hand closed around his fingers, he pulled, and his lost daughter was with him once more.

"Let them go," he said pathetically, knowing that there was nothing he could do.

"It's our turn to go home to the other world," one of the people said. And that was when Lee realised that their eyes reflected nothing; no moonlight, no glimmer from the naked flame. Nothing.

"Run, Lee! Run, Moll! Before it changes its mind!"

Pay the Ghost

Lee hoisted Moll up and she clung to his shoulders, her legs resting on his hips. She did not say anything. He so wanted to hear her voice, but he wanted to live as well. He wanted all of them to live.

He stared at the people—the things—from the estate and saw that there was no help there. They were completely in thrall to the shadow.

"Kate—"

"I'm dead anyway, Lee," she sobbed from the pit. "You've seen me. Take Moll. Save one, it's better than none at all."

So Lee ran along the edge of the trench, constantly expecting to be tripped by an unseen foot or pushed by one of the motionless watchers. Soon he was in the bushes, Moll clinging to him and burying her face in his neck. He could not imagine what she had witnessed or been through over the past year, but she obviously did not want to see any more. He felt her body heat pressing through his wet clothes, her breath on his skin, her hair tickling his face, and he could not believe that he had ever given up hope.

The night sky lit up behind them. There were screams, searing screams, but they did not last for very long. He could not help turning around to look, to see…people leaping across the pit, some falling into the flames, screeching with delight as they found their way home, wherever home was to them. And a shadow before the flames, guiding the dispossessed into the other worldly fire.

Lee fled, running into bushes and trees, stumbling, falling, expecting to feel hands on his shoulders or around his ankles at any minute. Moll grunted and whined when he fell, but said nothing. A shadow loomed, moonlight reflecting from sharp teeth…but it was only the burned out car.

As Lee emerged onto the road with his stolen daughter clinging to him, the fire reflecting from the clouds had dimmed to almost nothing.

—⚏—

Lee lost his wife on Hallowe'en. He knew…he *prayed*…that she was never coming back.

He also lost any pride, dignity or humanity he should have regained at rescuing his daughter, and any feeling that there was more to it than this. There was not. There was life and death and everything bad in between…like leaving children burning in a ditch to save himself.

Lee found Moll's mutilation: her tongue had been sliced out just after she had been taken, so he could never remember his daughter's voice. She did not attempt to communicate with him by any other means.

He guessed that during her year trapped in that out-of-the-way house, some of those doomed children he had left behind had become her friends.

Kissing at Shadows

"I'm going to visit Helen."

"She's dead, Dad. Mum's dead."

"I'm going to see her, Charley. You know you mustn't try to stop me."

"Dad, it's the same every year. You know how dangerous it is out there now. You know it's getting worse, getting even colder. And—"

"Don't try to put me off, Charley. She's your mother, you should want me to go to see her, ask how—"

"She's dead! She died with everyone else, why do you insist on not believing that?"

I paused for a moment and smiled. I knew that infuriated Charley, an unfair ploy in our yearly argument.

"Dad, what about the things living—existing—out there in the ashes? You know what happened to Marc and the others." She was crying now. I hated to see that but perhaps it was simply a tactic, like my wry smile.

"Marc didn't take care. I will."

Charley tried for another half hour but then she realised that I would be going, as I did every year, no matter what she said or did. Going to visit my dead wife, kiss her, share recollections of our last good times together. And then, God willing, I would be back.

Though with all God had willed lately, this was far from certain.

I remembered sitting with new-born Charley cradled in my arms. They were sewing Helen up after the Caesarean and they'd hustled me from the operating theatre, sat me down and placed this new life in my hands. Then they left me…us…alone. They didn't even tell me what to do.

She was not crying. She was looking around, all wide-eyed and shocked and vulnerable and beautiful. And I could say little, other than *hello, sweetie…hello, sweetie.* Minutes before she had not been here, now she was in our world. In a way she did not look too happy about it, but it was my job to make her happy, make her safe. Protect her as much as I could.

That was still my job, even after all that had happened. But to protect her, I did not necessarily have to be around her all the time. Helping myself was helping her, and sometimes I thought it was only these yearly visits with Helen that kept me going. A highlight in a year when everything else was low, when mutation and death and suffering held sway.

For a while, Helen would drive all of these things away.

Kissing at Shadows

—⚋—

Charley came to see me off. It was a brave thing for her to do, it meant swallowing her pride. I loved her for it. I kissed her on the forehead and told her I'd be back soon, and she tried once more to dissuade me from going.

"Dad, you don't even know where she is."

"I do. I've seen her. I told you last year, I saw her."

Charley looked at her feet and shook her head sadly. "I couldn't bear to lose you as well."

She did not look up but I saw dark rosettes of tears flowering on the dusty ground. I squeezed her shoulder once, turned away and started walking. I had to. There was too much holding me back, and another moment of indecision could have changed things forever. Besides, I could not let Helen down. She was expecting me.

I felt Charley's gaze on my back as I emerged from the mouth of the tunnel and walked along the old tracks. They were barely visible now, subsumed beneath a nature gone wild; creepers and weeds and red-flowering orchids fought over the rusted track and in most places hid it from view. Every now and then my booted feet would strike metal, reminding me of mankind.

When I was far enough away so that I would not see the look in her eyes, I turned to wave to Charley. She was still there, a tiny shape dwarfed by the half-moon tunnel surrounding her, the entrance festooned with rampant weeds, their colours and shapes mutated by a change we had brought about. She waved back, and it was as if she were trying to grab these hanging vines, haul herself from the tunnel and escape the strange community it now enclosed, survivors and those who simply could not be bothered to die. Perhaps she was jealous of me and my temporary freedom, however dangerous it may be.

At last I rounded the first slow bend in the track and Charley, the tunnel, home, fell out of sight.

A sense of emptiness closed quickly around me. Or rather a feeling that I was alone, a definite idea that the world had changed to such an extent that I was now one of a kind, unique. It was rare that anyone came out of the tunnel on their own. Even groups came only as and when materials or new food supplies were needed, such were the dangers outside. Now here I was, a rucksack of food on my back, dogskin coat tied around with dried creeper, a rifle slung across my shoulders with a precious handful of rounds in my pocket.

Alone. The world went on around me without seeming to notice my presence. Had things changed so much? Was I now so different that I did not even cause a ripple, a stir, did not turn a head? The birds in the sky were unafraid, unseen things ran quickly through the undergrowth either side of me. Even the plants seemed to spring back up behind me, as if my boots had never crushed them down in the first place. I wondered what effect a shout or a scream would have. I wondered would they even be heard in a place where there was no one to listen.

Things had changed a great deal, even since my previous journey this way the previous year. I worked my way along the old railway cutting, and where once the ruins of houses had stared down upon me from the tops of both banks, now they had crumbled and been worn by the harsh rains, overgrown with weeds of such a deep green colour that they appeared, from a distance, black. Some buildings still erred tenaciously to the vertical, but even those were more plant than stone. There were bones in there, I knew, skeletons of past lives laid bare by humankind's own impetuousness, the flesh stripped from civilisation by the corruption of nature's most basic components. Humankind was a rapist, and its victim still displayed the scars of its most recent and deadly assault.

It was cold, Charley was right about that. The sky was a uniform, heavy grey, pregnant with dust and sparkling here and there with electrical discharge. There were storms up there, great swirling spots like the surface of Jupiter, history blasting around in trillions of fragments of what had once been. I stared up for a time and wondered who or what I could see.

Looking closer at the plants I noticed the diamond glint of ice crystals winking at me, reflecting the negligible sunlight that fought its way to the ground. Each one could have been someone's condensed final breath. There would be billions of crystals.

Even before I was out of the cutting I sensed that I was being followed.

One night I almost lost Helen and Charley. A drunk driver nudged them off the road on the way home from the dance hall, and then he went on his way. Our car ended up on its side in a ditch.

Helen rang me from the hospital and told me what had happened. I was in work—overtime, so that we could have the holiday to Italy we'd long been promising ourselves—and she told me that Charley was in a bad way.

Things shrank from me. Experience grew stale, all the good aspects of life became nothing under the onslaught of Charley's potential death. Somehow I found the breath to run to my car and drive to the hospital, and when I saw Helen my heart broke. She had not even mentioned her own injuries: the dozens of facial cuts from the shattered windscreen; the broken cheek; her gored arm where the muscles would never be the same again. She stared at me, totally selfless, existing purely as a mother concerned for her terribly injured daughter. I hugged her and there was a blackness between us.

Together we stood at Charley's bedside and listened to the doctors tell us how there was hope, she would pull through if she was strong, people had recovered from these types of injuries many times before. The doctors would not catch my eyes.

For those few weeks Helen barely left my side, and she made me swear that the three of us would be together forever. It was a promise I could not make, but I did all the same. I promised her with my heart, my soul, I swore on everything I held dear, which was her and Charley. I hugged her close and promised, and several months later Charley came home and we all began the long haul back to a new kind of normality.

The driver was banned for three years and fined eight hundred pounds. "Bastard's got a lump of coal for a heart," Helen would say. Like a curse.

Kissing at Shadows

By the time I made my way into the first of the shattered streets I was certain that something or someone was stalking me, and had been since leaving the cutting. It was as if something had been waiting for me. Even though I guessed it was Charley I still unslung the rifle and chambered a round. I kept glancing back, afraid that I would be attacked from the front when my attention was turned, but I saw nothing. I thought of calling out to her, telling her to go back, but I knew it would do no good. Besides, there was always the chance that it was not Charley. Just a chance.

It had once been Clover Street. An early girlfriend of mine had lived here with her parents, but now it was just another ruined row of houses. I tried to recall which one she had lived in but they all looked the same. I tried to remember what she had been like, our times together, her smile and her laugh and her sigh, but it felt like a betrayal of Helen. I coughed, shouted, called out my name and that of my old girlfriend, suddenly wondering what I would do if I heard her shouting back. The thought made me pause and glance warily about, but there was nothing to be afraid of here. Whoever had once lived in these houses was now dead and gone, or just gone, or perhaps just dead, their bones mixed with tumbled masonry to build a sculpture to the past. I was half tempted to investigate, to see if I could find anything worth keeping.

Another noise behind me started me moving again.

I could not tell exactly what it was. It could have been a giggle quickly thwarted, or a grunt between fingers. It may have been human, but if so there was something basic and primeval in the voice. I hoped it was animal. All I could be sure of was that it came from behind me, so I started quickly on my way. I glanced back occasionally, praying I was alone.

I had been coming this way once each year for six years. Every time I followed the same route to Helen, and each year she had faded away some more. One day she may be gone for good, I knew that; but I also knew that this would change nothing. I would still take this walk. I must always visit her, however vague her memory was in my mind. I had made a promise.

I stepped onto the bus and nodded to the driver. It was a number 18, heading through town, over the motorway bridge and out towards where the industrial areas and mega-markets had been springing up for a decade before the war. I had used it often. I had gone to work on it a few times, when Helen needed the car or I was going out for a drink with friends straight from work. Now it sat still and silent and ruined, and the driver was little more than a fat man with whiskers haunting my memory. But every year I stopped here and sat on the bus, and looked out the window to despair at what had become of the old neighbourhood.

The seat had rotted down to the metal frame and I did not stay seated for long.

As I stood, somebody else got onto the bus with me.

I did not see them. I did not hear them or smell them. I did not even sense them, with that strange sixth sense so many of us seem to possess *in extremis*. I simply knew that there was someone else on the bus with me, perhaps sitting down, maybe just standing there and holding onto the overhead rail as the vehicle swayed and rocked over badly repaired potholes many years before.

Kissing at Shadows

"Charley?" I said, but there was no answer and nothing changed. "Helen?" Again, nothing. I sat back down and closed my eyes. They felt wet. My cheeks were cool with tears. I rarely cried at nothing.

There was a sudden noise from outside. It startled me and the tenuous presence on the bus disappeared. This sound was not secretive but overt, a heavy grunt like something hitting the ground from a height and having its wind knocked out. I grappled with the rifle across my shoulder and succeeded only in wedging it between the buckled ceiling and a rusted pole.

In the twilight no shadows moved, but there was something out there watching me. I could hear it wheezing heavily, walking across grit and broken glass. It sounded as if it had claws. Not Charley, then. Certainly not Helen.

I thought of what had happened to Marc and the others. They'd foolishly believed it was safe to go out and start rebuilding; we had found a few bits of them the first time we went to visit the house they were working on. There were teeth marks in their bones and heaps of shit around the place, as if whatever had killed them had chosen to foul their memory with its faeces.

The thing growled and strode into view. I gasped and managed to untangle the gun from the broken bus as the old dog sidled towards me. It had been a German Shepherd once. Now it was a mass of growths and contusions, even its teeth shoved out at crazy angles by cancerous gums. There were bits of stuff on its teeth, stuff I didn't like the look of. Its various boils oozed a black, rotten blood.

I raised the rifle and sighted on the pathetic creature's head—

—and paused.

Helen and I once had a dog, a scruffy mongrel called Pepsi. It had been a daft old thing but we'd loved it, enjoyed its company, relished its personified affection without trying to think too much about the animal reality. Perhaps someone had once loved this dog; combed its fur; clipped its nails; tickled its stomach in front of a fire before the ruin had spread fire indefinitely.

I lowered the rifle and the dog hobbled past the wrecked bus. I'm sure I actually heard its joints creaking, its bones grumbling as stresses promised to snap them at any moment.

I watched sadly until the dog was lost in shadows. Then I waited a few more minutes to make sure it had gone on its way and started out again.

—✽—

Something still stalked me.

The dog had gone, and I was now certain that the stalker was not Charley, either. The thing that followed me threw memories my way, steering me past places where Helen and I had stood and stared and talked, or just held hands and let time go on around us. Here, a cinema blackened by fire where we had shared our first tentative kiss. And here, the tumbled remains of the pub where I had told Helen that I loved her and she had almost choked on her gin and tonic. Outside, leaning against a wall that was now no more than dust, she had told me that she loved me too.

I stopped and ate tinned peaches, sitting on a rusted seat in what had once been a park. The ordered landscape had

Kissing at Shadows

gone wild, mocking humankind's semblance of control by contorting and twisting into new, incredible shapes. Trees grew horizontally and splayed their roots at the skies. A stream of melted glass had flowed downhill from the business district, trapping leaves and rubbish and air from before the ruin in its opaque depths. And I knew that I had once sat here with Helen, watching kids feeding ducks on the now absent pond, feeling the electric touch of her bare leg against my own.

I had to see her now, I had to be with her, and knowing where she was made that need all the more urgent. I had to make it clear that no matter what had happened, we were still a family.

There was a pile of skeletons against the twisted remnants of the park's railings, as if ghosts had been tidying up their former Earthly vessels. Some of them were rich in dulled jewellery. Others wore leathery skin where animals or the elements had not been able to steal it away. They had not been there on my previous trips, I was sure of that, and their appearance did more to unsettle me than anything I had yet seen. The naked bone collection hinted at organisation. Somewhere out here, someone was still alive.

I thought of the dog. And I wondered what state any survivors were likely to be in.

—⚇—

Charley's scars had been terrible. Helen and I had spent most of our daughter's childhood years dealing with them in one way or another, while Charley herself grew and developed into a normal, healthy, if slightly arrogant girl.

Tim Lebbon

The arrogance was a defence against the glances and smirks her scars drew, and rather than discourage it I left her alone to adapt in her own particular ways. She had to learn how to survive, because we would not always be there for her. Helen made me promise it so, she made me swear; but I knew that one day we would both be gone, and Charley would still be there.

Still I made my promise to Helen. It would have broken her heart had I not.

—⚘—

Helen was exactly where I expected to find her. The wall of the dance hall was still standing. No plants had rooted in the sterile powder of shattered concrete blown against its base. I stood for a while and stared at her.

The old hall was a graveyard of memories. The nights we had spent here, kissing and whispering as we glided around and between other couples, never winning the prize, but never caring. We had each other, and that was always enough.

Bad memories resounded, as well. Shattered windows echoed screams long gone, and against the outside walls the shadows stood in panicked, contorted poses, flash-fried there by the blast so long ago.

Helen was crucified into the brickwork. Her arms were held out, her head thrown back, all her beautiful features superimposed by my faltering memory onto a vague, dark smudge on the cracked and dusty wall. Sometimes memories have to be enough, but in this place, for one day each year, I still had Helen. Her arms were wide, her hands open. She

Kissing at Shadows

was wearing a flowery dress the day she died—the one day she had gone to the dance on her own—she liked floral print because it reminded her there was more to life than the city. I could not see it but I pictured it in my mind.

Her arms were ready to embrace me, and though they never would again, the intent was there for all to see. Love can survive. I saw it in her stance. And I saw it in her eyes as my memory placed them there against the old stone wall. They closed. I walked slowly forward, leaned in so that my shadow touched her own, and then I kissed the dusty stone where her mouth should have be. For a second I tasted her breath. Then a cool breeze blew and I felt ice forming on my lips.

—⚯—

I was followed back to the cutting and the tunnel, though it felt like I was led.

Charley was waiting there for me; the relief in her eyes made me cry, she begged me not to go again, held me tight and bled tears of grief onto my shoulders. Each year I went to see Helen renewed the wrench of Charley losing her mother. I closed my arms around her and cried as well, then the others gestured impatiently for us to go back into the tunnel so that they could shut the doors.

As I turned for one final look across the blackened landscape, I wondered if what had followed me would wait for me to come out again next year. I hoped it would. And yet at the same time I hoped that it would set me free, be gone, gone to wherever it needed to be. Helen had been dead for a long time. I could not keep my promise forever.

Hell Came Down

I went looking for him where it was dry and parched, where the skeletons of cattle decorated the outskirts of town like grotesque, bleached baubles, where children lay on pavements and breathed shallowly, painfully as their mothers tried to squeeze a drop of moisture from sagging breasts, where the sun had leached all colour and the facades of buildings presented a uniform paleness, where stream-beds were crazy paving punctuated here and there with dead weeds, where people wandered in a haze to and from the watering hole that was little less than mud now, mud that could be squeezed for a few precious drops, sometimes, if they were lucky. A place where death was sometimes a release, and cadavers were never put to waste. Dead fathers gave their children a source of sustenance for a day or two. They would have wanted it that way.

I knew that Lucien would be here. Where better to find a rain-maker?

Tim Lebbon

Heads turned my way as I entered the town. The dying people heard the slosh of water in my canteen, a sound that doubtless haunted their dreams, waking and sleeping. Some looked pleadingly, others scheming. They saw the rifle across my shoulders and perhaps thought better of it, but even without that I would not have been concerned. I had other ways of protecting myself.

I looked for signs of his presence. It was no use asking because they all thought he was trying to help them: Lucien, bringing down rain onto parched lands, urging the clouds to form and the droplets to condense, conjure life back into a dead place and a dying people. They thought this even though he had yet to bring a storm...of rain, at least. In Birmingham a shower of frogs had emerged from the clear blue skies and splattered across the ground around him. I had not seen it happen, but I had heard others talk of it. In Bristol, dogs and cats, clogging the remaining streams and watering holes with rancid bodies crawling with fleas and God knew what else. Some of the cats had two tails. Some of the dogs were new breeds.

Still, they worshipped him.

I stopped at a bakery devoid of bread. It was selling dried potatoes, their skins wrinkled around withered insides. I picked one up and it rattled like an egg containing a mummified chick.

"A drink from your canteen," the man in the shop said. He was still in his twenties, I guessed, but he looked fifty.

Hell Came Down

"It would kill you." I touched the metal canister on my belt, then briefly adjusted the gun across my shoulders. It was not what I meant…I wouldn't shoot him, the water itself would finish him because it was not of this world…but he got the message.

"Well then, what will you trade me?"

"For these?" I picked up a handful of potatoes and weighed them. There was hardly any mass there at all. Certainly no goodness.

"They're all I have," he said wretchedly.

I looked around the shop and saw old posters displaying rich cakes, thick with cream and bleeding with jam. "I used to work for a baker," I lied. "He was a good man. Jesus was a baker, you know."

The young-old man frowned, confused. He licked his dry lips with a drier tongue. I heard it, like a boot scraping across sandy ground.

I tried a smile. "You help me, and I'll do what I can to help you."

"What do you mean?" Still he glanced at the canteen on my hip.

"I told you that will kill you. But I have other water… purified. Filtered."

"Where?"

"Help me first." I sat on the inside window sill, wondering how many had rested here in the past waiting for their order of bread and doughnuts. In the street someone was wailing, but it was a common sound now, as regular as the beating of the sun. "I'm looking for the rain-maker."

"Lucien!" The baker's tired eyes brightened.

"You've seen him?" I sat forward. The black water moved in the canteen, shifting it against my leg like a living thing.

"I fed him!" the man said. "He came to me and took some food, and gave me…something in return."

"What?"

The man shrugged, looking as embarrassed as a man slowly dying of thirst and hunger could. "A frog." He had eaten it—his expression made that clear. Its blood, its mucus, its fluids…moisture of a kind.

"I need to find him," I said. "He's making all this worse."

"No, he's making it better!"

"Then where are the rains?" I roared, standing and advancing on the man, angry and desperate and so willing to cause pain…though I had caused enough already. The trail of Lucien's devastation across the land displayed that so well. "Show me how he's helped!"

"He said…he said that if I talked—"

"I'll give you water!"

"No, I can't, he said—"

I grabbed him by the shirt, lifted him and pressed him against an old poster for Chelsea buns. "Tell me where he is!"

"The Courthouse. Last I heard he…he was…" The baker gagged, his eyes turned up in his head, he bit straight through the end of his own tongue.

I dropped him. I didn't want to be covered in his mess.

The young man who looked so old slipped to the dusty tiled floor of his shop, twitching and twisting himself into unnatural shapes, arms and legs entwining as whatever was inside sought escape. His eyes bulged, as did his stomach.

Hell Came Down

He screeched, a high keening sound that scared the few remaining birds outside into flight and set a rabid dog growling somewhere in the distance. His hands clawed. I backed away. His nails scored into his throat and chest as he ripped at himself.

I was standing outside on the pavement when his stomach ruptured and a sickly grey mess spilled across the floor, steaming precious fluids to condense and dry on the walls of his shop. He twitched one more time, then was still.

Lucien was covering his tracks well, but not well enough. Perhaps, despite all his powers, he was not expecting me.

I had to find the Courts.

I was not a bad teacher. It was Lucien who was a poor pupil. My real mistake was in not seeing that, and this is why I had to pursue him across the country, closing in day by day, until that time I confronted him in the old Courts in Usk.

He had come to me as a boy and begged to be shown the weird ways, and even then he displayed some level of barely restrained potency that made me seem an amateur. I took him in. He had fled his family years before, his peculiar gift effectively ostracising him even from them. He had worshipped, venerated and heeded me, absorbing what I taught, listening when I warned. He was a strong young man haunted by what his mind contained. And that should have been my first warning: it haunted him, but did not control him. He fought it. He fought his gift from God.

I should have killed him there and then.

Tim Lebbon

I walked along the town's main street, trying to smile at one or two people but seeing only pain and fear sent back at me. The heat had been so great for so long that some of the buildings were crumbling, their brick and stonework destroyed from within, heated and expanded and cracked to ruin. On the left, an old antiques store had lost its window and surround. The sign still hung above, letters faded and forgotten, but all it housed now was a mountain of yellowed books. A fire waiting to happen. And indeed, further along the street there was a charred gap in the row of shops, a place where fire had come and taken its due. A few roof members had survived, protruding from the black mass of stone and concrete, thinned out by the flames. There was something else lying there as well, in amongst the wreckage. It glinted white, but only because carrion creatures had picked its cooked bones clean. Carrion creatures and, perhaps, carrion humans as well.

I reached an intersection of two roads. There was a banner strung across the street from years ago, a bitter in-joke that the townsfolk seemed still to be playing upon themselves. It read: *Usk in Bloom*. They had been gardeners, flower growers, feeding into the ground the water which they so craved now.

It had not rained for over a year. The country was in ruin.

I saw a bank, a restaurant, a clothes shop, all totally redundant now that famine and disease were grinding the last dregs of humanity into the soil. Some people still tried to keep a hold of what they had once been, and I was sure I saw the shadowy movement of someone behind the bank's counter. Perhaps even now they counted useless millions

Hell Came Down

and slipped out with a secret note here, a note there, slowly accumulating a fortune as worthless as the dry river bed, or the underground water pipes that had cracked in the heat and given their final precious drops to the dry earth.

"You!" someone shouted. "Hey, you!"

I could not locate the caller at first, so I closed my eyes and found them in my mind. Above and behind. I turned and looked up at an open window. There was a woman leaning out, naked and filthy, hair knotted and skin cracked beneath the dirt. Dried blood clotted around her joints. Her eyes were wild, at least the one I could see, squinting at me along the length of a shotgun.

"The water. Throw it up."

"You really think it will save you?"

"You think I give a fuck? It's for my baby." She was mad with thirst and hunger, I could tell that much at least, but her aim never wavered: my head. I could see right into the barrels.

I closed my eyes again and moved up to her, felt into the gun, saw that it was loaded. No bluffing, then. She really meant it.

I opened my eyes and leaned slowly against the wall beside me. I made certain that my hands stayed at my sides. There was no way I could reach my rifle in time. Besides, there were other ways of stopping her.

"Don't make me kill you," I said quietly.

She laughed. "Your head will be all over the road before you even touch that gun. Now throw up the canteen and you can go on. I mean it. I won't kill you."

"I know you won't," I said, "but the water will kill your baby. It's black water."

"He's drunk dirty water before."

"Never black."

I closed my eyes one more time and moved back up there, fingering my way into her mind this time, desperate not to see what was inside there but more desperate not to have to kill her. I knew how risky this was. I could spend precious seconds convincing her, or I could just slip in and throw a switch, kill her painlessly and without a sound, drop her to the floor and go on my way. I had killed before, many times. I would do so again, soon, when I found Lucien. But it was ironic that now, with my own head framed by a shotgun's line of fire, one more life seemed so precious amongst a billion dead.

She was mad. There were visions in there that terrified me, perverted truths that lied even to themselves, a fragrant paranoia that stank of neglect and pain and decades of abuse, stemming from long before the drought and famine, rooted in a past so dark that even the black water would taste sweet in comparison. I closed my mind to these places and tried to pass through, feeling the soapy touch of terror attempting to drag me from my path and lose me in the depths, places where direction was lost and simply being was all there was, being awed, being feared, being trapped.

At last I found the centre of her, the place where all sanity had been driven and where, even now, madness was eating away at its edges like an eternally patient caterpillar chewing at the boundaries of the mightiest forest. She had been a good woman once, a mother and a wife and a librarian, fighting a difficult past by revelling in a content present, little suspecting what the future held.

Then I showed her the black water.

Hell Came Down

"Get that fucking shit away from me!" she screeched, seeing instantly, not giving me a chance to withdraw before panicking.

I pulled out and went back to myself, opened my eyes, stunned by her quick reaction and suddenly knowing my mistake. She may be mad, yes, but she was desperate as well. She had a child to save when her own life was already wasted.

I had time to slip inches down the wall before she pulled the trigger.

Most of the shot struck the brickwork directly where my head had been a second before. Shattered brick rained down on my head and shoulders, and I felt something plucking at my forehead and right eye, something that felt cold but quickly turned hot, white hot, burning its way into my head and down through my neck. I screamed, fell to the ground and put my hands to my face. The ruin of my eye was leaking from its socket. My good eye was blinded by the pain. The blood and fluid was thick and slimy like a broken, raw egg.

Any normal man would have died or curled up with the pain. I stood, unslung the rifle from my pack and opened up at the window. I tried to probe at the woman but the pain was too great, I could not detach properly, and besides, I had the feeling she had fled. The sight returned slowly to my left eye, fading in from a bright white to a semblance of what was around me, and I emptied the clip at the window and those either side of it. Glass smashed, stonework spat out powdered eruptions, a bullet ricocheted along the street and starred the windscreen of an abandoned car.

Then I turned and ran. In my blinding agony I ran without direction. I automatically replaced the magazine in the rifle, but no one seemed keen to stop or tackle me. I must have presented a fearsome sight, a big man with bloodied face, ragged eye socket, water canteen and rifle, sprinting along streets where nowadays people could barely crawl.

I ran for five minutes. My blood pumped, my heart thumped, I bled out the pain. By the time I stopped my eye had ceased bleeding and was already scabbing over. The pain had reduced to a bright throb, flashing into my head as if my eye was still there and I was looking directly at the sun. I slumped against a garden wall, unhooked the canteen and took a swig of the black water.

It tasted awful, but it invigorated me, giving sustenance and strength and power of mind and will with one swig.

And I suddenly realised the truth. Things had come to a head without me even instigating it. I had to catch Lucien now, within the next few minutes, because he would have heard the shooting, and if he'd learnt anything good from me it was an aggressive instinct for self-preservation. Wherever he was, whatever he was doing, he would be readying to leave. If I lost track of him now it would take me weeks, or even months to find him again, wounded as I was. Weeks or months may be far too late for this place. I may not even have days.

In Devon I had found a whole village killed by the scorpions Lucien had brought down from the sky when he was trying to conjure rain. When I arrived the air was still tainted with his pain, his guilt, his growing madness. He was trying, trying again, striving to get it right, but wherever he went things were getting worse, the manifestations matching his increasing frustration. There were over five hundred bodies in that place. They were swollen and bloated and

Hell Came Down

burst from the effects of the scorpions' poison. Some of the creatures had been as big as my hand. Many had possessed a sting at both ends.

It could only get worse.

I pushed myself from the wall and went to the nearest house showing signs of habitation. I probed inside, saw that they had no weapons of threat to me, smashed on the door until it gave way. There was no time for niceties.

A little girl scampered into a room to my left. Her father stepped into the corridor, a short-bladed knife in his hand and a look of resigned terror in his eyes. He was ready to die for her. He looked about set to die anyway, all the signs of hunger and thirst evident on his face. It was obvious that he had been giving all the food and drink he could scrounge or steal to his daughter.

I grabbed him, shoved him against the wall, knocked the knife aside.

"I'll let you live if you tell me where the old Courts are in the next three seconds."

"Your…your eye."

"One."

I was choking him. He could barely talk.

"Two."

"I…I…"

"Three."

"Show you…I'll show you…"

I let him slide down until his feet touched carpet, then I let go. He looked down at the knife on the floor but obviously thought better of it. Rubbing at his bruised neck, he glanced into the room at his daughter, tried to smile at her. She cried at his grimace.

"That way," he said, pointing out the front door and to my right. "Two streets along, then turn left. Iron railings. But I don't know what you want with the Courts…they're haunted."

"I know," I said, and although I was lying—I didn't know whether they were haunted or not—I was sure they soon would be. I turned to leave. "Sorry," I muttered. I felt the man's stare, felt him beginning to crumple. His daughter ran to him and he was trying to hide his tears, but he was nearing the end of a life of weakness and loss, hopelessness and shame.

Sometimes I saw far too much to bear.

Lucien was still there.

As I neared the Courts, I saw signs. Cracked paving slabs at first, whatever falling things that had caused their destruction long since vanished. A row of houses with shattered slates, the holes in the roofs adorned with wispy material, flickering like spider-web in the subtle breeze. It could have been roof lining, or dusty webs snagged on the broken timbers, or skin. Then living things: a beetle with two heads, scurrying along the gutter on twelve legs; a butterfly spiralling in lazy, pointless circles, its wings a death mask with bleeding eyes; a hummingbird, probing at withered flowers in its useless quest for sustenance. Alien animals to these shores, perhaps even alien to this world.

Especially the rat. It was as big as a tomcat, and as it ran across the road I saw traces of bloodied ginger fur around its jaws. A tomcat's match as well, evidently. It had a horn

Hell Came Down

protruding from the centre of its forehead, serving no purpose other than to give it a hateful appearance.

I turned away and jogged along the street. Each footfall provoked a spike of pain in my head from my destroyed eye socket, but I welcomed it. It told me that I was still alive. The chaos Lucien had caused was my fault, and if half-blindness and constant pain was all the punishment I would receive for such a heinous mistake, then it was light indeed, for I was as guilty as sin.

The Courts were large and imposing. Columns graced the entrance, leaded windows on either side stared out like grey dead eyes, iron railings contained the building within its gardens, once lush but now brown and dry and dead. There was an old fountain in the front courtyard with a body curved around its central spout. Perhaps whoever had crawled here to die had believe that, if a miracle did occur and water flowed again, they would be revived. Most of the flesh had been chewed away. A denim jacket covered the ribcage. Rings, a silver necklace and a glittering anklet all touched bone.

I probed inside, carefully so that Lucien would not sense me. He was powerful, but mad with it, a twisted genius. If I was careful he would not notice me.

I gasped. There were things in there…I had felt ghosts before but never like this, never in such profusion. And the strangest thing was, they were all new, all recently dead, all inhabiting the same place in this doomed town.

Here, an old woman wandering in a circle, in and out of this world, seeking her husband both here and elsewhere. *Have you seen my Gerald?* she asked. *He's a farmer…*

Tim Lebbon

A young girl too, barely into her teens, crawling around the ceilings inside as if too afraid to touch the ground. Her mouth was open in a permanent scream. Her skin was raised in grotesque humps, each of them capped with a poison-filled pustule. The ants, the ants, the ants, the ants...

A man and a woman, husband and wife, twisted together and merged where something had gored them to death. *I love you...love...love you...* their voices entwined madly, neither of them realising that they had no reason to haunt.

Lucien's dead, I knew, those who had perished because of his failed efforts, killed by creatures they knew or monsters they did not.

I probed further, trying to ignore the anguish and the pain and the resentment that only the dead can truly feel. I sensed old ghosts too, ground back into the shadowy realms of this place by the new, fresh anger of the recently dead. And then I found him: Lucien, sitting at a table in the old library, reading from a book written in Latin, able to understand if he so desired but merely skimming the pages, relishing the peace to muster his energies.

I realised how late I had left all this. He was going to try again in minutes, try one more time to put things right where he had done so much wrong. I opened my good eye and glanced at the sky. Thunderheads were forming from nowhere as his energies converged, darkening the sky and bringing yet another false promise of rain. Guilt should have driven me after him sooner, but pride had held me back. The two had torn me apart. They were still tearing, deep inside, sparring with accusatory feelings and a dreadful home truth: that I had created a monster.

You.

Hell Came Down

He had sensed my furtive probings. I withdrew quickly and ran to the front doors, unslinging the rifle. So damn clumsy of me! If he hadn't found me I could have slipped into his mind, distracted him, shot him through a window then torn him apart inside as he lay there bleeding. I did not want to do it. I hated to have to kill him. But like all mistakes, if I let him live I knew he would only come back to haunt me again. And there really was no other way to stop him.

I kicked open the doors and ran into the lobby, already lifting the rifle, ready to fire as soon as I burst into the library.

Surprise had gone, but I had speed and strength…

…which I knew, instantaneously, to be outforced.

He slammed me back against a wall without touching me. The rifle tumbled from my hands and disappeared beneath a bench in the lobby. The ghosts screamed and I tried to shut them from my mind, but I felt Lucien's fingers in there, rooting around and opening up all the routes to my self, letting in his victims, giving him respite as they poured their rage into me.

I screamed. My wounds bled again.

He emerged from the library. "You," he said, standing before me.

"Lucien, you have to stop!"

"The world is dying! And what have you done to help it? Nothing."

"You'll kill it yourself," I shouted, barely hearing myself above the screams of the dead.

"I'm giving it life," he said. "I'm bringing a storm. A flood. Can't you feel it brewing? Can't you feel the electricity in the air, the hairs on yours arms standing on end, your teeth tingling? A storm to wash away the bad and bring goodness once again."

Somehow, I formed words around all the pains in my head, forcing them out, not knowing whether they made sense or not. "Lucien…help me help you. I made a mistake with you, I admit it—"

"Admit this, old man! That you're proud and arrogant, and you cannot…for…a…second believe that I've taught myself more."

He pressed me harder against the wall and I felt my lungs compressing, my heart being forced flat, blood pounding in my ears and pouring from my eye.

"Your dead are screaming at me!" I tried to shout, not even knowing if my voice was working any more. "How many more are you going to make?"

The noise stopped. I fell to the floor. I hugged myself, trying to make sure all my parts were still there.

"Look at me," he said.

I looked up. There was the Lucien I had known, a thin, short man with long hair and a face to match, down-turned eyes that gave him a begging-puppy look, clothes that never seemed to fit. Someone who had never seemed able to leave the angst of his teens behind. Someone with so much power, but who looked so weak.

"I'm a good man," he whispered. "You told me that. I'm here to bring good. I'm going to bring rain and end the famine, because I'm the rainmaker. You told me that, too."

I went to say that he was wrong—that I had been wrong—but my voice did not work.

It had gone dark, an instant dusk. "The storm's beginning," he said. Then he turned his back on me and went outside.

Hell Came Down

I heard it from where I lay, unable to move, paralysed by fear and defeat. Lucien roared. I imagined him standing out there with his arms outstretched, his palms facing skyward as he invoked what he thought would be a downpour to save this blighted land. I sensed the ghosts in the building cowering from the fury he imparted, hiding themselves away, the dead fearing something far worse than death.

I tried to stand. I could not. Perhaps it was failure, because I knew even then that I could not stop him. He was right. I was arrogant. I had not for a second believed that he could face me and win.

For a time, I thought he had prevailed. There was a glass atrium in the Courthouse's lobby, and for a long few seconds something pattered wetly onto the frosted glass canopy above me. I lay on my back and so wished that he had succeeded, but then I knew that was not the case. Rain did not crack glass. Rain did not leave bloody smears behind. Most of all, rain did not scurry away after it had landed, searching for dark places in which to hide.

No, I felt Lucien say in my mind. He must have seen something horrible coming down. I resisted the temptation to say I'd told him so, it was too much effort, and I had no energy left.

No...

Something massive hit the ground outside. The lobby windows blew in, letting in a terrible stench of rot and insides turned out.

Oh no, Lucien said again. *I'm sorry...*Perhaps he was even talking to me.

Other things began to fall, bigger and smaller, growling or roaring when they hit. Many of their calls halted instantly, but some went on. Some survived.

I sensed Lucien extinguished like an ant beneath the foot of a giant.

His death should have stopped it. It did not. The storm went on all night.

Lucien was right. He did cause a flood.

I managed to crawl to a place of safety while that long night brought chaos down to earth. I remained hidden in the basement of the old Courts for two days, recuperating and using my battered powers to hide myself when anything came inside to investigate. Once, I heard a creature on two feet drag something across the mosaic tiled floor above me. It grunted, chewed, spat. Sniffed the air. Held still.

I closed my eyes and had to use all my energy to turn it away from me. Its mind was revolting. And victorious.

When I left the Courts I fled the town as quickly as I could, shielding myself from view with simple but energy-consuming invisibility. The flood was diminishing, but only because the things that had fallen that night were spreading out. I saw a tiger strolling carelessly along the main street; a bulging black mass hanging from a telegraph pole, dropping spiders as big as my head to the ground; something that looked like an alligator but had wings; a wolf and a bear hunting together. I saw carcasses stripped clean, and the living results of Lucien's final storm were well-fed.

Hell Came Down

The town was obliterated. Every building was damaged, most completely shattered, and as for the inhabitants…a limb here, a blood-smeared pavement there. Most of the things that had come down, I knew, were carnivorous. Lucien's final, desperate, anguished attempts had made them so.

—⚡—

I've been hiding in the hills for several weeks, hiding like a criminal…and I suppose I am. I trained the person that ended the world, after all.

Sometimes I sense Lucien, a wandering ghost whose powers are ineffectual now that he has moved far, far on. But he still cries, and I cry with him. He was an innocent. I'm the one to blame.

When the things that fell that night finally find me, it will be only what I deserve.

Black

She *only screams for the first two minutes. Some of the screams may be words in her own language, but if so they are a curse. She still makes noises after that but they are unconscious and reminiscent of death, not echoes of life. He hears the knife going in, whispering through skin and flesh, grating on bone, its serrated edge sucking like a jelly shaken from its mould as he pulls it out. He is changing this mould radically. She sighs, but it is gas escaping her rent body. She coughs, but it may be blood bubbling in her throat. Still he stabs, slashes and gouges, just to make sure. He tries to concentrate on the white-hot anger and rage he feels, propagating them in the hope that they might camouflage the worrying excitement. The pleasure. He's enjoying this. She begins to drip from the edges of the table, more solid scraps of her following soon after, and a steady rain of fluid patters down onto the flagstone floor. He closes his eyes and listens, trying to distinguish the cleansing rain outside from* *that within. He's still shaking with fury, fear and dread, and even though he knows that what he's doing is so wrong, he cannot take it back. He* will *not take it back. It's her fault, it's the fault of her kin and kind, and this is his release. At least he can smell the truth of that.*

―∞―

Ed carved another niche into the damp plasterboard wall. As the knife penetrated and pink plaster squeezed out he expected blood to well from within, the wall to quiver and scream and smell of insides. He expected this every time, and every time it did not happen. Yet the fear was always just as fresh. Sometimes he believed that every memory he had was made up, pulled together hurriedly by his still-waking mind before he could become fully conscious and realise that he was actually nothing at all.

The only real memory he could never doubt was of the murder that had changed his life.

"Thousands," he said, standing back from the wall and surveying the damage he had wrought. The bare painted partition was scarred across its surface with a mark for every day he had been here. They started in the left bottom corner as inch-high, delicately cut indicators, the tender slices of a surgeon operating on his own child. But now, the latest was the hacking of a murderer. Tracing them from left to right did not tell his story, because at some point he had decided to mix in the marks, make them disordered and confused. Not his story, no, but perhaps his state of mind.

"Thousands of days." He'd counted to begin with. Each mark added to the number he kept in his head, the length of

Black

time he'd been here, and because back then his memory still was not too bad he would wake in the morning and remember the number from the night before. Then he'd started to forget, and it had become necessary to re-count the marks several times each week. He did not mind—he had nothing better to do—but it was tedious and, as the violence of the knife strokes grew, all but impossible.

So now he left it at this: thousands. With what he could remember of his life, it was as good as forever.

The flat was sparse and dirty. He ate takeout food mostly, and old boxes and bags and sachets were piled on the kitchen surfaces, plates in the sink waiting to be washed when all the clean ones were used. The bin stank of mould and rotting meat. Ed liked that. It reminded him of what he had done, and he only wished he had the conscience to view it as a punishment rather than simply an annoying smell. He paid for his food with a debit card from a bank account that seemed always to honour the transaction. He had an idea that he'd once had a good job. Perhaps he was still being paid. He didn't deserve it—he felt that he was deserving of very little, and he knew the dead woman would agree—but it was there, and he needed to eat, and any morals he'd once had had been slaughtered by that knife.

The same knife he now used to mark the passing of his own life.

He'd have laughed at the irony if he didn't make himself so sick.

Ed put down the knife and went for a walk. He did this most days, wandering past the greasy takeaway food bars, the tacky cheap jewellery shops, money lenders and video emporiums and dingy pubs, their closed doors and smoky interiors almost begging potential customers not to enter. Passing faces he did not know, he acknowledged no one and, in turn, was ignored. He was certain that sometimes they did not even see him. He'd read somewhere that the human mind filters out everything not required from its surroundings, otherwise the information input would be far too massive. He liked not being a part of anybody else's life.

Ed preferred living in the city because he could be just another mystery, even to himself. He deserved no less. As happened every day, flashes of what he had done haunted him: tastes, sounds, feelings, smells of his crime assailed him at every step, either reflected in shop windows, carried on the air or manufactured inside his head. Trying to ignore them was like trying not to breathe. Accepting them, suffering, was all he could do to make amends.

He certainly did not deserve to meet Queenie.

On that hot July afternoon when he first saw her, he simply watched. He hadn't had sex since the war, rarely even masturbated, but seeing the woman in the park stirred feelings that surprised him with their intensity. He wanted her, yes, but he was also interested by her. The strange things she did went some way to explaining that, but also the way she moved, the clothes she wore, the way she flicked her long hair back over her shoulder quickly and impatiently, as if it was merely an annoyance.

Ed sat on a bench by the pond and tried to blend into the background. He hated being noticed at the best of times, but now, watching this woman, he craved invisibility. The more fascinated he became with her and her actions, the less he wanted to meet her.

Black

She must be planning something, he thought. Scouting the area for a film. Or perhaps she was an artist. She was lurking beneath a clump of trees at the edge of the park, holding something up to the sky—a light meter, Ed guessed—taking photographs, scratching around at the foot of each tree with a small trowel as if looking for buried treasure. She kept out of the sun. If she did emerge from beneath one group of trees, she would quickly cross the sunlit grass to another area of shadow. Her skin was dark and weathered—she obviously spent a lot of time outdoors—but she seemed to much prefer the comfort of shadows to the hot caress of the sun. Ed could relate to that. He wondered what crime she was trying to hide away from.

It took over an hour for her to notice him. In that time he sat motionless on the bench, the sun slowly burning his bald pate, hardly even twitching as a group of teenagers cycled by so close that one of them touched his shoe with his wheels. He watched her set a camera on a tripod and take one photograph every five minutes, fix small boxes to several trees with nails, sweep leaves away from the bole of a lightning-struck tree as if to reveal its skeletal underside. She finally sat down and took a bottle of water from a rucksack… and that was when she saw him.

Ed held his breath, startled, as she froze and stared across at him. She was too far away for him to see her expression clearly, but she put her bottle down and stood without looking away from him.

His heart began to race, sweat popped out on his skin, his sunburned scalp tightened. She was not only standing, she was walking, coming out into the sun and seemingly oblivious of it for the first time, striding across the grass and glancing away now and then, though infrequently and not for long.

He felt her attention upon him, like fresh sunbeams cooking his skin.

Ed stood, turned his back on the woman and walked quickly away. He aimed through the kid's playground, dodging toddlers as they darted around his legs and hoping that he could lose her through there if she chose to follow. But when he looked back over his shoulder he saw her standing by his bench, hands on hips, staring after him. She shielded her eyes as he looked and he thought perhaps she smiled. But it could have been a shadow pulling at her lips, making him see something that was not really there.

He has smelled insides before, of course, but never like this. In the war he has seen more dead bodies than anyone ever should, two of them—the rebel unwilling to give up his guns, the government solider angry and aggressive at his intrusion—the results of his own actions. He hates every single corpse because they remind him of why he is here, what these people are doing to each other, and each shot, shattered or gutted body seems to be one more mocking taunt aimed directly at him: we're doing this, they say, and you can't stop us. So he has smelled insides...but never this close up. Never this fresh. Blood mists the air as he strikes, copper tints overlying the rich tang of burning from outside, strong and vital as he breathes it in, sticking inside his nostrils, embedding itself to remind him of this moment forever. The smells change as his stabbing arm becomes heavier and the

Black

knife impacts further down his victim's body: sickly-sweet as the heart is punctured; acidic as the stomach is torn open; piss and shit. Underlying it all is the cloying stench of cheap perfume. It's intended to remind him of roses and honey, he supposes, but in reality it's the aroma of desperation. Any idea that a clean and scented body can superimpose itself over the horrors happening here must be desperate, and he wonders when she found the time or inclination to buy this. He imagines what he is doing as some sort of alternative perfume advert for TV and he almost smiles...almost... because then the mouth-watering smell of roasting human flesh hits his nose from outside. He wonders what he will eat tonight. He swallows a mouthful of saliva and tastes death.

He didn't know he was going to return until he opened the door of his flat and ventured out into the twilight.

The park closed at eight o'clock, but he knew plenty of ways in. He spent a lot of his time wandering, day and night, and the park was always a convenient and innocuous venue. No one would see him in there, if he so chose, and he could hide and watch and wonder just what he was missing. Sometimes he saw someone walking on their own, but their expression was always happier than his own. On other occasions he spotted couples sitting or strolling hand in hand, and they reminded him that he had forgotten so much. Once he'd seen two people making love on a park bench, trying to be secretive about it but the woman's increasingly frantic movements and gasps revealing their passion. He had stayed and watched until the end. The movements and sounds reminded him of the woman he had murdered, even though their cause had been much different. Perhaps he knew why it was called the little death.

They had all made him mad, every single one of them. Every word and gesture and smile that marked what they were doing to their country and kin as normal drove him into a frenzy. He'd been sent there to protect them from themselves—he'd killed for them—and yet they willingly went about their continuous self destruction.

Sent there to protect them. Ironic.

He walked along darkened streets, moving quicker through pools of light. He'd been here for a long time, the marks on his wall testified to that, but still he found his surroundings unfamiliar. It was as if the scenery was frequently rebuilt and reordered, mostly to resemble its former self but with a few vital differences that prevented him from recognising it fully. It stopped it from ever feeling like home.

He reached the park and climbed the wall at one of its lower stretches. He could hear kids playing around near the bandstand, glass smashing as they lobbed bottles down the concrete steps, so he turned the other way. The pond was just around the corner, and next to it the trees, and within their deeper evening shadows perhaps he would find the secret of why the woman had been there.

Ed looked up and saw the full moon. Stars quivered with atmospheric distortion. He tried to appreciate the beauty of the view, but he could not realise any sense of wonder. It was long gone. The shadows pooled around the bench he'd sat on earlier seemed deeper than normal, thicker, untouched by moon- or starlight. He wondered whether someone had spilled something there, but he had no wish to venture close

Black

enough to find out. The shadows seemed to be something, not nothing. A definite presence rather than an absence of light.

Ed moved his head to get a full view with his peripheral vision. He did not like what he saw, but then he rarely did. Someone—perhaps it was his mother, although she was swallowed up along with most of his early memories—had once told him that if he was stressed or wound up he should see the beauty in things. The movement of a tree, each leaf performing its own independent dance to create a wondrously pure choreography. Or the way light fell on a puddle, a reflection of the world in there, a whole universe in a splash of water. Roses swaying in the breeze, waves of that same breeze rippling across a field of long grass, a flock of birds twisting and turning like one organism, not a thousand. All things of beauty, none of which Ed could see. Now he would see only a stump blown apart by shellfire, a porridge of blood and oil in a landmine crater, a hand clawed in the still air...and his knife stealing what little beauty he'd managed to find in that foreign country.

Before they sent him there, he'd never even heard of the place.

"Look just to the side of what you want to see," a voice said. It was deep but evidently female, husky and knowledgeable.

Ed spun around, knowing straight away that he'd found her. Or rather, she'd found him. He suddenly wished that he'd stayed at home. "Who's there?" He was not used to talking with people. *Scared of the dark*, she'd think. Maybe she was right. Ed liked to exist in shadows, but perhaps it was his fear of them holding him there, a guilt-induced masochism.

Tim Lebbon

"You saw me earlier." She came from the night beneath the trees, stopped a few steps from him and switched on a torch. His vision was stolen for long seconds. "Come back for another look?"

"I was wondering what you were doing." Ed could see the woman silhouetted before him. She pointed the torch at the ground behind her, throwing her face into deep shadow. He wondered whether she had two eyes, a nose, a mouth, or something wholly different.

"Why?"

It was not a question he had expected, although he'd been asking it for hours. He was not used to interacting, and to find something of interest like this was a surprise. Anything of pleasure would be mocking the life he had taken. Sometimes, on the worst of days, even breathing felt bad.

Everything went back to that. His life began in a foreign country when he was a murderous twenty-two.

"Well, you seemed so...intent. What is it? Animal research? You filming squirrels, or something?"

"I'm waiting for a murder."

"Murder." Ed felt cold, his balls shrivelled and an icy, accusing finger drew a line down his back, nail cutting to the bone. *Murder.* One day he feared they'd come visiting, the fellow soldiers who'd brought him back and released him, letting the incident fade into the shadows of war, honour amongst thieves, that sort of thing. There's always been that fear...but it was a yearning as well. He could not bring himself to account for what he had done because he was a coward. It would take someone else to do it for him.

Murder.

Black

"There'll be one here very soon. That's why I'm here. I'm sort of an early warning system, I suppose. Dark, isn't it?"

"Yes." He'd noticed. The woman turned the torch off and for a moment, an instant, it was pitch black. Then his night vision moved in and he could see the shadows forming around them. The woman seemed closer than she had been before. And when she spoke again he was sure he could smell her breath.

"They call me Queenie."

"Why?"

"Avoidance Queen. I avoid most of the important things in my life."

"Like what?" Ed saw her shadow shrug but she offered no response. "So what's your real name?"

"You can call me Queenie, too."

"So what are you avoiding here? Searching for a murderer, you say?"

"That's not what I said. I'm looking for a murder, not a murderer."

Ed thought that she was playing games, but perhaps it was simply because most of the time he talked to himself. He stepped back a couple of paces, shoes whispering across the soft carpet of pine needles. The air felt thick. Movement was difficult. "You can't have one without the other."

"Well…" She giggled quietly, little more than a heavy breath through her nose. "Sometimes a murder is just a death brought on too soon."

This was too close. Ed felt memories tapping the inside of his skull like insects, flying around and seeking escape, trying to force themselves upon him once again. They often used devious means, these memories: jumping out of doorways and the TV screen, emerging fully-fledged from single phrases, smells and sounds and sights inspiring their own dark memory cousins. He lived that time often enough without actively bringing it on.

"I have to go," he said. The instant he spoke everything went quiet, a deathly silence, the air swallowing movement and sound and seemingly solidifying around him. Even the shadow of the woman became solid and still, from living to statue in an instant. He turned to leave. She touched him.

"Don't go," she said. Her fingers bit into his arm, but in desperation rather than anger. "Please...I don't get to talk about this much. It'll go dark, it always goes dark, and in the blackness there's murder. Please! People just don't listen, they say I'm mad and walk away. Don't walk away."

"What are you *doing*?" Ed said. Was she playing with him again?

"I've put light meters on the trees. And time-lapse cameras. I hope they aren't stolen. I'm waiting for it to go dark."

Ed almost stayed. She'd piqued his interest, demanded his attention. Some of those things she was saying...*Sometimes a murder is just a death brought on too soon*...He wanted to become involved.

But he could not allow that. He was nothing, no one, and he did not deserve anything like this.

"It *is* dark," he said. And as he walked away, trying not to hear her muttering behind him, he whispered to himself: "It's *always* dark."

Black

She asked him to taste her. Maybe that's why he's killing her, but he thinks not. Her underwear is still tangled around her ankles, and as if to taunt him the taste of women comes out from behind his teeth, dripping from the roof of his mouth like ghost memories burrowing down from his brain, laying tangy caresses on his tongue. Perhaps if he'd accepted her invitation his rage would have been subsumed. Maybe she would still be alive. But time could not be reversed. Drowning out that sweet taste of love is the bloody taste of death. Her blood is in the air, misting when the knife comes out and permeating the dank atmosphere of the alley, more spilled blood in this bloody land; soon the air itself will taste of blood if the killing goes on, the hate and murder borne of the differences passed down from father to daughter, mother to son. He wonders whether their respective gods find it all amusing. And he tastes a bitter, furious anger swimming there in the blood, black spots of rage camouflaged in the very physical taint of the woman's death. He swallows, rubs his tongue against the roof of his mouth in an effort to distil the taste...because it scares him. It scares him because he knows it cannot be his own, his anger is false because he does not truly know what these people are going through, why, what they really feel. His is a tourist's rage at something that offends him, and it could never taste this bad. He spits and it lands on the woman. The taste grows worse. Hands rest on his shoulders, heavy and invisible, but for now they do little but help him thrust the knife in again. There is no one else here but him and the woman, but those hands have the feel of him, and the bitter tang of dread floods his mouth as blood arcs across his chin and teeth.

Tim Lebbon

This time, he knows the dread is his own.
And he sees what he has done.

Ed woke up from dark-soaked dreams to a dawn barely any lighter. He glanced at the clock blinking beside his bed. Must be wrong. It should have been daylight by now. Even through the hangover, the searing pain behind his eyes and in his throat that was testament to his binge the previous night, he knew he should be seeing more than this.

He rubbed his eyes but it did not help.

Queenie. She sprang into his mind and ambushed his thoughts, turning them away from the urge to vomit and then drink some more. If he went back to the park today she'd still be there. Sitting beneath the trees perhaps, or adjusting the equipment she'd placed around the little copse, replacing batteries, examining film and data tapes. *Light meters?* Strange.

Ed managed to haul himself upright without puking, but then he stood and swayed as his senses spun and swapped places, and he vomited down the wall. Standing there, leaning against the woodchip wallpaper as he heaved gushes of liquid poison from his guts, he noticed how each splinter of wood in the wallpaper had its own definite shadow. Most of them were small, little more that smudges, but one or two of them seemed far too large. As he gasped in air and tasted foulness, he picked at one of these wood chippings and felt it crumble between his fingernails like a desiccated fly. He dropped the dust to land on the puddle of puke, and seconds later the shadows faded away.

Black

Ed rubbed his eyes and sat heavily onto his bed. He was used to waking like this, even welcomed it sometimes, but it often lowered whatever defences he'd managed to erect against the memories plaguing him. Trying to rub the ache from his eyes he saw her face as she realised what he was about to do, her eyes widening and filling with something that would have scared him had he not had the upper hand. Pinching his nose and snorting to force out the damp remnants of vomit, he smelled insides other than his own, parts of her that should never have been touched by daylight. And the ringing in his ears, the rapid pumping of his heart as it struggled to purify his system, both could have belonged to her, a fearful whine and her heart galloping with fear.

It'll go dark, it always goes dark, and in the blackness there's murder.

Ed tried to revive himself because he needed to think, and like this it hurt. He drank a pint of water and washed down three aspirins, opened the windows to his dank flat and leaned out to let the fresh air do its worst. He could just about make out the park from here, its oldest and tallest trees peering over rooftops. The sky was clear but the streets were shaded, not shadowed but unclear nonetheless. The brightness of the day had been turned down. Some cars had their sidelights on. A young couple were standing on the street corner, whispering like lovers, though Ed thought not.

There was a knock at the flat door.

He spun around and leaned back against the window sill to steady himself. The knock came again and he nodded, yes, he hadn't imagined it. No one had come to his front door for years other than to collect monies due. He usually had it to give them, but still he resented their intrusion into his own private world. They looked at him like voyeurs, their eyes cameras to record and incriminate…or perhaps he just imagined it.

"Who is it?"

"It's happening," a voice said. Queenie. So much mystery in that one statement, so many possibilities (*you're caught, they know, you're a murderer, time to run, run again*).

"What's happening?"

"It's growing dark. The light's losing out, no one has noticed yet but all the readings hold up. Let me in. The landing light's bust."

Ed stepped to the door, drew the bolts and swung it open. Queenie entered without an invite, wafting cheap perfume and the smell of cleaned clothes. If she *had* slept in the park, she'd made an effort to be presentable before coming here this morning.

"Nice place," she said, looking around at the scarred walls and the refuse littering the floor and tables, and Ed hated the sarcasm, really hated it, his resentment running deep.

"I live like I live."

Queenie's eyes widened

her eyes widened and filled with something fearful, frightening

and she started talking excitedly. "The murder's soon, it has to be, the darkness is here and soon it'll be black, black as night without stars or moon, blacker than last night, but in the day." It sounded like she was looking forward to it.

"Eclipse?"

She shook her head. "No, not eclipses. Every time it's happened before it's been localised and has gone unreported, even from the authorities. I've followed the places it's

Black

happened, always got there after the event, been trying to narrow down future locations…find a pattern." She looked pensive for a moment, glanced around Ed's flat at the mess of his life, then back at him. "Maybe I've found it," she whispered. Then she became animated once more, excited. "There's been no film of it, little talk about it in the media. Well, *Fortean Times* picks it up sometimes, of course, and other folks like that." She looked at him and, as if knowing how all but his worst memories were lost, she smiled. "Blackouts."

Ed frowned at this strange woman who seemed to have some sort of claim to him. He'd seen her twice but already she was confiding in him, passing on something she was obviously passionate about, letting him in. "I really don't want any part of this," he said, and even as he spoke it was a lie.

She looked at him, eyebrows raised and lips pressed together. "You'll see it soon enough," she said, and still he could not read her.

"Why should I see blackouts?"

"Why shouldn't you? You live here and this is where it's going to—"

"But why do you think I of all people should see it? Why pick on me?"

Queenie was silent for a while. She seemed confused. "Well, I didn't. You came looking for me."

Ed could only stare at her, standing in the middle of the room he had yet to invite her into. And suddenly, amazingly, there was a stirring in his groin, a hardening so uncommon in all the years since his time in Eastern Europe, another use for the blood he now thought of as impure and tainted with the murder.

That made up his mind. "Out," he said.

"But I have to tell you. Don't you want to know? Don't you understand what I'm saying here?"

"No I don't, it's a load of shit you're trying to feed me, I don't know what's wrong with you and I really, really don't want to know. Out!" *He* did *want to know...*

"But I've been told I can give you a chance."

Ed shook his head, loosening those strange words from where they had stuck. Denying them. It was just too complicated. "Get out of my flat!" he hissed.

Queenie made to move toward him, faltered, took a step forward. Ed really thought that she was coming for him, her hands would come up and she would hold him or hit him or something equally as inexplicable. But after standing there for a few seconds, glancing out the window over Ed's shoulder, looking into his eyes and searching for something in there, she turned and left.

The door snicked shut and Ed looked at the clock. Not even midday.

He picked up his knife from the bedside table, looked for an unmarked spread of wall and carved in his mark for today.

—∞—

And kept carving. Silent, his breathing even, his eyes open but unseeing, hands clenched around the haft but unfeeling, the *scratch, scratch, scratch* going unheard, Ed carved days that never were into his wall, spanning midnights

Black

and middays without blinking, weeks passing with only a spot of blood where he'd nicked his finger, the wall filling faster and faster as months sliced by.

Fooling himself, an ironic deception with cuts.

By one o'clock, when he opened his first bottle of wine and stared at the sun hanging weakly in the clear blue sky and the shadows hunkering unreasonably around doorways and beneath cars in the street down below, Ed had been in the flat for another six months.

Four o'clock came. Ed had consumed two bottles of wine and was slowly working his way into a third. Bad Hungarian red. There'd been a scare a while back about anti-freeze in the wine, poisonous, bad for you, and Ed had been concerned and worried. That was before he'd been sent to Eastern Europe. Now, he wished it were true. Not brave enough to take his own life, he often thought that a freak death like that would be rather poetic.

As usual when he got drunk it was not the shimmering loss-of-control felt by most other people. His limbs went numb, yes, and his voice would undoubtedly slur had he cause to use it, but the main effects were more insidious. He felt the light leaving him. Both metaphorically and literally his light was fleeing, bleeding from organs pickled and ruined by bad alcohol: metaphorically, because he was losing the last dregs of hope, decency and guilt that still held out against the dark cancer of his soul; and literally, because on occasion he saw the dark.

He could never mention that to Queenie. He rarely even remembered because it happened so infrequently.

He saw the dark.

Shades of grey where there should be colour. Light bulbs fading and flickering as if gauze were being waved before them, the black gauze of mourning, not wedding-white. Shadows on the sun. And just as soon as he became sober the next day he forgot about it, cast it back into the depths of his mind where other memories dwelt like monstrous sea creatures, cruising the darkness and rising only occasionally to assault the small barren island his life had become.

Strangely enough, he did not feel under siege. Sometimes it was the exact opposite: sometimes, he thought he was a threat to everyone else.

—⚡︎—

He can see her. Obviously he can, he's murdering her after all, but he can really see her. Not the composite image of a human being our brains usually perceive—that face, those grey-green eyes, two arms, birth-mark on the neck... all go together to make someone we know and whom we never really see—but the actuality of her as a person made up of many, many things. He's destroying those things, slicing them asunder as if working on an item in a biology class, and perhaps this is why he sees her as she really is. Because her eyes are wide open and filled with something he hates, hates and fears, while she is still alive they are filled with anger and rage and something that can only be a curse, a horrible look that he wants to slice out, the look of someone who has won, someone who knows that victory

Black

is not hers now but will be in the future. So he slashes at her eyes and it takes several stabs before they both go. Her right arms begins to twitch, jumping on the concrete paving slabs, blood is pulsing from several cuts down near her hand where she'd initially tried fending him off, and every now and then her limbs enter his peripheral vision like curious ghosts watching over his shoulder. He feels the rage rising, something so basic and pure that he fears it more than he can understand, because it is not his own. He can almost see it. Black spots dance before his eyes, speckling in and out of existence like flies popping in and out of the dying woman's flesh. At first he thinks they are in *his eyes, because he's in a white-hot panic as he keeps stabbing, slashing, gouging. But then he blinks and wipes blood from his face with his left hand, and the spots are still there. He moves his head from side to side and they do not move with him. They are separate from him, more of the woman than him, and her rage must be far, far more powerful than his own. He realises then how pathetic and self-obsessed his murdering this woman is. As if he could possibly solve anything by taking one more life, a life he had come here to protect at that. But he sees the knife rise and fall, rise and fall, sees flesh opening up, sees parts of the woman that should never have been seen, ever. When he was young he'd peel a banana and think* I'm the first and last human to ever lay eyes on this piece of fruit flesh. *Now he is the first and last to see a different flesh. He feels the warm dampness of it on his skin. And the rage rages on.*

—ɯ—

Tim Lebbon

Ed surfaced slowly from another drunken, dream-filled slumber to find that it was early evening. And at the window in his flat's messy living room, something was fluttering against the glass.

He sat up quickly, trying to shake the fuzziness from his eyes, and he listened for the scraping across the glass. There was nothing. He stood, pulled the net curtain aside and thought he saw a bird. It took a few seconds to realise that whatever was out there was not solid. It was like a breeze given form, physical yet with nothing firm enough to be seen, stalking across the glass, trying to gain access.

"Get lost," Ed said, opening the window. The thing dissipated when there was no longer glass between them. Perhaps it had been a shadow cast from somewhere far off.

The street was quiet and still, but Ed saw that things were wrong. The dark, he thought, it's the dark come before the murder, but he was thinking in Queenie's voice.

He needed to go and find her. He needed to know what she knew of the dark. The dark, and the rage he sensed was drawing near again.

He left his flat as he had so many times before: without hope.

—∞—

Outside, night was forcing daylight into hiding. House windows no longer reflected the cloud-smeared sky, the cars and people travelling through the streets or the facades of buildings standing opposite. Now they were black, as if the light had already been sucked from the buildings' innards leaving only a void to press against the glass on the inside.

Black

Ed sensed a pressure behind these windows—he could almost see the glass bowing outwards—and he walked closer to them. Moving away from the road toward a more noticeable danger felt good. Once or twice he thought he saw himself reflected in there, but the light was fading fast and he could just have been a shadow. Perhaps it was even someone walking behind him and keeping pace, but when he glanced over his shoulder he was alone.

The animals knew that something was amiss. Pigeons huddled together on window sills, heads tucked beneath wings but looking up frequently, unable to sleep. Occasionally some of them would take flight, as if touched by nothing that could be seen. Cats sat behind several windows observing the street, watching the pigeons roost and panic, their heads turning here and there, none of them licking their paws, none outside in the street. There were no dogs sniffing along the gutter or pissing against garden walls, no magpies or crows or sparrows fighting over the remains of burgers trodden into pavements, no bees buzzing between gardens, no flies aiming for nostrils or eyes.

Another flock of pigeons lifted from a garage roof, their wings applauding the strange silence that had fallen over the streets. Even though cars travelled back and forth and people walked the pavements, sounds did not seem to echo, and Ed constantly brushed at his ears as if expecting some deadening material to be draped there. A car passed ten feet away, but its motor could have been coming from the next street. He coughed and felt it thrum through his head and chest, but its sound was dull and muted. He saw other people acting in the same bemused manner: rubbing their ears; watching cars drift quietly by; stamping feet or making some other noise to test their perceived deafness. It was as if the air were thickening, damping sound and diluting echoes into dull mumbles of what they should have been.

Cars approaching from the direction of the park had their headlights on full. Those moving the other way soon turned theirs on as well. The traffic was moving even slower than the usual rush-hour crawl.

Ed left the residential street and walked past the first of the shops. A man was busy pulling down a shutter and padlocking it into place, glancing warily over his shoulder as Ed approached.

"Who are you?" the man asked.

"No one."

"Something's going to happen," the man said, eyes dancing in their sockets like loose ball-bearings. He couldn't keep his gaze in one place. "Something soon, and something bad. Maybe there'll be a riot. Do you think there's going to be a riot?"

Ed looked along the shopping street at the cars wending their way home, the people minding their own business even more than usual as they hurried, heads down, inexplicably trying not to bring attention to themselves. "I quite doubt it," he said, but the man was already hurrying away.

A motorcycle passed by accompanied by an explosion of shadows. They buzzed the bike like the dregs of a bad dream, black butterflies, negative snow, but totally without form. The motorcyclist was waving his left hand around his head, flicking his hand at the air as if trying to sign to someone behind him. Ed watched his hand and wondered what he meant.

Black

The shards of shadow darted at the rider's helmet and disappeared.

Ed saw what was about to happen but he could do nothing to help it. He tried to draw breath but it was like breathing in the middle of a thick fog. His lungs felt heavy and full, but not with air. And then the bike flipped sideways, the rider left his mount, the machine hurtled up onto the pavement and through a shop window—the smashing of glass sounding like wind-chimes in the distance—and the street came to a standstill.

At last, Ed could shout. "Watch out!" he croaked, realising how foolish it sounded now. Realising too that he had allowed someone else to die. If only he had shouted…if only he had been able to warn…The man lay half-beneath a parked car, his helmet askew on his head, the car body dented where he had impacted. Someone was kneeling beside him and reaching for the helmet and lifting the visor, tugging, taking it off…

Ed ran across the street, not wanting to see what gushed out when the man's head was released. He dodged between the stalled cars and the drivers staring in blatant fascination at the scene unfolding in the gutter behind him. He did not look at any of them. He knew what they were feeling because he felt it himself sometimes, a revelling in the pain of others that helped him live with his own agonies. It was necessary, he supposed, and it kept him going however much he had no desire to carry on. They were shocked, and excited, and pleased that their own troubles had been unloaded—for however long—on someone else. Something strange was happening right here and now, but a man was dying in the road. For a while that would give these people an escape.

Tim Lebbon

Looking down, Ed saw shadows writhing across his legs as he ran through the beams of car headlights. They seemed to be stitched into his trousers, swathes of dark fluttering behind him like loose cloth. He ran on without looking down again.

"Oh, God!" he thought he heard from behind him, but it may as well have been a cry from hidden memory.

He had to find Queenie. Night was falling too early. And try as he might, Ed could not shake the ever-increasing certainty that he had seen it all before.

—⚋—

He can feel blood on his hands. The hard haft of the knife in his right hand counterpoints the warm wet thing he holds in his left, his palm pressed flat to the body's chest to hold it against the wall as he drives the blade home, again and again. A few moments ago he could still feel its heart beating, but that gave out with a spasm as if the big muscle was trying to force the knife back out with its own violence. The blood from there seemed warmer than the rest, more sticky, like sweet treacle instead of runny syrup. The body is sliding down the wall so he pushes harder, trying to keep it upright, his blows striking its shoulders and neck as it moves down, then its chin and face. His finger slips inside a cut as he pushes and he turns it around in there. He can't help comparing the feeling with one more loving and sensuous. Something scratches his finger—a bone splintered by the heavy knife—and he moves away, letting the body slump to the ground. His face is dripping with sweat, cool where sprayed blood dries there, soon to be a crust, cracking and

Black

flaking away like red autumn leaves. Something else settles around him. Heavy and dark and intimate, it reaches out formless hands to steady him, or perhaps to push him down. It enters his throat and makes it hard to breathe. For a second he feels a sudden, total rush of antagonism, fear and hate... unbridled hate...and then he is running. His feet slap on the pavement, rain taps patient fingers on his forehead and scalp, there's plenty of time, *it says, and his clothes catch and scrape where he is sweating. He is running. Again.*

As he reached the park the dark had already won.

The street lamps were still on but their light was weak. Car headlights struggled to part the air, their beams all but ineffectual now. Since running from the crashed motorcycle Ed had seen two cars hugging lampposts, and another one burning where it had come to rest on its roof. Burning, blazing, the stench of roasting meat bringing back dreadful memories, the sight of flames...but the flames looked weak and far away as if he were viewing them on a video tape, a copy of a copy of a copy. They appeared weaker than they should, too. Perhaps the fuel was trying its best not to burn today.

The normal had changed. People were not coping.

And then he wondered why he was running. He was searching for Queenie because she'd told him about this, and deep inside beneath those noxious memories he thought he knew much more than he'd like to believe. But he'd just seen someone die, smelled more people burning in their crashed car, and even then he could hear the muffled sound of smashing glass and a scream, penetrating the darkness as effectively as a sigh into a pillow. He sought danger, felt more comfortable in its presence, so why was he running? Why not stand still and let it come? He would not fight. He would accept whatever the darkness had chosen for him because he knew it, he had seen it

(and smelled it and tasted it)

and although he could not accurately recall when and where, he knew it must have been at the murder. When he was killing that woman, subsumed by his own rage and impotence and anger, the darkness must have touched him.

But a greater rage had been with him as well, something far beyond his own.

And that curse in her eyes.

He climbed the wall. The park was much darker than he had ever seen it. No stars peered through the cloud cover, no street light bled through the railings, but Ed knew where to go. He'd been there before and she would be there now. He would find his way in the dark.

"Can you feel it?" Queenie said as he neared the copse of trees. "Can you feel the rage?"

Ed stopped and tried to locate the voice. It had come from his left, he thought, over where the trees gave way to the shrubbery bordering the stream. He paused, held his breath and waited for her to talk again.

She whispered in his right ear. "I've never known it so powerful." She touched his shoulder and walked behind him, drawing her hand across the back of his neck and scratching him with her nails. It was not sexual, he knew that right away, because it hurt. She was trying to hurt him and he didn't know why.

Black

"What's happening?" he asked. If felt like a foolish thing to say. He should know. But right now, standing here in total darkness, a strange woman threatening him and turning him on, he was more confused than ever.

"I've always arrived afterwards." He could smell her breath, garlic and staleness, no vanity there. "After the event, watched them clean up the bodies and take them away, seen them put it down to just another murder." Her voice sounded stronger than it had before, and her accent was breaking through. He'd not noticed it before now, perhaps because it brought back way too many memories. She was foreign but her grasp of English was perfect. Ed wondered if she knew that she was letting it slip. "But with each one the blackouts lasted longer, because they were searching...searching for you, Ed."

"Me?" He could taste her hate. "*Me?*" He felt her breath caress his ear and neck. She was standing so close that her heat touched him in waves.

"You fuck!" She spoke quietly but her voice was heavy with venom and anger, and rage. And her accent, far from distorting her words, made them all the more clear to him.

"You've tracked me down," he said, wondering if Queenie was a daughter or a niece to the woman he had killed. In a way, he was glad. He waited for the attack.

"I didn't. They did. My mother and the other dead. You're not as invisible as you think. Every time you kill she sees, and she knows your mark, and together...they track you again. It takes time. But they find you."

They?

"Their hate for you blocks out the sun."

Ed stared up into the blackness and wondered just what he was looking at. "I don't understand."

"Murderer."

"Yes...But I still don't understand. Was she your mother? I can't see you. I'm so sorry, whoever she was I'm so sorry, but I've lived with it...really, it's destroyed me, you don't know how much." He should have been crying, but he felt nothing, no sympathy or regret. He thought of all the things that could have been, but he could not remember any of them.

"Destroyed you?" Her voice was breaking now, rage giving way to tears and perhaps increasing because of that. "Destroyed *you*? I identified...I named my mother by looking at her jewellery. That's why we knew it wasn't just another ethnic killing in that bloody war: she still had her jewellery. Anyone else would have taken it. Destroyed? She was *ruined*. I couldn't even look her in the face to say goodbye." She sobbed as a memory came back. "It was gone."

Ed opened his mouth but there was nothing he could say. Darkness flooded in and sent searing pain into his teeth, dried his tongue. Why was she Queenie, the Avoidance Queen? Her life? All of it? Maybe she'd shunned her future just to do this, track him.

"So now you've found me—"

"*They've* found you. My greatest desire—my fantasy, my dream—is to see you in pain caused by me. It's what I've given up everything to achieve. But I dare not argue with them. They have much more reason."

They, they, they?

She touched him again, a calloused hand coming around his throat to hurt but not kill—there were others ready to do

Black

that, more in the dark than Queenie—and Ed reacted quickly. He grabbed her wrist and twisted, brought his other arm around to strike out at where he thought she should be. His fist connected with something, he didn't know if it was hair or her woollen sweater, and then he was running through the park, the ground invisible but still there for now, and behind him he heard Queenie shouting something after him.

He had to get home. Back to the flat, to relative safety, before she found him again. Before *they* found him...whoever *they* were. Already he could sense faces pressing against his mind demanding entry, requiring acknowledgement. They were still too far away to recognise.

Still running, he came to the park wall. The level of the ground was raised almost to the wall coping, but on the other side there was a five foot drop into the street. Ed tripped over the head of the wall and fell out into space, arms pinwheeling, a frantic squeal escaping him for a second before he struck the pavement below. His head met with the kerb, and it was only as he faded into a stunned daze that light seemed to offer itself, a flash of white pain from inside. In that light, as if borne of it, memories swam and enlarged, vicious memories of that time years ago when he had changed and destroyed his own life by taking someone else's.

But they were all wrong...

The woman lying on the compacted mud floor, yes, the smell of burning outside, her eyes cursing him as the knife came down again—

And the woman, already a corpse, pressed against a wall with one hand while the other carves in, her blood running down his arm beneath his sleeve, coating his teeth as it sprays—

And blood staining the clean white sheets beneath her as it rains outside, the stink of the city rising up as the violent storm washes them from the gutters—

And the knife grates as it slips from her outstretched hand and calls sparks from the pavement down by the river—

And in the back of the car, thinking she was there for something else, his shoulder and head pressed awkwardly against the roof as he tries to swing his arm back and forth, back again…

And others.

One tastes of cinnamon, another smells of vanilla; one feels cool and calm even under his attack, another is hot and fevered; one goes quietly, another sounds like a steam engine whistle as she screams…

Others. Many others.

And with all of them, the fury and rage.

—⚋—

Ed came around, dizzy with the shock of memory and the impact of this skull on the pavement.

What was he? What kind of animal, monster…he should stay where he was, wait for the sad heart of this darkness to find him and exact the revenge it had been seeking for years. Growing all the time, expanding, because every time it drew near he repeated his crime, fed it a fresh rage to find him with next time, more anger, and in a way he supposed he *was* providing for his own punishment.

So he should wait and submit…

But there was still time. It was looking for him, a deeper shadow in this blackness, even now he could hear a scream

Black

as someone was picked up and tossed away when the dark realised it had the wrong person.

I should submit...I'm an animal...all those people, all that life...there's still time...I should die...I can escape...I'll let her, let *them* kill me...I can find light again.

Confused, crying, terrified, wretched, Ed felt his way along the boundary wall of the park, knowing he was going the right way. Cowardice and an instinct for survival—for Ed they had become one and the same—drove him on. If Queenie were following he did not hear her or sense her, and she would be as blind as him. He wondered what time it was and whether anyone was even doing anything about this, this weird darkness that had fallen, no stars no moon no lights, artificial light swallowed and beaten back like clouds of leaves before a hurricane. And he realised that he did not care. Because no one could do anything.

This was all for him.

He ran, letting go of the wall and launching himself into space. He tried to steer by sound and touch alone, but every mutter he heard became the scream of one of his victims, every thud of his foot on the road was a knife driving home. He ran through the landscape of his murders, remembering more than he ever thought he could have forgotten. And there were always more memories to come.

Ed found his way home, read the house number by touch, kicked open the front door, ran up to his flat. He had no idea how. He wondered, as he fumbled the handle, how many times he had done this before.

He flicked on his light, expecting nothing, and seeing only a ghost before him.

"Mother!" Queenie shouted, screamed. "Mother, he's here, get him, get him!"

"Shush!" Ed hissed, almost laughing at how ridiculous that sounded.

"Mother!" She screamed again and again, the drastically weakened effect of the ceiling lights making her seem almost transparent, a smudge on his vision, nothing more.

"Just stop!" Ed shouted. He could hardly hear himself. Maybe the dark was eating at his ears, burrowing in to reach his brain because she, and *they*, had found him already. He wondered how many…

"How many?" he asked, but Queenie was screaming louder now, her own voice and rage seemingly able to penetrate the damping effects of this blackness, rattling the windows and setting his hair on end.

"Mother, mother, mother!"

He scrambled around, looking for the doorway and escape, hand alighting on something else entirely.

"Mother, mother…"

He lunged at her, the knife an extension of his fear.

"Mother…" And then Queenie was quiet.

He worked for five minutes, reminded of all the smells and tastes and sounds that haunted his memory, and taking in some new ones. Once or twice, as Queenie slid further down, the knife went straight through to the wall, marking a few more bloody days in his life.

He left the flat, feeling his way through the dark, feeling it thicker around his neck and heavier on his eyes, wondering just when it would become too hard to push through, too *there*. But it never did.

Black

He felt the rage, old angers rising and a fresh, new hatred giving the blackness an electric edge. "Sorry Queenie," he whispered, but really he wasn't sorry at all.

Perhaps soon, when the memories were lost again, he'd imagine that he was.

—⚬⚬⚬—

He found his way to the back door of the block of flats. It was rarely used and he had to kick it open, but outside he ran straight into a car. He could barely breathe now, they were coming, and pure instinct drove him on even though he knew he was finished. Like a man putting his hands over his head to save himself from a falling building, Ed continued to fight and struggle on. To pause, to wait for the inevitable, was too much for him to do. He was too scared.

He opened the car door, reached in and found a torch. And it was only when he clicked it on—shining it around the car at the other torches, batteries, gas lamps, flares, fireworks, cans of petrol—that he realised it was his own.

—⚬⚬⚬—

Ed carved another niche in the timber panelling above his bed. There were over two thousand scratches there already. It still didn't feel like home.

He waited for the timber to bleed red sap, but there was none, it was dry. He expected this every time, and every time it did not happen. Yet the fear was always just as fresh. Sometimes he believed that every memory he had was made up, a whole lifetime manufactured in his sleep and given vent in his waking hours.

The only real memory, the one he could taste and smell and feel, was of the murder that had changed his life.

The Stuff of the Stars, Leaking

There was a clear dividing line between grass and sand, as if the beach advanced further inland night by night and, as yet, no breeze had come to blur the latest step. Shrubs held their baleful heads above the golden tide, and the shells of dead things surfed long drawn-out waves.

Yet Brynn saw little of this. He passed across that sheer border between land and water with his mind elsewhere. His wife had died a thousand miles from here but she was never far away, and as he imagined her car plunging into the sea, he smelled seaweed and brine and rotting things. Gulls screamed in the waning light, mourning further losses. The sea always made him maudlin. As death edged closer day by day, it was a state he felt content with.

Sometimes he imagined her waiting for him, wherever she was now.

Brynn's legs were aching from the walk down the cliff path, and he was already beginning to dread the climb back up. Glancing along the beach to the west he could see the sun dipping into darkening waters. It caught stray clouds as it fell, bleeding pinkly across their backs. He paused, looked back at the cliffs, wondered whether he should leave this until morning.

But the path seemed quite safe. And of course there was the dead thing on the beach, past the dunes, down near the sea.

From the clifftops it had been barely visible, little more than a smudge across the sands, a shape losing clarity to distance. Even using binoculars the image had been unresolved, though it had presented a most disturbing insinuation of size. Brynn was awed, but dissatisfied. He knew he would need a trip down to view it firsthand.

He mounted the last dune. In the soft light of the setting sun he could see the shape just above the waterline. He made a trail across virgin sands, each step a gentle hush against the soporific sigh of the sea. Sometimes he wondered whether, if he succumbed to the ocean's hypnotic charms, he would wake up even when the waters rushed into his mouth.

Approaching the thing, he realised that it was far larger than he had realised. A whale, perhaps? The local newspaper had called it a monster, but of course it would. Good for tourism. Building sand bridges was their main concern.

He stopped fifty paces from the corpse, close enough to view it in some detail. It lay on the beach like a huge lump of wax, melted and congealed many times over, picking up imperfections with each burn and set. Mottled and split though its surface was, however, there were no barnacles suckered to its leathery hide, no seaweed hanging from its

The Stuff on the Stars, Leaking

appendages. It was as though all life had eschewed this creature.

Brynn knelt in the sand and took his camera from the rucksack, imagining what Helen would have thought of this. She'd have created a million stories about this thing's final hours, drawing in all manner of inconceivable ideas and waterlogged fantasies to construct her own version of events...

Perhaps she'd been daydreaming when she died. Living stories in her head, while death crept up from behind, pushed the car over a cliff and drowned her.

As he began taking photos, changing position every couple of shots, the stench hit him. It must have been there before, but shock had obviously dulled his senses. It was not putrefaction, exactly, nor was it the tang of insides exposed to the elements. He held a handkerchief over his mouth with one hand as he snapped photos with the other.

The size of the thing stunned him. It was so big, he could not conceive what may have killed it. Could it really just die, something this magnificent, and wash up on this innocuous beach? As he circled the creature he saw tentacles buried in sand, surfacing a dozen feet further on, dipping in again, giving the classic sea monster silhouette.

He nudged one tentacle with his shoe.

There was a sudden shrill cry, startling him so much that he dropped the camera, stumbled and tripped over his own feet. Several seagulls descended and tried to alight on the shape, but they could only hover there unable to land, repulsed by something, screeching in agitation until they flew away.

Brynn gasped and instantly wished he had not. The smell was even worse. He gagged, sought control of his stomach, then puked anyway.

Afterwards he grabbed his camera and left, walking faster than he would have cared to admit. He did not look back.

In his caravan, waiting for his soup to warm, Brynn wondered why the prickly feeling on the back of his neck would not go away.

Darkness tried to sneak through cracks in the window panes. Its pressure was almost discernible, pressing in like gas at a vacuum. He shivered and drew the curtains. It did nothing to hide the massive outside. He did not want to see out in case he saw someone looking in, their face bathed in light borrowed from the moon to scare him. Their eyes unlit, even from without.

He sagged into his chair and sighed. He was acting like a kid. He'd always been cautious of the dark, that's what he told people: cautious. Never really afraid, even when he was young. Cautious. Like he was around electricity, or acid. He treated them with respect lest they hurt him, and he respected the dark equally.

He thought it was the reaction most likely to be welcomed by whatever lived there.

As the soup plopped and blubbered in the saucepan he examined his camera. The damp sand had buffered its fall, but grains had somehow worked their way into the mechanism. He removed the batteries and put the camera

The Stuff on the Stars, leaking

away, searching through piles of notebooks and scraps of paper for his cheap spare.

The smell of artificial tomatoes hung heavy in the air. Brynn had a fleeting, aromatic memory of eating with Helen in an Italian restaurant in Cardiff—

—and then he was on the floor.

Throughout it all he knew what was happening, but he had no control. His arms and legs buffeted the cheap carpet. His heels beat hard, shaking the whole caravan. His head lifted, fell, lifted and fell again, as if an invisible hand gripped his hair, its owner determined to shatter his skull. His fingers flicked at the floor as his arms rose and fell, and he heard his nails cracking. His back arched, then jerked straight. He tried to grit his teeth against the pain, but they crunched together, and he tasted blood and the gravel of chipped enamel.

He thrashed like a landed fish.

And he saw things. His eyes turned up in his head to view the terrible fantasies he had created, the images of what Helen suffered during her final few moments of life. Violent waters surged, snapping things flitting in and out of the waves, then a cool, dark deepness promising only a cold death…and something down there, waiting.

Shock held him and whipped him around, but one thought swept insanely around his head throughout the whole episode: *I won't piss myself, I won't shit myself*, again and again. In that respect at least, his determination held out.

It was seconds or minutes before the fit subsided, instantly and without warning. As he lay still on the floor, panting and sweating and scared of the silence, Brynn's muscles continued to twitch and knot.

Tim Lebbon

Something sighed against the outside of the caravan. Through a chink in the curtains, silhouetted by a tentative half-moon, he saw a breath fading slowly from the cool pane, revealing the stars to him once more.

Eventually he made it to bed. He hid beneath the blankets and did not sleep.

—⚂—

In the morning, in the light, things seemed different. Brynn knew it was foolish, but the sun seemed to titillate the logical side of his mind. He'd had a fit for the first time in his life. He was scared, but thankful that he had not badly damaged himself. His fingers were sore, his head was bruised and thumping, but there were no broken bones. He would go to the doctor's as soon as he arrived back in Cardiff.

Everything was normal.

As he arrived at the edge of the cliff and began his descent, a dreadful smell assailed him. It was worse than the stink of the day before, far richer, more *gritty*. It reminded him of the colour brown and white noise, as if he was smelling everything at once. He gagged, sure he was going to be sick again, but somehow he kept control of his guts. Leaning over, staring down at the rough path, he watched a string of saliva stretch from his mouth and darken the soil where it made contact. *Stuff of me in there*, he thought. *Cells from my body, the stuff of stars, that's what we're made from.* He wondered who else he was looking at in the muck around his feet.

He stood, shaded his eyes against the sun and stared down at the beach. The tide was out and he could see the thing laying there, a great black hump on the smooth golden

The Stuff on the Stars, Leaking

sands. Its tentacles seemed more abundant this morning—longer, more numerous—although it could simply have been that the sands had shifted in the night.

Brynn tied a handkerchief over his mouth and continued the descent. He tried to remember coming back up the cliff last night—it had been dusk, the shadows deceptive—but he could not recall the climb. He must have been on auto-pilot. He was surprised he had not taken a fall.

He followed his own footprints back to the thing on the beach. As he came to the dunes, he realised that he was following more than the single trail he had laid yesterday. There were other disturbances in the sand, strange whipped prints like those of a snake, and more resembling the footprints of birds, though a hundred time bigger. They may have been carved there by the breeze, or left by seaweed which had been blown away. Perhaps they were caused by thousands of burrowing worms blowing bubbles through the damp sand.

None of these options explained why all trails led to the dead thing.

Brynn approached, trying not to step on the other prints, afraid he would sense what had made them. As a child he would avoid cracks in the pavement…step on a crack, break your mother's back. Perhaps old habits never died at all, but just lay in wait eternally. Seagulls still buzzed the corpse, and as they turned and spiralled away they called out in distress. The distress was echoed in his head; a phantom throb like someone else's pain.

The sun was hidden today, but it was not cold. A warm breeze blew in off the sea, carrying with it hints of the deep and desert islands. As Brynn came to a standstill he kicked a bottle washed up the night before. He picked it up, expecting a message, but it was empty of hope.

He squatted on his haunches and wondered at what the thing had seen, where it had been. Six miles down on the ocean bed perhaps its mate waited even now, moving through unimaginable pressures in a vain search for its companion. Or maybe there were more of them, a whole community. Searching. Rising from the bottom. Air sacs inflating, flesh billowing out as the pressures decreased.

He shook his head and stood again. The sand was soft beneath his feet, still wet, but drying now that the tide had left it alone for a while. He stepped forward, ready to touch the hide of the dead creature, run his hand along its tattered mass and look for signs by which he could identify it. Great clots of flesh hung from its torn skin, bulging, dried up in the sun.

He reached out. He was within one step of the thing. The sand became softer, as if hollowed out from below.

But something grabbed him and turned him around, an inherent sense of self-preservation, and before he knew it he was walking back along the beach. His spare camera banged against his leg, unused. His head pulsed with the headache that had been plaguing him since last night.

He'd had a fit. There had been a shadow at the window. Yet he felt more alone now than he ever had since Helen's death.

—⁂—

Brynn did not want to climb back up the cliff path—that would have felt too much like defeat—so he headed to the

The Stuff on the Stars, Leaking

base of the cliffs instead. Sand gave way to rocks, protruding like the petrified remains of unknown creatures. A seagull landed nearby, glanced at him and then took flight again, cawing its way out to sea.

Nursed among the rocks were pools, darkened by the sea plants clogging their edges. There was an occasional pink flash of a sea anemone feeling at the water, and secret scamperings hinted at crabs and other creatures hidden in their own temporary eco-system. Brynn wondered what it felt like to be trapped like that every day, and he squatted next to one of the pools, swishing the water and watching the reflection of the sky distort above his head.

He clambered over the rocks for a while until he found a spot out of sight of the beach. His jacket provided adequate protection against the damp sand, and he lay with his hands behind his head, eyes closed. He relished the cleansing warmth of the sun on his face. The steady beat of the sea was soporific, and he felt time drifting away from him, his senses withdrawing. Sound came to the fore, the sea singing different songs depending on where it struck the shore: from behind him, the soft hush of the salt waters shifting tonnes of sand; nearer, a roar as it stroked patiently at the receding land.

In ten million years, this would all have changed. The sea would have eaten this place. The sea ate everything in the end, wearing it down over massive expanses of time, which it alone could afford to expend waiting. Eventually, like a salmon to its birthing pool, everything went back to the sea. Somewhere in there was all of history, way beyond simple human understanding.

Helen had died in the sea. Her body had never been found. Perhaps there were bits of her in the massive dead thing on the beach, atoms she had owned now given over to something else.

She died a long way from here, Brynn knew. But something that size could swim forever.

He had always hated himself for not hearing her final words, and the nightmares he had were guessed-at versions, guilt trying to fill in the blanks. The worst times were when she blamed him. However much he tried to convince himself that it could never have been his fault, the words followed him into waking, and set terrible seeds of doubt in his mind.

Time passed, the sun moved, Brynn slid slowly into sleep.

When he stirred it was late in the afternoon, and the sun was already bedding down for the night. He stood stiffly, brushed himself down, shivered and wondered why the cold had not awoken him. His head was still thumping, and his body had begun to ache even more from the battering it had received last night. His fingertips were bruised blue.

He picked up his rucksack and noticed how far in the tide had come. Creeping up on him, patient, unhurried. One day, if he was not careful, it would have him. Just as it had taken Helen.

He made his way back along the beach until he came to the top of the dunes. The thing was still there. He was tempted to approach again, but something warned him off.

The Stuff on the Stars, Leaking

He tried to convince himself that it was a simple matter of not wanting to invade its grave privacy.

He climbed the cliff path, panting, breathless, his knee joints burning and his sides stabbed with ice-cold stitch. He had to stop three times on the way up, and for the last fifty feet—when the sun had truly set and he felt that he was navigating by memory alone—he constantly expected to feel nothing beneath his next step, a wide, black nothing that ended with him broken on rocks a few frantic heartbeats below.

At the last, he had an incredibly clear urge to turn around and go back down. In the dark. Along a path that would certainly spill him to his death.

Sense and logic prevailed and he found his way back to his caravan, where something that had been working at the back of his mind for the entire climb came to the fore: the memory of what he had seen in the setting sun. The dead thing laying there with its tentacles—barely visible before—spread out across the sand like the spokes of a giant wheel.

Just laying there and waiting to turn.

Brynn tried to prepare something to eat, but his eyes were forever drawn to the window. He kept imagining a face there, staring in at him, a face made of the same stuff as the dead thing on the beach…the stuff of unknown stars…so he closed the curtains.

It did not work. The outside was now merely hidden from view, allowing anything the opportunity to approach unseen. And seeing slivers of night through the threadbare curtain was worse than seeing a whole pane of glass: one eye, bloodshot and reflecting his own fear, would be more dreadful than a complete face.

Soup burned to the side of the saucepan, blackened and coagulated into something barely resembling food. Brynn cursed and began to eat.

Later, he took out his notebook and began jotting observations of the dead creature. He made rough sketches of the corpse, estimated its size and weight and frightened himself in doing so. He was writing *The Book of the Sea*. He had been writing it ever since Helen died, but every chapter seemed to increase the distance between him and her memory. Still, he hoped a resolution would reveal itself soon, a twist in the forked tail of his grief—

He arched off the seat and hit the floor, pen and notebook sent flying. A groan of despair escaped him as he realised what was happening, then nothing else, because his neck was in tension as his head banged against the carpet once more.

This time the fit lasted longer and was more extreme. Light seemed to flee the caravan, scared by his thrashing, and the sounds of various parts of his body impacting the floor, doors and cupboards faded to a whisper. Something stank, something worse than burnt soup, more rancid than the chemical toilet he had not been tending properly. Faintness snowflaked his eyes. He vomited and felt the warmth across his face and neck. The thump of pumping blood filled his ears, sounding vaguely like the sea, and as coherent thought retreated he was sure he heard words in the rushes.

More ideas of Helen came in, but this time they were new visions of what she had suffered. So new, so detailed,

The Stuff on the Stars, Leaking

so obviously heartfelt, that Brynn could not have possibly created them himself. They were put here for him to see. Helen in the car, shattered windscreen shards opening her to the sea water and spewing dark clouds as she sank, trapped, toward the ocean floor. A final breath held dearly, going stale inside of her, slipping murderous fingers through her lungs to clasp her heart as she saw…below, down past the car's bonnet…a total darkness. Not just a lack of light but something more.

And she kept on falling.

And Brynn would never know when or where she struck bottom because, as her lungs expelled their last, the image and the pain faded away to nothing.

—⚇—

His senses crawled back like whipped dogs seeking succour. He gasped at the air, moaned, tried to scream but puked again instead. This time, he was able to turn on his side so that he did not have to swallow it.

The caravan door was swinging in the morning breeze. The place stank, and he was rolling in his own filth. He must have been out all night.

After much struggling he stood and peeled off his clothes. His arms, legs, back and buttocks were tender and bruised; his head throbbed as if his skull had been shrunk to compress his brain; he had bitten his tongue and the insides of his cheeks. Yet he took solace in the pain each breath gave him.

He found some clean clothes, dressed, made a pot of tea over the primus stove.

Tim Lebbon

The cold hit him all at once, retrieving memories of last night like hypnotic suggestions. He suddenly needed to leave the caravan. The smell of vomit and shit hung heavy in its staid atmosphere, and he could make out dents and scrapes where he had been flipping about during his fits. To stay there would be to tempt fate. And though fate was about as believable as malignant demons, given a choice Brynn would tempt neither.

So he left the caravan and headed to the cliffs, and on the way he saw trails in the dew-laden grass, slick sweeps of disturbed moisture where something had passed by not too long ago.

Soon, he found himself at the head of the path leading down to the beach. Daylight, fresh air, the eternal hush of the sea onto the rocks below, all helped to clear his mind of what had happened, both the fear of the fits and what he had seen while he was incapacitated. The pain felt good, because it was good to be alive.

The thing was even darker than before, almost black, and its tentacles were once again stretched out in dead abandon. Some were buried, others snaked along the sand as though seeking a comfortable resting place. From this high vantage point, the dead creature looked like a huge drift of oil on the beach.

On the way down, Brynn wondered yet again at how he had navigated this path in the semi-darkness. It was so narrow at times that his shoulder brushed against the cliff face as he passed, and showers of stones and sand snickered down onto the rocks below. And still the sea mocked his fears with its incessant song.

The Stuff on the Stars, Leaking

He had not brought his camera with him, nor his notebooks. He had left his jacket in the caravan, and now he shook and shivered as he waited for the sun to purge the shadows he was descending through. The path was slick with dew.

On the beach, a line of seaweed indicated high tide. Brynn thought it was further up the beach than he had yet seen it. He knew about tides and surges and seasonal highs—the sea had been his obsession since Helen had been lost to it—and he knew that there was nothing extraordinary about last night.

Really, he thought. *Nothing at all? What about that fit and those dreams? What about the trails in the grass?*

The sea was quite rough today, whipped into a frenzy by westerly winds, and where it struck the rocks near the base of the path it threw sheets of spray into the air. The wind carried it to Brynn, cooled his face, spotted his clothes. He opened his mouth and closed his eyes, wondering if some of Helen were splashing across him now, bits of the stuff that had made her spread across the oceans after so long.

He would touch the thing today. It must have been here for several days and decomposition was splitting it and venting its gases and melting its insides, but he would run his hands across those tentacles, feel its hide. Feel the truth of it.

He walked through the surf so that he did not leave a trail in the sand. It seemed the right thing to do. Because there were other prints there already, strange snake-like patterns winding to and fro across the beach. And as he neared the thing, he saw that it had begun to change. It was flattening, settling down into the sand, spreading a dark stain and becoming a new bridgehead between land and sea, known and unknown. The tentacles stretched further than ever, but even these were breaking down and giving themselves to the beach.

Brynn fell to his knees and scooped up a handful of the darkened sand. It was sticky and heavy, warm and sweet smelling. He stopped himself from tasting it…though he yearned to know its true scent.

He fell on his back next to the corpse and stared up at the new day. He could almost hear the thing rotting, a series of rips and tears over and above the constant hypno-surge of the sea. He closed his eyes.

His muscles clenched, then shook in the grip of the sudden, violent fit. His eyes turned up in his head. Senses drifted away like breaths in a storm. A gust caressed his skin and then he was gone, a berserker in the dawn, flopping and flipping in the sand like a thing of the sea.

Black grit entered his mouth and eyes and ears, worked its way beneath his clothes, trying to make him a part of the beach just like the dead thing. He saw darkness, felt unbearable pressure and the icy cold of unknown depths. Helen was in his head—or he in hers—and he finally knew what she was thinking at the moment life left her body to its doom. He knew but it did not comfort him, not as it should have. It scared him. Even in the depths of his strange fit, he wondered how her final wish would come to be fulfilled.

She never wanted to leave him. Someday, she would be with him again.

Her last thought had been of him.

—ꟽ—

The Stuff on the Stars, Leaking

Brynn opened his eyes, blinked rapidly and rolled onto his side. His bones felt brittle and liable to break at the slightest impact.

The thing had all but gone, now little more than a hump in the sand. It had spread as it came apart and as he stood, Brynn saw that most of the beach had taken on a dark tint. He walked across and tried the path to the clifftops, but he could not climb. He willed his limbs to take him up but they rebelled, showing him instead the trails in the sand that led down to the edge of the sea, and further. He doggedly sought other routes to the ground above, shambling along at the base of the cliffs, looking for handholds and cracks. But all paths were lost to him now.

The gale increased, driving the sea into angry white breakers, going from nowhere to nowhere with ferocious intent. He was sure the wind started on the beach and ended on the beach…he could see a horizon, but it seemed false, a trick done with mirrors.

The top of the cliffs looked a million miles away. He felt like crying but the tears would not come.

It was only as he finally followed the trails to the water—felt the sea close around his thighs, tasted brine on his tongue, sensed new depths opening up to him as he moved further and further out—that he felt truly in control once more.

Life Rained Off

The first leak appeared above the stairwell. It cried on Grim as he went to bed, dappling his bald head. He cursed, looked up, caught a drop in the eye and cursed again. A bucket took the spill, providing aural torture until he stuffed cotton wool in his ears and drifted to sleep.

In the night he found it hard to breathe, dreaming of smothering darkness and a cool fluidity kissing his skin. He gasped awake. His sweat and piss had soaked the bed. Saliva mottled sheets.

Next day, before he went to work, he was busy. Busy placing buckets and towels as other cracks opened up in his house to let out the wet. Busy turning off the appliances it had been his habit to leave on for so long, as if his whole life were on standby.

So busy, in fact, that he failed to notice the dry pavements and blazing sunshine outside.

Tim Lebbon

After tea that evening the first wave rippled across his living room floor. It broke against his feet and swished around his chair, amazing him. For a crazy moment he was scared to go into the kitchen to fetch newspapers and towels, afraid that he would be trapped there by a high tide and washed away when no one came to help.

His slippers cut through the water, leaving angry surf in their wake. By the time he reached the kitchen he could hear more than just drips from upstairs; gurgles, roars and *tides*, a liquid monster waking and shaking sleep from fluid bones. The dust of yesteryear popped up between floorboards.

"What the hell...?" He made it to the kitchen. By then the water was sloshing over the soggy lip of his slippers. And it was warm, sticky, sensuous, like freshly squeezed blood.

He spent the rest of that evening mourning his new carpets.

It was hot again the next day. The sun bathed the front of the library while Grim sat inside, silently poring over old books: Coleridge; Kafka; a curious tome on alchemy of the mind. He did not know what he was looking for, nor did he find it, so he went to work that afternoon concerned and afraid. He developed a slight fever, the moistness around his collar sending advance guards down between his shoulder blades. He left work ill.

Downstairs was awash and upstairs was dripping. Stains had risen and popped on ceilings, like boils on a grizzled

Life Rained Off

face. Plasterboard lay crippled across his bed. Wet electrics sent flares of distress across the pools.

He started back downstairs and the wave hit him five steps from the bottom, smashing him against the front door. He spluttered, kicked for the surface, but his feet would not touch bottom. His whole life flashed before him and he opened his mouth to laugh at the clichéd truth of it. Water flooded in, filling his lungs.

Grim bobbed through the downstairs. From outside he resembled a drowned fish, nudging against the distorting glass.

Skins

He found himself tugging at his eyelids, pulling the edges of his nostrils, plucking at the corners of his mouth to try to work his fingernails beneath the skin, peel it and tear it and roll it back to reveal whatever might lay beneath. He stared at the mirror, into eyes that mirrored a stranger seeking himself. Only the reflected reflection of his pupils gave away his desperation and the awful possibilities he had to consider.

He found himself standing with hands pressed either side of the mirror, face moving in close, glancing away and back again, trying to see the cracks, thinking that he could trick himself into revealing the joins, the seams that would open out into certainty and truth. His hands left sweaty marks on the walls that faded quickly when he stood back. Into the air, he knew, the moisture was evaporating, but he also knew that was a lie…it was sinking into the wall, being drawn through its solid skin into the depths, and once there it revelled in its freedom.

He found himself wondering who he really was.

—⚎—

Daniel saw the raw flesh of the office building one cold winter's morning.

His own block of flats was the taller of the buildings by a dozen floors, and he enjoyed walking slowly down the glassed-in staircase and staring across the void between the two, watching people hunkered over their desks, picking noses, drinking coffee, flirting, working, talking on the phone, staring out into space and seeing him looking back, smiling at their boredom. It pleased him that he could look in from the outside mostly without being seen, observe bad habits and the unconscious gestures of those reaching terminal boredom. And it amazed him that people sitting so close should think themselves invisible.

Sometimes he stood on a landing, staring long and hard at an office worker until they looked up and stared right back.

The morning he saw the flesh the office block was closed, haunted only by the ghostly flickers of a few computer monitors left on, the surreptitious movement of a fax slowly oozing from its slot and floating to the floor, a tall plant twitching in some unseen breeze. As he came level he paused and looked down, thrilled that he was seeing into these private spaces, seeing what the workers could not see, knowing what was happening. The knowledge empowered him. He sometimes closed his eyes and tried to imagine movements on the sunken Titanic, what was swimming

Skins

there now, whether a few bones were still visible above the silt, what the tiny crustaceans dulling the cold-polished chandeliers thought of themselves. This view he had now was similar…a place unmanned, meant not to be seen, yet laid out plainly in his line of sight…

And then he saw the skin of the office roof peel away.

A carpet of leaves had fallen onto the roof that autumn, rotting down and melding together in the cool rain, the rot making the slime, the slime bonding them together as one. Now, dried out by days of cool wind and nights of vicious frost, the breeze had lifted one corner of the leafy carpet and hauled it skyward. It hung there, undecided as to whether to rise higher or fall back down, waving, hesitating in the fluctuating breeze.

And beneath this carpet, this skin, lay the pink, pulsing, moist flesh of the building. No asphalt or grit or roof linings here, only what lay beneath, the honest body of the office peering from the skein of reality today of all days, today when it knew there was nobody inside.

Daniel gasped and stepped back.

The carpet dropped quickly back down, spraying a gush of leaves over the parapet to drift slowly to the pavement below, rotten suicides fleeing their proper resting place for one more remote.

He shook his head, stepped to the window again, wiped at the condensation his shock had left there. The breeze blew. The layer of leaves on the office roof remained motionless. Daniel ran down two more floors and stared straight across into the tenth floor office. The computer screens were off now, the fax was still, and the shifting plant had somehow moved out of the breeze.

Looked like flesh, he thought as he completed his descent. *Looked like* blood.

Out in the bustling town, movement and noise soon hid Daniel's worries away.

—⚏—

"Our mothers wrap us up," Daniel said. Kathleen lay with her head resting on his chest, breathing hard, stroking his dwindling wet erection.

"What?"

"They wrap us up. Conceal us from the world in skins of their own making. They think they're trying to protect us, but it's more damaging than they know."

"Dan, just what are you on about?" Kathleen raised herself on one elbow and frowned down at him. Her chest was flushed, her face reddened with friction from his stubble. "Where the hell does that come from?"

"Just a thought," he said. "Lying here with you on top, seeing where I go into you, made me remember some things my mother used to say. She told me that babies come from a woman's belly button. That was a lie. I only found out the truth when I was nine or ten, and I resented the lie for years, years…"

"Well, she could hardly tell you the truth, could she?"

"Why not? What's the difference between a pussy and a belly button to a six-year-old?"

Kathleen sat up, shook her head, reached across for a cigarette. "Jesus Dan, you know how to put the coolers on a moment."

Skins

He lay there remembering other things his mother had told him, which he would never tell Kathleen.

"I just think it's wrong," he said.

Kathleen puffed smoke into the steamy air. "Yeah, but why bring it up now?"

Daniel barely heard. "I mean, there's enough lying going on in the world. Things are rarely as they seem. Why should our own mothers lie to us like that? It must be so hard for them to remember all the lies. Mark Twain said that if you always tell the truth, you never have to remember anything. Our mothers…no wonder they age. No wonder they stress. They bring this perfect, innocent, ideal child into the world, and the first thing they do when it's old enough to understand them is lie. 'If you stay like that your face will stick', and 'Father Christmas is looking to see if you're good', and 'If you eat all that you'll have curly hair', and 'Granny has gone to sleep up in the sky', and 'There's no such things as monsters'. So many in so little time. No wonder most adults are just fucked up kids."

"Maybe they do it because they love us," Kathleen said distractedly, more interested in her cigarette, her distraction itself a lie. She was pissed off and trying to hide it.

"Love us?"

"Of course. Sometimes the truth hurts."

Kathleen pulled a sheet around, hid her nakedness, puffed away on her cigarette. Daniel stared wide-eyed at the ceiling, seeing fallacious shapes in the smoke that slowly gathered there.

Tim Lebbon

He always took the lift to the ground floor now, not wanting to see the office block's roof. Since he had glimpsed beneath its skin, viewed the very flesh of the place, his spying had not felt so secretive. A secretary had glanced his way and smiled slightly, maybe seeing him, maybe not. A man feeding sheet after sheet of paper into a shredder had stared across the open space separating them, seeing through two panes of glass and into Daniel's eyes, destroying secrets, unconcerned at his act, staring, dead black eyes boring into Daniel until he had to turn away and take the remainder of the stairs without looking up from his feet.

Since then, the lift, searing through the guts of his building yet revealing nothing of its inner workings.

—⚊—

During the day, Daniel dug holes. He worked for a groundworks contractor, spending much of his time excavating trenches and laying drainage runs. However deep he went there was always further to go.

The day he saw the things that changed him, he was working on a new site.

A hospital had once stood here, but now there was only acres and acres of rugged concrete slabs, stepped in places where basements had been infilled with crushed brick, rippled here and there with rough walls. The buildings had been demolished and removed months ago, leaving a cold pale wasteland as testament to the thousands of people that had died here, the thousands more that had regained their health. His firm had been employed to complete the job the previous company had left undone: the removal of the ground

Skins

slabs. Houses were to be built here eventually, three hundred new homes as part of the city regeneration plan, bringing people in from outside with the lure of nearby amenities and subsidised mortgages.

The demolition firm had been unable to employ anyone to work on the site. Their men had sworn that the place was haunted, and that the ghosts were angry at the hospital being torn down. Upon seeing the place, Daniel could well understand. This was nowhere to live or die.

He loved digging holes in virgin ground. The idea of laying open the earth and viewing sights that no person had ever laid eyes on…he felt honoured and humbled, excited and nervous, and terrified that one day he would see something he could never understand. Mud and rock, mud and rock, occasionally a shred of bone or something older, but he always found what he expected. Perhaps that was because he expected to find it; perpetual cause and effect, the truth steered and created by his own beliefs. He would grab a handful of the mud as it tumbled from the walls of the hole, crunch it in his hand and let it crumble or squelch, raise it to his nose and inhale its scent, squeeze it again next to his ear so that he could hear its gritty whisper, its wet suck. Sometimes the men working with him gave him strange looks, but most of them were used to him by now.

It took three hours of working with breakers, loading giant skips with mechanical diggers, cutting through troublesome reinforcement with disc cutters, before he saw the first ghost.

As a child, Daniel was fascinated with what was beneath the ground. He would ask his father, 'Daddy, what's under the road?' and his father would tell him stones, mud, rocks. 'And caves?' Daniel would ask, 'And dragons, and treasure, and monsters?' No, none of those, his father would tell him, turning the page of his paper or increasing the volume on the television.

Daniel would pace his garden, kicking at the turf again and again until it raised and he could get his fingers beneath, tugging hard, gasping at the tearing sound as the grass tore up in a rough layer to show what was beneath. Sometimes he closed his eyes for minutes on end before looking, always afraid of what he would see, giving the uncovered things time to bury themselves again. Sometime he could even hear them scurrying away or panting and rasping as they dug down into the exposed mud, eager to escape his gaze.

When he finally looked there were the tail-ends of worms withdrawing into the cool soil, earwigs scuttling to and fro, smaller things, white and almost impossible to focus upon. Everything he expected to see. And again and again he found himself dropping the turf back with a disappointed sigh.

Maybe one day, he used to say to himself. *Maybe one day*. But he had no idea what he was waiting for.

"You know me so well," Kathleen said to him. "You see right into me. You touch the heart of me, and that's why I love you."

Skins

Daniel never truly believed her, not about the touching and not about the love. But she believed herself. That is what made things so complicated.

—⁂—

There was something grey peering out from the dark wet earth. He halted the machine's mechanical arm, bucket still filled with shattered concrete, and jumped from the cab. *It must be concrete we've just broken up.* But something about the way the bucket had revealed the thing had caught his eye. It was from below, not above, hidden all these years, comfortable in the absence of light.

As he approached the large hole in the concrete slab, the grey thing did not move.

One of the men shouted over and asked what he was doing. "Hit something," Daniel called, not looking the man's way, eyes concentrated on what was exposed. Down there, given daylight and sun and air, several grey things waved damp material at the sky. Daniel paused and held his breath, heart stuttering, eyes locked wide, but then he too felt the breeze that had set these things shifting. He'd thought the day calm and still, but he had been in his cab for several hours, sheltered. Exposed now, like these things. Given back to the day.

There were three of them, dried out even though they resided in the ground, shells hard and brittle, arms folded beneath their slender bodies, legs drawn up, hair long and brown and flicking at the air like horses' tails bothering flies. One of them stared at him, eyes blinded by cataracts of clay.

And they were so wrong, forbidden, that it was like glancing at the face of God.

Daniel's first thought was that they were corpses somehow left over from the hospital, lost from the morgue perhaps, mislaid, buried secretly after some terrible mistake. But then he realised that they lay below the slab, deep, deep down, in places that sunlight had not touched for aeons, and that was when he turned around and raced away for help.

He stopped after a few steps. A couple of the men were watching him, one resting on his mechanical hammer and scratching his forehead. "What did you hit?" the man asked.

Daniel shook his head, not knowing why, and told them, "Nothing. Just a rock. Nothing." He avoided their quizzical stares as he turned away, sure that the frowns had broken into smiles as he presented them with his sweat-soaked back.

Back at the broken section of slab, deep in the hole where even now the sun was drying anciently dampened earth, there was nothing to be seen. The skin on this wound had scabbed over.

Later that afternoon Daniel slipped and fell into the hole. Scrabbling at the sides, he reached out for the reinforcement protruding from the concrete slab, gashing the back of his hand. He was in a frenzy, desperate to escape the hole, and even as his work companions gathered at its edge and reached in to help him out, he expected their faces to be dimmed, their eyes fading out as new skin cut him off from the rest of the world.

Skins

He would be down there with *them*.

He looked at his wound for the first and last time as he climbed from the van and walked through the automatic doors into Accident and Emergency. The pink, pulpy flesh around the cut seemed denuded of blood, and inside his hand there was only the dull grey, papery flesh of something long dead and gone. Like the mummified ghosts he perhaps had never seen, there was dead stuff hiding inside.

He tried to cry out, but a faint placed a sudden barrier between him and the truth.

And later, as the nurse stitched him together, she kept glancing up as if to catch his eye.

—⚘—

That night he slept alone, and dreamed of Kathleen sewing him up. She sat beside him on his bed, holding together pursed wounds in the skin of his chest and stomach with one hand, trying to thread a needle she held in her teeth with the other. She sweated and cried silently, the drops merging saltily on his open flesh and stinging him to the core. *What is it?* he kept asking, as if he could see nothing wrong. But she only shook her head—which made the threading of the needle more difficult still—refusing him any answer, denying that there was one. He tried to look at the rents in his flesh but she nudged him back down with her elbow, not letting him see. She had the needle threaded, tied cat-gut ready to stitch his cuts firmly shut, but now he decided he needed to see, pushing himself up, feeling the cool fluid movement of his loose guts as he shifted position, and he *had to see*. Kathleen shoved him back down again and swung one leg over his chest, sitting astride him, facing his stomach where he felt the needle begin to slide in an out, in and out, silver cool metal and white hot pain. She was keeping his insides from view, refusing him access to what lay beneath his skin, and even though he lived with himself every day he felt a terrible sense of lost opportunity as he felt the wounds pulling shut, Kathleen shuffling back to stitch his chest.

Eventually, finished, she slid from him and walked into the bathroom so that he could view himself. He saw only a spread of puckered, livid pink skin. He had once claimed to know himself, but he now knew nothing of what truly lay within.

"You need to see someone," Kathleen said. She stood beside his chair and plucked at his sleeve. Perhaps she was trying to pick him up. "Maybe you're depressed, or stressed, or something. But you need to see someone, do something."

"I'm alright."

"*Nothing's* alright!"

Her voice threatened rage but there was not enough life in her for that. Perhaps he bled it without knowing.

"I'm fine," Daniel said, raising his hand as if to show her the cut beneath the spread of bandage and gauze. He thought of removing the dressing, but he was suddenly terrified that there would be nothing there to see.

Skins

He did not go to work the next day. He rang the site foreman, who was understanding and sympathetic, and said that he would likely be off for the remainder of the week. His hand was stiff and sore, bruised from the trauma, his fingers fat black sausages.

And besides, he was afraid.

As he woke from more murky dreams of Kathleen shielding his wounds, something dry rasped on the sheets beside him, rucking across the space that Kathleen had refused to occupy that night. It sounded like something made of dead leaves dragging across the sheet, slipping from the bed and disappearing into shadow as Daniel opened his gummy eyes. His bedroom seemed different from the night before, larger, its dimensions altered unevenly so that his feet looked farther away than they should have, the window incredibly distant, light from the blazing morning sun travelling from another galaxy. Closing his eyes did nothing to hide the effect.

He slipped back into a disturbed unconsciousness. Sounds from outside combined with dream images to form something new and unknown. The toot of a car horn in the distance was the cry of something buried alive. A weightless presence hauled its dead self across his bed, though it may have been his nails as he thrashed through another dream. The *baa*ing of sheep from the fields beyond the village attacked the air, and it was the distance screaming in at him.

The phone startled him awake, and for a few seconds he looked around, trying to place his surroundings. The window frame he recognised, but not the view beyond. His clothes were scattered across a floor that was not his. And in the mirror a stranger sat up in bed. He closed his eyes and let the phone ring some more, then opened them again and knew, at least, who he was.

"Daniel?" Kathleen said. "I didn't think you'd be there."

"Then why ring?"

The pause seemed just too long. "I was just making sure. Are you okay? How do you feel? How's your hand?"

She was asking different questions below the surface. Daniel pretended not to notice. "It's still sore, and it feels light, like some of it has gone. Can you come over?"

"Yes, I'd like that." Kathleen told him she loved him and hung up.

Daniel washed and shaved, avoided wetting the dressing on his hand. He was very careful not to cut himself with the razor, as he was unsure what it would reveal.

Blood?

Something else?

Kathleen was right...he needed some help, someone to talk to, someone impartial with no interest in him or the truth of what he claimed to know. *Perhaps everyone's truth is different*, he thought. *In which case, everything is a lie.*

It was only later that he noticed he'd nicked his chin with the razor. Blood had already scabbed there, and he picked it and saw the fresh smear on his thumb, glad.

—⁂—

"It's just the atmosphere about this place," the foreman said the following Monday morning. They were sitting in the site cabin drinking scalding tea, and Daniel was sure the foreman was hedging around something. His manner was flustered and vulnerable, not harsh and confident as normal. Daniel felt that the big man was opening up, and the idea frightened him immensely.

"The guys are still out there," Daniel said, nodding at the open window. The grind of machines, the growl of trucks never let up. Half the site was now cleared and surfaced with a deep layer of hardcore, exposed earth hidden once again beneath a healing skin that Man himself had applied.

"Some are the same blokes, most are different." The foreman trailed off, looking at the small dressing still covering the back of Daniel's hand, staring hard as if trying to see through. His eyes, normally bright and filled with a harsh humour, were a pale grey. "What exactly did you see?" he asked.

Daniel could not frame an answer. Partly because he could not put what he had experienced into words—it was seeing those grey things, yes, but the smell of old dry history too, the sound of the air touching them for the first time in ages, the sense that a staggering truth had been inadvertently revealed to him—but also because he found the question so intimate. Coming from this man who usually asked how many pints he'd downed the night before, how many fucks he'd had at the weekend, which TV celebrity he'd like to lick to within an inch of her life, the question was as personal as the orgasmic gasp of a lover.

"Nothing," Daniel said. He stood and left the cabin, venturing back onto the slabs that were being ripped open, torn up, wounding the land.

He did not see them again, but he knew that they were there. He could feel them all around. He worked in the cab of his machine, lifting concrete like old peeled scabs, and while the ground beneath never held those old dead grey things, he knew that they were present somewhere else. Deeper perhaps, farther down, teasing him to pursue them…but he could not. There was so much importance in what he already knew, and he was far too frightened to discover more.

At lunchtime he peeled his banana, and as he glanced away the fruit beneath was grey and dead, light and dried out by time. He looked back quickly, and it was the yellow flesh he always expected to see. He took off the rest of its skin, trying to keep an open mind, but the only abnormality was a slight bruise on one side. He threw the fruit away, uneaten.

After lunch, grey clouds crowded in the distance, grouping over the horizon in a cumulous attack. They bore down on the site, obliterating all colour from the streets and the small park at its boundaries with their curtain of warm rain. By the time the windows of his cab were streaked with the first spits of water, the foreman had called a halt to the day's work. Daniel sat in his machine for a while longer as the scene outside was blurred by the downpour. He thought he saw the yellow safety hats of his fellow site workers turn in unison and stare at him, but he could not be sure.

—⚒—

That night he and Kathleen made love. She sat astride him in her favourite position and worked at him with her eyes closed, mind turned inward, and later she told him what a wonderful lover he was. But he had lasted an hour not

Skins

through sexual prowess, but because his mind was distracted, torn elsewhere. At first he had watched his fiancé riding him, the light from the landing outside his bedroom sliding softly across her goosebumped chest and shoulders, moulding itself around her muscles as she strained and writhed. Even then his interest had passed from sexual to something else; a consideration of what lay beneath her skin, what thoughts hid behind the Kathleen he knew and professed to love. Her eyes were closed, yes, and that small act shut him out and, tonight, made her a stranger. The more he dwelled on it, the more her thoughts became more mysterious and introverted, ideas he could never even begin to understand because they were totally alien to him. However much they spoke, however much they made love in this most personal, abandoned way, they would always be strangers.

The room took on those strange dimensions again, walls bowing in or out, pressed or sucked by the grey things beyond, ghosts of dead things that teased him with their insubstantial, dried husks, their skins whispering against the very edges of his perception like mocking voices shouting secrets from distant hilltops. The house disappeared around him—the house, the street, the trees, the town, the sky and the Earth—leaving only this misshapen room, and this stranger Kathleen with her distorted face.

He scratched the skin of her shoulder and she hissed, paused briefly, surprise overtaken by the distant sensations she was feeling. The scratch was darker than her skin, but in the weak light he could not make out whether it was red, or grey.

Later it was red and livid, and he told her he was sorry, kissed it better, embarrassed and ashamed.

She only smiled. Perhaps it was relief.

—∞—

Daniel thought that by catching the truth unawares he had opened his eyes, imbued himself with a knowledge of what to look for, what to see, what to believe and deny. Most people refused to see what they did not expect to see, but now he was forewarned. He walked through town on his own the next day, lying to Kathleen about his plans but feeling no guilt. Everything was a lie, after all. The truth was elusive at best, and not for the likes of them.

He thought of her face last night, her eyes rolling up as she came, and he wondered whether that was the only time that control was lost and reality was truly within reach.

—∞—

He found himself staring into the mirror every morning, leaning closer and closer as the days went by, vision eventually blurring but, in truth, becoming far more clear. He shone lights in his eyes and tried to see deeper inside. He opened his mouth and prodded the skin of his throat with a knife, gagging at the running warmth, punished by the painful healing.

Kathleen told him constantly that he needed help, but he knew it would be help to deceive him again. Cover up what he was beginning to know. Hide away everything that should be concealed and which should never be exposed.

And as the nights drew in and winter cast its grey veil across the land, he found himself more and more often holding

Skins

a knife close to the skin of his face, closer, waiting for the day when his own truth screamed at last for revelation.

The Horror of the Many Faces

What I saw that night defied belief, but believe it I had to because I trusted my eyes. *Seeing is believing* is certainly not an axiom that my friend would have approved of, but I was a doctor, a scientist, and for me the eyes were the most honest organs in the body.

I never believed that they could lie.

What I laid eyes upon in the murky London twilight made me the saddest man. It stripped any faith I had in the order of things, the underlying goodness of life. How can something so wrong exist in an ordered world? How, if there is a benevolent purpose behind everything, can something so insane exist?

These are the questions I asked then and still ask now, though the matter is resolved in a far different way from that which I could ever have imagined at the time.

I was on my way home from the surgery. The sun was setting into the murk of the London skyline, and the city was undergoing its usual dubious transition from light to dark. As I turned a corner into a narrow cobbled street I saw my old friend, my mentor, slaughtering a man in the gutter. He hacked and slashed with a blade that caught the red twilight, and upon seeing me he seemed to calm and perform some meticulous mutilation upon the twitching corpse.

I staggered against the wall. "Holmes!" I gasped.

He looked up, and in his honest eyes there was nothing. No light, no twinkle, not a hint of the staggering intelligence that lay behind them.

Nothing except for a black, cold emptiness.

Stunned into immobility, I could only watch as Holmes butchered the corpse. He was a man of endless talents, but still I was amazed at the dexterity with which he opened the body, extracted the heart and wrapped it in his handkerchief.

No, not butchery. *Surgery*. He worked with an easy medical knowledge that appeared to surpass my own.

Holmes looked up at me where I stood frozen stiff. He smiled, a wicked grin that looked so alien on his face. Then he stood and shrugged his shoulders, moving on the spot as if settling comfortably into a set of new clothes.

"Holmes," I croaked again, but he turned and fled.

Holmes the thinker, the ponderer, the genius, ran faster than I had ever seen anyone run before. I could not even think to give chase, so shocked was I with what I had witnessed. In a matter of seconds my outlook on life had been irrevocably changed, brought to ground and savaged with a brutality I had never supposed possible. I felt as if I had been shot,

The Horror of the Many Faces

hit by a train, mauled. I was winded and dizzy and ready to collapse at any moment.

But I pinched myself hard on the back of my hand, drawing blood and bringing myself around.

I closed my eyes and breathed in deeply, but when I opened them again the corpse still lay there in the gutter. Nothing had changed. However much I desired to not see this, wished it would flee my memory, I was already realising that this would never happen. This scene was etched on my mind.

One of the worst feelings in life is betrayal, the realisation that everything one held true is false, or at least fatally flawed. That look in Holmes's eyes…I would have given anything to be able to forget that.

His footsteps had vanished into the distance. The victim was surely dead, but being a doctor I had to examine him to make sure. He was a young man, handsome, slightly foreign-looking, obviously well-appointed in society because of the tasteful rings on his fingers, the tailored suit…holed now, ripped and ruptured with the vicious thrusts of Holmes's blade. And dead, of course. His chest had been opened and his heart stolen away.

Perhaps he was a dreadful criminal, a murderer in his own right whom Holmes had been tracking, chasing, pursuing for days or weeks? I spent less times with Holmes now than I had in the past, and I was not involved in every case he took on. But…murder? Not Holmes. Whatever crime this dead man may have been guilty of, nothing could justify what my friend had done to him.

I suddenly had an intense feeling of guilt, kneeling over a corpse with fresh blood on my fingertips. If anyone rounded the corner at that moment I would have trouble explaining things, I was sure, not only because of the initial impression they would gain but also the shock I was in, the *terror* I felt at what I had witnessed.

The police should have been informed. I should have found a policeman or run to the nearest station, led them to the scene of the crime. I was probably destroying valuable evidence…but then I thought of Holmes, that crazy grin, and realised that I already knew the identity of the murderer.

Instead, something made me run. Loyalty to my old friend was a small part of it, but there was fear as well. I knew even then that things were not always as they seemed. Holmes had told me that countless times before, and I kept thinking *impossible, impossible* as I replayed the scene in my mind. But I trusted my eyes, I knew what I had seen. And in my mind's eye Holmes was still grinning manically…at me.

With each impact of my feet upon the pavement, the fear grew.

Holmes was the most brilliant man I had ever known. And even in his obvious madness, I knew that he was too far beyond and above the ordinary to ever be outsmarted, outwitted or tracked down. *If his spree is to continue*, I prayed, *please God don't let him decide to visit an old friend.*

I need not have worried about informing the police of the murder. They knew already.

The day following my terrible experience I begged sick, remaining at home in bed, close to tears on occasion as I tried

The Horror of the Many Faces

to find room in my life for what I had seen. My thoughts were very selfish, I admit that, because I had effectively lost my very best friend to a horrendous madness. I could never have him back. My mind wandered much that day, going back to the times we had spent together and forward to the barren desert of existence which I faced without him. I liked my surgery, enjoyed my life…but there was a terrible blandness about things without the promise of Holmes being a part of it.

I mourned, conscious all the time of the shape of my army revolver beneath my pillow.

Mixed in with this was the conviction that I should tell the police of what I had seen. But then the evening papers came and somehow, impossibly, the terrible became even worse.

There had been a further six murders in the London streets the previous night, all very similar in execution and level of violence. In each case organs had been removed from the bodies, though not always the same ones. The heart from one, lungs from another, and a dead lady in Wimbledon had lost her brain to the fiend.

In four cases—including the murder I had witnessed—the stolen organs had been found somewhere in the surrounding areas. Sliced, laid out on the ground in very neat order, the sections sorted perfectly by size and thickness. Sometimes masticated gobs of the tissue were found as well, as if bitten off, chewed and spat out. Tasted. *Tested*.

And there were witnesses. Not to every murder, but to enough of them to make me believe that the murderer—Holmes, I kept telling myself, Holmes—wanted to be seen. Though here lay a further mystery: each witness saw someone different. One saw a tall, fat man, heavily furred with facial hair, dressed scruffy and grim. Another described a shorter man with decent clothes, a light cloak and a sword in each hand. The third witness talked of the murderous lady he had seen…the lady with great strength, for she had stood her victim against a wall and wrenched out the unfortunate's guts.

A mystery, yes, but only for a moment. Only until my knowledge of Holmes's penchant for disguise crept in, instantly clothing my memory of him from the previous night in grubby clothes, light cloak and then a lady's dress.

"Oh dear God," I muttered. "Dear God, Holmes, what is it my old friend? The cocaine? Did the stress finally break you? The strain of having a mind that cannot rest, working with such evil and criminal matters?"

The more I dwelled upon it the worse it all became. I could not doubt what I had seen, even though all logic, all good sense forbade it. I tried reason and deduction as Holmes would have, attempting to ignore the horrors of the case to pare it down to its bare bone, setting out the facts and trying to fill in the missing pieces. But memory was disruptive; I could not help visualising my friend hunkered down over the body, hacking at first and then moving instantly into a caring, careful slicing of the dead man's chest. The blood. The strange smell in the air, like sweet honey (and a clue there, perhaps, though I could do nothing with it).

Holmes's terrible, awful smile when he saw me.

Perhaps that was the worst. The fact that he seemed to be *gloating*.

I may well have remained that way for days, my feigned sickness becoming something real as my soul was torn

The Horror of the Many Faces

to shreds by the truth. But on the evening of that first day following the crimes, I received a visit that spurred me to tell the truth.

Detective Inspector Jones, of Scotland Yard, came to my door looking for Holmes.

"It is a dreadful case," he said to me, "I've never seen anything like it." His face was pale with the memory of the corpses he must have been viewing that day. "Different witnesses saw different people, all across the south end of London. One man told me the murderer was his *brother*. And a woman, witness to another murder, was definitely withholding something personal to her. The murders themselves are so similar as to be almost identical in execution. The killing, then the extraction of an organ."

"It sounds terrible," I said lamely, because the truth was pressing to be spoken.

"It was," Jones nodded. Then he looked at me intently. "The papers did not say that at least three of the victims were alive when the organs were removed, and that was the method of their death."

"What times?" I asked.

"There was maybe an hour between the killings, from what we can work out. And yet different murderers in each case. And murderers who, I'm sure it will be revealed eventually, were *all* known to those bearing witness. Strange. *Strange!* Dr Watson, we've worked together before, you know of my determination. But this...this fills me with dread. I fear the sun setting tonight in case we have another slew of killings, maybe worse. How many nights of this will it take until London is in a panic? One more? Two? And I haven't a clue as to what it's all about. A sect, I suspect, made up of many members and needing these organs for some nefarious purpose of their own. But how to find them? I haven't a clue. Not a clue! And I'm sure, I'm certain, that your friend Sherlock Holmes will be fascinated with such a case."

Jones shook his head and slumped back in the armchair. He looked defeated already, I thought. I wondered what the truth would do to him. And yet I had to bear it myself, so I thought it only right to share. To *tell*. *Holmes, my old friend*...I thought fondly, and then I told Jones what I had seen.

He did not talk for several minutes. The shock on his face hid his thoughts. He stared into the fire as if seeking some alternate truth in there, but my words hung heavy, and my demeanour must have been proof enough to him that I did not lie.

"The different descriptions..." he said quietly, but I could sense that he had already worked that out.

"Disguises. Holmes is a master."

"Should I hunt Holmes? Seek him through the London he knows so well?"

"I do not see how," I said, because truly I thought ourselves totally out of control. Holmes would play whatever game he chose until its closure, and the resolution would be of his choosing. "He knows every street, every alley, shop to shop and door to door. In many cases he knows of who lives where, where they work and who they associate with. He can walk along a street and tell me stories of every house if he so chooses. He carries his card index in his brain, as well as boxed away at Baker Street. His mind...you know his mind, Mr Jones. It is *endless*."

The Horror of the Many Faces

"And you're sure, Dr Watson? Your illness has not blinded you, you haven't had hallucinations—"

"I am merely sick to the soul with what I have witnessed," I said. "I was fit and well yesterday evening."

"Then I must search him out," Jones said, but the desperation, the hopelessness in his voice told me that he had already given up. He stared into the fire some more and then stood, brushed himself down, a man of business again.

"I wish you luck," I said.

"Can you help?" Jones asked. "You know him better than anyone. You're his best friend. Have you any ideas, any reasoning as to why he would be doing these crimes, where he'll strike next?"

"None," I said. "It is madness, for sure." I wanted Jones gone then, out of my house and into the night. Here was the man who would hunt my friend, stalk him in the dark, send his men out armed and ready to shoot to kill if needs must. And whatever I had seen Holmes doing…that memory, *horrible*…I could not entertain the idea of his death.

Jones left and I jumped to my feet. He was right. I knew Holmes better than anyone, and after many years accompanying him as he had solved the most baffling of cases, I would hope that some of his intuition had rubbed off on me.

It was almost dark, red twilight kissing my window like diluted blood, and if tonight was to be like last night then my old friend was already stalking his first victim.

I would go to Baker Street. Perhaps there I would find evidence of this madness, and maybe even something that could bring hope of a cure.

Tim Lebbon

The streets were very different that night.

There were fewer strollers, for a start. Many people had heard of the previous night's murders and chosen to stay at home. It was raining too, a fine mist that settled on one's clothes and soaked them instantly. Street lamps provided oases of half-light in the dark and it was these I aimed for, darting as quickly as I could between them. Even then, passing beneath the lights and seeing my shadow change direction, I felt more vulnerable than ever. I could not see beyond the lamps' meagre influence and it lit me up for anyone to see, any stranger lurking in the night, any *friend* with a knife.

I could have found my way to Baker Street in the dark. I walked quickly and surely, listening out for any hint of pursuit. I tried to see into the shadows but they retained their secrets well.

Everything felt changed. It was not only my new-found fear of the dark, but the perception that nothing, *nothing* is ever exactly as it seems. Holmes had always known that truth is in the detail, but could even he have ever guessed at the destructive parts in him, the corrupt stew of experience and knowledge and exhaustion that had led to this madness? It was a crueller London I walked through that night. Right and wrong had merged and blurred in my mind, for as sure as I was that what Holmes had done was wrong, it could never be right to hunt and kill him for it.

I had my revolver in my pocket, but I prayed with every step that I would not be forced to use it.

Shadows jumped from alleys and skirted around rooftops, but it was my imagination twisting the twilight. By the time I

The Horror of the Many Faces

reached Baker Street it was fully dark, the moon a pale ghost behind London's smog.

I stood outside for a while, staring up at Holmes's window. There was no light there, of course, and no signs of habitation, but still I waited for a few minutes, safe in the refuge of memory. He would surely never attack here, not in the shadow of his long-time home. No, I feared that he had gone to ground, hidden himself away in some unknown, unknowable corner of London, or perhaps even taken his madness elsewhere in the country.

There was a sound behind me and I spun around, fumbling in my pocket for my revolver. It had been a shallow pop, as of someone opening their mouth in preparation to speak. I held my breath and aimed the revolver from my waist. There was nothing. The silence, the darkness felt loaded, brimming with secrets and something more terrible…something…

"Holmes," I said. But he would not be there, he was not foolish, not so stupid to return here when he was wanted for some of the most terrible murders—

"My friend."

I started, tried to gauge where the voice had come from. I tightened my grip on the pistol and swung it slowly left and right, ready to shoot should anything move. I was panicked, terrified beyond belief. My stomach knotted and cramped with the idea of a knife parting its skin and delving deeper.

"Is that you Holmes?"

More silence for a while, so that I began to think I was hearing things. It grew darker for a moment as if something had passed in front of the moon; I even glanced up, but there was nothing in the sky and the moon was its usual wan self.

"You feel it too!" the voice said.

"Holmes, please show yourself."

"Go to my rooms. Mrs Hudson hasn't heard of things yet, she will let you in and I will find my own way up there."

He did not sound mad. He sounded different, true, but not mad.

"Holmes, you have to know—"

"I am aware of what you saw, Watson, and you would do well to keep your revolver drawn and aimed ahead of you. Go to my rooms, back into a corner, hold your gun. For your sanity, your peace of mind, it has to remain between us for a time."

"I saw…Holmes, I saw…"

"My rooms."

And then he was gone. I did not hear him leave, caught sight of nothing moving away in the dark, but I knew that my old friend had departed. I wished for a torch to track him, but Holmes would have evaded the light. And in that thought I found my continuing belief in Holmes's abilities, his genius, his disregard for the normal levels of reasoning and measures of intelligence.

The madness he still had, but…I could not help but trust him.

From the distance, far, far away, I heard what may have been a scream. There were foxes in London, and thousands of wild dogs, and some said that wolves still roamed the forgotten byways of this sprawling city. But it had sounded like a human cry.

He could not possibly have run that far in such short a time.

Could he?

The Horror of the Many Faces

Mrs Hudson greeted me and was kind enough to ignore my preoccupation as I climbed the stairs to Holmes's rooms.

—⚏—

There was another scream in the night before Holmes appeared.

I had opened the window and was standing there in the dark, looking out over London and listening to the sounds. The city was so much quieter during the night, which ironically made every sound that much louder. The barking of a dog swept across the neighbourhood, the crashing of a door echoed from walls and back again. The scream... this time it *was* human, I could have no doubt of that, and although even further away than the one I had heard earlier I could still make out its agony. It was followed seconds later by another cry, this one cut short. There was nothing else.

Go to my rooms, back into a corner, hold your gun, Holmes had said. I remained by the window. Here was escape, at least, if I needed it. I would probably break my neck in the fall, but at least I was giving myself a chance.

I've come to his rooms! I thought. Fly to a spider. Chicken to a fox's den. But even though his voice had been very different from usual—more *strained*—I could not believe that the Holmes who had spoken to me minutes before was out there now, causing those screams.

I thought briefly of Detective Inspector Jones, and hoped that he was well.

"I am sure that he is still alive," Holmes said from behind me. "He is too stupid to not be."

Tim Lebbon

I spun around and brought up the revolver. Holmes was standing just inside the door. He had entered the room and closed the door behind him without me hearing. He was breathing heavily, as if he had just been running, and I stepped aside to let in the moonlight, terrified that I would see the black stain of blood on his hands and sleeves.

"How do you know I was thinking of Jones?" I asked, astounded yet again by my friend's reasoning.

"Mrs Hudson told me that he had been here looking for me. I knew then that you would be his next port of call in his search, and that you would inevitably have been forced by your high morals to relay what you have so obviously seen. You know he is out there now, hunting me down. And the scream...it sounded very much like a man, did it not?"

"Turn on the light, Holmes," I said.

I think he shook his head in the dark. "No, it will attract attention. Not that they do not know where we are...they must...fear, fear smells so sweet...to bees..."

"Holmes. Turn on the light or I will shoot you." And right then, standing in the room where my friend and I had spent years of our lives in pleasurable and business discourse, I was telling the truth. I was frightened enough to pull the trigger, because Holmes's intellect would bypass my archaic revolver, however mad he sounded. He would beat me. If he chose to—if he had lured me here to be his next victim—he would kill me.

"Very well," my friend said. "But prepare yourself Watson. It is been a somewhat eventful twenty-four hours."

The lamp flicked alight.

I gasped. He looked like a man who should be dead.

The Horror of the Many Faces

"Do not lower that revolver!" he shouted suddenly. "Keep it on me now, Watson. After what you think you saw me doing, lower your guard and you are likely to shoot me at the slightest sound or movement. That's right. Here. Aim it here." He thumped his chest and I pointed the gun that way, weak and shocked though I was.

"Holmes…you look terrible!"

"I feel worse." From Holmes that was a joke, but I could not even raise a smile. Indeed, I could barely draw a breath. Never had Holmes looked so unkempt, exhausted and bedraggled. His normally immaculate clothing was torn, muddied and wet, and his hair was sticking wildly away from his scalp. His hands were bloodied—I saw cuts there, so at least for the moment I could believe that it was his own blood—his cheek was badly scratched in several places and there was something about his eyes…wide and wild, they belied the calm his voice conveyed.

"You're mad," I said, unable to prevent the words from slipping out.

Holmes smiled, and it was far removed from that maniacal grin he had offered me as he crouched over the dying man.

"Do not jump to conclusions, Watson. Have you not learned anything in our years together?"

My hand holding the gun was starting to shake, but I kept it pointing at my friend across the room.

"I have to take you in, you know that? I will have to take you to the station. I cannot…I cannot…"

"Believe?"

I nodded. He was already playing his games, I knew. He would talk me around, offer explanations, convince me that the victims deserved to die or that he had been attacked…

or that there was something far, far simpler eluding me. He would talk until he won me over, and then his attack would come.

"I cannot believe, but I must," I said, a new-found determination in my voice.

"Because you saw it? Because you *saw* me killing someone you must believe that I *did*, in fact, kill?"

"Of course."

Holmes shook his head. He frowned and for an instant he seemed distant, concentrating on something far removed from Baker Street. Then he glanced back at me, looked to the shelf above the fire and sighed.

"I will smoke my pipe, if you don't mind Watson. It will put my mind at rest. And I will explain what I know. Afterwards, if you still wish to take me in, do so. But you will thereby be condemning countless more to their deaths."

"Smoke," I said, "and tell me." *He was playing his games, playing them every second…*

Holmes lit a pipe and sat in his armchair, legs drawn up so that the pipe almost rested on his knees. He looked at the far wall, not at me where I remained standing by the window. I lowered the revolver slightly, and this time Holmes did not object.

I could see no knives, no mess on his hands other than his own smeared blood. No mess on his chin from the masticated flesh of the folks he had killed.

But that proved nothing.

"Have you ever looked into a mirror and really concentrated on the person you see there? Try it, Watson, it is an interesting exercise. After an hour of looking you see someone else. You see, eventually, what a stranger sees,

The Horror of the Many Faces

not the composite picture of facial components with which you are so familiar, but individual parts of the face—the big nose, the close-together eyes. You see yourself as a *person*. Not as *you*."

"So what are you trying to say?"

"I am saying that perception is not definite, nor is it faultless." Holmes puffed at his pipe, then drew it slowly away from his mouth. His eyes went wide and his brow furrowed. He had had some thought, and habit made me silent for a minute or two.

He glanced back up at me then, but said nothing. He looked more troubled than ever.

"I saw you killing a man, Holmes," I said. "You killed him and you laughed at me, and then you tore him open and stole his heart."

"The heart, yes," he said, looking away and disregarding me again. "The heart, the brain…parts, all part of the one… constituents of the same place…" He muttered on until his voice had all but vanished, though his lips still moved.

"Holmes!"

"It has gone quiet outside. They are coming." He said it very quietly, looked up at me from sad, terrified eyes, and I felt a cool finger run down my spine. *They're coming*. He did not mean Jones or the police, he did not mean *anyone*. No man scared Holmes as much as he was then.

"Who?" I asked. But he darted from his seat and ran at me, shoving me aside so that we stood on either side of the window.

"Listen to me, Watson. If you are my friend, if you have faith and loyalty and if you love me, you have to believe two things in the next few seconds if we are to survive: the first is that I am not a murderer; the second is that you must not trust your eyes, not for however long this may take. Instinct and faith, that is what you *can* believe in, because they cannot change that. It is too inbuilt, perhaps, too ingrained, I don't know…"

He was mumbling again, drifting in and out of coherence. And I knew that he could have killed me. He had come at me so quickly, my surprise was so complete, that I had plain forgotten the gun in my hand.

And now, the denial.

Doubt sprouted in my mind and grew rapidly as I saw the look on Holmes's face. I had seen it before, many times. It was the thrill of the chase, the excitement of discovery, the passion of experience, the knowledge that his reasoning had won out again. But underlying it all was a fear so profound that it sent me weak at the knees.

"Holmes, what are *they*?"

"You ask *What*, Watson, not *Who*. Already you're half way to believing. Quiet! Look! There, in the street!"

I looked. Running along the road, heading straight for the front door of Holmes's building, came Sherlock Holmes himself.

—⁂—

"I think they will come straight for me," Holmes whispered. "I am a threat."

"Holmes…" I could say little. The recent shocks had numbed me, and seemed now to be pulling me apart, hauling reality down a long, dark tunnel. I felt distanced from my

The Horror of the Many Faces

surroundings even though, at that moment, I knew that I needed to be as alert and conscious of events as possible.

"Don't trust your eyes!" he hissed at me.

That man, he had been running like Holmes, the same loping stride, the same flick of the hair with each impact of foot upon pavement. The same look of determination on his face.

"Faith, Watson," Holmes said. "Faith in God if you must, but you *must* have faith in me, us, our friendship and history together. For there, I feel, will lie the answer."

There came the sound of heavy footsteps on the stairs.

"I will get them, it, the thing on the floor," Holmes said, "and you shoot it in the head. Empty your revolver, one shot may not be enough. Do not balk, my friend. This thing here, tonight, is far bigger than just the two of us. It is London we're fighting for. Maybe more."

I could not speak. I wished Jones were there with us, someone else to make decisions and take blame. Faith, I told myself, faith in Holmes.

I had seen him kill a man.

Don't trust your eyes.

He was bloodied and dirtied from the chase, hiding from the crimes he had committed.

I am not a murderer.

And then the door burst open and Sherlock Holmes stood in the doorway lit by the lamp—tall, imposing, his clothes tattered and muddied, his face scratched, hands cut and bloodied—and I had no more time.

The room suddenly smelled of sweet honey, and turning my head slightly to look at the Holmes standing with me at the window, I caught sight of something from the corner of my eye. The Holmes in the doorway seemed to have some things buzzing about his head.

I looked straight at him and they were no more. Then he gave me the same smile I had seen as he murdered that man.

"Watson!" Holmes said, reaching across the window to grasp my arms. "Faith!"

And then the new visitor smashed the lamp with a kick, and leapt at us.

I backed away. The room was dark now, lit only by pale moonlight and the paler starlight filtering through London's constant atmosphere. I heard a grunt, a growl, the smashing of furniture and something cracking as the two Holmes tumbled into the centre of the room. I quickly became confused as to which was which.

"Away!" I heard one of them shout. "Get away! Get away!" He sounded utterly terrified. "Oh God, oh sanity, why us!"

I aimed my revolver but the shapes rolled and twisted, hands at each other's necks, eyes bulging as first one and then the other Holmes presented his face for me to shoot. I stepped forward nonetheless, still smelling that peculiar honey stench, and something stung my ankle, a tickling shape struggling inside my trousers. I slapped at it and felt the offender crushed against my leg.

Bees.

"Watson!" Holmes shouted. I pulled down the curtains to let in as much moonlight as I could. One Holmes had the other pinned to the floor, hands about his neck. "Watson, shoot it!" the uppermost Holmes commanded. His face was twisted with fear, the scratches on his cheek opened again

The Horror of the Many Faces

and leaking blood. The Holmes on the floor thrashed and gurgled, choking, and as I looked down he caught my eye. Something there commanded me to watch, held my attention even as the Holmes on top exhorted me to shoot, shoot, shoot it in the face!

The vanquished Holmes calmed suddenly and brought up a hand holding a handkerchief. He wiped at the scratches on his face. They disappeared. The blood smudged a little, but with a second wipe it too had gone. The scratches were false, the blood fake.

The Holmes on top stared for a couple of seconds, and then looked back at me. A bee crawled out of his ear and up over his forehead. And then the scratches on his own cheek faded and disappeared before my eyes.

He shimmered. I saw something beneath the flesh-toned veneer, something crawling and writhing and separate, yet combined in a whole to present an image of solidness...

Bees left this whole and buzzed around the impostor's head. Holmes was still struggling on the floor, trying to prise away hands that were surely not hands.

The image pulsed and flickered in my vision, and I remembered Holmes's words: you cannot trust your eyes... instinct and faith, that is what you can believe in...

I stepped forward, pressed the revolver against the uppermost Holmes's head and pulled the trigger. Something splashed out across the floor and walls, but it was not blood.

Blood does not try to crawl away, take flight, buzz at the light.

My pulling the trigger—that act bridging doubt and faith—changed everything.

The thing that had been trying to kill Holmes shimmered in the moonlight. It was as if I was seeing two images being quickly flickered back and forth, so fast that my eyes almost merged them into one, surreal picture. Holmes…the thing…Holmes…the thing. And the thing, whatever it is, was monstrous.

"Again!" Holmes shouted. "Again, and again!"

I knelt so that my aim did not stray towards my friend and fired again at that horrible shape. Each impact twisted it, slowing down the alternating of images as if the bullets were blasting free truth itself. What I did not know then, but would realise later, was that the bullets were defining the truth. Each squeeze of the trigger dealt that thing another blow, not only physically but also in the nature of my beliefs. I knew it to be a false Holmes now, and that made it weak.

The sixth bullet hit only air.

It is difficult to describe what I saw in that room. I had only a few seconds to view its ambiguous self before it came apart, but even now I cannot find words to convey the very unreality of what I saw, heard and smelled. There was a honey tang on the air, but it was almost alien, like someone else's memory. The noise that briefly filled the room could have been a voice. If so it was speaking in an alien tongue, and I had no wish to understand what it was saying. A noise like that could only be mad.

All I know is that a few seconds after firing the last bullet Holmes and I were alone. I was hurriedly reloading and Holmes was already up, righting the oil lamp and giving us light. I need not have panicked so, because we were truly alone.

The Horror of the Many Faces

Save for the bees. Dead or dying, there were maybe a hundred bees spotting the fine carpet, huddled on the windowsill or crawling behind chairs or objects on the mantelpiece to die. I had been stung only once, Holmes seemed to have escaped entirely, but the bees were expiring even as we watched.

"Dear God," I gasped. I went to my knees on the floor, shaking, my shooting hand no longer able to bear the revolver's weight.

"Do you feel faint, my friend?" Holmes asked.

"Faint, no," I said. "I feel…belittled. Does that make sense, Holmes? I feel like a child who has been made aware of everything he will ever learn, all at once."

"There are indeed more things in Heaven and Earth, Watson," Holmes said. "And I believe we have just had a brush with one of them." He too had to sit, nursing his bruised throat with one hand while the other wiped his face with the handkerchief, removing any remaining make-up. He then cleaned the blood from both hands and washed away the false cuts there as well. He seemed distracted as he cleansed, his eyes distant, and more than once I wondered just where they were looking, what they were truly seeing.

"Can you tell me, Homes?" I asked. I looked about the room, still trying to imagine where that other being had gone but knowing, in my heart of hearts, that its nature was too obscure for my meagre understanding. "Holmes? Holmes?"

But he was gone, his mind away as was its wont, searching the byways of his imagination, his intellect steering him along routes I could barely imagine as he tried to fathom the truth in what we had seen. I stood and fetched his pipe, loaded it with tobacco, lit it and placed it in his hand. He held on it but did not take a draw.

He remained like that until Jones of Scotland Yard thundered through the door.

"And you have been with him for how long?" Jones asked again.

"Hours. Maybe three."

"And the murderer? You shot him, yet where is he?"

"Yes, I shot him. It. I shot it."

I had told Jones the outline of the story three times, and his disbelief seemed to be growing with each telling. Holmes's silence was not helping his case.

Another five murders, Jones had told me. Three witnessed, and each of the witnesses identified a close friend or family member as the murderer.

I could only offer my own mutterings of disbelief. Even though I had an inkling now—however unreal, however unbelievable, Holmes's insistence that the improbable must follow the impossible stuck with me—I could not voice the details. The truth was too crazy.

Luckily, Holmes told it for me. He stirred and stood suddenly, staring blankly at me for a time as if he had forgotten I was there.

"Mr Holmes," Jones said. "Your friend Dr Watson here, after telling me that you were a murderer, is now protesting your innocence. His reasoning I find curious to say the least, so it would benefit me greatly if I could hear your take on the matter. There were gunshots here, and I have no body,

The Horror of the Many Faces

and across London there are many more grieving folks this evening."

"And many more there will be yet," Holmes said quietly. "But not, I think, for a while." He relit his pipe and closed his eyes as he puffed. I could see that he was gathering his wits to expound his theories, but even then there was a paleness about him, a frown that did not belong on his face. It spoke of incomplete ideas, truths still hidden from his brilliant mind.

It did not comfort me one bit.

"It was fortunate for London, and perhaps for mankind itself, that I bore witness to one of the first murders. I had taken an evening stroll after spending a day performing some minor biological experiments on dead rodents, when I heard something rustling in the bushes of a front garden. It sounded larger than a dog, and when I heard what can only have been a cry I felt it prudent to investigate.

"What I saw...was impossible. I knew that it could not be. I pushed aside a heavy branch and witnessed an old man being operated on. He was dead by the time my gaze fell upon him, that was for sure, because the murderer had opened his guts and was busy extracting kidneys and liver. And the murderer, in my eyes, was the woman Irene Adler."

"No!" I gasped. "Holmes, what are you saying?"

"If you would let me continue, doctor, all will become clear. Clearer, at least, because there are many facets to this mystery still most clouded in my mind. It *will* come, gentlemen, I am sure, but...I shall tell you. I shall talk it through, tell you, and the truth will mould itself tonight.

"And so: Adler, the woman herself, working on this old man in the garden of an up-market London house. Plainly, patently impossible and unreal. And being the logical minded person I am, and believing that *proof* defines truth rather than simply *belief*, I totally denied the truth of what I was seeing. I knew it could not be because Adler was a woman unfamiliar with, and incapable of murder. And indeed she has not been in the country for quite some years now. My total disregard for what I was seeing meant that I was *not* viewing the truth, that something abnormal was occurring. And strange as it seemed at the time—but how clear it is now!—the woman had been heavily on my mind as I had been strolling down that street."

"Well to hear you actually admit that, Holmes, means that it is a great part of this mystery."

"Indeed," Holmes said to me, somewhat shortly. "My readiness to believe that something, shall we say, out of this world was occurring enabled me to see it. I saw the truth behind the murderer, the scene of devastation. I saw…I saw…" He trailed off, staring from the window at the ghostly night. Both Jones and I remained silent, seeing the pain Holmes was going through as he tried to continue.

"Terrible," he said at last. "Terrible."

"And what I saw," I said, trying to take up from where Homes had left off, "was an impersonator, creating Holmes in his own image—"

"No," Holmes said. "No, it created me in *your* image, Watson. What you saw was your version of me. This *thing* delved into your mind and cloaked itself in the strongest identity it found in there: namely, me. As it is with the other murders, Mr. Jones, whose witnesses no doubt saw brothers

The Horror of the Many Faces

and wives and sons slaughtering complete strangers with neither rhyme, nor reason."

"But the murderer," Jones said. "Who was it? Where is he? I need a corpse, Holmes. Watson tells me that he shot the murderer, and I need a corpse."

"Don't you have enough already?" Holmes asked quietly. I saw the stare he aimed at Jones. I had never been the subject of that look, never in our friendship, but I had seen it used more than a few times. Its intent was borne of a simmering anger. Its effect, withering.

Jones faltered. He went to say something else, stammered and then backed away towards the door. "Will you come to the Yard tomorrow?" he asked. "I need help. And…"

"I will come," Holmes said. "For now, I imagine you have quite some work to do across London this evening. Five murders, you say? I guess at least that many yet to be discovered. And there must be something of a panic in the populace that needs calming."

Jones left. I turned to Holmes. And what I saw shocked me almost as much as any event from the previous twenty-four hours.

My friend was crying.

—ɯ—

"We can never know everything," Holmes said, "but I fear that everything knows us."

We were sitting on either side of the fire. Holmes was puffing on his fourth pipe since Jones had left. The tear tracks were still unashamedly glittering on his cheeks, and my own eyes were wet in sympathy.

"What did it want?" I asked. "What motive?"

"Motive? Something so unearthly, so alien to our way of thinking and understanding? Perhaps no motive is required. But I would suggest that examination was its prime concern. It was slaughtering and slicing and examining the victims just as casually as I have, these last few days, been poisoning and dissecting mice. The removed organs displayed that in their careful dismantling."

"But why? What reason can a thing like that have to know our make up, our build?"

Holmes stared into the fire and the flames lit up his eyes. I was glad. I could still remember the utter vacancy of the eyes I had seen on his likeness as it hunkered over the bloody body.

"Invasion," he muttered, and then he said it again. Or perhaps it was merely a sigh.

"Isn't it a major fault of our condition that, the more we wish to forget something, the less likely it is that we can," I said. Holmes smiled and nodded, and I felt a childish sense of pride from saying something of which he seemed to approve.

"Outside," said Holmes, "beyond what we know or strive to know, there is a whole different place. Somewhere which, perhaps, our minds could never know. Like fitting a square block into a round hole, we were not built to understand."

"Even you?"

"Even me, my friend." He tapped his pipe out and refilled it. He looked ill. I had never seen Holmes so pale, so melancholy after a case, as if something vast had eluded him. And I think I realised what it was even then: understanding. Holmes had an idea of what had happened and it seemed to

The Horror of the Many Faces

fit neatly around the event, but he did not understand. And that, more than anything, must have done much to depress him.

"You recall our time in Cornwall, our nightmare experience with the burning of the Devil's Foot powder?"

I nodded. "How could I forget?"

"Not hallucinations," he said quietly. "I believe we were offered a drug-induced glimpse beyond. Not hallucinations, Watson. Not hallucinations at all."

We sat silently for a few minutes. As dawn started to dull the sharp edges of the darkness outside, Holmes suddenly stood and sent me away.

"I need to think on things," he said urgently. "There's much to consider. And I have to be more prepared for the next time. Have to be."

I left the building tired, cold and feeling smaller and more insignificant than I had ever thought possible. I walked the streets for a long time that morning. I smelled fear on the air, and one time I heard a bee buzzing from flower to flower on some honeysuckle. At that I decided to return home.

My revolver, still fully loaded, was warm where my hand grasped it in my coat pocket.

I walked along Baker Street every day for the next two weeks. Holmes was always in his rooms, I could sense that, but he never came out, nor made any attempt to contact me. Once or twice I saw his light burning and his shadow drifting to and fro inside, slightly stooped, as if something weighed heavy on his shoulders.

Tim Lebbon

The only time I saw my brilliant friend in that time, I wished I had not. He was standing at the window staring out into the twilight, and although I stopped and waved he did not notice me.

He seemed to be looking intently across the rooftops as if searching for some elusive truth. And standing there watching him I felt sure that his eyes, glittering dark and so, so sad, must have been seeing nothing of this world.

Making Sense

I'm sorry. There is no way I can let him live. I'm battling with my conscience, spending long sleepless nights pondering my position, weighing the moral wrongs against the heartfelt rights, the law versus instinct, and I've come to the only conclusion possible: he has to die. It's hatred, true, but with the decision finally made it's also pure logic. He has no right to life. I know people will disagree, but when it comes down to it I will have no regrets. I'll kill him slowly because it's what he deserves. He should feel the pain both you and I are going through…though that's impossible, because he has no feelings. He should experience the torture, the unbearable emptiness I wake to every day and fall asleep with at night. But that, too, is impossible. He's inhuman. He's…nothing. That's all he seems to me, and it's what he will actually be soon. I don't believe in Heaven and Hell, I don't believe in an afterlife, so he will be nothing. Not even a stain on my memory. Not even a smell. Because I'm doing the right thing.

Aren't I? You have to know where I'm coming from on this, don't you? You have to understand.

He's the cunt who killed your baby girl.

The letter lay on Dan's desk, one corner curled over like a scorpion's sting, the threat apparent. He held his head and closed his eyes, pushed fingers through thinning hair. Perhaps his hands would hold in his thoughts and help him realise just what the hell was going on.

"I don't know what to do with this," he muttered.

"What's that?"

Dan jumped in his chair. He hadn't known that Mel was behind him. "Jesus!"

She laughed and came to him, put a cup of tea down on his desk, gave him a hug. "Sorry, I thought you knew I was there." She saw the letter. "Another one?"

He nodded. "This one's like the others. Same tone, anyway. He's talking me through it. I wonder what I'll get when he finally kills the bastard. A video? That's if he has actually got him, if he's not just a whacko, mad, a stalker..."

Mel sighed. "You should give these to the police, I've told you before. He's disturbed. And it's frightening you."

Dan shook his head, but he wondered just how right she was. Was it scaring him? If not, what exactly was that heaviness in his gut, the lightness in his head? "I'm okay, Mel, really. They're just...not very nice. And if I give them to the police they'll ask me questions, what I know about this oddball, and…well, you know." It would drag it all back up.

"I know, babe," she whispered, and kissed the top of his head. She scanned the letter, reached the last line and grunted. "Whoever it is, he's sick. Come on. I'm cooking curry, you're chopping the ingredients."

"Well, apparently I am."

They left the study and Dan closed the door behind him, shutting the letter away, trying to lock it out of his mind. It would have been easy, he thought—as he cried when onion juice hazed into his eyes, enjoyed the tangy smell of fresh chilis—had it not been one of a dozen such missives he'd been sent over the past four weeks. All on the same subject. All about death.

It would have been easier to forget if he hadn't lost his daughter all those years ago.

—⁂—

"I love the smell of curry in the evenings," Dan said in a passable American accent. Full of wine and Indian food, he and Mel had slumped onto the settee and were listening to nondescript background music while they waited for the meal to go down. Afterwards, there would be going down of another kind—Mel seemed in the mood, and although Dan had received another letter today, the wine had gone some way to dulling its import. He was with the woman he loved. He felt good. He was trying not to think about those things.

The television remained unplugged because Dan did not like to watch the news. He was the nearest thing to a hermit living in the big city, and although he sensed that

Mel resented this at times, he could not bring himself to be involved in the outside world. The news depressed him, chipped at his resolve and whatever life he had rebuilt over the years, and when something sickeningly familiar came on…another child missing, another pathetic, ragged body found in a shallow grave…he simply could not take it. He withdrew to a place he could never remember, plunging into an introverted depression that could not be bled out by the love of his girlfriend, nor the lure of drugs, prescription or otherwise. It was somewhere special inside of him, a place of retreat, though it had as many stings and barbs as the world outside. On emergence he would be damaged again. Weighted with memories and regret. Heavy with tears.

It was a shell, and he needed it. What he didn't know, he reasoned, could not hurt him.

He leant over and rested his head on Mel's shoulder, her familiar scent—Obsession perfume; the spicy tang of breath; her own particular body smell that he'd come to know and adore—providing a sense of calm and peace. He was where he was meant to be. His living room was large, sparsely furnished, victim of apathy as opposed to intentional minimalism. Mel kept trying to persuade him to buy more stuff to fill it, but his reply was always the same: when you live here. For now this was Dan's territory, and she was a visitor.

Her smell reminded him of a long weekend they had spent by the sea the previous year. It was their first time away together. They'd been sitting on the seafront eating chips from a crinkled newspaper, fending off seagulls as they dive-bombed their lunch, and then Dan had told her about Emily. He'd not intended telling her, it was simply something that

Making Sense

he'd thought would take its course and come out when the time was right. Cold, snuggled together and sharing a bag of chips had obviously been that time.

Mel had listened silently, but Dan had sensed her shock. It was not something she had expected to hear. Nice chips, honey? And by the way my daughter was kidnapped and killed eight years ago when she was six. And they never found the killer. And my wife left me two years later, and it's taken me this long to get to where I am now, which in truth is pretty fucked most of the time, so I feel I should warn you now, it's only fair, because I'm falling in love with you and it's something you need to know before, just in case, on the off-chance you feel the same about me...

It had been a strange day. Mel had not relinquished physical contact with him for the rest of that afternoon or evening. It had been their first time openly in love with each other, and even now it was a landmark for Dan.

"Love you," he whispered.

"Me too. Big time."

"Fancy some wine?" Dan had several racks in the cellar, and he bought two bottles for every one he or they drank. Soon he would need a new rack. He was nowhere near a connoisseur but it was something he enjoyed, and it gave him a distraction for those evenings when Mel was not there.

"Absolutely. In fact, as it's Friday, bring two bottles. I feel like getting gloriously drunk and then having a long session of oral sex."

Dan's eyes widened and his groin stirred. He kissed Mel, drew in her breath and loved it and her as much as ever. By the time he returned from the cellar with two opened bottles, she was naked.

She took a bottle and splashed rose-red wine across her breasts. "Let's sup."

Dan thought briefly about those letters stored in his study; generally, no specifics, no phrases or sentences leaping at him. I'm doing the right thing, he thought. If he's genuine, if he has got the fuck that killed Emily…I'm doing the right thing.

I am.

"I've told him he should go to the police."

"Of course he should. Christ, what sick bastard sends letters like that to someone who's lost his child and his wife?"

"A sick bastard who has the guy that did it."

A crackle of silence over the phone line.

"You really think these letters are genuine?"

"Dan thinks they are."

"How can he know? It's some crank, Mel, some sick swine who knows about Dan's loss and gets off on taunting him with it. He may even be watching you and Dan when you leave the house, go out—"

"Dan identifies with it."

"You know how unutterably worrying that sounds, don't you?"

"Well…yeah. I suppose. But he does. He reads those letters and I see his eyes…he's going back eight years. He's feeling it all again, and his anger—"

"That's just what the sicko who's sending the letters wants! Whether he's watching you and Dan or not, that's what he's after, he's bringing the pain back again, making Dan suffer when the poor sod's taken this long just to get back on his feet. Jesus. He lost his daughter, then his wife left him…Jesus."

"But what if the letters are true? Mum…I really think Dan really wants it to happen."

More static, like ghosts trying to make themselves heard.

"I'd never thought of that."

Dan was excited. He was living again. He loved it, he relished the verve he felt when he woke in the mornings, but he felt guilty as Hell…not because of Emily and his wife, though they were always there, but because of Mel, and the fact that this new-found dynamism was more to do with the letters than her. For years he had been static, a rock stuck in a moving river, an unblinking presence in the dark watching the lights of progress flitting by. Now, for the first time in years, his life was really moving on.

Someone had the sick fuck who'd killed Emily, and he was going to kill him in turn, and he was seeking Dan's approval. There was never a return address, but Dan was sure that his not going to the police was signal enough. Yes. Do it. Kill the nobody.

He parked outside his business unit, switched off the radio, sat there for a while with the car windows down and the early morning chill cold on his lips and ears. It was still only six o'clock, and most of the other owners would not arrive until seven. He liked being here early. The air smelled almost fresh. And he enjoyed the silence, the chance to open up, carry in whatever materials he'd brought with him for the day's work and lock up the car without being forced into inane exchanges. A selfish act, he knew, but he'd been like that for years. Even before the destruction of his family he'd been a quiet man. Since it had happened, he'd been driven much deeper.

He'd been renting the unit for five years. It was smaller than the one he'd worked in before the bad times, but nowadays he did not produce so much. He made expensive furniture to order, commissioned by rich people who'd heard of his skills from friends and acquaintances. Chairs, tables, bookcases, beds, cabinets, dressers and a whole host of other pieces, carved and whittled with the creative gift he'd had since his school days. There were lathes and saws and other machinery in the unit, but his favourite part of any creation was the final construction, the gluing and jointing that brought the disparate parts together to make a whole.

Lately, that was how his life seemed to him. There were many separate aspects to it—dread of the past; fear of the present; hope for the future—most of them shoved apart by Emily's murder. Now they were coming together again, merging back into one person, a single Dan who could handle them better as a whole than in their individual, untempered states. Mel was beautiful, intelligent, and she loved him. He would marry her one day. He knew she wanted it and over the past couple of months, he'd realised that he wanted it too. The fact that she was so open about Emily's murder, so easy to talk to about something unmentionable, he appreciated greatly. And when he plainly did not want to be reminded, she kept silent. It was as if his past were her past too, even

Making Sense

from long before they had met. What more wonderful thing could a couple share?

By the time the business park began to buzz and roar, Dan was sitting at his lathe working on his new piece. It was a selfish week this week, because he was building a new rack for the basement. As the machine hummed and the smell of hot sawdust filled the air, it brought back memories of how Emily had loved to watch him work. A young, active child, she had still found the patience and fascination to sit, without fidgeting, without asking for anything, as he worked the wood and brought out whatever he could find within. She'd loved the lathe especially, she said it changed the wood like magic. The scent of hot timber brought her sparkling eyes to mind. He stopped the machine, made a slight adjustment to the angle of the cutting chisel, turned around without even thinking about it…of course, she was not there. She never would be again. But he knew he would always turn around just to make sure.

With his first cup of tea he ate some chocolate. Emily had often smelled of chocolate when she spoke to him. It made its taste now that much more important. And candyfloss in the summer, and cordite in November, sweet hot biscuits from when his wife baked, sickness and heat from those terrible midnight illnesses, Kouros when Emily spilled his aftershave…a tragically short lifetime constructed of little more than memories, no less than total love and devotion.

Soon it would all be over. He would receive the last letter, the one he wanted so much.

Three days, Dan thought, and the rack would be ready. Then he would take it home and install it, and next week he'd begin work on the dining table the Palmers had commissioned for Christmas. Three thousand pounds, he'd quoted them, and they'd jumped at it.

He was thinking of booking a weekend break in Verona to ask Mel to marry him. He was sure the answer would be yes. He already had a ring to give her.

—⁂—

She smelled of chocolate. I remember you saying that in the news conferences, I read it in the papers, all those times you were hassled by the press outside the police station while the search was still going on, while there was still hope, some note of optimism in the police spokesman's statements. That really brought it home to me at the time. A missing girl, terrible, a father's and mother's worry, awful…but your comment about the chocolate humanised it somehow, drove the story past the TV screens and radio news, made it real, solid, so much easier to empathise with. The chocolate and the peach shampoo, the one Emily used to have her hair washed in. That conference the day before… well, before they found her…that sticks in my I mind more than any other. Because you were sitting there crying, holding your wife's hand, looking down at the table as you pleaded for her safe return, and without any outward sign you turned inward, whispering about how she smelled of peaches after she'd had a bath in the evening, and how in the middle of the night you always knew if she'd got up and was standing by your bed even before you opened your eyes because you could smell her.

It was the last time you believed she might still be alive.

Making Sense

I smeared chocolate over him. I rubbed squashed peaches into his hair. I was hoping it would make him remember, make him feel some sense of remorse, but of course it did not. It only affected me. So I cut off his ears and rubbed peach juice into the wounds.

That was last week. I still use those things on him. Now it makes him scared.

I will kill him, you know that. I'm just telling you these things to make it right. And I hope, above all else, that it will help you to know how he's suffering.

"I'm sorry I opened it, I couldn't help it. I knew it was from him, I recognised the handwriting from the other envelopes, so I just…I'm sorry, Dan."

"Hey, Mel," he said, taking the envelope from her hand. "Don't worry."

"He's sick."

Dan shrugged, slipping the single folded sheet from inside and reading it quickly. "She liked Curly Wurleys," he said. "And Mars Bars most of all. She said you could never beat a Mars, and I agreed with her, and I still do now. They've come up with loads of other chocolate bars since she died, you now, but they never have beaten a Mars. Not in my opinion. Strange how memory affects taste so much."

Mel slipped her arms around his neck and rested her head on his shoulder. They were silent for some time. Dan breathed in her perfume and closed his eyes. There was a hint of peach in there, perhaps from a new skin exfoliant, and the smell both scared and saddened him. Even with his eyes closed he knew she was there…

"They disgust me," Mel said at last.

"What do?"

"Those letters. They're so horrible!"

Dan shrugged instead of speaking. He didn't find them horrible at all. He stroked the back of Mel's head, running his fingers through her hair and touching the nape of her neck, squeezing her just how she liked it.

"Most of all," she said, "I hate the thought that it's all going on now. And that it's me here with you, but you're living so far in the past. Living those times again."

Dan was angry for a second, resenting her intellectual monopolisation of him, but then he smiled and patted the back of her head. Really, she had no idea what it had been like…what it was still like…and always would be.

"Hey, don't worry babe," he said. "I'm more in the present than you can guess." He thought of the ring in the box in his office, so desperate to tell her here and now. He held back. He hated spoiling surprises. Over the past few years he had become adept at keeping things inside, not forcing himself upon people but restraining the thoughts he knew would upset, offend or damage. Which was good for other people. Sometimes, though, it was terrible for him. Sometimes he felt ready to explode.

Mel lifted her head from his shoulder and looked into his eyes. She was slightly taller than him, a fact which, at times, he found unbearably sexy. Like now. That look in her eyes… well, every time he saw it he became more and more certain that she would say yes in Verona.

Making Sense

"Just make sure you stay here," she said. As usual, she had a way of relaying an awful lot in only a few words.

—⚜—

Later, Dan went naked to the cellar to fetch them a bottle of wine. He chose a Zinfandel, rich and full bodied. They sat up in bed drinking, reading, chatting. And all the time Dan thought of those letters piling up in his study, what they represented, the optimism they inspired in him.

He hoped another would arrive tomorrow.

—⚜—

"It's unhealthy. It's…gruesome. And if Dan's allowing this to happen, he could be an accessory to the fact. Really. You should tell the police."

"But sometimes I think this is all to do with him. You know what I mean; I'm excluded. He's told me all about it, and I've told you, but neither of us knows what he really went through. How he really suffered. Can you just imagine?"

"No, I can't, ever. If anything had happened to you I don't think I could have handled it. Especially something like that."

"Mum, he's still struggling."

"You love him?"

"You know I do."

"You're losing him."

Breathing, breathing and sighing because somehow she knew the truth. "I'm not losing him, Mum—"

"Listen, Mel, can't you see he's relying on you? He needs you to rescue him. How will he feel? How will both of you feel if they find that bastard's body in a couple of weeks time, cut up, tortured, abused. He may be the one—the killer—but could you live with that?"

"Don't go all religious on me, Mum."

"Screw religion. This is common sense. It's…being civilised. Dan needs you. However right he thinks all this is, it's wrong. Go to the police. Tell them everything. Show them the letters."

Another pause while the truth sank in. "The letter-writer will probably still kill him anyway."

"Yes! At last you see. And then everyone wins, don't they?"

"Everyone wins," Mel said, thinking of the man tied in a basement, the letter-writer rubbing peach juice into his open wounds. If living with that was winning, losing was beyond comprehension.

There were two more letters.

Mel was out with a friend when Dan returned home from work the next day. He checked the mail and saw the familiar envelope. Brown, nondescript, his name and address scrawled across the front as if in haste. He's only got time for torture, Dan thought, and the idea pleased him. He dropped the other mail back onto the mat and tore the envelope open.

By the time Mel arrived home an hour later, he'd read the new letter a dozen times. Each time the images therein impacted harder, his face turned grimmer, his mood sank

Making Sense

as he realised that soon it would all be over. In a way—a terrible, shameful way—he was enjoying this tease of death. He felt like a lion when the lionesses were out at the hunt; awaiting his taste of blood. Soon, he would have his pound of flesh. And then there would be Mel to think about, and a new life, and the past would be just that, to be resurrected in dreams and memory, not lived out every single day, every hour. Mel didn't truly know how bad it was. How could she? He had never told her. That wouldn't be fair. And Dan was a fair man.

Not long now. Soon I'll be killing him, and I hope and pray that it will be with your blessing.

I think you should know the mechanics of how I will do it. I'll come to that soon, but first I'd like to tell you about something he did today.

He begged.

I was pleased because it means he knows what is happening, and why, and what the end result will be. So I let him continue his useless act of contrition, his sickening play that seemed to say, hey, I'm sorry, I'm so sorry for what I did, but I can make amends. He can't, not for what he did to Emily, not for those terrible crimes he committed. Because when he did those things he did them to all of us, all fathers, not just you and your lovely daughter. People like this kill one little girl but their crime is against everyone. Some may not see it that way but I do, and I'm sure you do too…his evil is all-encompassing. By killing him, I'm only doing good.

Tim Lebbon

I made him suffer as he has made so many suffer, as he made Emily suffer, as near as I could. I used a bottle. But I smashed the neck first.

Soon I'll kill him. I think he knows this…perhaps it was the way I looked at him as I left the room this evening. Maybe he sensed it in the smell of my sweat, or the way I spread chocolate around the room, placed rotten peaches in all four corners, the Kouros aftershave I splashed on his open wounds. He had the audacity to cry for mercy then, so I did some more. A whole bottle for his ears, another for his stomach (which, by the way, I've been slicing slowly over the past couple of weeks…shallow enough to keep him alive, deep enough to hurt).

I have no choice but to kill him soon. I suspect you want this over with…I'm sure you have a new life to lead… and besides, he's beginning to smell. I think he may have gangrene.

The letter went on to explain how the kidnapper was going to kill the fucker who'd killed his daughter. It was only a paragraph long but it was very precise. Dan read this part two-dozen times, trying to imagine the pervert's face as his captor went about his work, enjoying the certain knowledge that it was going to be slow. It was going to hurt. It was written like an instruction manual, curiously devoid of emotion or reference to Emily or Dan himself, as if the captor had gleaned the description from a book instead of made them up in his own sick, twisted, wonderful mind.

Making Sense

Dan wanted to shake his hand, but he knew that could never be right. He would have to live with the fact that once it was done, it was done. Mel at least would be pleased.

Now, at last, he could book the trip to Verona.

The next day in work, Dan completed the rack for the cellar. He took it home, struggled to drag it into the house, denting doorframes and cursing as it snagged on the living room carpet.

"Dan, honey. What the hell is that?"

"New rack."

Mel helped him with the heavy wooden cabinet, steering him as he walked backwards towards the cellar door. "Hey," she said, "no new letter today!" She sounded pleased. Maybe she thought it was all over.

Dan worked the door handle with his elbow and leaned the rack against the wall, catching his breath.

"You okay honey?" Mel asked. "You look exhausted."

Dan smiled. "Not yet. Hey, I've got a surprise." He threw something at her. She caught it, dropped and caught it again before it hit the carpet. It was a brown envelope. Her eyes went wide and she held it carefully by one corner. Dan gasped, seeing why she may be so shocked. "Hey, no, don't worry, it's tickets! Open it."

She did. "Dan…"

"Verona," he said. "Tomorrow. I've asked your mum to pack a suitcase for you. I wanted to keep it a secret until the morning, but .. well, I love you. I can't keep secrets from you anymore."

Tim Lebbon

She stepped forward and hugged him, kissing his neck. He could feel the dampness of tears on his skin. He closed his eyes and breathed in her scent, wondering what beautiful memories of now it would evoke in the future. He imagined her mouthing Yes under the starlight of a warm Italian evening, red wine catching the moonlight on the table before them, a breeze drifting through the old city carrying with it the promises of good times to come.

"Where do the bottles go?" she asked.

The rack was the shape of a deckchair, but twice as large. Dan indicated the canvas slung from end to end. "Here. Broken. Smashed." From the top and bottom hung cuffs made of steel.

"Dan?"

He reached into his pocket and gave her the final brown envelope. "I found him five weeks ago," he said. "It's only now that I know it's right. I'm sorry, Mel. It'll be over soon, but right now there's no way I can let him live."

He nudged the basement door with his foot.

"Dan? Dan? I don't understand…"

He turned back to his girlfriend—his eventual fiancée and wife—and smiled. "Read the letter, honey. And always remember: it tells you how much I love you."

He hauled the rack inside and slammed the door behind him. Wafting out, like the final exhalation of a dying man, the smells of chocolate and peach.

In Perpetuity

Have you ever lost something? I don't mean your keys or your voice or something you've always meant to shed, like your virginity or that smoking monkey on your back. And I don't mean something less quantifiable, like losing your nerve in a darkened street-fight or forgetting an important fact about someone: their name; their age; their reason for being in your bed.

I mean something precious, loved and protected.

Your son, for instance. Your own flesh and blood. Have you ever lost your son?

—⚉—

"Sammy? Sammy?"

For now it remains a vaguely worried shout, tinged with embarrassment at the people glancing up from across the street and tempered by the thought that I must be mistaken, I *must* be, because stuff like this just doesn't happen.

"Sammy!"

He had come out of the shop and sneaked away, that was it, hide and seek, slipped across the street and found his way down the steps to the car park and river. He was only four-and-a-half, but he was resourceful and mischievous and perfectly capable of hiding down there behind a bush, giggling as he listened to me slowly but surely going mad up here on the street. He would eat those last few chocolate buttons he'd kept in his pocket—they'd be melted mush by now, all the better to make a mess for his poor Dad to clean up—and he'd laugh as he heard me fading out and fading in as I ran back and forth, because now I was panicking, retracing my steps, passing the place where the shop had been and should be again and again and—

"*Sammy!*"

First signs of madness there. My voice was louder, changing surreptitious glances from others in the street to longer, blatant stares. One of them crossed the road and approached me, holding back as I leapt at a six-foot timber fence, pulled myself up, straining to see over, looking for the shop.

A garden. Kids' toys scattered about, a well-manicured lawn, a dog taking a shit in a flower border, glancing back at me as if offended at my intrusion.

I dropped back to the pavement and muttered my son's name under my breath. It came as a gasp.

"You got a problem, mate?" The guy was a punk, purple Mohican out of place amongst the antique shops and cream tea parlours of the little village, too colourful to be seen

In Perpetuity

against the wan greyness of the centuries-old tumbled down cathedral by the river. A tattoo of a dragon crawled out of his black tee-shirt and a silver Celtic ring pierced his nose, and I remembered a story my old headmaster once told me at primary school. He was long-since dead, that wonderful man, but his words had stuck with me, the tale of a leather-clad, heavily tattooed and pierced biker pausing in a multi-storey car park and going back up the stairs to help a woman with two kids and a buggy. Don't judge people by their appearances, the story had ended, the moral hammered in but utterly memorable, something he said would be with me for ages and had been forever.

"Yeah." I ran further along the street, jumped at a stone wall and saw an old man washing his car before I slid back down. The stone snagged my jeans and scraped my legs. If only my senses were as keen as my pain, I may have perceived that something was wrong early enough, soon enough...

The skinhead had wandered after me, frowning. He looked very young. The tattoo was vivid and fresh.

Sammy was four-and-a-half.

"My son's missing," I managed to whisper.

"Sammy, right?"

I nodded. The skinhead ran back across the road, signalled down the bank at someone in the car park below and turned back to me. "Where'd you last see him?"

"In a shop," I said, raising my voice as a car passed by, its inhabitants unknowing and uncaring. "An antique shop, but with lots of other stuff. It was called 'More Things'. I think. But I'm not sure..." I trailed off, ran along the street for a few seconds and tried the front door of a house. It was locked. Nobody came to open it. Fear presses in, panic, a terrible need to do something, *something*. "I'm not sure where it is now," I said.

I looked back across the road and three other youths had joined the skinhead, a boy and two girls, similarly attired in metal and leather and honest attitude. They huddled together for a few seconds and I was suddenly, inexplicably certain that they would step apart and there would be Sammy, laughing as they laughed at this cruel joke, but at least it *was* a joke, only a gag, at least he would still be *there*.

"Sammy!" they yelled, a couple going either way along the street. "Sammy, your dad's looking for you! Sammy!"

Their voiced faded, I crossed the street and looked down at the car park, and I was surprised that I could still see my car. The fact that my son was missing had not changed the way it looked one bit.

Shop's gone, I thought. *Car's still there*. It is truly panic now, but then fragmented memory starts to swing in and take a stab at me, a foe parrying and prodding until my defences are totally clear.

I'll give you access, the shopkeeper had said. *To your hidden thoughts and the places they lead. To pathways that most people cannot or will not see. I'll give you vision.* But that was later after Sammy had been taken and the keeper had charged me with my task, something I was still not sure of, a puzzle like a jigsaw thrown to the wind, waiting to land and be turned up the correct way. Right now I didn't even possess the corners.

"Sammy!" a voice called in the distance.

"Proof of love," I said, trying the words in my mouth, discovering that they sounded less ridiculous than they should have by any sane benchmark. *Access*, the keeper had said. *To pathways*.

I wondered where they led.

As more memories sliced through my shock, forcing the truth into parts of my brain that were surely never designed to deal with such things, I remembered Sammy locked in that room. His eyes staring out, my vision blurred with tears that may have been mine, or his.

And he's thinking of me, seeing me, wondering why I've left him in such a place.

He's *missing* me.

Fleeing is all I can do to help.

"No law," the shopkeeper said.

It was at that precise moment when I knew something was amiss. Sammy was at the window display, looking down at the wood carvings that had so grabbed his attention as we walked by outside. His eyes were wide as he took in whole new worlds. I was browsing the books, dusty old tomes I had never heard of before, used to fill old oaken bookcases to give the place some warmth. There seemed to be several copies of the same book there, though the title refused to imprint itself on my mind.

The shopkeeper was ironing his hand on an old pool table.

"No law," he said again, turning his hand and pressing his palm. There was hissing and steam. When he took the iron away there were no markings on his skin, no burns, no lifeline.

Tim Lebbon

Everything changed. Not visibly—there was no movement, no shift in things—but I noticed things I had not seen before. A display of recently acquired roadkill graced one shelf behind the counter, dripping slow red stalactites to the floor. A cat gazed at me with glazed eyes. A hedgehog bristled, guts hanging out of its arse. A magpie pointed one sad wing skyward, mourning its loss. Further along the wall a row of six coffins were stacked upright, timbers blackened and weakened by long submersion in the soil, the wet mud spilled around their bases holding treadless, nameless footprints. One had ruptured, and I saw something white trying to break free.

"What is this?" I whispered, not intending the shopkeeper to hear. He was ironing his other hand now, watching me as I glanced over at Sammy. "Son!" I said.

Sammy turned around and pointed down at the carvings, eyes wide, a big grin on his face. "Horses!" he said. "Pigs! Daddy, pigs and horses!" From where I stood they were not likenesses of anything known.

"No law," the shopkeeper said for the third time, and he placed the iron on its base and turned to look at Sammy.

I moved towards my son. The shopkeeper raised a hand and I felt stupidly threatened; stupid because he was hardly there, little more than five feet tall and probably a measly nine stones to my sixteen. His hand was red-raw from the iron. I felt the heat coming off him in sickly waves, but he did not seem to be in pain.

"Sammy, get out," I said. "We're going now. We're going for an ice cream!"

"No," the shopkeeper said, "you're not."

In Perpetuity

"What is this?" I asked again rhetorically, totally believing what he said. We were not leaving. The mere possibility of going for an ice cream was almost laughable. The view from the window was already film of a country I had never visited, a place I could never go. The shop felt darker, heavier, deeper than it had when we had entered five minutes before. Sun shone through the windows stronger than ever, but it was as if a haze of dust had been lifted from the floor, vision tinted with a sepia brush.

"This is something far removed," the small man replied. He smiled. It was a pleasant smile, toothy and fresh and it touched his eyes like all good smiles should. There was nothing unkind about it at all, and for a moment I wondered just why I was worried, why I'd concerned myself with a few strange exhibits, he was a little quirky, that was all, and quirkiness was needed to make a living in a place like this, so much competition in the village, so many others trying to ensnare the tourists.

It was a good smile. An easy smile.

But it was ancient.

"Sammy, out you go son," I said. "Wait for me on the pavement." Sammy was standing by the window, not far from the counter and the exit. The shopkeeper was in the middle of the shop, the central exhibit in a place lined with strange wares. I stood to one side, next to ranks of loaded book cases, shelves sagging like a fat man's jowls, tomes askew.

Sammy pouted and frowned heavily for a moment—his not-on-your-life look—but then he saw how serious I was. In that moment, that final moment, I think even Sammy knew just how much trouble we were in. He moved quickly to the door.

"Daddy!" he said, tugging at the handle with a kid's conviction that it would do exactly what he wanted it to do, and *now*. "It won't open!"

"Want sweeties Sammy?" the shopkeeper asked.

"No he doesn't!" I said.

"No thank you," Sammy said. "Daddy said I mustn't. Not from strangers or nasty people."

The shopkeeper turned back to me, not bothering to correct Sammy's depiction of him. "If you want him back," he said, "I need you to find something for me."

Everything shifted. Minutely, almost imperceptibly; I felt it in my bones, my cells, although I did not actually see or hear or feel any movement at all. The change was instantaneous, so fast that my senses dizzied themselves catching up.

One second he was there, the next he had vanished.

Sammy.

"Sammy?"

"Let me show you," the shopkeeper said. He made to walk past me, a faint smile holding his lips up. He stank. Dirt and grime and sweat and worse, a miasma of stenches I had not noticed upon entering the shop. The roadkill had gone rotten, slicking a greenish mess down the wall. The broken coffin had spewed its content across the floor. It wore a dress.

Sammy had gone.

"Where's my son?" I hissed.

"As I said...let me show you. Listen to me and you'll know." He held up his hand and pointed, a filthy fingernail

In Perpetuity

aimed straight between my eyes. "But no law. Any interruption from outside, any efforts to reveal the truth, and you will never see your son alive again." He walked past me and pushed aside a dark curtain hiding a doorway. The weight of further rooms beyond was immense.

I was speechless, actionless, stunned by how things had changed and how outside, everything seemed so normal. Cars passing by, people sitting on a wall eating bags of chips, fluffy clouds dancing across the sky. All the same but an infinity away.

"You'll see him dead, of course," the shopkeeper said, holding the curtain aside as an invitation. "Here and there. Now and then."

Where is Sammy? Where am I?

"Somewhere neither here nor there," the shopkeeper said. "This is my place, my real place. I'm the keeper of it. Come inside if you want to help your son, and I'll tell you what you have to do."

"Tell me now," I said.

The keeper shook his head, face still holding that smile, begging to be melted off with a blowtorch. And I would. When this was over, when I had Sammy back, I would go along with this madman's demand for no law and assert my own.

The smile broadened slightly, and he knew what I was thinking. "Come," he said.

"No. Tell me now. Tell me, or I put a chair through your window and leave."

He knew I would not. He knew I *could* not, not without my son. He disappeared behind the curtain, laughing softly as I heard Sammy crying out for his Daddy.

It is panic now, but a panic somewhat tamed by the memory flying at me. I cry. I sob. And I think of the things the keeper had said.

No law, he said. *Any interruption from outside, any efforts to reveal the truth, and you will never see your son alive again.*

I froze on the edge of the pavement, the car park down the slope before me, the road behind, the row of shops and cafes staring at my back. 'More Things' was not there. Maybe it was further along the street, or in an alleyway I had forgotten fleeing only minutes before. But I thought not.

"Sammy!" I heard from my left. The skinhead and his friend were at a junction in the road, hands cupped to their mouth, their shouts so desperate that they could well have been my own.

I wondered whether asking them for help had been revealing the truth. Maybe even now the keeper was opening the door I could not touch, smiling his benevolent smile as Sammy cried out for me, drew back from the little old man, knowing danger when he saw it...

I had to go. There was nothing I could do here, not anymore, because my life had changed in the last hour. It was more than realisation or experience, it was something fundamental about my existence that had drawn previously held truths from my mind and diced them, hacked them, slaughtered them on the threadbare carpeted floor of the keeper's back room. I'd watched them die, those beliefs, heard their final whimpers through ears still echoing with

In Perpetuity

my young son's pleas for help. Those cries were imagined—nothing could get through that door, not sound, not smell, not me—but they were no less cutting because of that. I had failed him. It was my job to look after Sammy, he was my boy my blood my son and I had failed him. I had left him.

But there was no other way. I believed what had happened, what the keeper had told me and demanded of me. Later I would question this instant belief but right then, right now, there were places I had to be.

I slid down the grass bank and ran to my car. It was hot in the afternoon sun. It needed a wash. I saw Sammy's handprints where he had insisted on opening and closing the door for himself, always learning, always striving for experience and knowledge, *Daddy, why is glass hard, where are the dead people, is there a dinosaur in the sea...?* The car was familiar and unaltered over the last hour, so I clung to it and hoped it might change things back. It did not. Sammy remained not there.

Sammy! I heard from the distance, but if it was still the skinhead it was an echo at most. They were only trying to help, and I should have stayed to thank them, but I had to go. I had to leave and find the pathways that most people could not or would not see. The keeper had given me the key. There was nothing in my pockets, my hands, around my neck, but somehow he had given me the key.

I looked across the river at the ruined cathedral that was this village's life-blood, and for a moment I saw a colour I did not know.

"I have many things," the keeper said as I pushed the curtain aside and followed him in. Sammy's cries had ended without echo. "Many, many things. Here. See this."

He paused beside a glazed picture frame. It held a neatly written one page letter, an admittance of guilt and dishonesty, signed Lucan.

"I almost had the man himself, but he's a slippery beast." The keeper gave me his smile, sickening in sincerity. "Must be all that seaweed."

He walked on and I followed on behind. The corridor opened out until we were walking down the middle of a long, high-ceilinged room. It was huge, its end lost in a haze of perspective, and it could never be here. The shop Sammy and I had entered had been sandwiched between two others, small, a dwelling house with a converted downstairs. Not this place, this somewhere else. Its crannies were lit with gas lanterns hung from impossible heights, the light too strong and even to be only from them. The floor was covered with old carpet, worn in places by countless footfalls until the darkly stained floor showed through. There were smells… they were familiar, the whole rank stew of them, but I could place none. Individually they seemed to conjure secret memories I could not consciously recall; images and places and people and comments and feelings I must have experienced once, such was the sense of familiarity. But they remained unknown to me.

"Look," he said, and "Look," raising his left hand, his right, pointing up and down at the strange exhibits hanging and lying and living in this place. And quickly, shockingly, I began to realise that I was somewhere else. I had moved on, sideways, aslant, and the things I saw here…they were

In Perpetuity

genuine. I believed that instantly and without doubt, as if the air itself were a truth drug and the keeper and I were breathing deep.

A glass case containing the smashed skull and torn brains of Kennedy, still glistening and wet, unclotted, sitting there like the incorruptible remains of a saint.

Further on, hanging in mid air with no visible means of support, something that looked like a blinded eyeball plucked from its socket. *Hitler's testicle*, the keeper whispered, and I believed him.

Sitting on a wide wooden bookcase were a collection of bones, skull ridged and distorted, ribs twisted as if melted and reset a dozen times. The skeleton of an Orc. It even displayed battle damage, knots smashed from the pelvic bone by the repeated impact of an axe.

I saw something else long before we drew level. It struck me and held my attention, obvious, unmistakeable, but when the keeper spoke its name I sank to my knees. Not in worship, but in fear.

The one true cross.

He moved on quickly, as if there were more important exhibits deeper in the room.

Pacing a cage, too large to be inside but here nonetheless, a sabre-toothed tiger. It looked at me with pale, wan eyes, dipped its head and strode one way, dipped again as it came back. There was madness in its gait.

Turned to the wall, sat on a table, an open suitcase cast its unknowable golden glow against damp stone.

More things, more, and the shop's name suddenly held meaning as I remembered the quote from Hamlet. I looked at the back of the keeper's neck, within easy reach of my hands, and suffered the same indecision as that Danish prince.

"A door," the keeper said. He stopped and looked back at me, his arms crossed, waiting.

There was a glass viewing panel and I looked in, saw Sammy huddled on a dirty bed. He had been crying for a long time.

"Sammy!" I shouted, reaching to bang the door and grab his attention. The door drew back from me, like someone drawing in their stomach muscles. "Sammy!" I said, quieter this time, but he merely looked across the room at the far wall, lost, forlorn, forgotten, shoulders shuddering and bottom lip protruding.

I cried. It did no good, there was no power in my tears, but I could not hold them back.

And a few seconds after the tears, came anger.

"Give him back to me!" I hissed. I launched myself at the keeper. My hands were clawed to grab, my heart aching to give pain, but as my fingertips brushed his thick shirt Sammy cried out.

"Daddy!"

I held on to the keeper, pulling him toward me so that I could head-butt him in the face. I wanted to break his nose, see his blood. I abhor violence, and this rage was a thrilling shock to my system.

"*Daddy!*" Sammy shouted again, his voice cutting into me, misting my vision red with furious tears.

"You're only making things worse," the keeper said. He was still smiling. I wanted to rip off his face, turn that smile upside down into a grimace of agony. People had done bad

In Perpetuity

things to me before, but never to my son. This feeling, this anger, was fresh and new and primal. It felt good.

I *growled*. Veins raised on my forearms as I squeezed harder, feeling pinches of the man's flesh caught in his rumpled shirt. He did not seem to notice or care.

"The more you hurt me, the more your son will feel that hurt."

Sammy had stopped shouting but it was replaced with a cry, something worse than the shouting because I recognised it. He was in pain. If he'd been play-acting, the cry would have been loud and forced.

I let go of the keeper and sprang to the door. It shivered away from me as if suddenly swallowed by a heat haze, a mirage formed from the heat of my anger and fear. Yet I could see through the viewing panel. Sammy was still on the bed, but he'd shifted until he was leaning back against the wall, brushing at his chest as if to wave off a wasp or fly that had landed there. There was no insect. There *had* been my own hands on the keeper's shirt…perhaps that was it.

"Daddy," Sammy said again, and my heart broke, I *felt* it. I've heard the expression before, but now I sense the rupture, feel the coolness of shock and then the white-hot rage as blood floods my chest cavity, my insides, drowning me in grief quicker than I can choke.

I turned to the keeper. "I want him back."

"And you'll have him," the old man said. "I'm almost certain of that. Come with me, I'll tell you how." He turned and walked away, further along this wide room that I knew could not be, without a single backward glance.

I suppose that was when I gave in and realised that he had me. Any normal person would have remained behind with their son, tried to get through the door, ignoring the impossible flexing and distortion as their love blinded them to the intolerable and insulated disbelief. But the irony was that no normal person would have seen this. I may have been normal half an hour before, but I had witnessed things, felt things, which destroyed normality as surely as a dream given life. I had seen the one true cross and known it to be genuine, smelled sabre-toothed tiger faeces and not even touched my nose to question the scent. I had queried nothing. That made me not normal.

So I left my son and followed the old man, ready to hear what he had to say. We passed more displays—cages and tanks and echoes and smoke-filled rooms and chattering artifacts—but I ignored them all. I concentrated on the back of his neck, seeing the lines worn in by years of looking up. He was a little man. I wondered how strong he really was.

"Here," he said eventually, turning left and shifting a curtain from a doorway. He motioned me through and I did not pause, not for an instant. If he wanted Sammy and me locked away together he would have had us. I could not have protected myself. My only hope was that he was telling the truth.

"Come into my office," the keeper said, giggling as he dropped the curtain behind him and entered the room.

Outside, the village street. It was still sunny. There were a man and kid across the road, paused on the pavement as the man knelt and wiped ice cream from the boy's shirt. The boy—not much older than Sammy, maybe five or six—continued licking his ice cream cone, smiling wickedly as another chocolate blob dripped down onto his Dad's hand. The father looked up and growled, held his son's arms, shook

In Perpetuity

him and buried his face between his shoulder and neck to give a playful bite. The boy put his head back and laughed. Sunshine glittered from his ice cream tongue. His Dad was bald, his scalp pink from the long hot day he had spent with his boy. A happy day. A day without concerns.

Half an hour earlier, that had been me.

"Where's Sammy?" I said, turning to look at the curtain.

"He's not back there," the keeper said. He shuffled around and sat behind the desk taking up half of the room. It was a chaos of paper and envelopes. I tried to see the addresses on some of them but they were all the same, and equally nonsensical. They had no street, town or city names, and the intendees were little more than smudged names.

"Then where?" I said.

"He's waiting for you."

"Waiting for me to do what?"

"To find something for me."

I saw that strange room again, long as the world, shrunken to nothing at the end by perspective, fading into time and space even though the walls still sprouted miracles and impossibilities. I looked at the keeper. I could read nothing in his face other than enjoyment.

"You've seen my display," he said. "You've seen the things I have in there."

"They're not real," I said, but it was a lie in my throat. I flushed red and looked away from him.

"I think you know they are." He opened a small wooden box and, ridiculously, offered me a cigar. I refused. He chose one, clipped the end and lit it, taking care to puff as much as he could to fog the room. It did not cloud my vision. I could see him just as well, and I would remember his eyes as long as I lived.

"You've seen *Fargo*?" he asked.

"Huh?"

"The film, *Fargo*? You've seen it?"

I nodded.

"Last year I took a child from a car and told its mother that I wanted the money the criminals had buried in that film. She flew to the 'States to look for it. She went to Fargo and froze to death."

I could only frown. There was nothing else to do. I could not, do not understand.

"Don't die on your quest," he said. "If she'd worn warm clothing, gone prepared, she may yet be alive. And the child may not be where it is now…wearing what it is."

"What quest? I'm going nowhere, you have my son, I have you in my eyes, I'm not going anywhere without him."

"No law," the keeper said quietly. He had seen into my mind, that flicker of an idea about leaving here and going straight to the police. "Tell no one of this. I'll know if you do. If they come looking—if they think they can find me just by looking—I'll know."

"What quest?" It was barely a whisper, because I was beginning to see the hopelessness of this. He had me, trapped not by strength but by the surreal, imprisoned in some strange psychotic dream where truth was a lie and everything unreal was as real as my loss. I thought of the cross I had seen out there and felt the holy truth of it. And Sammy, sitting in his room as he cries and wishes for me, wishes I could go and find him.

In Perpetuity

"I want him back," I said. It was an admission of defeat.

"Good," the keeper said. He stood to move his game one step forward.

—⚉—

I had not even left the village before I saw someone who would know me.

The woman was walking along the pavement, glancing into shop windows, pausing to stare at the sky, but I knew from the instant I clapped eyes on her that she was out of place here, out of time. Her clothes were old, tattered and grubby. Her blouse was ripped and bloodied, an old denim jacket draped around her shoulders bearing signs of some ferocious attack. She only wore one shoe; her other foot was clod with blood, and it left a single trail of red footprints along the hot pavement. No one saw them but me.

She passed a young family—sporty father, sexy mother, cute little girl with a chocolate beard—and paused. They walked away without acknowledging her, and even though the father moved to one side to let the woman pass, I was certain he had not actually seen her.

She looked at the sky again and seemed to sigh, shoulders drooping, cheeks glistening with tears or blood.

I rolled the car to a stop and sat there unmoving, wondering whether I knew this woman. I had never seen her before, but the way she blinked and stroked her ear inspired déjà vu, ten seconds, twenty, such a long spell that I felt giddy with possibilities. I clasped the wheel tightly and closed my eyes, and when I opened them again the woman was walking toward me. Staring. Seeing me through the sun-glare from the car windscreen.

"Have you seen him?" she asked. Her voice was like a fox's yap in the night, secretive and instantly lost.

"The keeper?" I asked.

"Of course, the keeper." She sat in the road and rested her forehead on my door. A car approached but the woman seemed unconcerned. It swerved to avoid her without its horn sounding, and with no angry look from the driver.

"So long," she said. "I've been looking for so long…"

I leaned against the door so that I could look out the window, and she looked up at me quickly and smoothly. She knows that I have just left him, she can smell him on me, that stench of cigar smoke and calm deceitfulness. She sees the terror of him in my eyes, and I blink to try to clear the memory of him.

"You'll never forget him," she whispered. "And you'll never see him again."

"I have to! He has my son, locked up crying and thinking I've left him…" Tears came then, and I wished my guilt could be purged with them. Instead they seemed to feed it and lend it strength.

"I'll keep looking," the woman said. "I'll just keep looking. One day he'll slip, one day I'll see the door." She stood and walked away.

"Wait!" I jumped from the car and followed her across the road, running the last few steps as a car honked. I met the woman on the far pavement and reached out to grab her. She evaded my grasp without moving.

"Been looking a long time," she said. "Never found what I was sent for. He has my daughter." Her eyes, deep and dark

In Perpetuity

and all but dead, seemed to deepen more, like the zoom lens of a camera. "I'll see her again, just one more time…"

She moved away and I could not stop her. The same young family she had paused by minutes before had turned around, and now they passed us by. The father gave me a look loaded with suspicion. The woman brushed by his shoulder without him even noticing.

I watched her leave, wending her way along the pavement and turning eventually into a car park shielded by trees. Tears still blurred my eyes, but they could not explain how the woman seemed to skip and jump across the street, as if the scene were part of a jumpy old cine 8 film.

When she had gone, the street was normal once more.

I got into my car and drove from that village. I drove at breakneck speeds along country lanes, and in the back there was Sammy's booster seat, a plastic dinosaur he'd been playing with that morning, a shower of crisps speckling the seat, a half-empty bottle of water which he would never finish…

I thought of that lonely woman, wandering the streets as if that was all she had ever done, her body and clothes and eyes making her invisible to people around her. Because she was somewhere else, somewhere not here, in a place where the keeper had sent her. And where she had found nothing.

She was somewhere I had to go.

—⚉—

"I have many things and want more. I'm a collector and a admirer, an artist and a consumer. I covet what I have not and treasure what I have, because I respect the stranger things in life. Sometimes, so strange. Sometimes too strange to be. But I've never let that rein in my desires." The keeper puffed on his cigar and gave more smoke to the room. I felt queasy. "This is when you ask me what they are," he said mildly. His mouth made a *pop, pop* noise as he obscured the room.

"You have my son in a locked room," I said, my throat clogging, eyes stinging. "You think I give a shit about your desires?"

The keeper sat forward and took the cigar from his mouth. His face seemed to part the smoke as he leaned across his desk toward me, eyelids drooping, the smile as sick and sincere as ever. "Oh, I think you do," he said. "You've seen what I have and you believe in me. That's a good start. Better than most. And while your child cries out for the father who's left him, try to tell me there isn't a little part of you that's *fascinated* with me!"

I shook my head but smoke shapes spoke of my lie, dancing in amusement as swirls of air stroked my still-damp cheeks.

Those things he had out there…such things! And still he wanted more.

"You're a magician?" I asked.

He snorted. "That's like saying you're a master of life, simply because you live. No. I see and accept more of the world than most, that's all."

"How does that help me get my son back?"

"You'll see more soon, too. You'll accept. I want you to find me a new addition to my collection."

"And if I bring it to you?"

"Yes. Your son. Of course!" His voice vented outrage at any hint of mistrust. Again, I believed.

In Perpetuity

"What do you want me to find?"

He sat back in his chair once more. It creaked and sighed as he rested his feet on the desk. I wondered how many times he had done this before.

"Well, I have many things, as you've seen. Some of them you will have recognised, some perhaps not. The cross that Christ was crucified on…that took some finding, and some getting." He stared up at the time-yellowed ceiling and sighed, then leant forward like an excited child. "The fleece, did you see the fleece?"

I shook my head, although I could remember little of that strange walk now. I was concentrating on just one impossible exhibit, unbearable to recall: Sammy locked in the room. The door shifting from my hand, as if diffracted through water. Sammy was my one true treasure.

"Pity. Well, there's more that I want of course, much more. The Grail would be nice…I have a corner where it would look very effective." He grinned, and for the first time something savage showed through. I was almost pleased. "There's someone out looking for that right now," he said, sifting a sheaf of papers and perusing a book I could not see. "Ah yes…more than one, in fact. I suspect they may be some time."

"Me," I said. "What do you want me to find? Tell me what and how and I'll go. I don't care about your habits or your collection or how the hell you came to be here, today, just when I brought Sammy to visit."

"Fate," he said.

"I don't believe in fate."

The keeper shrugged. "It doesn't need your belief. Unlike God, it works just as well without."

I stood, ready to leap across the desk. He was playing with me, like a cat toying with a mouse before the kill.

"Find me proof of love," the keeper said. His words hung in the air between us for a few seconds, sinking slowly in. And then that saccharine smile again, like an evangelist or a talk-show host. "I apologise, of course. I appear to be turning abstract in my old age."

"Proof of love." I stared at him, waiting for the smile to break into a laugh, his façade to fracture and the truth come tumbling out. And once started, my mind continued down that route. I looked around for the hidden camera—what foul TV programme had they dreamed up now, how many deluded and brainwashed sheep-people were phoning in their votes on my fate?—but there was no camera and I had never felt so alone.

The keeper gathered some papers from his desk and knocked them into a pile. None of them were the same size. He wore a ring on every finger, all of them different grades of gold, silver, platinum and other metals, no two colours the same, each design unique. A leather thong hung around his neck bearing several large teeth. They clinked together as he moved and spat a tiny flame, and I knew they were from a dragon. This man was beyond belief.

"That's all you need to give me," he said.

"I loved my wife."

"Prove that to me."

"Sammy is the proof. He's our love made real. Now give him back to me."

The keeper shook his head. "Not good enough. And besides...I can't keep words on display. I can't catch your alleged love for your wife and hold it captive, to muse upon

In Perpetuity

as I grow even older. What would the sabre-tooth think of me listening to nothing? How can I sit before Dracula's lower jaw bone and feign interest in meaningless, long-gone echoes? No. I need something. Something physical, tangible."

"I loved my wife," I said again, and he sees that this is the truth, he looks inside my head and sees the frantic memories of Anne that have been coalescing over the past few minutes. He sees and believes but it is not enough for him. He needs something *tangible*…and stealing my thoughts is way below that.

"I know," he said, almost with pity. "But I need to know forever."

A car passed by outside, a child shouted, a dog barked. Normality mocked me.

"Now you can leave." He looked down at a blank sheet of paper and started to write, dismissing me entirely.

His attitude disarmed me and I slumped to my knees in front of the desk. I watched the keeper write, saw my name appear in a beautiful script on old parchment-like paper, bleeding from his pen as if passing out of his mind, down his arms and through his fingertips.

I had never told him my name.

He looked up. "Are you still here?"

"How long do I have?" I asked.

He shrugged. "How old are you? Do you look after yourself, are you healthy? Looks to me like you may have forty, fifty years in you yet."

"I don't know where to look, what to find, who to ask. I have no idea where to go."

Tim Lebbon

"I'll give you access," the shopkeeper said. "To your hidden thoughts and the places they lead. To pathways that most people cannot or will not see. I'll give you vision."

And he reaches out and touches me for the very first time.

—m—

Twenty minutes after passing the village outskirts, I was still driving through countryside.

Monmouthshire is a beautiful part of the world, but it is hardly wilderness. There are country lanes that seem to lead to places unvisited for years, hillsides and valleys seen only if one abandons the car and proceeds on foot, and here and there stand dilapidated houses and farms buried by vegetation and time, echoing with memories of the dead and stories too long forgotten to ever be told again. The spirits of Romans wander these vales and meadows, the clinking of their armour quieter now than the tinkling woodland streams, subsumed beneath the waters just as their true selves lie buried in the earth, hidden in graves lost millennia ago. So the place is wild, true, but not wilderness. There is little of that left on the planet, and none here. The roads are short, the distance between neighbouring villages and towns small. I had been driving hard, and by now I must have covered almost twenty miles. I should have been out of the county. I should have found civilisation.

Instead, more hills and valleys surrounded me, and wild woods hunkered down on hillsides with no evidence of planned planting. I searched for electricity pylons and plane trails in the sky, but there were none. There were no road

In Perpetuity

signs, either, and the road was more contoured than before, raised and dipped all over, every imperfection exaggerated and put on display.

Looking back up at the wooded hillside, I saw not only trees: there were ash, oak and sycamore, interspersed here and there with rashes of tall, thin pine. Branches raised up and pointed down, to and away from the sun, and even from this distance I could see that the leaves held no uniformity of shape. A willow hung curtains of colour at the lower edge of the forest and two dead, lightning-struck trees were the skeletal hands of the earth, trying to push up and out of the smothering woodland. The canopy was like an amplified reflection of the uneven road surface, and it was just possible there were no two trees in there even approaching a similar height.

I was seeing more.

I glanced at the car's dashboard and every number on the speedometer registered, every crease in the cheap plastic trim was a size, length and shape of its own. The motor rumbled, and I could distinguish the slick hush of pistons from the whirr of the drive shaft. The crackling of tyres on the hot road surface changed sporadically as I ran over a snail, a leaf, a puddle of pitch melted by the blazing sun. Smells parted and gave themselves to me individually, and I felt as if I had a dozen nostrils acting independently, not two. I breathed in deeply and smelled bluebells in the woods, the corpse of a hedgehog by the road and the sweat of a running man.

I was seeing, experiencing and understanding more, much more. Everything was being fed to my conscious mind, not filtered and sorted into important and unimportant, foreground and background. For a few seconds the sensory input was too great and I felt faint. Wheels growled as they encountered grit at the edge of the road. Opening my eyes and biting the inside of my cheek, I tasted blood. I was still in an unknown wilderness. And there is no wilderness; not in the here and now, at least.

I pulled over, trying to ignore the weight pulling me back. The gravity of my abandonment drew at every cell in my body, every slight electrical impulse in my nerves and muscles and brain. I could almost sense Sammy far back through the hills and rock and underground caverns, as if his presence were so strong that mere physicality could not hinder its effect nor tarnish its glow. He is sitting there now, still crying and afraid and wondering why his father has not come to rescue him from this room, where water drips down one wall as if the building is crying in sympathy.

I jumped from the car, suddenly sick and cold and needing to sit and look out across the countryside. The engine ticked behind me as it cooled, and I imagined the sounds a body may make soon after death, the gurgles and farts and sighs as if the soul could mourn its own demise.

Anne had been dead for two years, but she was always here. She was present in my actions, my beliefs, my morals, my faith, my behaviour and my habits—more than anything, her memory was a pleasant habit—and now I sat and actively thought of her. It brought tears as always, but I needed the love we had felt to be fresh and rich.

I *needed* her.

I needed my dead wife.

And then a man ran along the road with a sack full of heads over his shoulder.

In Perpetuity

———m———

"Have you come to collect me?" he said.

"No." I knew there were heads in the sack; I could hear them talking. Several different voices muttered the same short sentences, again and again. It was a light hessian sack, stained red. It dripped.

"Oh," the man said, face dropping. "Only, I've been walking a long time, and I think it's time I got to the shop."

"Who are you?"

He looked instantly suspicious. "Who are you to want to know?"

I shook my head and stood up. "I need to go," I said.

"No! Wait! You have to see, are you from him? You have to see." He shrugged the sack from his shoulder and upended it on the verge next to my car. "I have as many as I could find," he said. "Is it enough? Do I get it, do I get what I was promised?"

He wittered on and I let him, I could not stop him, I was too busy recognising the heads rolling and spinning and coming to a stop at my feet. Jayne Mansfield, a milky Ian Holm, David Warner still muttering omens under his breath, a head wearing a hockey mask and someone who had surely once been a princess.

"Do I get my reward?" he asked again.

"But these have been dead for years," I said, feeling naïve and childish in my assumptions. I had been in the keeper's rooms. I had seen his displays.

"You're new," the man said, obviously disappointed. "Oh. Well, you'll soon see. What has he promised you?"

"My son," I muttered, but I said no more. My quest felt foolish, and I was certain that this man could not help me. He looked like he'd been out here for a long time.

He gathered his heads, picking them up by the hair and dropping them back into the sack. Still they muttered, the same phrases over and over. Perhaps they were the final words they had spoken before their decapitation.

It was impossible. They should not be here, just as everything I had seen in the keeper's shop could not be. I had been duped, drugged, driven temporarily insane by Sammy's disappearance, and now here I was miles away, talking to a madman. He had picked up his sack and slung it over his shoulder, and there could be anything in there.

Above the hills I saw a plane trail drawing slowly westward. Reality.

"I need to go back and get him," I said. I was speaking to myself. "I should call the police, tell them, then find him and—"

"No!" the man said. "You go back looking and you'll be looking forever. You'll lose sight of what you have to do... which is exactly what the keeper says. He never lets anyone return without whatever it is he's sent them to find. He's not that kind of collector. He doesn't take failure."

I thought of the sad, bedraggled woman I had seen in the village, dead but walking, forever lost even though she knew exactly where she was.

"I have to go," the head-man said, almost apologetically. "I've finished, now. I have to find him again."

I felt a rush of jealousy, warm in my guts and cold in my head. The man walked away and he had found his charge—

In Perpetuity

the heads of famous dead people—and however impossible that was, at least they had been a physical, tactile request.

The keeper's challenge to me, however…even if Anne were still alive, where was my *proof?*

"One more bit of advice," the head-man said. He turned and he had changed, his skin more flushed, eyes wider and a subtly different shade of blue. He looked like a final chapter, and the broken veins in his eyes were maps of where he had been. "Keep away from the Green Man. He's lost, but still out there. He's gone mad, forgotten his quest, so he tries to steal from others. Just…stay away from him."

"Green Man?" I said, only more confused.

He looked back one more time, standing there in the road between me and my son. I could ask him to rescue Sammy, I thought. I could go back with him and when the keeper lets him in…

But he had been out here for a long, long time. Why would he jeopardise his reward for me?

"How long have you been looking?" I asked.

He seemed confused for a few seconds, shrugging the sack higher onto his back and paying no attention to the whispering coming from within. "Long enough to find these," he said.

He turned away from me for good. He did not turn or pause or wave, and so I closed my eyes and turned my face to the sky. The sun felt good on my skin, but after a few seconds it began to burn like bad memories. I had enough of them, and I wished for no more.

When I looked back, the head-man had vanished. The road was long and flat, and although there were ditches and undergrowth on either side I did not believe he had hidden himself away. The distance shimmered with heat haze, liquefying the way I had come and the man had gone, turning it indistinct. I blinked again, but the haze grew thicker.

Noises came at me from across the fields, through the woods, beyond the hills. At first I thought they were the voices of giants—grumbling as they awoke, moaning as they hauled themselves up out of the ground and climbed the hills—but then a lorry came around the corner, a helicopter buzzed by high overhead, and within thirty seconds I came to recognise my surroundings.

Cars passed me by, occupants sparing me bored or vaguely curious glances. Perhaps they saw that I had been crying. Maybe some of them realised, in the couple of seconds they had to see, that I was not as wholly here as they.

The motorway was nearby. I had to sit down, plan, think about what had happened and how best to rescue Sammy. I thought that home, a thirty minute drive from here, would be the best place to do so.

Now I had a plan. But desperate as I was, I could not know just how much had changed.

The journey home was haunted by strangeness. Thoughts of the Green Man and the bag of heads and the lost woman intruded, casting themselves alongside careless lorry drivers, angry sports cars and people stuck inside their own little worlds, staring into distances I had seen and they could not imagine. I saw a man driving an MR2, shaving cuts lined on his cheek like claws marks, or scratches impersonating razor slashes. A white van was spotted here and there with bloody

In Perpetuity

stains, most of them smaller than cigarette burns, probably rust but perhaps blood, evidence of a careless dog or a recent hit and run. In a new Mini, a woman frantically frigged herself with one hand and steered with the other, nodding her head slowly up and down while she kept to fifty in the slow lane. I saw all this, and more.

"Daddy!" Sammy calls. "Look Daddy, I'm riding my bike!" I have been at work all day and I've missed this milestone, it's been witnessed only by Anne's mother Jean. "He's riding his bike!" she says. I smile and nod. Sammy is wobbling in an uneven circuit of the garden, joy in his eyes, a sense of achievement in the way he glances up at me every few seconds. He is six years old.

"What the fuck," I whispered, and the image vanished, washed away by a new rush of tears.

I went home. The house was more detailed than it had ever been. The street wavered in heat-haze, and with each flicker of my eyes I could see something more, something extra. It was as if layer upon layer of lies were being peeled back, sheets of air ripping it away until I could see reality peering out from beyond. My front lawn held hillocks and hummocks and battlegrounds for ants and woodlice. Acid evidence of their encounters seared the grass. The corpse of a small slug lay beneath a piece of tree bark, stinking and humming with microscopic life.

Detail, detail, so much detail came at me without my being able to filter it. I had stopped lying to myself, but it was all too much. Sensing more let me understand less.

I tumbled through the front door, ignoring my neighbours where they stood like wax dummies, staring at my red eyes and the empty space around me where Sammy should have been. It was none of their business. How dare they even think about asking.

In the dining room at the back of the house I sat at the French doors, keeping them closed. There was too much going on out there. I had to think. I had to plan. I had to prove love and get my young son back.

Each time I considered returning to the village and breaking into the shop, I saw something else that reminded me of how things now were. A hummingbird drinking nectar, where there should only be sparrows and blue tits eating seed. A shape staring at me from the darkened window of a neighbour's house, glass smudged with too much breathing. Two dogs in the next door garden, mirror images, tails swinging at the same time…every hair, every whisker distinct, and all of them exactly the same. My mind was holding a mirror up to this world and reflecting reality back, telling me to accept, to believe. I realised no sense of glee that I had to inhabit both sides to save Sammy.

I stood and stalked the ground floor of my home, full of empty spaces now without Sammy's shouting, his chattering, the rumble of toy cars on the timber floor, the crash of book towers being built and demolished, whole worlds making up his game. And suddenly, being home alone, Anne was more there than she had been since her death. She may as well have been breathing the same air.

There was a spread of paint on the dining room wall that did not match the rest, and Anne grins at me and says, *You just have to leave your mark everywhere, don't you?* I smiled and shook my head at the memory, and a second later she is sitting at the table, eating the meal I cooked for our first anniversary. She smiles across at me and nods

In Perpetuity

appreciatively. There is a smudge of food on her chin but I do not say anything, we don't know each other that well yet, life is still an adventure of discovery and the future is luscious and long.

Anne is pregnant with Sammy right then, although neither of us knows it at the time.

I turned and left the dining room. In the hallway was what we used to call our holiday wall, a place where we hung photographs and paintings and etchings from the places we had been together. One of the frames held a sketch that Anne had made of a Saracen watchtower on Italy's Neapolitan coast. It was not a very good drawing—it had been the end of her brief foray into doomed artistic ambition—but I loved it more because of that. I stared at the picture, and I can see Anne sitting on a chair in a pavement café, brow furrowed and hand dancing across the paper as she tries to bring the image to life. Her stomach is full and round with our child. There is a drop of ice cream splashed on her chest from moments before, slowly running its way down between her breasts, and I reach over and wipe it away with a delicate stroke. She does not even smile, but it is that familiarity and acceptance that makes me feel so loved. Anne's drawing was my favourite of them all, although each inspired different memories, smells and sounds and rich golden days which, at the time, had seemed nothing special at all. Fate contrives on occasion to make the normal extraordinary. If only we could recognise those times when we were there, not years later.

Two paintings away from my dead wife's drawing was a photograph of a harbour wall in Cornwall, the sun slipping down behind craggy cliffs and setting fire to the oily waters. I could remember taking that picture, turning to Anne, kissing her, telling her how proud I was…simply how proud. Like déjà vu in the making, that brief and seemingly normal moment springs back at me now so that I can smell the sea, feel the weakening sun on the right side of my face, a cool breeze on the left. I turn, alone in my hallway, and although Anne is not there my memory conjures her smile and the taste of her lips.

I walked upstairs, and outside our bedroom was a place where her smell so often lingered. Perhaps her perfume was in the carpet or ingrained in the walls themselves. I could almost hear the perfume bottle being shaken, see the haze of spray drifting in the afternoon sunlight. I began to cry and even that brought a memory; Anne holding me when news of my grandmother's death came through. And my own lonely tears, shed so often in this room as night hugged me close, cried into the pillow so that Sammy did not hear them and come running, asking why are you crying again Daddy?

Still I had no proof.

I looked at the ring on my finger; metal, that was all. Mouldable, meltable, easy to lose, a token rather than a product of our love. A wedding band signifies the traditional, not the spiritual. I had never taken it off, but that meant nothing.

Sitting on the top stair, looking down at the empty hallway and hearing the empty house around me, I began to have an idea of what I had to do. I could not catch a kiss, or the component parts of a muttered I love you long since stolen by the winds and shattered against distant hillsides. But just as love itself is not one thing but many, so its proof would need to be a collage. Physical, spiritual and imaginary, all these pieces would go to make up a big picture, just as

In Perpetuity

devotion, attraction, respect and a dozen more subtle aspects combine for love. I would have to make a collection.

A ghost from the past hit me right then, and suddenly I knew where to begin.

There was still time before the sun went down. I had maybe an hour to drive up the gentle hillside and then climb the final steeper two hundred feet to the summit. On the other side, where part of the hill had fallen away in some million-year-old cataclysm, mine and Anne's names faced out across the lowlands of Monmouth. A foolish greeting-card heart wrapped them together, intent so much more complex than execution. No one ever saw them, but that had not been the point. I had carved them in rock in the hope that they would become as timeless. A teenaged idea of romance, when love exulted in physical form was love made stronger. I smiled as I remembered climbing down the cliff face, heart thudding, sweat tickling my sides as if to make me lose my grip. It was thrilling and tempting, that chance-taking, and I had felt naked and so alone. Anne had been in college. It was all my own effort, and I had fully intended bringing her up here to show her my handiwork, show her just how far my love for her went. For one reason or another, however, days and weeks passed by, and eventually I decided that the carving was best left unseen. It was my own private statement and eventually it faded from my mind, as if worn by an aeon of erosion.

I had not thought of that carving since Anne's death.

Tim Lebbon

As I parked and stepped from the car I was assaulted by detail once again. The sun came in low over the hillsides, dazzling me and giving me clarity of vision at the same time. It was as if its fresh, filtered light was washing my eyes, clearing out the cobwebbed corners where traditional vision held sway, and truth was hidden away. Looking down at my shoes I could see the teeming life around them. Wood ants scurried through pine needles, both blown here by the wind. They moved with purpose even though they may have been lost. Some carried leaves, others locked antennae in brief embraces. I wondered what they shared, and for a terrifying instant I thought I could know. But tiny and insignificant as they were, the working of their minds was way beyond me. There were woodlice too, an earwig, a grub squirming its way blindly between grass stalks and danger. Perhaps I was shielding it from a bird's attention simply by standing here. Once I moved it would be under threat again. For now I had control over this thing's life and death, even though I had never seen it before.

I probably killed things walking from the car, but if it changed the world I would never know.

And then Sammy called out to me and I saw nothing. Strange that his voice sounded so loud even though he was forty miles behind me. "Daddy," he said, not calling or crying, just talking. "Daddy, I'm seven now, I've been playing football for the school team. My knees are scraped and I've knocked out a tooth, but I don't care because I scored the winning goal and the tooth fairy will leave me a fiver."

"You're a very clever boy," I say, and my voice spread across the hillside and startled a big bird into flight. It was a buzzard or a goshawk, and as it took off I saw something squirming in its talons. For an instant it looked as if the victim wore some sort of clothing, but it must have been a splash of blood.

I started walking up the hillside. This place had the reputation of being a favourite suicide spot, although I could not recall ever hearing of anyone jumping. Maybe it was too beautiful. Perhaps here, suicides never quite happened.

The ground shimmered, wavering in and out of focus as if through tears, but I was not crying. It kicked lightly against my feet. I wondered if I was feeling the world's heartbeat.

I looked up again, and there was someone running up the hillside ahead of me.

He was not dressed in green, and as he glanced back down at me his face looked pale, almost white. Yet I was terrified. He had not been here moments before, and now he was above me, legs cutting through the bracken as he ran for the summit and the potential plunge beyond. He was two hundred feet away, yet I could hear his panting, smell his sweat, almost feel the itch of rough cloth against skin as he increased the distance between us.

"Wait!" I called. The man surprised me by stopping and turning around. He leaned forward and rested his hands on his knees, gasping for air. "Wait!" I said again, the word redundant now that he was still.

I started up the slope, but my movement set him running again. I shouted, called, tried to be friendly and then threatening, but he seemed not to hear me anymore. He had even slowed somewhat, his attitude calmer now. His shoulders were not so tense, his breath came easier…and perhaps he gave an occasional giggle.

Why should he be laughing?

Tim Lebbon

He could help me, I think, *if I tell him what I'm doing here maybe he'll help me find the carving, chisel it out, preserve my romantic intentions from so long ago.*

I tripped, stumbled forward and hit the ground hard enough to wind myself. My hands sank into the soft loam, and I felt things moving beneath my palms and between my fingers. The living earth, the mud awash with life, felt more keenly now, smelled and heard and as I looked down, seen. I could *see* the ground moving around me, such was the potential it held. The history, too. It held the past like the coveted lushness of a recently-buried corpse.

When I looked up the man had vanished. I hurried on, passing rocks I remembered from my last time here, years ago. My visit from then was clear, the intention certain. Déjà vu struck me hard as a breath of wind blew dandelion seeds across my path. I looked left and saw a bird drifting low across the hillside. Down by my feet, a scrap of sheep's wool lay tangled in a thistle, all as it had been years ago. I even had the same tools in my pocket, the chisel and hammer… but inside, I was so different.

I sighed as the déjà vu drifted away on the breeze, and then I heard a bird calling from somewhere higher up. A bird of prey, I thought. It was powerful and confident. But I had never heard a call like this. It would not have surprised me to see an unknown species hovering up there. I looked around cautiously, and although the calling continued I could see nothing.

Detail came in at me again, and I realised that I was hearing two sounds, not one. Metal on metal; and metal on stone.

In Perpetuity

Tap tap tap, as the man ahead of me tried to carve something from the cliff face.

There could be no other reason for him being here. Or if there were, the coincidence would be huge. Coincidences happened, I knew that—I believed in much more right then than I had mere hours before—but on this scale it would be unthinkable.

He was the Green Man, here to steal.

I ran. If this really *was* the Green Man, and if the head collector had been right, then he was dangerous. Yet I had to confront him. It was barely a conscious decision, simply something I had to do next, like breathing or blinking.

Tap tap tap.

He *had* been laughing. Because he was here to steal away part of my proof, take a small part of what I could use to save Sammy. The reasons hardly mattered. The fact that it was happening gave me the only impetus I needed. I did not let tiredness or pain slow me down, and the raw anger went to speed me up. A pair of birds were startled from the heather to my left, and I heard their feathers stroking the air as they drifted away. They spoke to each other as they flew. I could have known what they were saying, it was almost within my reach, yet right then it would not have been of interest.

I reached the summit and the world fell away. I was looking out over the countryside I knew so well, grateful to see roads and electricity pylons and the smudge of a village in the distance. Anne and I had eaten at a pub there once, sitting outside in the summer heat and swapping her cheese for my slice of ham. We had often shared meals. There was little we called our own.

Yet there were differences here, and they disturbed me greatly. The village looked larger than it should, some of the buildings taller. And the landscape itself had changed. Like a face grown old, its proportions were now subtly different, the rises higher, the dips deeper.

Tap tap tap.

I looked down and there he was, standing on the narrow ledge fifteen feet below me, one hand holding a small hammer, the other tracing a chisel against the carving I had not seen for years. I almost leaned out to take a look. It was mine, I had put it there and I owned it, and the need to see was great. But then the man looked up at me and grinned—rotten teeth, eyes so empty that I wondered how he could still be alive—and I knew I had to climb down. He sees me and hates me, he sees purpose and a love still burning strong. But he feels nothing because there is nothing to feel, no past, no history, no course of action other than to steal someone else's route back to the keeper.

"That's mine!" I called down. "I came here for that!"

"Stake a claim on the rock of the world, do you?" the Green Man said.

"Do you?"

He kept tapping, harder now, faster. "I just steal," he said. His voice was gruff, as if unused. His clothes were torn, his hair knotted with filth, and he had a long beard that must have been home to things. He had been on the outside for so long that he seemed to have forgotten himself.

I knelt, edged backwards over the cliff and planted my toes against the rockface. It was actually about ten degrees from vertical, but the memory of exquisite danger came back hard. I stood there for a few seconds, my arms stretched out

In Perpetuity

across horizontal ground as if to keep hold of safety. I did not want to let go. I had no idea what I would do once I got down there.

"Please," I whispered. "I need it for my son." But the words must have been swallowed by the ground before me, because the man's only response was to tap harder at the rock.

I heard the patter of small stones tumbling down the cliff. "No!" He'd broken it, shattered my clumsy heart and torn our names apart. They would never be found now, not in a million years could I gather the stones and shards and piece it back together. It would be like grabbing a handful of air and trying to reconstruct Anne's final breath.

"Got it!" he said. I looked down over my shoulder and he was mocking me. Not content with stealing, he was waving a fistful of stone at me, a small rock faced with my expression of love for my dead wife.

"That is mine!" I hissed, the anger pure and enlivening. I felt so *wronged*.

"Which means it's now mine." And then the Green Man began to scurry down the cliff. He descended incredibly quickly, using only one hand, the other retaining its grip on the rock. He stared down at his feet as he went, effectively dismissing me. There was a mole on the back of his neck. His crown was thinning, showing browned scalp beneath. He'd lost a finger on his left hand, ages ago, and I wondered if he had once been a carpenter. He must have loved things then, coaxed shapes from wood, taken time, taken care. He must have been a normal man once.

"What did you lose?" I asked. The Green Man did not seem to hear. He continued his descent, jumping down several feet from one ledge to the next, nails scraping on the rock face so harshly that I felt the vibration through my toes and fingertips.

I started down after him. The thought of what he was stealing urged me into action. I actually wanted to see it so much, I *needed* to see it, because not only was that carving old proof of my love for Anne…it was proof of myself. A confirmation of my existence, my past and history, and evidence of that would make what was happening in the present easier to handle. There was a whole history to me, not just the panicked, useless here and now.

I moved far slower than the Green Man, trying to never have more than one foot or one hand away from the rock at any one time. The thief was shifting with the speed and grace of a spider, whereas I was the slug. So thinking, my hand slipped into a crack and found something cool and wet in there. I drew it out quickly, gasping, hearing and sensing the animal shock of whatever I had touched. I slipped down a few feet. It wasn't until I kept slipping that the shock really kicked in; the realisation that my heart had stuttered and my fists opened and I had relinquished my trust in the rock.

I'm here and there, I think, *at the back of beyond and the forefront of things, and I'm already sure that this is not a place where normality is what I'm used to.* I grab at the rock and see Sammy's face, older than I remember it, sadder, as if all he knows of me are his memories of my abandoning him with the keeper.

My right foot struck a rock and tumbled me out into the air, and I was truly falling. Distance and orientation left me. My views span, but two sights stayed with me and accompanied me down: the village across the valley, larger than it should be, more bulbous, like a cancer that had jumped several years of growth; and the face of the Green Man as I fell past him. Turned to look at me. Knowing I was falling. Nothing in his eyes, no guilt, no pity. Not even victory.

As I struck the ground, I felt every twist of pain.

—⁂—

"Dad," Sammy says.
Dad. Not Daddy.
"This is me when I'm nine. I'm with my friends in town and there's this boy, a bit older than us, he's got an earring and a leather jacket and he's only ten. He pretends he's the Man, and most of us are scared of him, but I remember what you and Mum told me, Dad, to not judge people by their appearances. I talk to Jack and offer him a sweet. He likes Jelly Babies, just like me! And his granddad was in the army too, *and* he likes Willard Price books and Thunderbirds, and we make friends."

Silence for a time. Darkness and silence. I can hear a breath being held and the space between heartbeats, and I wonder if they will go on forever, potential winding incessantly until it folds in on itself and this vision withers and dies.

And Sammy is there again.

"Me and Jack will be best of friends, Dad," he says. "If you let us."

If I let them? Why wouldn't I? Sammy is a growing lad, no reason why…

He's four and a half.

I open my eyes. I hear the Green Man's thought, even though he must surely be long-gone by now: *another one dead.*

I was lying on my back on the ground, the dusky sky filling half my field of vision, the cliff face the other. The sky was beautiful, the cliff face angry that I had even tried to better it. Its ledges scowled, the cracks running vertically were slit eyes that closed even as I looked at them, hiding itself away from me once again. Shadows merged and softened its expression as the sun dipped in the west.

Pain kept me bright. I sat up and agonies coursed through my body, lighting my limbs and chest and neck, exploding in my head. I groaned out loud, and it was louder than I would have liked. The darkness was there, and anything could be hiding within it, listening for me. I had seen that in the keeper's shop, the fact that everything was out there should we but choose to acknowledge it. He had given me a key, a doorway to the locked routes of my mind, but by doing so he had also opened me up to their dangers and threats.

I should have been dead. The top of the cliff was high in the sky, and I should have been dead.

I should be dead!

There were bumps and bruises and cuts, half my body was stiff with dried blood, sticky where my movements started the bleeding afresh, but I was still very much alive.

I fell...I fell a hundred feet!

Yet I could still taste the cold and hear the mysterious distance.

The Green Man had stolen what was mine, but if he was already seeking the keeper he would be fooled. He only had a part of what I needed. The carving was a portion, and there

In Perpetuity

were more to gather before I could join them together, make them react and give the keeper what he had asked for.

Another idea came. The fall had perhaps cleared my confusion like a windstorm through a dusty attic; the impact, maybe, knocking in a knowledge I had only been grasping at up to now.

I knew what I needed next.

—ɯ—

On the way I passed a police car. It was cruising, lights off, perhaps trawling for a final speeding ticket to fill their quota for the day. I almost flashed them down. I would pull them over and go to the driver's window, lean in, breathe in all that had happened to me over the past few hours. The shop, Sammy, the bag of heads, the demand, the door I could not touch, the one true cross, cross at its incarceration, the Green Man, my fall from the cliff—

—and why my bruises were fading, not expanding. And why my bleeding cuts had already scabbed over. I could sense the pain, smell it, taste it, but because I was so in awe of what my senses knew, I was also certain of my recovery. A rib may have been broken, but I could hear it knitting. For now, I could not think about these things.

I'd wave them down and tell them all I could. There was nothing else to do.

No law, I remembered, and the voice was with me in the car. I spun around but there was no one there. The keeper is thinking of me then, sitting at his desk puffing at another cigar, feet crossed on the huge open book, my name scratched in there already, a scrawl of a beginning with an ambiguous middle and an ending waiting to be written.

No law.

I pressed my foot on the gas and drove on. I had to be the author of my life, until I next saw the keeper. I could not let him ghost me. That would take Sammy away and I would forget myself forever, a lost identity wandering the streets, struggling to remember a dead family, their memory chased every day and night to the bottom of a bottle.

There was more proof out there, waiting to be found. The photograph was next. Like the carving it was something I had not thought about for years, yet now its place in my collage of proof was so obvious. A good photo holds and echoes lifetimes, that's what my mother used to say. It was the reason Anne and I had never bought a video camera to record Sammy's early life; we'd wanted photo albums. His smiles frozen, those milestones retained forever for us to see. And sometimes, only rarely, everything that we were was caught within the lens. Just once I could remember, all three of us.

I tapped in the phone number as I drove. For a few seconds I wondered whether my mobile would work here, between many places and beyond most, but it rang and was answered.

"Hello?"

"Jean," I said. "It's me. I have to see you, I'm in trouble."

"Oh God…" she said. Nothing else. I did not even hear her breathing, and for a panicked few seconds I thought of the Green Man. Somehow he had known of the carving. That was something I'd been trying to ignore up until now,

In Perpetuity

shuffled away in the 'To Be Considered Later' part of my mind along with the fact that I'd survived the fall relatively unhurt, and those injuries I had picked up now seemed far less serious than even half an hour ago.

He'd known of the carving, and maybe now he knew of the photo.

"Jean, I need to borrow a photo. That one of me and Anne and Sammy at the hospital, the one—"

"Oh Christ, is Sammy missing?"

That threw me. I even swerved the car, hissing across the gravel at the roadside.

"How do you know?" I whispered.

"As soon as you rang I had a bad feeling." She was Anne's mother. She still treated me like a son. And, like a bad son, I took her for granted far too much. "I don't know," she continued. "I've not been able to do anything all afternoon. I rang but I remembered you were taking Sammy out for the day. The police, have you called—"

"No law," I said. That brought the keeper's face flashing back at me, and I didn't like that. The thought that he was thinking about me, listening in, actively following everything that was happening— "No law, Jean. It's something I have to handle on my own, I'll tell you why later, just please trust me, *please*. It's Sammy, Jean." I began to cry, and for a moment I thought it was raining. I even turned on the windscreen wipers, but they were powerless against my guilt. "He's all that matters."

Jean was silent, weighing up everything I had just told her. Anne had been like this. She was rarely wrong or misinformed in what she said, because she invested such effort and time thinking about things, letting her thoughts coalesce instead of bump together. Our arguments had often lasted for hours, consisting mostly of heavy silence. Like mother, like daughter.

"Are you sure you know what you're doing?" Jean said.

It was a question with no sensible answer, yet instilled with a trust I did not deserve. This world was a place I had never known existed, one where there was much, much more than normal people. Even now, with car lights blinding me at every curve in the road, I heard things moving in the fields.

"Yes," I said, "I'm positive."

There was another silence while Jean digested my lie. She knows it for what it is, but her real dilemma lies in trying to decide whether I am lying for the right reasons. She knows me as well as anyone—grief does that to people, lays them bare, strips their souls to scrutiny—and now, although she is confused and worried at my take on things, she knows that I am doing what I think is right.

"How far away are you?" she asked.

"Ten, fifteen minutes."

"I'll find it for you. See you soon."

It had never been the sort of photograph to grace a wall or sit on a sideboard or desk. Those were always safe, comfortable snaps of smiling faces and casual hugs, sunburnt cheeks and dopey smiles. Vacant images of people loved and perhaps lost, but empty nonetheless, harmless and fun, if melancholic at times. The photograph I wanted had been taken at the hospital when Sammy was two. He'd come out in a rash and we pressed a glass to his spots, neither of us remembering whether they should have faded away or not, and panic had been my guide as I drove to the hospital through rain-sodden midnight streets. For a couple of hours

In Perpetuity

we were certain that our son had meningitis, and the whole world had been swallowed by the darkness outside, none of it mattering, most of it already vanished in readiness for the grave news we both expected. It would not have returned if Sammy had died. We were already all but empty when the doctor told us that everything was going to be alright.

A nurse had taken a photograph of us at Sammy's bedside. I never knew why, but over the months and years following that night I wondered whether it was because she knew what she might capture. She worked with emotions, not just people, and perhaps she had known the magic of that place, wanted to retain some of it for herself. She had sent us a copy. It showed us not as a family but as a single, united whole. We were bonded by more than blood, right then. It was love that held us together.

We were all crying, so Jean kept the picture hidden away. It was too extraordinary to put on show.

"I can't lose him, Jean," I said, "not after Anne." There was a crackle and static stole her immediate response.

"—have to get it for you," she said.

"He thinks I've left him. He thinks I've abandoned him."

"I'm sure he knows that isn't the case, whatever has happened. Sammy's a bright boy. He's quiet, like his mum, but he thinks like her too. He'll know the reasons for whatever you've done, even if you think he can't."

A long line of cars passed in the opposite direction, headlights dazzling me. There was a flash in the sky above the hills to my left, bright as lightning but the wrong colour. Something dark fell from the boiling clouds' underbelly and skirted the hillside. A huge flying shape beat at the thermals and rose once again, belching fire, steaming its way into cover once more.

"There's so much more, Jean," I said. "So much more than what we know or believe. More than we even imagine."

Jean was silent again, and I began to think she had put down the phone.

"I think you should tell me when you get here," she said. "I'll get that photo. And I'll put the kettle on."

"Ten minutes, Jean," I said. I wanted her to stay but knew she had to go. We could talk when I arrived. I should concentrate on my driving, wrapping the car around a lamp post was not the way to help Sammy at all, even though… even though the accident's only cause would be my quest, driven by my utter, desperate love for him.

No proof in death. But there was little conviction in the thought. And for a second Anne was sitting next to me, scolding me for considering such foolishness.

I drove more carefully than ever after that, keeping to speed limits, expecting the dark to surprise me at any moment. As I drove into the city I became aware of the weight of things hiding beyond car lights. Before today I had known nothing in the night, other than golden flashes of car windscreens and garden hedges lit by headlights, the monochrome puddles of pavement around street lamps, the landscape startled into guilty immobility by lightning. Beyond, there was only more night. But now…

…now I can feel the solidity of reality hiding behind the dark, a truth unhindered by the lie of daylight, which itself is simply a trick of the eye. There are threats and promises out there, and promises of threats, skirting the oases of natural vision like tigers and bears at a camp fire, far enough away to

In Perpetuity

stay hidden but close enough to make their presence felt. I felt eyes upon me, ears tracking my car motor and the motoring of my heart. There were fingers searching for me in the dark. Thoughts probed outward and found me wanting. I tried to close my mind, but I was not used to this way of thinking and really, truly, I was only a child here.

Yet people walked the streets and welcomed the night, unaware of what it held, the massive potential they could not perceive and the countless unknown things enjoying the cool night air with them. I had been one of these people this morning, and I knew that however much they tried to think up and out of themselves, in reality their thoughts were turned inwards. So far, in fact, that they almost reflected themselves, holding their originators in a spiralling trap of self-deception.

I had to ignore this new insight. But it was not easy. I drove along the town's main street and saw a child with a ghost at her shoulder, a shop built on an ancient graveyard which hummed with energy, a woman kissing a man in a shop doorway, a man who had horns and no face to kiss... but I drove on. Jean was waiting for me.

And Sammy was spending his first ever night alone.

—⚹—

I had not been to Jean's house for several weeks. She spoke to Sammy almost every day on the phone, but I always found excuses as to why we could not visit. They were empty and meaningless, more so because I loved Jean and bore her no ill will. Perhaps she reminded me too much of Anne. Or perhaps, not enough.

Tim Lebbon

There were several lights on in her house, and music mumbled through the windows. I felt the reverberation of something classical, a soft string section coaxing me up the garden path with promises of hot tea and Jean's understanding smile. I would not tell her everything, I knew that, because however much she trusted me she could not keep this quiet and private. She would frown and nod and agree as I explained the need for secrecy, but once I left she would be on the phone to the police. Jean had lived a long life and seen her husband and daughter into their graves, but I was sure she had never seen anything beyond the world she knew. She had not walked the keeper's rooms and witnessed proof of how little we knew. She would not be able to understand.

I stood at the front door and reached for the bell, but smiled at the formality. It was my first smile since leaving the keeper's shop. It made me feel sick. I rang the bell anyway, and then tried the handle. The door slipped open and let me into the house.

"Jean!"

I could smell freshly-poured tea from the kitchen at the end of the hallway. She must have seen me pull up in the car. The music paused between tracks right then, and as I held my breath I heard the steady *pop pop pop* of trapped air escaping from beneath a hot mug.

"Jean! I'm here!"

She must have been cooking, because there were other smells from the kitchen. The sweet tang of burnt gas. Old grease on her oven. Blood.

"Jean?" I glanced into the living room before walking down the hallway. A cigarette had burnt down in the ashtray next to her favourite armchair, leaving behind a delicate

In Perpetuity

skeleton of ash. The television was dead, screen hazed with a thick layer of dust, and a tatty paperback was steepled on the table beside her chair. Also on that table lay her cordless phone. My voice had shaken that earpiece not ten minutes earlier.

At the end of the hallway I could already see into the kitchen, and before I acknowledged or understood the writing on the wall I knew what it meant. Perhaps I had put it there by dialling Jean's number. *Down,* the word on the wall said, running from the tails of the 'w' and the feet of the 'n', because it had been written in blood.

I could not move. To go forward would be to reveal the full message and the source of the dreadful ink. To back away would be to deny my responsibility. So for a few seconds I stood where I was, watching a bubble of blood slip down my dead wife's mother's kitchen tiles, slowing because it was already growing thick.

Someone laughed, and the back door from the kitchen to the garden slammed shut.

I did not even think about moving. It was as natural as breathing or eating, or loving my son. I leapt forward and held onto the door jamb, swinging around so that I faced the back door. The full message revealed itself as I did so—*You're slowing down!*—and then I saw something at my feet. Momentum took me forward, and there was rage there as well, because I already knew what had happened and why and who was to blame.

I stumbled over Jean's corpse and held my hands out to break my fall. But there was so much blood there, pooled and splashed and smeared by whoever had killed her, that I slipped forward and landed across her chest.

She gasped, a short, sharp exhalation that made me cry out.

"Jean, Jean, holy shit!" I pushed at the floor until I was kneeling, glanced at Jean, at the back door, at Jean again. She'd gasped but she was dead, she must be. If she *were* somehow still alive I would have wished her dead, the injuries were so severe. I looked back at the door again, and the bloody handprint on its frame drew me to my feet.

Jean gasped again, and a bloody bubble grew slowly from her nose before popping. She was alive. Barely, alive.

The hand that made that print had already thieved something from me, and now it was stealing more, fleeing with the memory of Jean's life already drying under its fingernails and in the crease of its lifeline.

He'd been laughing, and my last memory of Jean was four weeks ago, when she had given Sammy a hug and kiss goodbye and he'd reached up and tweaked her nose and told her that he'd stolen it away.

I stood and ran to the door, feeling the slickness of blood beneath my feet. The next track began on the stereo.

"You bastard!" I shouted as I opened the door, but then borrowed light from the neighbours' houses quietened my voice. It was guilt that silenced me, the certainty that I had hauled Jean to this moment simply by calling her…perhaps even from the moment I thought of the photograph. She gasped again behind me but it must have been involuntary, a death rattle, she surely could not live, and it was hopeless me staying here now…

The murderer laughed one more time, though he may have been streets away by then. I knew without searching

In Perpetuity

the house that he would have the photograph in his bloodied hand.

You're slowing down, the gruesome message on the wall read, scrawled over cigarette-yellowed magnolia paint. And so where next? What else could the Green Man see in my immediate future that I had not yet even considered? He'd already taken the carving, and stabbed Jean for the photograph.

He must have arrived minutes after she hung up the phone. Jean already knew that this single old image was important, vital, and her love for Sammy had helped her clasp it to her chest. She was no spring chicken but this intruder, haunted and haunting to look at, had not fazed her enough to give in. Perhaps he had mentioned me. Maybe he had even told her whatever he knew of Sammy.

I had to go after him. There was a trail, I could smell it now, an unnatural taint on the air that had silenced barking dogs and made twitching curtains fall back into place. Whether I had a hope in Hell of catching the Green Man or not, it was essential that I followed him. If luck was on my side I would catch him unawares and take my possessions out of his grasp.

I stood on the threshold, undecided, torn between staying to watch her die and continuing onward. Looking again at the clotted writing on the wall, I could already perceive the final shape it would make. Food for thought for the police.

That decided me. The police would have to know—or they would find out—and I would be trapped. *No law,* the keeper had said. Jean would not want me being useless here when Sammy was still out there somewhere, awaiting my return but perhaps, hour by hour, trusting its certainty less and less. *How does a four-year-old think?* I wondered. *Does he have any concept of next month, next year? Or is it all 'later' to him?*

"I'm sorry Jean," I muttered, hoping that she could no longer hear. The door slammed shut behind me, sucking in the light and giving me back to the night. I stood there for a few seconds, sniffing the air, listening, and in the distance I heard an area of silence, felt an aura of disquiet. That was where the Green Man must be.

"Am I too late?" a voice asked from the shadows. It was quiet, so low and wretched that it was androgynous. "I am, aren't I? Too late again. Could I really expect anything else?"

"Who are you?" I hissed. I tried to appear taller than I actually was, wincing as wounds from my fall fought back, but maintaining the posture. The pain was deserved. Better still, it felt *right*. I should have been dead, after all.

"I'm always too late," the voice said, as if that could be an answer. A tall woman stepped away from the house, appearing from shadows I had thought were nothing more.

"I have to go," I said, unnerved.

"You won't catch him."

"Who?"

"Green Man. He's more removed from this world than any of us, and sometimes he slips even further. If you did get close he'd just…jump. Go so far out you wouldn't even see him."

I looked out beyond the garden and neighbouring houses. Out there was an element of my proof, part of the key that would rescue Sammy. The Green Man, his own quest

In Perpetuity

long forgotten or lost, had taken on my own. The sense of uselessness was dreadful.

"I *have* to catch him," I said. Yet I waited there on Jean's patio—her pot plants' shadows were wilting, as if already aware of her death—and stared at this strange woman. Tall, dressed in dark clothes, black hair cropped short, her face was as white as the moon and equally melancholy. It seemed to reflect light from long ago, a time when things may have been all right.

She shook her head once and I heard the creak of her neck muscles, felt her short hair part the darkness, and she looks at me and sees a man as desperate as she. She thinks my eyes are shaded and my soul hidden in greater darkness. I despair at how quickly I have changed to these new ways.

"I'm like him," she said, "except that I remember my quest. He'll never find his way back and his reward is lost forever. I may never fulfill my charge…and so my daughter is similarly lost to me. It's not fair. In a way he's luckier because of his madness. It's unfair."

"What are you looking for?" I asked.

"The final sigh of a violent death," she said. "He wants it in a jar. From a man, a woman or a child, he doesn't mind which. Maybe he'll unscrew the lid and breathe the sigh in. Perhaps he'll just put it on a shelf and forget about it. Nothing to him, everything to me. She's everything to me." The woman sobbed and her thin shoulders shook, but there were no tears reflected in the moonlight. Time had cried her dry.

"How long?" I asked.

"I don't know. Years? Decades? I'm never in time…I sometimes know when there's a murder, but I'm always too far away to catch the final breath. I'm nothing more than a ghoul. I seek murder but only find its aftermath."

"Do it yourself."

She seemed to freeze before me, like a tortured artist's vision splashed on the living canvas of Jean's garden. I heard her withheld breath and felt her tensed muscles. "Would you?"

I shook my head slowly. "I have to go."

"I'll come with you!"

The offer struck me as ridiculously kind, and a lump formed in my throat. She seemed to know what the Green Man was capable of, and yet she would accompany me as I tracked him down. And then I considered her true motives, how tied in they were to the keeper's demands on her, and the offer felt suddenly hollow.

When she looked at me, perhaps she saw murder.

"No, I'll—"

"You can't stop me," she said. "I can follow, I know where we are much better than you. You've seen some things already, I'm sure, seen the detail all around, stepped some way down the path the keeper gave you. But there's so much more yet to see and feel and taste. I've been there already."

"How do you know about murders?" I asked. "How do you seek out death?"

"Worried I can see a knife in your back?" she asked quietly, smiling, and although the smile should have been cruel it seemed to light up her face. For a moment I saw the beautiful mother she had been so long ago.

Years. Decades. How desperate must she be?

"What's your name?" I asked.

"Elizabeth. What's yours?"

In Perpetuity

"I'm not telling you. I feel better that way."

She shrugged, smiled again. "I'll allow you that."

"How kind." I turned away and hurried to the back of the garden, feeling around in the dark for the gate latch. Elizabeth was behind me, I could feel her eyes concentrating on the back of my neck, perhaps finding some comfort in staring at something new to her old, old world.

I turned and took a final look at Jean's house. The kitchen light was still on, spilling through windows like the blood that had flowed from her body. The music was still playing. Perhaps the CD player had been set on 'repeat'. It seemed fitting that such beautiful, intricate music might be the warning sign to her neighbours that something was amiss.

I hoped that Jean lay still at last.

"I'm glad you didn't get here in time," I said to the tall woman. "I knew her. Her last breath was her own." *If she's breathed it,* I thought. I *had* to get away.

"But it wasn't," she said. "The Green Man saw to that. Strange, I don't think he's actually killed before. Not quite."

"He's getting further away." I set out along the lane between gardens.

"You won't catch him."

"Then why the *fuck* are you tagging along!"

"I want to fill my jar." Her reply was quiet, and in her calmness I discerned the utter obsession that kept her going. Years had passed and her daughter, if still alive, may be little more than a living mannequin by now, put to whatever use the keeper had found. Yet Elizabeth's single aim was still the fulfilment of her given quest. The final sigh of the dying.

She kept the jar in a leather bag around her waist, tenting her jacket like a pregnant belly.

We walked in silence for half an hour. After emerging from the lane we kept to the main streets, blending in with the twilight and feeling the world flowing around us, unaware, uncaring. People saw us but did not respond. Dogs trotting along the pavement sniffed at us but let us be, as they would a breath of wind, a fallen leaf scratching along the street, a shadow hiding in a shop doorway. They didn't even growl.

The Green Man had been this way; I could smell blood in the air and I knew it was Jean's. But his trail was cooling with each passing minute. The blood was aging, the stench of his sweat old and musty rather than fresh and rank. And if I paused and breathed out slowly, I could hear his footsteps still echoing between buildings, fading, edging themselves eventually to nothing.

"What are you looking for?" Elizabeth asked.

"The man who stole from me," I said, but I knew before finishing the sentence that was not what she meant.

"What *really?*"

We paused outside a pub, static rocks in the river of life that flowed around us: the noise of enjoyment; the smell of food and drink; laughter soaking the air like that river's ebullient spray.

"*Really,* I'm looking for my son Sammy. The keeper has him, just as he has your daughter. It's only been since this afternoon. The keeper showed me his collection. He said that proof of love can give Sammy back to me."

She surprised me by reaching out and touching my cheek. Her fingers were rough and calloused, as if she had spent a

In Perpetuity

lifetime looking under rocks. "That's not an easy one," she said.

"I have no idea what he really wants."

She pulled away. I was glad she kept her hand away from the bag on her belt. If I ever saw that—her eyes on me, hands opening the jar—I would have to run.

"Neither does he," Elizabeth said. "I've met someone looking for the first pacemaker, a woman searching for the sledge from Citizen Kane and a man collecting screams. The keeper makes demands, but I wonder if he ever knows what he's really asking for. Like me. How does he know what a final sigh will comprise? What will it be?"

Elizabeth continued talking but I had drifted off, staring through the pub window, its insides coloured by the old brewery name set in stained glass, and also by my perceptions of how far I already was from this reality. If I stayed out here for days more, weeks, years like Elizabeth, how different would I be if and when I finally had Sammy back? People inside were chewing at the air with their laughs. They were eating the atmosphere. They had no idea about the truth of things. I could go in and tell them, point out just how much there was that they would never see. Like the shape in the corner by the bar, a toothed wraith from centuries before, perusing its flock. Or the things swimming in the air like fish out of water, ducking into and out of the patrons' mouths as they drank and laughed, eating of them as they ate the air. Perhaps they were cancers looking for a home. I pressed my lips close.

The noise increased suddenly as the front door opened and two girls emerged. They were teenagers, their attire begging attention, their eyes defiant and challenging as I approached them.

"Have you ever loved?" I said. "Do you have proof?"

"Fuck off, weirdo!" one of them said, setting the other one giggling. They shoved past me, burning my forearms with their cigarettes as they did so. I could smell the singed hair and bubbled skin, and the fact that one of the girls had recently had sex. Raucous laughter erupted inside the pub, perhaps at their departure.

No. Love was older than this.

I walked along the street, Elizabeth tagging along beside me. I sensed that she had much to say, but perhaps she realised that I had started something here. I had fired an arrow into the dark and had no idea where it was going to land, even though there lay my destination.

"Have you ever loved?" I asked an old woman walking her dog. She looked startled for a moment, but then something in my eyes must have convinced her that I was no threat.

"Oh yes," she said, nodding, walking on, her eyes greying as tears and time took her back to somewhere I could not see. But she's also thinking of me as she walks away, trying to come to terms with the strangeness in my eyes. It would have been terrible of me to pursue her, so I walked on again.

A man stood at the front door of a house, rapping on the wood. "Sue!" he shouted. "Sue!" He knocked again, shouted again. I stopped and stared over the garden hedge. The man stepped back and flung a stone at an upstairs window. Not a pebble; a stone. It *snicked* from the glass and left a bright line of white, like a scar already healed.

I could have asked this man, but it did not feel right.

In Perpetuity

Further down the street, away from the man's shouts, a shadow stepped from an alleyway a few steps ahead of me and walked in the same direction.

"Do you know love?" I asked. Elizabeth giggled behind me, but I tried to ignore the feeling that she knew something I did not.

The shape stopped and turned, and in the weak streetlight I saw a young man, younger than me but with age burned into his face. He began to cry. His tears were silent as they fell to the pavement, forming splashes of shadow on the concrete. His shoulders shook but he did not whimper, did not speak.

"One of us," Elizabeth whispered in my ear.

How could she know? I thought. But as I looked harder, so the truth of the statement manifested before me. The man did not belong on this street: his colours were out of synch, his presence an anachronism that seemed to ignore light and weight and the sounds of civilisation. He opened his hands and raised his sleeves, showing me the wounds of Christ that can only have been given in mockery, never received in hope. Whatever the keeper had asked of him it was too much. Too much for this man, and too much for me to take in.

"I know love," he said quietly, wincing as if speaking burst blisters inside his throat. He said no more, but turned and walked away, tying the buttons on his sleeves and never once looking back.

"Give me proof!" I shouted back, but he passed out of sight. I was glad. My own love was all I knew, and someone else's proof may be fake or meaningless. I could not return to the keeper with proof of which I was not totally convinced, something that may be false as a lover's smile… the authenticity of which is known to them, and them alone.

I turned to Elizabeth, held her shoulders and pressed her back into the hedge bordering the road. "How many are there?" I asked. "How many like us, wandering the streets?"

"Streets?" she asked, surprised. She did not seem perturbed by my behaviour. Indeed, she thinks of me as a poor, panicked young boy, younger than her daughter is now, if she's still alive. "More than just streets. Hillsides. Valleys. Sewers. Parks. Woodland. Shopping centres. We're everywhere. The keeper is old, and he's always been this way."

"But I've seen so many already!" I said. It had only been hours since I'd left him, *hours*. How many wanderers could Elizabeth have met through her decades of slow mourning?

"I've met so many more." She shrugged and I took my hands from her shoulders, looking into her sad eyes, hating that my own were reflected in there.

"I'll never do this," I said, turning away from her in despair. "I have no idea what I'm doing. I'm *useless!*"

Elizabeth shocked me then by coming to life. She pushed me against the hedge and breathed into my face. Her breath smelled of old times and places we should never know. I breathed deep.

"Never give up hope!" she said. "It's been hours, and already the Green Man is onto you. That means you're on the right track, because he sees you as someone who can get him back to the keeper. So don't you ever give up hope. Your son depends on you. You may have no idea what you're doing, but that doesn't mean it can't be done from instinct. You have to protect your son. You're still a man, a person, far more so than me, so that's what your blood is telling

In Perpetuity

you now, your soul, the darkest corners of your mind are all rallying to save your son. It's human nature. It's *nature*. Survival instinct at its most basic. You have more hope than I've had in years." She turned away from me and I heard her tapping her glass jar with a ring on one of her fingers. She must have given up on whoever gave her that ring years ago. I was humbled that she refused to give up on me.

"I'm sorry," I said. It sounded and felt hollow, so I did not say it again.

"So where next?" she asked.

I closed my eyes and thought. Jean was there, the image of her alive and loving and dead and bloody combining in my mind's eye.

Sammy was there too.

Where next?

And then I knew.

"Not where," I said. "When. Come on."

I had no desire to go back to Jean's house, but I needed my car. Walking the streets at random would take weeks to cover the town, and even then speed would not be available to me when required. I thanked whatever Fate may have been watching over me that Jean's body had not yet been discovered. And then I wondered if that Fate was the keeper, and paranoia had him watching me again.

We paused at the end of my dead mother-in-law's street, hiding in the shadows between streetlamps, pushed into a hedge for added concealment. Elizabeth had followed me silently and effortlessly, so that from time to time I forgot she was with me. She kept her hands away from the jar on her belt. I was fine with that.

There was little activity in the street, and what I could hear and see and sense—inside and outside the houses—seemed relatively normal. No police sirens, no gawping neighbours. We walked from shadow to shadow until I heard those gentle piano strains still playing, and to the theme of Mozart we got into my car and left that murderous place.

At last I had time to feel pure rage toward the Green Man, not for what he had stolen but what he had done. And that belated fury shamed me terribly, to the point of tearing me away from myself, lessening my predicament, numbing the fear and dread I had lived with every second since leaving that impossible shop. He had killed, and I had been angry because he had stolen an old photograph. *Perhaps I could have saved her?* My self-loathing clouded my vision for a time, and I found yet more shame in the gratitude I felt for this.

I owed it to Jean to succeed, and when it was over and Sammy was back with me I would go to the police. They would track the keeper down somehow, and then the Green Man would be found as well. I would enjoy being at that bastard's trial. I would relish the look on his face when he was imprisoned for life. Mad he may be, but my blame still found him a deserving target.

"The police will never find him," Elizabeth said. "He's not of this place, not anymore. You should know that. You should know from the insight the keeper has given you."

"How do you…?" I began. Lights dazzled me, too many lights.

In Perpetuity

"You've been silent for so long. You *must* be thinking, and even after all this time, I remember what I thought about those first few weeks. I'd find her, somehow, whether I fulfilled my charge or not. Then I'd go to the police. Make him pay for what he'd done. Except sometimes people like him don't pay, they grow old and fat and sated on their own particular perversions, and they never pay, and the poor people like us suffer until we die. That's why there is no God."

"He has the one true cross."

"I never said Jesus didn't die for us," she said. "I just wonder if it worked. Maybe we killed him in more ways than we know."

"Believe what you like," I said, and Elizabeth turned to look at me, and she is amazed. She sees a man who has lost his son and seen his mother-in-law slaughtered on her kitchen floor, and still he keeps his faith. Amazed, yes, but she also feels vaguely superior. She had been here longer.

"I do," she said. "After you've been here as long as me, you will too. I've seen more things than you can ever imagine. And amazing as they are, it's ironic how each one convinces me more that God is dead."

"So how do you explain them?" I had once spent months looking for a miracle, and when Anne finally died I knew, too late, that our final time together was what I had sought.

"The universe is a fucked up place. Humans are lucky enough to not usually see this, not fully, never clearly." She trailed off and I concentrated on my driving, my aims, the idea that had put me back in the car.

There was proof of my love out there, I had only to find it. Instead of wracking my brain, I would drive around the streets for the remainder of the night. There were places here that had seen our courtship, places we had been, things we had seen, and sooner or later something else would come to me. Location would reveal it in my mind, unearthing it from the grave where Anne's death had buried it. The smell of a tree, the sound of a stalking cat, the way the car bumped on a particular stretch of road, any one of these could inspire the memory of something that I could take to the keeper. And being so near, I would reach it before the Green Man. He would have no warning.

I would not let him steal the rest of my life away.

We drove until the traffic thinned to a few taxis and police cars, night deepened, and I realised for the first time just how much more was revealing itself to me. As normality went to bed, so everything that was not normal stood out. People wandered the streets, more fleeting than shadows yet concrete to me, their purpose clear in all those frightened eyes caught in my headlights. Sometimes they ran, and once there was a thump as someone leaped onto the car, clawed at the roof, screaming as their nails flipped off and sprayed bloody droplets onto the windscreen. We passed a parked police car and the driver gave me a careless glance. I used the windscreen wipers to smear blood across the glass, giving the night a new hellish tinge.

The person fell from the roof and I saw a shadow fighting in the rear-view mirror.

"What the hell were *they* after?" I asked, but Elizabeth remained silent for the whole drive. I thought perhaps she

In Perpetuity

had died, and I gently removed her jar from its bag and held it before her mouth. The glass misted and cleared, misted and cleared. I wondered whether she had thought of providing its fill, and knew that she must have.

I drove to areas where Anne and I had lived, partied, made love, shopped, drank and visited friends. The town was as familiar to me as my own eyes, but at the same time I felt as though I were rediscovering it after decades away, living a whole night of nostalgia for a place I saw every day. Elizabeth snored gently beside me. Her history was long but her story short, a beginning and a middle with no end in sight. I pitied her, but it also disturbed me that she had come along. Surely it was not out of a desire to help? She must have seen something in my eyes, known that I was death walking, or a short walk to another death.

I could stop the car and kick her out here and now. But she would only find me again.

This world, these people, amazed me no more. In fact I felt little for them—a trace of pity, a tinge of disgust, a healthy dose of fear for something I had not been aware of until today—because my thoughts were for Sammy alone. A day had passed and another would go by quicker, another, and then the first week would be a milestone in the history of my loss, and then weeks would flow by easier like a baby's second, third and fourth real steps following the impossible first.

So I drove. And inspiration finally came with the dawn, after I parked the car in a garage forecourt and slipped easily into an uneasy doze.

"I'm thirteen now dad," Sammy says. "This is Helen. She's in my class at school and she likes martial arts movies too, and westerns. Cool, huh? I would have liked her if you'd let me, shared my first kiss with her, maybe more. She's really pretty." His voice is a teenager's croak, but it sounds as if his throat is constricted by tears. "I know these things don't usually last, but maybe one day she'd have been a part of your family. If you'd allowed it."

Something crashed by my ear, and I felt the impact on my head. *Hitting me,* I thought, *it's the Green Man caving in my skull with a hammer and he'll never have his proof now...unless he's looking for it inside. Trying to find the bits of my brain that matter, no pretence, no deceptions, love laid bare to the sunlight...*

I sat up and saw the petrol station attendant staring through the window. Her expression changed to one of disquiet as she backed away. She'd seen Elizabeth. She was not easy for me to look at, let alone someone who knew nothing of what and where we were.

"Inside my head," I said. "It's all inside my head."

And then I knew the next place we had to go, the next thing to try to collect.

"Wake up!" I shouted. Elizabeth stirred slowly, as if accustomed to being woken by violence. "We've got half a mile to drive," I said. "Half a mile to what I need. He *can't* beat us there, surely. I've only just realised. Only just thought of it."

"What?"

"The poem. I've only just remembered, it was so long ago. It came from inside me. Deep inside. Anne didn't really understand it or like it, but I think that's even better proof right there. The fact that I could show it to her and she didn't understand, and still it meant so much."

In Perpetuity

I twisted the ignition key and rammed the car into first. A motorbike swerved to avoid us as I pulled out onto the road and Elizabeth perked up, watching to see whether the rider would spin into a lamp post.

As I headed home, I tried to remember where the poem would be packed away. I had written it in a notebook, and it lay huddled between other bad poems that had bled from me over the course of a couple of years, revealing itself only to the back of a previous page. Anne had not liked it, true, but perhaps it had matured with age, ink blending, words transmuting, gathering meaning and import as it lay hidden away from corrupting opinions.

"What poem?" Elizabeth muttered. She had slumped down in her seat as if unused to the bustle of the morning rush-hour.

"I wrote it…" I said, and then trailed off. I wrote, Anne hid it away. And now, looking for it, perhaps I was drawing the Green Man to it as well. "No poem," I said. "There's no poem." To think of it, perhaps that is all he required of me. The carving on the cliff and the photograph in poor Jean's house, he had stolen these after nothing more than a glimmer of an idea in my mind. Now, minutes away from home, I feared that he was coming closer again.

"How does the Green Man travel?" I asked. "How does he move around?"

"Same as you and me," Elizabeth said. "Same as everyone. Mostly."

"Mostly?"

She looked across at me. "There are other ways in the world. Most don't dare use them. He does."

As we turned into the cul de sac where I lived, the truth of her statement revealed itself all at once. Because my front door stood open, and disappearing inside—almost as if he'd been waiting to offer me that one glimpse—the Green Man. Other ways in the world, she had said, and I shuddered to think what routes he had trodden to reach here so quickly. There was an animal smell about the place, I could detect it even with the windows up, and the light was strange too. Not the clear light of morning, but tainted and greyed, as if this day had been left out in the open for too long.

"He's here!"

"This is where you live?"

"That house. He's here, he's in there already. How can that be? It was minutes ago I thought of coming here, only minutes, how the hell is he here already?" I looked at Elizabeth but she seemed not to have heard. Her eyes grew wider as her hands had strayed to the glass jar. She froze as I looked at her. I wondered what she could see of me now; whether it was my life or death that she imagined as she stared back into my eyes.

"I'm going," I said.

"I'm coming too."

I parked and ran across my front lawn. Elizabeth came after me for her own reasons, with her own mission in mind…and yet I was glad. Any company felt welcome here, whatever its objectives.

I paused at the front door. It was dark inside, I remembered coming home after Anne had died, dark then too, dark and foreboding and *wrong,* as if I should never have returned alone and the house itself had noticed an absence and frowned upon it. From inside came noise of the Green Man's

In Perpetuity

destructive search, and I tried my best not to imagine where the book could be, certain now, convinced that he could see and use my mind, and I thought *fuck you,* and the noises stopped for a moment.

And then, with a laugh, they started again.

The house was an alien place. As I stepped inside the front door and looked down the hallway—the pictures on the holiday wall, the carpet, the telephone table with several of Anne's grandmother's Toby jugs standing guard—I could have been returning home after years at sea, decades away. Because the house was exactly as I remembered it…and yet things were so very different. The detail was stronger. Threadbare carpet, damp plasterwork, a dip in the ceiling, shadows moving where there should be no shadow or movement, echoes of my life playing back again and again. I closed my eyes but could not see less, so I opened them again and there he was, the Green Man, striding from the living room and nudging past me to head upstairs.

"Stop!" I said. He glanced around, his eyes awash with more shadows than my home. I wondered why they called him the Green Man. He mounted the stairs and started climbing, his only intention to tear my house apart until he found my book of bad poems, because that was what I'd returned for. Bad poems, and one bad poem that could be part of my proof of love.

I darted forward and grabbed his jacket, pulling hard. He grunted and turned, lashing out, catching me on the face with his fisted hand. I fell back and staggered against the front door screen, trying to shake the *stench* from my nose, the slickness from my cheek, the dizziness from my head. He must surely have been dead.

Halfway up now, and as I watched him climb I remembered where the book of poems lay hidden and forgotten. I could almost sense its pleasure as I thought of it, as if rediscovery had always been its game; but the real smile was on the face of the Green Man, and he turned to show me before disappearing into the spare bedroom.

"Are you going after him?" Elizabeth asked, and at last she was holding her jar, not trusting the time it would take to pluck it from the bag. She wanted death here today. She wished for it, she craved it, and there was little else that really concerned her. The lid of the jar muttered slightly, pressure from within or without.

I ran upstairs. Sammy had come down this way just yesterday, laughing and giggling as I chased him because he was still not dressed. I'd been impatient and flustered because it was taking too long to get ready. I may even have raised my voice. As I ran up now I pounded my feet in anger and shame. Elizabeth was suddenly forgotten, the memory of a shadow behind me. This was my house, and familiarity closed in, feigning safety. This place had been my refuge after Anne died. She was everywhere I looked—her memory scattered like dust—and that had comforted rather than upset me. I always liked the idea that she was still here, watching over me. I hoped her eyes were open now.

I burst into the spare bedroom. The Green Man was standing at the wardrobe with his back to me. He'd pulled down a box from the top shelf, dropped its contents across the floor, sifting with his foot. His long hair hung down either side of his face, shadowing the shadows. He moved like a shadow himself.

"You got here quicker than last time."

In Perpetuity

"Fuck you," I said. "This is my house. You're stealing my life. I don't care what you've forgotten…I hope it hurt, I hope it was a son or a loved one. I might have seen them in the keeper's rooms. Maybe it was that living corpse, crawling with insects and maggots and feeling every bite!" I despised what he was doing but my words, my attitude, shocked me still. This hateful manner felt so alien.

Lights swam about his head like fireflies. Even though the curtains were drawn light from outside lit up his face, and I could see so much more than I ever had in that room: dust furring the skirting, Sammy's skin and Anne's last breath combined; an echo of an old friend who had stayed here, a man who may have helped me had he still been alive; and the Green Man's rank breath filling the room, spreading something old and desperate and, essentially, sad.

He bent down and picked up the little hardback notebook I was looking for. It contained the bad poem that Anne had pretended to like even though she knew she could not lie to me. For a second I thought it was pointless—this was stupid, this chase for tokens of love could never constitute proof, it could not be what the keeper sought—but then the anger came back, and I reached out to grab the book.

"That's mine!" I said.

The Green Man sidestepped and slowly, casually, pushed a long-bladed knife into my stomach.

The action did not register for a few seconds. My attention was on the book, that was all, the red cover faded by years of being forgotten. It seemed redder around his fingers where he grasped it tight, as if blood were leaking out to make the book his. I managed a clumsy step, wondering why the distance between me and the Green Man increased the closer I came. My fingertips actually brushed the tatty spine—for a second I had it, and I spied freedom and success somewhere in the vague, hallucinatory distance—but then the Green Man stepped back, tugged the knife from my clenched stomach muscles and thrust forward again. I heard the scraping of metal on bone, and that convinced me of what was happening.

I fell. I had hugged Anne against this wall when we were decorating the room, but now my blood stained the wallpaper, merging with traces of her left behind. I slid down, legs unable to hold my weight, as he withdrew the knife and stabbed me one more time. The knife passed straight between my ribs and struck something vital inside me, I felt it go, felt the pop and the cool rush of blood through my flesh, into my stomach, drowning my insides.

The Green Man grinned at me and then left the room. Yet still I was not alone. The space grew larger and distances faded, blending into one invisible horizon. The wallpaper was still there, the window and the wardrobes and the bed against the wall, but they were all endless, parts of a wider landscape now. And that landscape was not deserted. Anne was there in many ways, she peopled the place where I lay dying, and so many truths were made plain to me that I began to cry with the effort of understanding. There was nothing bad, nothing I could not have guessed or had not truly believed, but here things were so certain. The fact of her love for me, no longer relying simply on trust or hope, but now so definite. Here was proof, amorphous yet obvious in its intensity. Anne danced on our wedding night, strolled along a dusky shore on our honeymoon, and near the bedroom door she made

In Perpetuity

love to me, laughing and sighing and assuming that this was always the right thing.

And somewhere in that room Sammy was sixteen, confident and brash and full of my lost ambitions, still raging fires of aspiration rather than smoking embers that time had made them in me. "I'm going to be an actor, Dad," he said. "I'm going to be a contender, I'm going to shoot the devil in the back, I'm going to travel the world and help people and have adventures, like Cain in King Fu. I look for the door sometimes, Dad." And he was doing some of what he wanted, being a son who would make his father proud. I lost sight of him then because something blotted out the sun, something panting and excited, and for a second I thought that Anne had come back to me again, her image blurring with tears, and I felt hands on my stomach and chest, pressing and slipping in wetness…

It was Elizabeth. Her eyes were wide and frenzied, and still I could not see her clearly. I went to wipe my eyes and there was something hard in front of my face. I knocked it away and the glass jar skittered across the carpet, clanging hollowly as it hit the corner of the bed.

She hissed, crawled after the jar and hugged it to her chest, cooing as if it were her own lost daughter.

"Stay the fuck away from me!" I said, pushing myself into a sitting position. When I looked I could not believe that there was so much blood in me, enough to drench me from the chest down and spread across the cream carpet, soaking it deep crimson, a slick spreading from a holed tanker. "Just stay away," I said, quieter now. Shock was cutting in deeper than the knife.

Tim Lebbon

Elizabeth stared at me wide-eyed. She looked so old that I could never age her. Any sense seemed to have fled. Along with Elizabeth there were things watching me inside that room, eyes less substantial than smoke, further away than the future.

Carefully I lifted my shirt and brushed my hand down over my stomach, clearing the blood. There were three rents in my skin, lipless mouths seeping blood like silent pleas. Even as I watched the flow slowed to a dribble, the blood thickening and darkening as it coagulated. I felt sick, and my stomach twitched involuntarily as its muscles cramped, working its contents up towards my mouth. The wounds pouted as I leaned over onto my side, and Elizabeth tensed and leaned forward as I spewed what felt like a gallon of blood across the floor.

It felt as though I were there for hours, but it can only have been a few minutes. Eventually I was retching nothing but air. The cuts no longer gaped. I was feeling better. I let my shirt drop back down, not wanting to see or think about what I could not understand, content instead to stand and once again pursue that which I could: my only hope. My chance to save Sammy. The Green Man.

He knew where we were going before we got there. No amount of deception on my part would help, because he had been waiting here, ready to see me arrive before he stole what I had come for. Now he had the carving, the photograph, the bad poem, and even though I had started to suspect that these material things were less important than I imagined, still he was stealing. I could not show the keeper my dreams, could not let him view inside my head as I lay dying. I had to *give* him something.

In Perpetuity

"I'm coming," Elizabeth said, following me as I moved unsteadily onto the landing. Her surprise at my sudden recovery seemed to have waned quickly, and I remembered her words from earlier, how she had seen so much more. I had been here for a day, she had been here for decades. No wonder she was mad.

"Just keep that thing away from me," I said. "I'll smash it. You'll lose it, lose all hope. Or maybe next time I'll hold it to *your* mouth."

As I walked gingerly down the staircase—my stomach feeling hollow and not there, my upper body supported by nothing, hands grasping at air to support me—echoes came in, offering me peace and pieces of proof. If only I could retain memories and dreams…

I heard Sammy playing in the bath and Anne singing to him, hushing him to sleep when he had colic, and crying out in our bedroom on the night she conceived. Sammy again, running around downstairs and sliding across the living room after I'd laid timber flooring in there. All good times, all still here. I wanted so much to stay. Let these happy memories lull me to death.

Mourning the past, cursing the present, dreading the future, I stumbled down the final few stairs and fell out through the front door.

The Green Man was waiting for me. He stood at the neck of the cul de sac, reading my book of poetry, mocking me. Something bubbled in my lungs and I coughed up blood, but I did not go down. Instead I half walked, half ran to my car. Elizabeth made it into the passenger seat just as I pulled away. The Green Man had vanished, as I knew he would, but I drove anyway. In the golden morning light I saw invisible people looking for miracles. And I realised that I had found one myself.

"I should be dead," I said.

"The keeper has strange ways."

"I should be dead. I fell from a cliff yesterday. And he stabbed me today. I felt something die inside me."

Elizabeth shrugged but said no more.

Somehow my legs and feet worked, my hand found the gear stick, I did not crash. My stomach swelled with blood once again, my lungs throbbed and I felt slow bubbles popping at my nostrils. If I breathed through my mouth I tasted blood.

I saw him ten minutes later. Hurrying along a pavement. And even though he could not possibly have come this far on foot, I mounted the pavement and pressed down on the gas. His shadow was drawing level with a lamp post when it turned, and I saw the Green Man grinning as he flung himself sideways through a garden gate. I twisted the wheel sharply to the right and the car bounced back onto the road, the lamp post punching in both side doors. Elizabeth shook smashed glass from her hair, looking back to see whether I'd hit the Green Man. I pressed the brakes and looked in the mirror. The view shimmied as the car shuddered to a stop. No sign of him. He must have run through the garden, perhaps even into the house, and I would lose him.

"Shit!"

"He's heading east," she said.

"So?"

"East. Towards the keeper. Maybe he thinks he has enough."

In Perpetuity

The idea was crazy, but once uttered it played in my mind, even as I started off down the road away from the twitching curtains along the street. I found an isolated alleyway to park in, lowered the seat back and closed my eyes. And I can see the Green Man's feet hitting the pavement, feel his breath pounding in and out of my own ruined lungs, smell the stink of ages clinging to him like another layer of clothes. And then I know what he thinks of me. I jerk back in my seat. So much jealousy there. So much *hate*.

"He's on the main road," I said. "Heading east. He can't really have enough, can he? A picture, a lump of rock, a book? You've been searching for decades, I can't have found enough in a day?"

"Some tasks are harder than others," Elizabeth muttered. "I don't think the Green Man will ever finish his."

"Which is?"

"I never found out, but that's not the point. Can't you smell the doom on him?"

I closed my eyes again, welcoming the dark, comforted when I had no more rushes of the Green Man's thoughts. I felt alien enough in my own mind right now; I had no desire to be in someone else's.

I could not think of anything else, no more material items that would prove my love for Anne or Sammy any better than those stolen by the Green Man. Besides, I still did not know exactly what the keeper wanted. Proof of my love, proof of anyone's love, was all surely subjective. I could point him the way of charity, show him people who devoted themselves to others, claim that we are all still here because love triumphs in the end, regardless of wars and murder and death and hate, so much of which finds its way to us. Love wins out. And if I could believe this totally, perhaps I would find my way through.

Love wins out.

I wished it were Anne saying those words.

"I'm twenty-five, Dad," Sammy says. "I'm a musician. I'm working in America right now, but my heart's still in Europe along with Helen, my wife. She keeps it there for me. I know you'd be proud, I know you'd be happy, you and Mum together. Helen's a lovely girl…she will be if you save me. She is, she will be." I can see him, tall and more handsome than I had ever been, and before tears blur my vision I feel something so profound that it almost halts my heart: love. Total, unadulterated, unequivocal love for this, my son. He's so much a part of me and Anne, the sum of us and so much more.

"I go back and look for the door, sometimes," Sammy says. "I know I can't have dreamed it."

"Hey!" Elizabeth nudged me, shoved me against the door. I hissed in pain as the muscles in my stomach clenched, holding down the bloody vomit, holding myself together long enough to find my way back.

"Back," I said. "We're going back. We'll get him before he reaches the keeper. And if you help me, if you're here for me, I'll do my best to make sure you have his final breath."

She looked at me for a few seconds, eyes reflecting my hope with her own. "I didn't have to nudge you awake just now, you know. I could have sat here. I could have taken out my jar, and sat here, and waited."

"I'm not dying," I said. I did not know that for sure, but I meant it.

"How far away are we?"

In Perpetuity

"An hour, maybe more."

"An hour. Only an hour…" She drifted off, and I wondered how far she had wandered over the years. Perhaps she had always remained this close, looking for the dead and the about-to-die, and the realisation hit her only now. Her daughter was almost within shouting distance.

I started the car and headed off. When we found the main road I slowed down and drove carefully, not wanting to attract the attention of any police. The Green Man could travel quickly, and however he managed that, I could not let him reach the keeper before me. I had no idea what would happen if he did. Whatever his forgotten quest was, would the keeper let him steal mine? I guessed so but hoped not.

Our chase was drawing attention. People stopped to watch us pass by, and I recognised some of them as the keeper's seekers, hollow desperate eyes, some carrying boxes or bags, many obviously mad. They seemed lost to crowds in the daylight. I had never seen so many people unseen and unnoticed, and the thought that they had always been there, moving through places and spaces where normal folk did not look, their respective searches so removed from normality that they were beyond sight…it frightened and humbled me. Perhaps ignorance truly is bliss.

We drove out of the city and into the country lanes. It was like moving into the wilds. Neither of us said anything, but I felt any dregs of safety being left behind, wrapping themselves around the normal people to protect and insulate them from the terrible truths we lived. Cool air blew through the smashed side windows, but Elizabeth did not seem to notice. Her eyes were open but she could have been asleep.

She held the jar in her lap, the skin of her fingers grey like old pottery.

The rising sun tried to blind me as I steered through the lanes. I drove at it, yearning for the safety that daytime had used to bring. Even after Anne died, the days had not been so bad. Nights were quiet and promoted thought. Days were filled with Sammy. I was determined that they would be so again.

"I wonder if I'll always see," I said to myself, expecting no answer from the woman next to me and receiving none. *After Sammy,* I thought, *after I get him back, will I always see these people in the shadows? Will I always know more of reality than most?* There must be those who had succeeded, given the keeper what he wanted. He had a place full of impossible things.

I had stopped bleeding, but my stomach felt full and hard, and the knife wounds were still open. Perhaps the keeper's touch only went so far. I felt weak and tired, ready to lie down. It had only been one day. If the Green Man evaded me, if he fled and took those things with him, or if the keeper took one look at my proof of love and laughed...

I could be here a long, long time.

As if to lure us on, the Green Man appeared out of a hedge further along the road. He stood and stared me down, grinning, covered in freshly picked grass, ferns tucked into his clothes as if he were trying to become a part of the landscape. In his right hand he held the things he had stolen from me.

He did not seem to come closer as I drove faster. Instead he turned and walked back through the hedge, and as he vanished the car passed where he had been. I looked left

In Perpetuity

and saw his shape moving in there, pushing through the undergrowth, and I slammed on the brakes and spun the car on the dew-slicked road. He was still pushing through—trapped, he's trapped in there!—so I gunned the engine, tried to judge just how deep the ditch was next to the road, and launched the car at the hedge. Just as the bonnet parted the bushes I saw something wrong with the Green Man's shadow. It was too regular, his movements too defined, too rigid, and I knew that it was not him in there at all, just the memory of him left behind to confuse me and make me waste time. As the car powered through the hedge and shattered the struggling shadow to the sunlight, I knew one thing for sure: *He's afraid that I can beat him!*

It was the largest flash of hope since I'd left Sammy to the keeper.

The car's underside hit the earth bank and the engine screamed before I took my foot from the gas. I was flung against the seatbelt, puking blood across the windscreen and dashboard. The pain was immense, driving me under for a few seconds and bringing brief, awful visions of Sammy screaming in his cell. *Now?* I thought. *Is that now?*

The car rocked for a moment and then tipped back, rolling its rear wheels onto the road.

Elizabeth had strained forward in her seat, spinning the top on her jar.

"He's not there," I hissed. "He's fooling me. Distracting me. We have to get back now, as soon as we can, go to the keeper before he reaches him."

The engine had stalled, and for the first few seconds after I turned the key it coughed and complained. And this is what the Green Man had wanted; for me to break the car and destroy my only means of reaching the keeper. He could travel by some other means, his speed proved that, but even though I had the car he still feared me. Which meant that I could beat him. It was not all hopeless.

And then the engine caught and reverse gear worked and the car whined and creaked its way fully back onto the road, obviously wounded but, like me, willing to fight on through the pain.

I drove quickly, dangerously, heading for the village where this had begun a day ago, though it felt like decades. And unlike when I had fled the place, the village seemed to appear around a corner too quickly. I was sure it was further, much further than I had driven. It was as if the place was eager to welcome me back.

The village was bustling, though I knew now that it never really slept. Elizabeth was making small, terrified noises in the passenger seat, clasping her empty jar and perhaps fearing that her quest had truly failed, she was back, she was back and the keeper would see her failure and keep her daughter forever.

If I had my way, her jar would be filled before long.

I drove into the village. Heads turned at the sight of my smashed car—some people were surprised, and others seemed to know just why I was here—and I saw the Green Man running along the pavement.

"Open the jar," I said to Elizabeth.

We were several hundred yards from the keeper's shop.

—⁂—

"What would you do for love?" I asked.

In Perpetuity

"What do you mean?"

A car slowed in front of me and I swerved to avoid it, clipping its bumper and losing my own in a scream of metal and sparks. "How far would you go for love? For the love of your daughter? What wouldn't you do?"

"There's nothing…" she said, and then her voice trailed off as I aimed the car at the Green Man. He was running along the pavement, glancing back, dodging people where they walked their dogs or strolled hand in hand.

"Then why haven't you killed? Creep into a house at night, slit a throat, collect your sigh and set your daughter free?"

The car jumped its front wheels onto the pavement and I felt something tear loose inside me, flooding my insides with blood once again, bursting past the keeper's magical touch or perhaps obeying it to the full.

"I never even thought of it," she said.

I glanced across at this woman trapped by morality, cursed with this life because she could not think beyond what was right. Even after everything she had seen, all the truths laid bare and the impossibilities made real, still she was a good person.

"Then you'll never win."

The Green Man loomed large in the windscreen and his frown turned into a smile, just as I knew it would. I wondered whether those teenaged kids were still staying in the village, nursing hangovers and strange memories of the mad guy they'd tried to help yesterday. And they were, they were still here, because the Green Man suddenly moved ahead and he was amongst them, past them, reaching out to knock on the keeper's door even as my car bore down on the four youths, their eyes and mouths wide, limbs moving far too slowly as they tried to fling themselves out of my path.

There were three seconds when I could have changed my mind.

One of the girls had a pierced nose. The other showed bare midriff. The boy with the Mohican—he was the most likely to get away, I thought, because he'd been balancing on the kerb like a young kid trying to miss cracks in the pavement—he'd recognised me, and while the others were just screaming he looked confused as well.

Two seconds…

Elizabeth screamed, but I heard the sigh of the jar's lid being spun open. Something rattled beneath the car and it jumped slightly as the exhaust was ripped off. The wheel juddered in my hands. It tore to the right, struggling to steer away from the disaster facing it, the machine having more humanity than me for that split second, and I let the wheel turn because that was the natural thing to do, steer away, avoid the poor kids who'd come out of nowhere…

One second…

The Green Man would be turned away by the keeper, I was confident of that, but I could never be certain, *never.* That uncertainty held my hands straight. I would not get another chance. He was knocking at the door, I *recognised* that door, and it was the 'Open' sign that finally made up my mind.

I would not get another chance.

I closed my eyes and listened to the sickening sounds of death.

In Perpetuity

"I'm thirty-three now Dad. The age you were when Mum died. I've got a son and a daughter of my own, and I just know you'd love them so much. I tell them about their granddad and how he saved me, although when they ask how I find it difficult to explain. I'm not even sure myself; how do I tell my children? But I still go to look for the door sometimes on my own, though I never find it. I'm glad. I'm not sure I could just stay outside." I see Sammy, and it's like looking into a mirror. "I leave flowers here sometimes. The families do too, on the anniversary. I think it's only right."

I open my eyes.

We hit the wall next to the keeper's doorway. The seatbelt ripped into my neck and stomach, and I felt the wounds opening again, blood slick and warm against my skin. The car bounced back as Elizabeth grunted, exiting through the windscreen, passing straight over the body on the bonnet and striking the wall head-first. I heard her hit the ground as she dropped down between the wall and the corner of the car.

Somebody was screaming.

I could not see the Green Man.

Footsteps pounded concrete, another scream, the sound of a door slamming shut…and then for a few seconds, almost total silence. The engine ticked itself to death. Something was dripping, petrol or blood, and the girl on the car bonnet stared at me with one disbelieving eye. She may even have still been alive.

I clicked open the seatbelt and tumbled from the car, landing in the gutter. There was a small trail of blood running beneath me. I sat up and turned, looking back along the road, wishing I could forget. Two of the youths were dead, the one with the Mohican was trying to crawl with crushed legs, and where was the Green Man? Where?

I stood, holding onto the car, trying not to see the body on the bonnet as blood slicked the paintwork, slipping the girl down toward where Elizabeth lay crumpled against the wall. To my left the shop doorway was still there, but the sign had changed to 'Closed'. The keeper must surely be watching me, although I could see nothing past the drawn blinds. I stepped forward, expecting to find the Green Man's crumpled form pressed between the corner of the car and the wall, crushed there, burst open so that his sick fucking insides had spilled out, and I would pick up the photograph and the carving and the notebook of bad poems, wipe them free of his blood and go and knock at that door.

He was not there. Elizabeth stared up at me, shaking and twitching as she struggled to bring the jar up to her smashed mouth, but her arm was broken and useless.

No Green Man.

More footsteps.

He was running down the street, I saw him now, running and laughing and people could see him at last, he was pushing them out of the way if they had not already moved. And in his hands, waved above his head, were the things that could set Sammy free.

I knew then that I would never, ever catch him. I knew also that something was very wrong with me now, and it was not only the knife wounds in my stomach and the blood I spewed up into the gutter. It was something far, far worse than simply dying.

Elizabeth gurgled, and she blinked when I looked down at her.

In Perpetuity

The girl slid from the car bonnet and rested back against the wall, looking past the car and along the street at her friends.

People were running in to help now, the shock lifting.

"What have I done?"

Elizabeth gurgled again, uttering no reply but speaking volumes. Her eyes, I could see so much in her eyes, and whether I was actually speaking to myself through her or not, she was right. There was disgust there, and fear, and also something insistent. She was *demanding* that I help her.

I knew now why she had never killed, never sat over somebody as they slept and slit their throat and collected what the keeper had charged her to collect. Because it was wrong.

I reached down and grabbed the jar from her hands, stepping over the leather-clad corpse of the girl and trying not to faint, or puke again, or turn and run into the road in an attempt to outpace what I had done. I was sure I heard laughing from somewhere, echoing as if trapped within a room. I looked up at the shop and the sign had changed to 'Open' once again.

Elizabeth growled at me and blinked rapidly a few times, and I leaned forward and placed the jar over her mouth. She stiffened for a second or two, and then the jar misted with her final breath. Her eyes remained open, staring into mine, and I think I saw a reflection of my memory of Sammy deep in there. Either that, or Elizabeth finally saw her little girl one more time before she died.

Somebody was shouting and trying to pull me away, but when I turned they stepped back.

"Leave me alone," I whispered. I would haunt their dreams forever.

Knocking at the shop door, I wondered whether anyone would see me when I stepped inside.

—⚝—

The shop was exactly as it had been the previous morning. There were no new additions to the ugly displays, although the coffins seemed to have slumped down somewhat lower, and there was now a space on the road kill shelf that would be filled very soon.

"You don't look too well," the Keeper said.

"Give me my son."

"Do you have what I asked of you? Have you brought me proof of love?" He frowned and smiled at the same time, looking me over, shaking his head, mocking me because he knew the truth. Perhaps he even created it.

"I have this," I said, offering him the jar.

He took it gingerly and stared through its old, cracked sides. "Ahhhh," he said, "very nice indeed. Yes, I'll place this one later. A pity she couldn't have been here herself, but..." He did something then, sent a thought flying, I felt it leave the room like a cold breath. Within seconds the curtain at the back of the room billowed and a little girl walked through. She looked tired and vacant, as if she was sleepwalking, but she knew where to go. She passed us by, sparing one glance for the keeper—there was hate there, intense and keen, but a deep, almost religious fear as well—before reaching the door and stepping out.

In Perpetuity

The street was clear. My car had gone and there were flowers tied to a nearby lamp post, sad tributes rotting in the sun.

"Was that…? But she's still young."

"Because I chose to keep her that way. Sweet young Helen. But now, you, your son, our arrangement. You may have helped someone else, but I have to ask you again: where is your proof of love? I'm very busy today, I really can't wait around here for long."

I slumped down to the floor, leaning back against the pool table I had seen him ironing his hand on yesterday. "I had it," I said. "I had it ready, I knew what to give you, but he stole it all away. The Green Man stole it all away."

"Oh dear," the keeper said, frowning and smiling again. He knew everything that had happened and enjoyed my pain. "Well, he's forgotten why he's out there. You can hardly blame him for trying to get back here any way he can."

"What is he out there for? What did you task him with? Why is he called the Green Man?"

The keeper leaned down close to me, and I smelled his breath. I wanted to die. People were dead because of me, families were grieving, and it had not done me any good.

It had not done me any good.

"That would be telling," the keeper said. And then he stood up and sighed, held his hands together, looked down at me where I bled onto his floor. "You really have been through an awful lot in such a short time, haven't you?" he said. "Some of my people spend years just…wandering. You've certainly shown me how much you love your son."

I closed my eyes. I was crying because of what I had done, and because even if I could rescue Sammy I had already failed him. I would never be someone of whom he could be proud.

When I opened my eyes again I was in the cell with my son.

"Daddy!" he yelped, jumping from his low bed, leaping into my arms, burying his face in my neck and soothing my pain with his tears. "Daddy, Daddy, I knew you'd come, I knew you didn't really go away!"

I wanted to tell him so much, so much that my thoughts jumbled and my mouth failed to work, but it did not matter because he was so happy to see me. *Wear a tooth guard when you're playing sport,* I needed to say, and *Helen's a lovely girl,* and *I'm so proud of your children, Sammy, I'm so, so proud.*

And, *I love you.* I needed to say that. But he knew already.

—m—

I am forever dying. *Proof enough,* the keeper had said, and Sammy was gone from that cell, long gone, and I was there instead, unmoving, frozen, blood mid-drip, eyes mid-blink, my own wretchedness apparent in the way I knelt, the slump of my shoulders and the dip of my head. *Proof enough.*

I am frozen in a moment of time so that those who occasionally come by and look cannot even see the moisture glittering on my eyes. For me, every second is an eternity in which I think about what I have done.

Sometimes, when the keeper is standing there looking at me, I wish I could ask him how long this will last. But even

In Perpetuity

he must have some humanity to him. He does allow me my dreams.

"I'm a grandfather now, Dad. I haven't been to place flowers for a long time, and I've stopped looking for the door. Because the older I get, the more family I have to love and love me back, the more I think I can understand what happened. And I try to believe it was all for me, Dad, that terrible thing you did. I really try to believe it was all for me."

I'm comforted that my Sammy has had a good life. And much as I miss him and love him, I'm glad I've never seen his face staring in at me. Because there are lengths you have to go to for love, and places where you need to stop. I don't want Sammy to have to face the decisions I made.

I want him to be better.

Casting Longer Shadows

When the village came back into the world I knew that it was time to go home. Home is where the heart is, so the saying goes, and I had been adrift for so long. Travelling between village and town and city, making fleeting acquaintances here and there, never missing them when I eventually moved on. To stay in one place was to invite trouble back into my life. Sometimes I remained long enough to make friends, a few times long enough to take a lover, and once I think I even fell in love…but sooner or later the shadows would appear again and drive me away.

It had been one of the longest dry spells on record, almost fifteen weeks without rain. The city I was living in at the time—nameless, faceless, hopeless—had already implemented water rationing. Hose pipes lay coiled in garden sheds like sleeping snakes, while green lawns turned brown and flowers wilted to the ground in mimicry of their owners.

Tim Lebbon

There was no place here for shadows. It had been so hot for so long that they seemed to have been denied a home. The sun had burnt them away. The pavements were too bleached, my eyes too scarred by the heat, the light too tired to hide, so that when I first caught sight of a shadow from the corner of my eye I put it down to exhaustion. My eyes, I thought, were playing tricks on me. I turned to look at where it had been, and there was nothing but a row of dead trees and a scrawny dog panting dryly at me. I blinked, rubbed my eyes moist, looked again. Nothing there. And there was no sense of being watched, not like the previous times I had shapes haunting my vision. No feeling of being the centre of something's attention.

So I turned and walked away, and that evening I saw home on a television set. The news was the same—heat, rationing, global warming scaremongers and nay sayers—and it ended with the image of a village that had risen from the depths. The reservoir had all but dried up, and now the buildings and streets of the drowned village were laid bare to the sun once again, walls crumbling quickly after so long immersed in the waters, bricks tumbling into the mud roads where the ghost of the old reservoir still hung on tenaciously. There was even a church spire, a skeleton of its former self, draped in dead and drying weeds. Its cross had long since gone.

It was only a glimpse of the village slotted in amongst other signs and images of the crisis, but in those few seconds I knew that I had to go there. Home it may have seemed, but I had never lived there, I was sure. Not in this life, nor the last.

Casting Longer Shadows

A shadow saw me on my way.

"I could give you your bond back, Sean, but to be honest you haven't really..." I had already resigned myself to fleeing here with less than I came with. That would leave me without the money to get to the village. My landlady stood before me, explaining her selfishness as best she could, and I no longer heard a word she said. I was watching the sweat beading on her forehead and rolling down into her wild eyebrows, the occasional droplet finding its way onto her cheek, or through the small gap in her eyebrows above her nose. She didn't blink the sweat from her eyes when it ran in. She seemed used to crying.

I smiled and nodded and saw something in her eye. A flash of dark, like a moonlight blink, so removed from her that she didn't notice it herself. I spun around, sure that it was a reflection from over my shoulder. When I looked back something dark slipped across the room and hid behind my landlady. She was still talking, still trying to explain, so unconcerned that she didn't see the expression on my face.

"What was that?" I said, but I already knew. A shadow, to see me on my way.

"I said, haven't you noticed the curry stains in the carpet?" She trailed off again and I stepped quickly to one side, hoping to fool the shadow and spot it behind her. But it remained in the corner of my eye, so fast that if I spun around again it would still be out of reach and out of sight, behind me always.

"I have to go," I said.

"Well, Sean, I'm really very sorry..." Her blouse stuck to her skin. The endless talk was a defence against her disquiet.

I had that effect on people. There was still something behind her, I was sure, although it was so well hidden.

"I mean, I *know* I have to go," I said again, not expecting her to understand, barely comprehending it myself. I turned and walked through the front door out into the sun. I wasn't going to look back—she'd think I was doing so to say goodbye, and she had been nothing but selfish to me—but I did anyway. She stood in her front doorway and scratched at her neck, looking into the distance as if she'd forgotten me already. The first time I'd missed a rent payment she'd asked me for sex, but I'd refused. And the shadow had slipped away from her and now lay out on the lawn, in the sun, impossible.

Defying the heat and against all my better instincts, I ran along the street.

I used to think that they were ghosts, come stalking me from beyond death. Or perhaps they were facets of my own madness, wraiths from inside my head superimposing themselves over my eyes, hiding in their corners so that I never truly saw them, only suspected. Sometimes I even believed that they were the truth, hovering around me like fans around a superstar, or flies on shit.

I never dreamt that they could be all three.

I didn't move far and fast enough to throw the shadows. It was hot already, although it was still only early morning, and the town was bustling with people on their way to work or looking for something to do. The main street was chaos, and I chose to be there. I knew that I would not lose the shadows, but I hoped that being amongst so many people would protect me from them.

They had never touched me, yet still they hurt. They *offended* me, in the way that the stench of shit offends some, the sight of sadistic sex others. Their wrongness made me want to vomit. The sounds they made drove me cold. I knew that one day I'd find out what they were, not through asking but by being told. And shown.

The people ignored me. I was used to it and welcomed it, but as I sensed the first of the shadows on a display window across the road, I wished so much for a friend. It clung to the glass like oil on ice, disappearing in the sun's glare when I looked directly at it, manifesting again when I turned away and continued walking. Something's gaze cooled the sweat on my neck like a slow exhalation. My breathing became faster and sweat ran down my sides and back. It was a fear I was familiar with, but it stung all the same, thudding my heart far harder than effort warranted.

I wanted to run, though I knew that would not work. The first few times I'd tried to outpace the shadows, but they always caught up or were waiting when I stopped running. It was as if they were a part of me, mostly attached, but removed on occasion so that they could gaze back in.

Somebody bumped into me and moved on without apologising. I paused and looked at her, a young girl and her boyfriend exuding apathy and attitude. They wore very little and their skins were dark brown, as if the sun had baked them hard. "Excuse *me*," I muttered, never intending to be heard. I took the opportunity to glance back along the street at the window. It seemed clear and clean of all but grease and the brownish tinge of exhaust fumes. "Gone now, eh?" I said.

Somebody else nudged me from behind and I turned, expecting to see a dark flash across my vision as the shadow mimicked my movement. They could stay behind me for hours sometimes, all but out of sight no matter how desperately I searched for them. They were the visual equivalent to a name on the tip of my tongue.

It was a woman, old, grey-haired, cloaked in numerous layers of clothing even though the sun was all but melting the glass out of shop windows. "Clumsy oaf," she said. And her mouth was dark.

I stared. Her lower jaw hung down as she drew in heavy, shuddery breaths, and in there, behind her teeth, wrapped around her tongue…but why inside? I had never seen a shadow as a part of someone else.

"What are you staring at?" she asked, her voice far too loud and panicked for my liking. Behind and beyond her voice, the familiar growl and squeal. A few people stopped to watch. One or two of them looked at me menacingly. "Never seen an old woman before? My bag, where's my bag?" She ruffled through her clothing, and I saw one of the watchers' eyes flicker down to my hands.

For that instant—brief, but incredibly lucid—I considered what she had said, thought about snatching the bag from her left shoulder and running. Train fare to the village, at least. But I looked into her mouth again and, although her lips were downturned, the dark in there was laughing.

"You have death in your mouth," I said.

Casting Longer Shadows

"You have it in your eyes," she whispered. And then she started shouting and cackling again, and while the crowd went to help her I made my escape, feeling eyes on my back but not caring, because for once I knew where they came from.

...in your eyes. Did she see herself reflected there? I wondered. Or were the shadows so much a part of me now that there was really no difference?

I had to get home. I didn't know if I was being guided or hindered, but one way or another I had to find my way to that strange, unknown village. There, I was sure, I would find some sort of resolution. Something had to break, and all things end. In my memories there were nothing but the shadows, the ones I saw and the ones I inhabited. Every place I had been seemed dark and half-forgotten, and anything from before a few years earlier was a feeling more than a memory, a sense that things had *never* been quite right, and that hope was all I had left.

I closed my eyes for a moment to see if I could see anything inside, but there was no light in there.

I had begged before. I wasn't proud. As I sat there outside the train station—grey, bedraggled, pale and faint—the people gave me money. I don't think it was through guilt, pity or helplessness that they dropped their coins and notes into my T-shirt spread across the hot pavement. I thanked every one of them. None of them spoke. None of them looked at me, and many of them seemed disturbed, as if they'd just walked unexpectedly into a place they no longer recognised.

I think they gave because somewhere deep down, I made them aware of their own mortality.

Later, I bought a ticket and boarded the train. I resisted the temptation to keep looking behind me. If the shadows were following they would not be so obvious.

The train drifted out from the confines of the city and found countryside. There was a definite sense of leaving. I knew that from hereon, I was stepping out of the existence I had been leading for so long that memory failed. Something new awaited me. It was terrifying and thrilling, and I could not help but burst into fits of nervous laughter every few minutes. Some of the passengers looked at me as though I were mad. I silently agreed and laughed again.

I had known that I was dead for a long time, of course. But I didn't see why that meant I could never belong.

The first shadow I ever saw accompanied my first real memory. This was at a time when the world was not such a frightening place for me, when my wanderings were a living adventure, not a dead trail. I found myself in a little village in Devon. It was a strange place. It had a picture-postcard square bordered by thatched cottages, singing stream, arched stone bridge, tiny church and a pub defining the word 'quaint'. But the strangeness came from another part of the village, a district taken almost entirely by an electronics factory and the associated outbuildings, workers' housing and parking lots. It grew out of the village boundary and into the countryside like a tumour, grey and rank and utterly at odds with its surroundings. A totally opposing combination… and yet it worked. The village thrived because of the factory, the factory gave the village its life. There were even those who claimed that they could not remember it being any other way.

Mixed in with my earliest memories of that time, my first sighting of a shadow.

I was walking home one Friday afternoon after an early finish at the factory. Some of my colleagues had gone to the village pub to wash away the week's accumulated grime and sweat, but I was thinking more of my bed-sit. I craved sleep. I needed warmth and relaxation. And, in truth, I didn't feel that I belonged with those at the pub. Not really. The fact that they did not go to great pains to entice me along proved that they thought so too. Even alive I was something of a pariah.

The shadow slipped from beneath a wall and tickled my heels as it darted across the road.

I spun around, sure that a cat had just crossed my path, but when I looked at the hedge there was no tell-tale rustling of undergrowth as it passed out of sight. In fact there was nothing. Just a sense that things had changed.

And as I sat in my bed-sit thinking of where I could go to feel welcomed and wanted, I knew at once that home was somewhere else.

I left the next day. The village seemed more divided than ever: the secret beauty of age hanging from the old houses and the village square; and the modern wound of the factory swelling into the land. It was as though time were impressing itself upon me, and I could see the wrongness of what that place had become.

Eyes watched me leave, but they belonged to no one who lived there.

That strange feeling of being home came again as I stood on the hillside and looked down into the dried reservoir. The valley floor was a patchwork of greys and browns: the grey where the reservoir bed had dried and cracked in the sun; the brown where water still sat, hiding in mud. And like a corpse trapped in the muck, sinking slowly, drowning not waving, the remains of the village. A different place from that which provided my first memories—and hundreds of miles distant—this village was little more than a grid of tumbled walls, its streets dried mud flows, the church spire naked to the sky. No sign of anything resembling a factory. This place was truly old. The buildings stood stark and bare, surprised at their sudden revelation.

The valley resembled a moonscape, though bathed in blistering sunlight. There were places for shadows—huddled against the walls of the drowned village, hidden under folds in the reservoir bed—but it seemed that the sunlight had turned fluid in sympathy with the vanished waters, finding its own level, leaving nowhere to hide.

Maybe this really *could* be home.

Glancing back once the way I had come, hoping to bid farewell to my confused history, I started down into the valley.

Casting Longer Shadows

The going was easy at first. I was in the heart of gorgeous countryside, and there were many paths, small gravel car parks and landscaped areas leading down to where the edge of the reservoir had once kissed the ground. And this dividing line was a strange place, almost a convergence of two worlds. One, where normality and familiarity reigned; the other, where things normally hidden were now in plain view. A few small jetties reached out from the gentle slope, ending in thin air. I stepped from the dried grass onto a vague border of mud and pebbles, sand and silt, and with one more step I was standing on what had once been the reservoir bed. The ground became uneven and my feet hurt as I walked. It was only with a careful examination of the baked mud that I saw the reason: there were cans, bottles and old food containers buried there, metalled edges rusted by the water and sharpened by rot. The drought had revealed the disregard with which people held this place of recreation and beauty.

Still no shadows.

I wondered how many people had swum and sailed here, fathoms above a ghost village that had once sung with life and seen everyday folk going about their everyday lives. I wondered where those folk were now.

I walked on, heading down into this strange valley that was once green and lush and alive, and then drowned, and now dry again. Dry, and all but lifeless. There were a few birds flitting to and fro, the incessant buzz of insects complaining at the heat, but the greyness gave the place the look of a dried wound, a corpse on the face of the world. I was used to *being* dead, although I'd never got used to the *idea* of it. Perhaps that was why I was starting to feel so at home.

Tim Lebbon

It didn't take long to reach the first ruins of the village. It happened to be the church. Gravestones protruded from the dried mud like the ranked ribs of a buried giant. At first I thought they'd tumbled, but then I saw that they had been buried in sediment, only their very tops appearing above the dried bed. I walked amongst them, trying to see names, but they were buried too deep. As I neared the church I passed by a couple of larger mausoleums. They were both smothered by a black mossy growth, baked so hard now that I could not even scrape it off with my nails. Even where the moss had not taken such a tenacious hold, any words had been scoured away by decades of silt-laden water, until whatever they said was now less than a shadow on the stone. I was in a graveyard of forgotten people. Standing there in the blazing sun, looking at a wrecked church that hadn't sensed worship for fifty years, I wondered whether anyone outside this valley could remember me now.

No shadows. None pursuing me, none watching me and none, I saw now…none in the graveyard. None *at all*. I stood behind one mausoleum where the sun did not reach, and there was light there, and heat, nothing to suggest that the stone structure was an obstacle at all. I ran my fingers across the surface, dust speckling the hairs on my arm, and it felt solid and real to me.

"But then I *am* dead," I said, and a stronger silence was my answer.

I moved on to the church. I wanted to go inside. There would be nothing there, of course—it would have been cleared out before the valley was flooded, and half a century of submersion would have rotted anything inadvertently left behind—but still it appealed to me. To be the first person to pray there for so long.

Of course, I no longer believed. How could I? I'd never done anything wrong, yet here I was still…a dead man, a haunter haunted by shadows.

"Service starts at ten…" a voice said, fading away like a breath in a breeze.

I spun around, but saw straight away that I was still alone. The shadows had never spoken to me before, and I didn't think that this was them now—the voice had been too *human*. There was no echo, no remnant, nothing to tell me that I wasn't hearing things. It was as if I had heard a sound at the edge of sleep and snapped awake, never to know whether it had been a dream or not. Perhaps I was even talking to myself. I repeated the words quietly but the sound was all different.

I looked back up the slight slope to the picnic grounds and the small jetties reaching out plaintively into thin air. I was alone. And in the village, still no signs of life. Even the church was so obviously dead, a monolith to lost faith.

I was sure I wasn't hearing things, but equally certain that the words had come from inside my head. This place was too barren to offer up any glimpses of life. It even stank lifeless, a dried, dusty staleness to the nose that hinted of opened tombs and the forgotten dead. Further into the village there were a few lower-lying areas that still held water…and from these, I sensed the faint whiff of rot.

But it was not an unpleasant place. The smell was passive, a result of the drying and baking of the reservoir bed and the silts and plants that had dried with it. There was nothing aggressive here, it was just the way things were.

Tim Lebbon

I was pleased that I felt no fear or disgust at nature at its basest. A normal person might have been scared.

I passed by the church, deciding it should be left alone, and walked further into the village. It had been little more than a hamlet really, and I could see that there were not that many buildings left standing. I tried to imagine how the initial flooding of the valley had taken place. Images came of sweeping walls of water, tumbling boulders and trees, a mad frothing at its head that tore everything to pieces before hitting the earth dam and roaring back…pictures inspired by all the bad disaster films I'd seen. In truth I knew that it must have been a gradual process, the reservoir rising over several weeks until the houses disappeared, then the church, the waters lapping eventually at the head of the dam. Weeks, maybe even months…but still the village was a ruin.

There was not one building with a complete roof. A house to my left just behind the church—perhaps it had been the priest's home—bared its ribbed roof structure to the sun, but the timbers were rotted by the decades under water, and the sudden drying had shrunken and broken them. Other than that there were a few timbers here and there, one or two slates still hanging on valiantly against time…and nothing else.

I entered the remains of one of the houses. The doors, windows and frames were all but rotted away. The hardened silt level was halfway up the front door, so I had to go down on my hands and knees to enter.

"Watch your head," someone said, and I looked up sharply, cracking my head so hard on the stone lintel that I slumped to my stomach, breathing in dust and smelling wet-rot from somewhere else, all the while trying to see who had

Casting Longer Shadows

spoken. I was in what must once have been a small hallway. There was a stone staircase leading nearer to the sun and nowhere else, because all the timber floors had gone. That was all. Nobody there, no one who could have watched me coming in and spoken at just the right time. I scurried away from the door and stood upright.

And then I saw something.

It was not a shadow. If a shadow had an opposite then this was it. And unlike the shadows it did not try to hide from me, but simply faded away. One second it was splayed comfortable on the middle of the stone staircase, a few seconds later it had gone, eaten by the voracious sunlight from above.

And I smiled.

"No more shadows," I said, an expression of hope. I looked under the staircase and no darkness awaited me there, no feeling of dread or malicious observation. There was a painting on the wall, a watercolour representation of how the village had once been, and as I leaned in closer it disappeared, melting into the hot stone. I was sad that it had gone but not afraid. Dead people see lots of strange things, some of them not good. *This* was good. I don't know how I knew, but I did. Nothing bad could feel so right.

I moved through to the kitchen. The chimney breast was huge, occupying one whole end wall, although the fireplace was silted up. The walls were bare. I kept glancing left and right, hoping to catch sight of some fleeting adornment, but it seemed that this house was offering me nothing more.

I made for the opening where the back door had been and was stopped in my tracks by another voice.

"Won't you take tea with me?"

I wanted to turn around. In this strange silence the voice had seemed loud, perhaps amplified by death, and now the quiet was a paused breath expecting a response. It would be rude of me to ignore it. And really, I shouldn't be scared. None of the shadows had ever spoken. This was a *good* voice.

Still, I glanced over my shoulder first just in case I had to run. Only then did I turn around.

The aged woman was sitting at a battered oaken dining table. Her clothes were colourful and garish against the grey and brown backgrounds of the sunken cottage. Her shawl held all the hues of the rainbow and some new ones, its twists and twirls confounding me as I tried to make out whether it was a part of her, or she a part of it. She smiled and flashed her perfect white teeth, but it must have been a distraction. When I looked down again the table had taken on some weight: a huge steaming pot of tea; several cups and saucers; a jug of milk; a plate, bearing rich fruit cake. There was no sign of the village's fate in this scene, no grey dust smeared on the cake or forming a sheen on the milk. This was out of time.

"I'd love to," I said. I wasn't sure whether to expect a response. Dead I was, but I'd never seen sight or sound of any 'late' other.

The old woman smiled, and her teeth seemed slightly less perfect than they had moments before. Her shawl too, although still intricately wound, was losing some of its colour. "That's good," she rasped, "because I've baked a cake and I hate to…" She trailed off, but not in despair. Her voice faded, as did her image, until the only thing left

Casting Longer Shadows

was the table, darkening and splitting as if aging before my eyes.

"I love cake," I said into the empty room. "I'd be very flattered to..." It wasn't a conscious effect, but my voice faded in sympathy with the table.

I wondered who the old woman was, and where she was now. I scanned the room, the walls, the uneven silt floor, and whatever was buried there—the tiled floor she had walked on, the hearth where she had baked her cakes—would probably be there forever.

I didn't want to leave that room. It held such a sense of peace: the old woman hadn't seemed sad even as she'd gone. I wished I could join her, but wishing did nothing for me. I left instead, ducking low to slip through the door. Across an expanse of dried reservoir bed another cottage faced me. This one had a window left in place, most of the panes smashed but some of the ragged glass still there, grey with sun-dried moss, the wooden frame rotten and powdery. Through that window I saw a shadowy movement.

I paused, standing statue-like on that plain of dried silt as if I belonged to the village. I held my breath, narrowed my eyes against the sun as I waited for the shadow to move again. It had flitted behind the window even though the cottage had no roof and the sun was obvious through the shattered glass. A bird, maybe? But I had seen little wildlife here. There was nothing much to attract it. And besides, nature seemed to have forgotten this place along with everyone else. Another visitor from the past? Another fleeting ghost to invite me, urge me, warn me?

Whatever, I felt compelled to explore.

Tim Lebbon

Keeping my eyes on the upstairs window, I skirted around the stumped remnants of a tree and approached the door. The sun was heading down now, and I could see the first smudged shadows leaning out from walls, grudgingly cooling the ground with their touch. They did not frighten or disturb me, but I wondered what would happen come night. I'd made no arrangements to leave, walk back to the local town, find anywhere to stay. I didn't even know where I was going to go next. I'd simply come here, taking the day hour by hour, minute by minute. And I felt that where I ended up next was something that was being decided for me.

I did not pause outside the house. That might have dissuaded me from entering, and I needed to see—

Needed to see the skeleton suspended from one of the few remaining roof trusses. The rope frayed and adorned with dried plants, morbid decorations. The skeleton itself fragmentary, only the skull, ribcage and one arm still hanging there. Its legs had vanished, as if trying to avoid being swallowed by the rising silts of time. Weeds hung in its ribcage, dried now but still there, like the remnants of skin or guts. After all this time there was nothing left but bone.

I wondered why the hell this person had chosen to stay and die instead of leaving with the rest of the population.

And as I wondered, he told me.

"This has always been my home," the voice said, fading in as if a dozen doors were quickly being opened between us. "And when the time came, I decided it always would be."

"I'm chased by shadows," I said, thinking that a soul so tortured may know something about the affliction.

"Some like us never find rest, they just fade to glimpses. How did you die?" The skeleton did not move but behind

Casting Longer Shadows

it, in a deepening shadow thrown by the west-facing wall of the house, a face materialised from nowhere. It surprised me how young the man was. It surprised me more that he knew I was dead.

"I don't know," I said.

"How long have you been dead?"

"I'm not sure."

"These shadows. They talk to you?"

"No. Just…growl."

He was *there* now, as there as I was, and I thought that if I walked forward and batted his skeleton to one side I could touch and feel him. But it seemed impolite.

"I waited until the water was around my ankles," he said. "It took a while. I was in this room for a week without leaving, and by then I was hungry. But not thirsty of course. Of course not." I wondered whether his was the shadow I had seen. I still didn't feel spied upon, but the recent memory of something moving behind the smashed window still disturbed me. "And ever since, I've dreamt of water."

"Why are you still—"

"Going now," he said, and it seemed to be a surprise to him as well. He was fading, swallowed into the wall and the timber beam and the solidness of this place.

"But I don't understand!" I said, expecting no answer.

"Stay longer," he said from nowhere, "and when you come to terms…" And the rest was lost.

I fled the ruined house. I did not understand why I was scared—the man, the *ghost*, had not been threatening in the slightest—but for a couple of minutes I felt like I did when the shadows were stalking me. The air was hot, the ground radiating the heat it had been sucking in all day, and yet I felt a cool breath on my neck and left shoulder. Someone was standing right behind me, shifting as I shifted, letting out a constant sigh of pain onto my sweaty skin. There were eyes focused on me, I could sense them drawing the light and colour away, and I was no longer alone.

I'd never been the centre of anything, but now I felt that the whole of this dead place was watching me.

Looking up out of the village I saw the reason for my sudden coolness. In the distance, topping the mountains like grotesque black wigs, thunderclouds were beginning to boil.

—⁂—

I would be spending the night in the village.

The sun was kissing the hillsides now, and long before it actually set, the storm-clouds drowned it from me. I stared for quite some time, standing in what I guessed had once been the village square, but the sun never emerged again. Even its ghost would have been a comfort, a glimpse through the clouds, but I was not even afforded that.

Because the clouds were shadows, the largest I had ever seen. And they were striding in for the kill on lightning legs.

I hurried through the gathering gloom and entered one of the more tumbled-down buildings, little more than two perpendicular walls holding each other upright. Inside there were three colourful canvas chairs, and in each chair sat a corpse. At least I thought they were corpses when I ran in. For a crazy second my mind tried to find truth in what I was seeing—how could they still be here, sitting like that, almost

Casting Longer Shadows

untouched, after fifty years submerged? And then they turned to look at me, and one of them smiled, and I knew that I'd found another part of the village.

"Don't be scared," the smiler said. It was a little girl, pigtails and flowery dress and crooked-toothed smile.

"I'm not," I said, but it came out so false that none of them even countered me. I looked up at the storm in the hills. The first rumble of thunder rolled in and I could tell that rain was falling up there. Real rain, heavy rain, the torrential downpour that the whole country had been praying for for weeks.

"Coming closer," an old woman said from her chair. She sounded pleased. A table had appeared between them now, and behind the farthest chair the wall had taken on colour, lines of patterned wallpaper, one half of a large framed oil painting. Under the chairs and table was a carpet, several feet higher than it should have been but level and even for all that.

"I don't know what's happening," I said hopelessly, pathetically, but when they all smiled at me I felt more at home than I ever had. And that feeling on its own told me most of what I needed to know.

"It's safe here," the little girl said. "I died a long way away, in another country, but it's safer here."

"I see shadows," I said.

The third corpse, a man, spoke at last. "Your death following you."

"But I don't remember—" I was interrupted by a louder crack of thunder from the mountains, and my head whipped around as I awaited an impact from behind. The roar, the shout of fury, it was bringing something back.

Tim Lebbon

Something that started light and quickly turned dark.

I staggered from the room as memories threatened to unhinge me. Outside there were people moving about in what had once been the streets, each carrying their own oasis of history with them in sight, smell, sound. A cobbled street, the waft of freshly made bread, a cheerful song as someone went about their daily chores, all of this happening in this dead, strange valley. *It's safe here*, the little girl had said, and looking around I wondered just how many of these shapes and forms originated here.

The thunder cracked again, rolling down the valley like a precursor of the waters that must soon follow. It would not be a flood, I knew, but a trickle. Nevertheless, I had a choice to make.

—⁂—

And the memory returned, gushing through my mind as if a floodgate had been opened, one previously held closed by devious hands, vanquished now by a few careful words from dead folks. *Your death chasing you*, the old man had said, and I remembered when I saw a shadow for the first time. The first and last, I knew now.

Walking home from the factory that day, leaving my colleagues drinking in the pub because they hadn't really wanted me there anyway. It was hot, a scorching day, unseasonably so, and I was sweating, running my hand through my hair and watching my shadow go on ahead of me as if eager to reach shade.

And then the rumble and warning squeals I did not recognise through my heat-cooked senses. The growls, the

Casting Longer Shadows

whines. A shadow fell over me and I turned, thinking that a cat had run by and tickled my heels, as the lorry struck me and sent me spinning and tumbling away.

I was on my side looking into the hedge. The sun hit it and baked it dry. Nothing moved there. As I heard the creak of a door opening, the gasp of the mortified driver, the hedge slowly began to grow dark, dark…darkest.

I opened my eyes and felt the first spots of rain sizzle on my upturned face.

I looked around the village and saw houses with their thatched roofs, window-pots exploding with flowers, villagers exchanging pleasantries and aiming smiles at me as they hurried for cover. Shadows here, shadows there, none of them threatening anymore, none of them cruel.

Something tickled my foot and I looked down quickly, but it was only the first trickle of water. The ground darkened as it turned wet, and I heard the joyous sound of church bells ringing behind me, calling a congregation to worship.

I stood there for some time, feeling at home. And when the water had risen far enough to find its way into my shoes, I decided that I would stand there for some time more.

A Ripple in the Veil

A parliament of rooks passes over my house every day. In the morning they fly south, presumably to the fields and woods where they feed. During the evening they head back North, a great black cloud dragging dusk behind. I never tire of watching them; there's something intensely spooky about it, as if I'm witnessing something that should be unseen, or a sight so far beyond humanity's control—so *of nature* that we can barely understand it—that it seems truly alien. And yet I love to watch, because it offers me a glimpse of the grandeur and wonder of the power that sits around us all the time. Usually that power whispers its presence in the meanderings of a bee, or hums its possibilities in the slow turning of a rose to face the sun. But the rooks are a scream.

It amazes me how, when seen from a distance, they seem to move and flow like a single living organism. There's order in there, and design, and the movement of the flock displays instinct at its most fundamental level. They pass across the sky like a shoal of fish, each bird following the ones to the left and right, and up and down, never questioning the movement, and never apparently have designs of their own. They follow, swerving and dipping and rising and pulsing across the sky, and it is only when they are passing directly overhead that I make out the individual movements of each bird.

What fascinates me the most is that there must be one bird that decides their path. No democracy, this. No votes as to direction or intent. I know my idea holds no logic—indeed, it would probably be blown from the water by any ornithologist worth their salt—but it seems to me that every bird is controlled, steered and coerced to behave the way it does. And it is nature doing the coercing.

That idea would frighten most people. But not me. I like the impression of order. Chaos scares me, and it is while watching this parliament of rooks that I feel most at peace with the world, and my place in it.

—ɯ—

Until the day the lead rook disappeared.

As usual I heard them before they appeared. I was on my way to the bus stop to catch the bus to work, and the rooks were a familiar part of my morning routine. I smiled. From a distance their calls sounded like one *caw*, the combined chorus of one single existence. I paused to watch. They came from the north, preparing to see in the new morning, but even at a distance I knew that something was wrong. The call began to break up, panic cutting it into frantic shards that sailed to me across the village rooftops and through the

A Ripple in the Veil

orange smudge of autumn trees. I stood at the roadside and saw the rooks in the distance, a dark fluid cloud blurring the horizon and expanding as it came closer. It pulsed instead of flowed, breaking up, reforming, spreading out wider and wider until parts of it were no longer distinguishable from the wide blue sky.

I frowned, shaded my eyes and wished I'd brought my glasses. I was sixty next month, and I was doing my best to deny the ravages of age. Now I cursed my foolishness.

The birds drew closer, and I knew that something had vanished, some unifying force that kept rooks together, one flock, one community. Some of them collided in mid-air, a couple spiralling to the ground stunned or dead. Others flew away from the flock cawing in panic, as if fleeing something that wanted to eat them. One bird flew directly toward me, and a dozen other rooks followed as if in pursuit. They seemed to envelop the fleeing bird in their black mass, and when they came apart seconds later a torn shape fluttered to the ground a hundred yards down the road. A cat darted from a garden, grabbed at the bird, and it was gone.

I shouted, an incoherent expression of shock and anger and sadness. Animals did not do this to themselves! Murder for the sake of murder was a human foible! This should not *happen!* The greatest mass of rooks was directly above me now, throwing down a shower of cries and feathers. They flew every way, following nothing but the madness that must have infected their small minds. There seemed to be no final destination in mind. Bird crap spattered the pavement and struck the arm of my coat, and I walked quickly to try to emerge from beneath the cloud. It disturbed me. Their calls were not normal, their behaviour skewed, and the further

Tim Lebbon

I walked the more I sensed black eyes upon me. That was foolish, I knew, product of a wild imagination. But when I glanced up and back I saw several birds hovering, as if watching me on my way.

I reached a garden belonging to somebody I knew and went in through the gates, hiding beneath the porch over their front door. My heart was racing. Was I really *scared*?

The clouds of rooks moved on, expanding more and more, and soon it would reach the point of no return and split asunder.

The birds' order had gone.

I shook my head and walked back to the pavement.

And suddenly I knew what I must do. The rook they all followed—the bird there to keep order, exert nature's influence over the chaos of so many disparate minds—had gone. Perhaps it lay injured and needing aid. Or maybe mankind had stamped its mark once again, and killed it.

Either way, I would not be going to work. I passed by the bus stop and crossed the main road, heading up toward the canal and the woods that surrounded it. The chance of finding a single bird in such wide, wild countryside was miniscule, yet I felt that I should be the one to find it. I knew. I understood. Nature would recognise that, at least.

There could be little pretence at wildness where roads bordered fields, telegraph poles stood at the road's edge like the skeletons of trees, houses spotted hillsides with a rash of humanity, plane trails made a chequerboard of the autumn sky, hedgerows were trim and square and stark with cut

A Ripple in the Veil

shrubs, and the constant, unending background rumble of traffic provided a counterpoint to the birdsong and struggling silence of the fields. And yet I saw the skein of raw power that nature still held, evident in every falling leaf and every call of a bird unconcerned at humankind's intrusion into its world. I could smell the wet rot of leaves sinking down into the ground, and understand the miracle that lay therein. I could hear the hum of electricity passing through wires high above, in concert with the swallows that roosted on those wires, preparing to migrate. I appreciated the depth of things around me, and the more that appreciation grew, the more I saw.

This was a road I often travelled. It curved gently to and fro for a mile until it reached a steep humpbacked bridge over the canal. I walked quickly, glancing left and right and seeing nothing unusual in the hedges either side of the road. I paused at gates and scanned the fields, paying particular attention to the occasional clumps of trees the farmers had left standing. If I saw the injured rook, there would be something to display its location, I was sure, some upset in nature that would be obvious at first glance. I saw cows waddling in mud, but their stares told me nothing. I saw a constantly flooded depression in one field shimmer as a heron stood at its centre, waiting for a frog to break surface, but there was nothing wrong in that. A family of rabbits gambolled along close to one of the wild hedgerows, pausing every few seconds to sniff the air for dogs and shotguns. They looked my way and saw me watching them, but they were at the other side of the field. They played on, perceiving no threat in me.

I walked on, breathing in the damp autumn smells that went so certainly with the golden fall of leaves. The road here was well used by people travelling to and from the expensive houses up on the hillsides, and the few attractive country pubs hidden between folds in the land. Yet still fallen leaves coated the tarmac, much thicker at the edges, wet and rotting already even though the sun shone today. I kicked through the leaves, taking a great childish delight in the sound they made and the warm, damp smell that rose from them. A couple of weeks ago perhaps I could have picked them up and crumbled them in my hands, but now they were well on their way back into the ground, limp and wet and seeping their last. I shifted a pile aside here and there to look for the rook, but it would not be here.

My walk held a sense of such import that I felt I could never turn back. And yet this part of it—the walk between the village and the canal—was relaxed and sure, untainted by true purpose. Somehow I knew where the rook would be, and that was not down here. I looked forward and up, toward the distant line of trees that marched alongside the canal, and that was where the bird would be. From this distance I could make out little difference from normal; a silence, perhaps, and a stillness, but nothing obvious.

I drew level with the old deserted house that had been a part of the landscape since my childhood. It stood back from the road, smothered in ivy and hidden from casual view by a stand of trees that may well have once formed its garden boundary. Abandoned for so many decades, the house had been swallowed by nature, subsumed back into the natural order of things. I had gone in there once, when I was ten years old. My cousin had dared me. These were in the days

A Ripple in the Veil

when ten-year-olds explored the countryside instead of the inside of a TV set, and when tales of hauntings and spooky occurrences were as rich and textured as a living nightmare, rather than laughed at and barely discussed in school the next day. This house had supposedly been haunted by an old man who had been found dead in the kitchen, sitting upright in his chair with a glob of porridge still resting in his mouth. Back then, as a ten year old, the story had been terrifying. Fifty years later it had taken on an almost nostalgic hue, and yet every time I passed by the house I wondered why nobody had lived in it since. I had not been inside for fifty years, and now, so long after, it was barely discernable from the road. It was likely that local kids did not even know of its existence, and for me there was something poignant in a haunted house that drew no attention. I leaned on the hedge and tried to peer through the screen of trees, ivy and rose bushes gone wild, but I could see little of the hidden building. I wondered what was still inside, and whether sometimes that old man still sat in his chair, waiting to swallow his last mouthful of porridge.

I walked on, and turning a gentle corner in the road I saw the bridge over the canal. It had been built long before motorised vehicles decided to use it, and the new road surface was deeply scored and scarred from where the undersides of cars did not always clear. The metallic sheddings of ruptured exhaust pipes and dented chassis glittered at the roadside, and as I drew closer their shapes changed.

A chill went through me. I paused and looked around, expecting to see the hedgerows stirring from a slight breeze or a shadow passing before the sun. But there was nothing. *This is where it will be*, I thought. *In these woods alongside the canal. This is where they roost, and this is where they left the one among them that gives order.* I was suddenly very afraid. I was intruding into something here that mankind was not meant to see or know. This was nature in its basest form, and I, a human who had chosen to clothe himself, build a brick house, use electricity and read books and watch distant places on television, had removed myself from nature. Much as I still loved to walk in the country I was always a visitor, and though I hated that feeling it still gave me some comfort. The countryside was wild; returning to my home at the end of the day was always a relief. I often thought of camping out in the woods or digging a hole and calling it home, but none of these ideas were ever serious, or indeed possible. I was an intruder into the world I loved so much, and I often felt its gaze upon me.

Next to the bridge was a wide gate that led down onto the canal's towpath. This was the easiest route by which I could negotiate the woods that grew alongside the canal, and yet here was when the impossibility of what I was trying to do hit me, with the stark choice of left or right. If I turned one way I would be going toward the missing rook, if I went the other I would be moving away. There was no in-between, and each choice made thereafter would be equally bereft of hope. Whatever my belief in my appreciation of nature, I could not fool myself that it would lead me to one single bird in such a huge expanse. I had rarely even seen a dead bird—the most common sighting was beside a road—and trying to find one now was madness.

Was that it? Was there a madness about me? I was only sixty, still fit and healthy and involved in life, but perhaps age had hit me harder than I could have imagined.

A Ripple in the Veil

I shook my head, and that was when I saw the man crossing the landscape.

He was away to the east, several fields away, visible to me only because he was passing over a rise and heading across to the edge of the woods bordering the canal in that direction. As soon as I saw him he looked around, as if he felt the weight of my gaze. I did not think he could see me, yet his face turned my way and he paused for a few seconds. He wore a long coat, had long hair, and he was not like me.

I knew that straight away. *He was not like me.* Nature did not part around him, as if he were a rock in its flow, but flowed *with* him. He was a part of that stream. Birds dipped and sang as they passed him by, a family of rabbits played unconcerned at his presence, and even from this distance I could see that he walked barefoot. He was here because he was meant to be here, and I knew for sure that he too was looking for the missing rook.

I turned and walked quickly away from the man. Perhaps I was going the wrong way but I had no wish to draw closer, see his face, feel how his presence barely disturbed the world which I loved so much. I carried a silence with me—birds falling quiet, the woods holding their breath as I passed by—and the thought of the man being part of the noise instead of the silence disturbed me greatly. It was not anything so shallow as jealousy. If anything, I think it was fear. I knew that I should turn around and go home. He had probably disappeared into the trees already, and he would not see me hurrying down the road, away from the canal and woods and toward the village. Even if he did, I did not concern him. He would do whatever he had come here to do, and then leave.

Tim Lebbon

I walked faster along the towpath. It was quite rough here, with rocks protruding from the path and puddles of water threatening to slip me up at every step. Mud splashed my trousers, but I did not care. A family of ducks followed me for a while, keeping pace on the canal and setting tiny waves lapping at the shores in their wake. The reflected sky blurred, clouds dancing and folding in the ripples, the sun shimmering across the water as the canal turned to the right. Eventually the ducks realised that I carried no bread and gave up their pursuit.

Things splashed in the water. Bugs skimmed the canal's surface. A buzzard sat in a high tree, staring down as if assessing whether a part of me would make a meal. A squirrel dashed out onto the path and back into the woods, an acorn grasped in its tiny paws. Nature happened around me but not with me, not through me, and I sensed a sudden sheen of panic to my surroundings. It was nothing so obvious as the screech of a bird or the growl of something larger. Instead, the squirrel that had retreated came out again, just for a moment. It put itself in danger for a second time, and then ran and hid again. The buzzard flapped its wings and drifted to a lower branch, as if keen to draw closer to me. But it was not hunting. Its head jerked this way and that, left and right, looking up, looking down. It was as if the buzzard had lost something fundamental to its existence, and thought it could find it somewhere in the air around its head.

I walked on, and the sense of panic grew. It came to me like a cool fist in my stomach, sucking my heart down with its gravity, and I wondered whether I had picked up on nature's upset, or whether I had exuded it from myself in the first place.

A Ripple in the Veil

"So what is it?" I said, pausing and looking up at the sky. Clouds drifted by, unconcerned at my plight. My voice silenced the silence, stilling movement and sound that I had not even been aware of, and for a second or two there was nothing to be heard. Nothing close, nothing distant; nothing. It was an intensely eerie experience, and when the buzzard screeched—and nature answered by resuming its background rustling and whimpers—I felt so relieved that I sank to my knees. "So what *is* it?" I said again, quieter this time, and then everything around me pointed at what it was.

I had to go back. The canal showed me that in the way it suddenly rippled eastward, as though disturbed by a breeze I did not feel. The birds told me by flying in that direction as well, singing all the way. I looked up and the clouds flowed west to east, though I was certain that they had been passing directly across the canal moments before. Plants leaned that way, and a flower dipped its weight as a bee kissed its heart.

I looked west, along the canal towpath, and darkness seemed to wait there for me.

I turned and looked east, back the way I had come, back toward the mysterious man who had crossed the field, and sunlight dappled through the tree canopy to light my way. I began walking, and every step I took eased the panic around me, and the cool pressure that had been building in my gut.

I passed beneath the road bridge where I had come down onto the path, and continued moving on. The going became much easier; fewer rocks protruding above the ground, fewer puddles. I felt the sense of growing unease lift from me like an unseen fog. It was almost as if I had been meant to go this way.

I walked quickly, because I thought there was something I should see. The man I had spied crossing the field would have entered the woods at least ten minutes ago, and if I was ever to see what he was going to do, I had to get there fast. And suddenly the possibility of missing him brought panic of a different sort. He was someone I was meant to meet and see, and to miss him now would be like missing my first meeting with my dear departed wife. That would have changed my life beyond recognition, and so would this.

I would live on. I would work, come home, work. I would mourn Elizabeth, cut the grass, see our children several times each year, read myself to sleep every night, dream myself awake each morning. Time would ease me ever onward toward whatever reunion eternity may allow my wife and me, but in the meantime my life would be the same. Lessened, perhaps, by what I had missed; cheapened by the demise of the parliament of rooks.

I had to see. I had to change. Potential breathed down my neck, and on its breath I caught the sweet smells of autumn.

After five minutes I rounded a bend in the canal, and the man was there. He was squatting down on the canal path, his hand held low and flat over something lying on the ground. He did not move his head, but I knew that he knew I was there. His stance changed, his bearing, and his long coat shifted as his shoulders set themselves against my gaze. This close, his unreality was richer than it had been before. He was there, he was solid, and his feet would leave impressions in the soft ground, but he was not of this place

A Ripple in the Veil

and this time. I could not see anything that told me this, but I knew all the same. It scared me. Once, when I was sixteen, I had seen a ghost sitting on the end of my bed whilst on a family holiday in Cornwall. That had always remained a secret terror, something very much meant for me, and this felt the same. There was fear in me, but awe as well. And behind that, rich and vibrant, the astonishing realisation that there really were more things in Heaven and Earth.

I looked from the man to what his hand covered, and even before I saw the rook I knew that it was dead. There was no life in its pose. A feather on one wing fluttered, but only in time with a sudden breeze. The man looked up at me and then back down to the bird. I never looked into his eyes again.

"Fishing wire," he said. "Left lying here. Tangled and rancid with rotten bait. The rook took the bait, and entangled itself, and that's where we are right now."

"Where?" I said.

"Entangled," the man said. His hand lowered slightly until the flickering feather tickled his palm. Behind the fringe of long hair I saw his mouth break into a grim smile.

"Who are you?"

The man snorted and shook his head, as if I was nothing to him, or I should have known already.

His hand lowered some more, and from where I was standing—perhaps twenty paces away—I saw reality shimmer. His hand and the rook merged, sharing the same space. Nature took a breath; a sigh or a gasp, I could not tell. Trees moved, the canal rippled, the air and ground seemed to shift suddenly, as if I had been moved several paces. I staggered and went down to one knee, crying out in surprise, but the man ignored me. Instead, his hand worked around the bird and inside it. Feathers fell and reformed, something crackled, and seconds later the rook was standing on its own two feet.

"No..." I did not know what else to say. The dead bird stood. The fishing wire was a blur on the grass, as if melted away. The rook jerked its head left and right, up and down, and its obsidian eyes were amazed.

The man spoke once more before leaving, and still he did not look at me. Perhaps he knew that his eyes would show me things I was still not ready to see. "It's for you to follow and value, not me," he said. "I just maintain the balance." And then he stood, turned and left. He did not walk away, nor vanish. He simply left. One second I was in his presence and the next he was gone...and I was certain that elsewhere on this same world, someone else suddenly stood amazed.

I watched the rook take off and fly south. And on my way back down to the village I saw the cloud of rooks in the distance, swooping and flexing and diving, calling out in gleeful appreciation at what can only have been a second chance.

Forever

On Dana'Man the cold bit hard, ice informed thought, frost froze dreams of freedom, and duty and supplication were the way. On Dana'Man there was preparation for a war long in coming, with no sign of its beginning yet in sight. On Dana'Man—island of the damned, natural home only to glaciers and snow demons and the ice people—life was hard, but death was harder. The mages needed every man and woman for their army; death was unpardonable.

From a distance the island seemed huge and barren, a desert of ice and snow with a few silent volcanoes protruding like the fingertips of buried giants. It stretched east and west farther than the curves of the world, and its widest point north to south would take twenty days to traverse. Occasionally a localised melt would occur when the island's only active volcano erupted, and the resultant floods would rearrange its geography for generations to come.

Closer in there were settlements, scattered across the low-lying plains at the foot of the volcanoes, staggered along the seashore, a few further inland. Some were long-deserted, others appeared to be thriving. Smoke rose high from countless fires, boats bobbed between ice floating at the coast, and occasionally a hawk would drift down out of the constant cloud cover, disgorge its passenger and then rise up again to its customary heights. There were even a few farms where snow and ice had been painstakingly removed and the ground given over to sparse greenery.

Closer still, one settlement clung to a slip of rock that protruded half a mile out to sea, curving around and forming a natural breakwater and harbour. It was here at Newland that the mages and the remains of their army had landed over a century before, driven out of Noreela far to the south and sent into exile. Fitting, then, that their new Krote army called this place their home. Boats and ships of all sizes rested here, most of them small fishing sloops, a couple of transports for carrying materials and people around Dana'Man, and two larger vessels brimming with tools of war. The harbour was a busy place. It stank of freshly-landed fish—much of it rank and inedible, gone to rot—and echoed to the sound of metal on metal from glowing metal-smiths at its very tip. One of the war ships was moored at the breakwater, and once each day a giant trolley was pushed back and forth, the ship weighed down with more weapons.

At the landward end of the breakwater, on a slope where Newland spread and cast its roots into Dana'Man proper, a collection of timber and ice buildings was laid out in a regular, monotonous design. Pennants floated above some buildings, others were bare. Some were well maintained, others less so,

Forever

given over more to evidence of violent times than careful tending. Hundreds of men and women walked in and out of the barrack complex, sometimes in groups or pairs, more often alone. They wore furs and leathers, wrapped against the cold, and they all carried weapons of some kind attached to their belts or strung across their backs. But there was no fight in the air today. Dana'Man was their island, and theirs alone. The fight they existed for would come later.

In one of the rows of barracks there was a tent made of whale bone and cured horse skin, and in that tent sat a man named Nox. He was a big man and, like most of the Krote warriors he shared the encampment with, his clothing bristled with weaponry; knives, stars, maces, slide-shocks and throwing spikes. His hair was long and braided, more to keep it out of his eyes than for decoration. His skin was dark as leather, weathered by his four decades living on Dana'Man, and his eyes were as cool blue as the oldest glacier. He sat alone. Those sharing his quarters had gone for food. Had anyone entered, they would have seen instantly that something was wrong. Nox was slowly, deliberately slicing grooves into his arm, letting the blood well and flow from each cut before raising the knife to his face, scraping away a line of rough stubble and running the knife through each wound again. He was breathing hard and fast, swaying on the end of his cot, shaking his head slowly as if to spread and dilute the pain.

The stubble dug into the raw flesh of his wounds, stung him there, promising to keep them open and bleeding. When his wounds were noticed, he would be sent to the hospital barge moored at the end of the breakwater.

And from there, escape from Dana'Man—and the mages—was so much closer.

—⚇—

"How the hell did you do that?" Serville said. She was staring at Nox's arm with frank fascination. She had always been one for blood.

This is it, thought Nox. *This is the lie that changes me forever.* "Foxlion cub," he said. "I went down to the beach looking for crabs, and it was hiding behind a float of ice."

"A cub did that?" Serville leant in closer, removing her glove and reaching out. Nox pulled away, wincing as his arm flexed and the wound gaped. More blood ran. Serville licked her lips.

"You'll have none of me!" Nox said. He was sitting on his cot, furs splashed with blood, waiting for the words that may set him free. He thought it unlikely that they would come from Serville—she had been here much longer than him and was of the Western tribes, wild and hard even for a Krote—but the others would be back soon. He had to be ready.

"Did you kill it?"

"No, it swam away. Dived as soon as it took a swipe at me."

Serville glared at him. "A cub bettered you?"

Nox shrugged. "I wasn't there looking for trouble. I was looking for crabs. I wanted something different from that shit they serve in the mess."

"We eat to live, not for pleasure," she said, looking at his bloodied arm once again.

Forever

"You Westerns are so backward," he said, and Serville threw back her head and laughed. Nox glanced at her belt in the second she looked away, marking her weapons. Just in case. She was part of his troop, but they had never really been friends.

Jaxx and Morton came into the tent, belching and laughing, and a gust of cold air and snow followed them in.

"Nox had a fight with a foxlion cub and lost," Serville said.

Morton sat on his bunk, unconcerned. Serville went to him—they were together sometimes, these two, and Nox only hoped that they did not start right now.

"That looks painful," Jaxx said. He stood over Nox and stared down at the wounds. "It'll scar well. Better than mine!" He displayed a fleshy knot on his own arm.

"You're welcome to it," Nox said. "And yes, it does hurt."

"You should get to the hospital barge," Jaxx said. "Foxlions carry contagion. And no offence, Nox, but I don't want to catch anything you may have."

There they are, Nox thought, *the words that set me free.* "You think so? It's not that bad. The bleeding's almost stopped and—"

"How long ago did it happen?"

"Just after you went to eat."

"It should have stopped by now," Jaxx said. "Krote's don't bleed for long, you know that. Something's keeping your blood thin and your wound open. And I say again, I don't want to catch it." He stepped back, giving Nox room to stand. Serville and Morton were looking over now, sensing the threat of violence in Jaxx's voice.

"A warm bed and the attention of those medics!" Morton said. "Don't pretend you don't want to go!"

Nox did not risk a response. *Give myself away,* he thought, *they'll know I intend never to see them again. Serville and Morton I'll not be sorry to leave, but Jaxx has been something of a friend.* So he shrugged his weapon belt over one shoulder, held his bleeding arm beneath his outer jacket and exited into the open air.

Nox took in a deep breath and let it out. Somewhere in that stew of stenches, freedom.

Nox had been caught by the Krote armies when he was a child. He knew nothing but his current existence, even though there were sometimes dreams that he could never truly know or understand. Then, he saw the faces of kindly people, green fields, a village working for survival, not war. He had no idea what had happened to that place, nor those people, and mostly he pretended not to care. He was as much a Krote warrior now as those born here, and he lived, as did every Krote, to serve the mages. His upbringing and training had made sure of that.

Newland, the only named settlement on Dana'Man, was where the mages had landed after being driven out of their rightful home on Noreela. So it was told, so it was true. They had landed here, nursing wounds driven into their flesh by the arrogant Noreelan armies, and they and their surviving Krote warriors had made the place their home. The harbour had welcomed them in with its long, curved breakwater, protecting them against the storms that had raged for all their

Forever

weeks at sea, allowing them a gentle landing on this place of snow and ice. And now, though the mages were rarely seen away from their volcano lair miles inland, this harbour was still a special place.

Nox had lived here all his life, venturing away only to train on the mountain slopes inland, or to join a raiding party to the islands far to the east and west of Dana'Man. He ate here, trained for the promised war to come, slept, screwed, drank, made friends and lost them. He returned here to nurse occasional wounds suffered on raids. He relaxed here on those days given over to leisure, hunting sea snakes with his friends, wrestling and sparring on the harbour front. He called it home. And yet…there were those dreams. Fields of green, not white. Striving for survival and peace, not war. And Nox had begun to wonder more and more just where those dreams could lead.

He walked out of the barracks and headed down the gentle slope into Newland. From here he could see the whole expanse of the natural harbour, curved out into the sea like the arm of Dana'Man itself. Boats were docked all along the breakwater, but it was the two war ships that stood out. Five times larger than any other vessel, they sported huge masts and furled sails, ready for sailing at a moment's notice. Snow and ice made surreal sculptures of their rigging. From this distance Nox could barely make out individual people walking along the harbour, but there was a sense of continuous movement about the port which made him yearn, briefly, for the relative calm of the barracks.

But his arm throbbed, and the stubble in the wounds kept them open and leaking. He withdrew it from the cover of his jacket and was surprised at the amount of blood still running from the cuts. How ironic it would be to die from blood-loss, now that he had finally found the nerve to attempt escape. After all these years, all those vague notions of fleeing, no one would know. He would slump down here in the snow and, dreaming of green fields, his life would filter away into the ice of ages. They would find his corpse frozen into the hillside, thaw him and feed him to the trained hawks that came down on occasion from above the clouds. Killed by a foxlion cub, they would say, probably mocking him. And in weeks or days, he would not even be a memory.

Nox shook his head and bit his lip, the pain stinging him into action. He hurried on toward the harbour. He could make out the hospital barge now, right at the end of the breakwater past the weapons workshops. And beyond that there was open sea, and freedom.

When he was seventeen Nox already knew the meaning of faith. The subjects of his faith were the mages—sinister, elusive S'Hivez; beautiful, terrible Angel—and his belief was strong and profound. He had faith in the fact that he was there to serve them, and nothing else. Those brief memories of childhood were dream fragments frozen by the snows and ice of Dana'Man, their meaning lost, any emotion conjured by them scorched away by the frost. The mages were his masters, and everything he was, everything he *would* be, was because of them. He was a soldier, and one day they would call on his services to take revenge on the people far to the south that had driven them away. They owned his mind and, most of the time, his heart.

Forever

Most of the time. Because even pure faith is fickle. And one evening, lying in a sweaty tangle with a female Krote warrior, sated, sharing body warmth against the freezing air outside, he uttered a brief, illicit sentence. "One day, maybe we'll get out of here." The Krote mumbled something and shifted, her hands searching for the hottest part of him, and within minutes Nox had forgotten the thought that had conjured those words.

But above them, in shadows cast between the ceiling and wall of the tent, something blinked out of existence. It was a nothing, not even blackness; a shade, a ghost of a soul yet to be born. It too served the mages, though it had no mind to doubt, nor a heart to debate. It skimmed away beneath the surface of reality, back to its masters. And though the words meant nothing to the shade, the mages heard and stored them for the future.

Nursing his bleeding arm, Nox entered the outskirts of the harbourside. The iced road had been powdered with volcanic ash to make the going easier. Snow had been cleared from the rooftops, icicles hacked away from windows, and animal hides hung heavy across doorways. All the timber used in construction was brought in from other places, and along with the materials came slaves to do the building. There were dozens of them in the streets. Nox paid them as much attention as he did snow goats and sea gulls. They were below his contempt. Human, yes, but beyond that there was little to compare the slaves to the Krote masters they served. The mages used some arcane chemicala to drive down any rebellion in the imported slaves, and they strolled through the streets like dim-witted goats, heavily muscled and vacant. Nox met their gazes occasionally and saw no intelligence there. Instinct kept them out of the Krotes' paths, and interaction was unheard of.

He stepped aside to let some burden-beasts pass, ex-slaves that had been transformed even further by the mages' chemicala. It had taken time and interbreeding, but over two or three generations the mages had created large, strong beasts out of previously man-sized, weak slaves. These things had lost their sexuality, their humanity, and any remnants of dignity or pride that often still existed deep in a slave's mind. Their skins were sometimes stretched and split by accelerated growth, and the dusted roads showed trails of dried blood where burden-beasts had passed by. Nox watched these four snort and strain as they hauled a sled of food out of the harbourside and up towards the barracks on the hill. A Krote rode the sled, sitting casually amongst the crates, smoking and staring absently over the beasts' heads. He glanced down as the sled passed by, looked at Nox's bloodied arm and away again. None of his business, his attitude said, and Nox could only agree.

He walked further into Newland, and the closer he came to the harbour, the busier it became. The whole point of the Krotes' existence was to go to war; the fabled Great Return of which the mages spoke whenever they emerged from their solitude, a return to Noreela and vengeance upon the peoples that had made them outcasts before magic had withdrawn itself from humanity. Yet though the Great Return was their sole reason for being, generations of Krotes had been waiting for a long time. Over a century since the mages had landed

Forever

on Dana'Man—so it was told, so it was true—still the war seemed no closer, the final order to prepare and launch as distant as ever. In darkened taverns and the dead of night, some whispered that it was because the mages had lost magic. They had their chemicala, they had their *rage*, but without magic they were powerless against the land that had driven them out. Others said it was because the mages were too old. Most that spoke bad of them rarely did so more than once. Punishment was silent, and swift.

Nox felt suddenly dizzy, and he had to lean against a wall to gather his strength. He glanced inside his jacket and saw the weak sun reflecting from fresh blood. *Maybe I've killed myself*, he thought, and smiled grimly. *Maybe that is an escape of sorts.*

At the age of twenty Nox went on his first raid. He and his troop of thirty Krotes took a coastal sloop and travelled east for three days, dodging icebergs, whirlpools and giant cold-whales until they reached the far end of the isle of Dana'Man. Here they came ashore overnight before heading out across the sea. The small boat was not built for the swells and storms of the open ocean, and on more than one occasion Nox was certain that they would capsize. He knew very well that to be tipped into these waters meant certain death, either from the intense cold, or the things that lived beneath the waves. They saw them sometimes, white movement in the depths like wraiths floating by at twilight, and though the Krotes were not cowards, they *could* feel fear. Fear keeps you alive, the female mage Angel once said at a gathering.

And it was fear that saved Nox and his fellow Krotes that day. Close to being swamped they took up oars, rowing all day and night and into the next day until they reached their destination.

Then, after days travelling without sleep, freezing, hungry and weak, the Krotes had to fight.

The tribe they went against were not warriors. Perhaps decades before they had held some semblance of organisation and civilisation, but after a century enduring regular Krote raids their society had regressed to something base and pitiful. Some had fled, but most stayed because their island was all they knew. And though they were all but resigned to the regular pillage, some still fought. They used rocks and sharpened whale-bone, fiery blubber bombs and fists, and to begin with the Krotes toyed with them, giving the islanders a brief sense that victory was possible. After an afternoon of running, hiding and fighting, however, the mages' warriors' exhaustion took over. They stormed the islanders' stronghold, slaughtered anyone who offered resistance and took what they had come all this way to steal.

They returned to Dana'Man with their hold filled with food, spices, and seedlings for the farms on Dana'Man's volcano's flanks. Also in the hold were several men and women from the island, and each Krote, man and woman alike, took turns pleasuring themselves.

"There has to be more than this," Nox whispered to himself that night. It was not guilt or shame, but a hollowness that seemed to fill him as he lay on the deck, staring up at a sky so filled with stars, it seemed to be snowing. It was not a sensation he was familiar with, and he put it down to post-fight fatigue. But he felt empty, wanting, and perhaps then more than any time before he perceived a fraction of the potential his life could have borne. "*Has* to be."

As he slept he dreamed of green fields.

And a Krote that had been lying near him remembered his words, sensed their rebellious potential, and pledged to confer them to her superior.

In Dana'Man, anything out of the ordinary had a way of making itself known to the mages.

―m―

"Nox, you snow goat's cock. Where are you off to in such a hurry? Am I missing a fight?"

"No Sir," Nox said. *Of all the luck!* The woman standing before him was at least two hands taller than Nox, wider, heavier, older, and scarred from countless fights and battles. A Krote took pride in his or her scars, displaying them whenever possible, and despite the cold this Lieutenant wore only bands of hide around her chest and hips. Her bare stomach was a network of livid red disfigurements, and her shoulders, though broad, had great chunks of flesh missing, as if burned away by a white-hot iron. *Of all the bloody luck!* Lieutenant Lenora was something of a legend amongst the Krotes of Newland.

"What have you done there, cut yourself shaving?" She nodded at the bloody patch on Nox's jacket, her bald head shimmering with frost.

"Foxlion, Sir," Nox said, changing his story slightly. He had to impress her now, pass her by, go on his way. If she thought he'd come out worse in a fight with a foxlion cub, she was likely to take a knife to him herself.

"And that's all you have? I'm impressed, Nox. I'll bet you cut the thing's head off as a trophy, eh?"

"Absolutely, Sir. It's back at the barracks. Serville is boiling it up for me even now. I'm off to the hospital barge to make sure I didn't catch anything from the shitting thing, then it's foxlion stew all round."

"Hah!" Lieutenant Lenora clapped him on his bad arm and laughed at the sky. They said she had the ear of the mages. Some even said she was one of the Krotes that had survived the rout from Noreela, immortal now, the ultimate killer. "So let me smell your sword!"

"My sword?"

"The blood of victory smells sweet, Nox, and it's months since I've bloodied mine in battle. A foxlion's a worthy opponent, that's for sure. Even though you shouldn't have been down at the beach on your own, eh?" She leaned in close and smiled.

"I...I was looking for—"

"Something better to eat. Yes, I know Nox. Can't blame you. The shit they serve you Krotes is enough to drive anyone to fend for themselves."

I'm being tested here, Nox thought. *She's probing, she smells something wrong, maybe it's my eyes, my guilty eyes.* The way she referred to Krotes as if she were not one disturbed him greatly. Far from sounding disrespectful to the mages, it showed that she thought herself above a mere Krote, a true warrior of the mages with countless scars to prove it. He had heard that her shoulder wounds were caused by a hawk gone berserk. It had grabbed her and flown so high with her in its claws, that when she finally burst its stomach with her sword it took her a whole afternoon to fall. Foolish legends.

Forever

But her eyes held a cool, dark humour, as if challenging him to doubt.

"Well, you don't have to agree with me, Nox, even though I know you do. So, your sword! I trust you didn't polish it clean, what with your arm half off?"

"Polish? No. No…" He felt suddenly faint. His arm began to burn where the blood still pumped through, and Lieutenant Lenora grew higher, wider, as he sank to his knees on the ice road.

—☽—

When Nox came to, he knew that he was caught. Lieutenant Lenora had known from the second she saw him that he had escape on his mind. It was obvious from the way he walked, the look in his eyes, the tint of his skin, and now he was being held somewhere awaiting punishment.

He had never, ever heard of a Krote trying to escape Dana'Man. He had never heard of anyone even entertaining the thought. It was bred out of them, and though he knew he was abnormal even considering fleeing, he did not waste time questioning why. Perhaps it was the grass-green dreams… but really, he did not care. Actions had meaning; musing upon such mysteries did not.

He had sometimes wondered whether there was a place on Dana'Man where attempted escapees were held. Now he opened his eyes, not knowing what to expect.

"You've lost a lot of blood," Lieutenant Lenora said. She was sitting on a bench before him, holding him upright. The muscles in her arms were knotted and hard. Even if he wanted to fall away, she would not let him.

"I'm flying," he muttered, and for a brief instant he thought he'd said, *I'm fleeing*.

"Nasty bastards, foxlions. They carry something in their spit that stops blood clotting. Helps them drink from their prey easier. You say you were scratched, not bitten?"

Nox only nodded. To elaborate would be to open his story up to scrutiny, and he was not level-headed enough for that.

Lenora frowned. "Hmm. Well there's *something* in there keeping you flowing like a holed goat." She twisted Nox's arm up out of his lap and licked across his wounds, slowly, her tongue fat and grey. She cleared a path through his blood, glanced up at him, smiling grotesquely. "Tasty," she said.

Nox looked away, unnerved. He had often seen Krotes blooding themselves after a battle—had done so himself—but he had only ever heard of cannibalism second-hand. *The immortal ones do it*, Serville had told him one drunken evening. *Those that came back from Noreela with the mages. They never die, so it doesn't matter if they're eating infected flesh, drinking bad blood. Imagine being like that...*

"Strange," Lenora said. She turned Nox's arm this way and that, examining the wounds. They began to seep and Nox was certain she was going to lick them again, and he was not sure he could stand it, that sandpaper tongue scraping across the pouting lips of his gashed arm—

"What?" he said, trying to draw her attention. "What's strange?"

"Something in there," she said, running her tongue around her mouth. "Gritty. We'd best get you where you were going, what do you say?"

Forever

Nox nodded, and his gratitude and relief were not feigned.

Lieutenant Lenora—allegedly immortal and over a hundred years old already—swung his right arm around her shoulders and held him upright. His feet could only just touch the floor, such was her height, but to begin with it seemed not to matter. She walked quickly towards the harbour, a path clearing naturally before her, and for a few seconds Nox began to believe his own lie. A few Krotes glanced at them, and he saw admiration in their expressions. Wounded in battle, he thought, and he wanted to tell them about the foxlion he had fought and defeated. But of course there had been no foxlion, there had been only his knife. And if Lenora asked again to smell the vanquished beast's blood on his sword, then his ruse was over.

He looked down at his feet trailing across the dirty ice. *Did I really believe I could get away?*

Yes, he had. And he may yet.

They reached the harbour, and Nox suggested that he walk himself to the hospital barge. "It's not fit for a warrior to be carried into hospital," he said. "Not unless he's missing legs and arms. Then, maybe, there's no shame in having a lift."

Lenora smiled and set him down, and Nox knew that he had impressed her. That was good. Perhaps it would ensure that she would ask no more about his foxlion-blooded sword.

"You're a brave Krote," she said.

"I'm surprised you even knew me, Sir."

Lenora raised her eyebrows. "I'm a Lieutenant. You think it's my duty to not know those under my command?"

"Of course not, Sir. It's just that you've never called me by name before."

"I never had cause to. You never impressed me before." She stared frankly at him, her eyes intelligent and filled with the cool threat of imminent violence.

Nox smiled weakly, and his genuine pain and faintness helped him on his way. "I hope this will not be the last time," he said.

Lenora laughed and clapped him on the shoulder, sending him staggering sideways into a mound of fishing baskets piled on the breakwater. She stepped after him and held him steady, still laughing.

"I'm sure it won't," she said. "When the time comes and we sail to Noreela, I expect you to be at the head of your troop. There'll be plenty of blood to spill there. Plenty of Noreelan women to be stung by your sword. The wait for revenge is cold, but its fulfilment is hot as blood."

Nox forced himself to smile. *Maybe I'll even be living in Noreela then*, he thought. How ironic that would be. "And when will that be?" he said. Asking questions like this was usually frowned upon, but he seemed to have gained Lenora's respect. And, truth be told, the idea that he may well be away from this place and on his way to freedom by nightfall made him more daring.

Lenora raised her eyebrows. "Keen, are we?"

"Of course," Nox said, suddenly afraid that he had gone too far.

Forever

"Good. That's good, Krote. Because whenever the mages call on us, we need to be ready to make them proud." She turned to walk away, and through his queasiness Nox felt a warming sense of relief. And then she turned back to him. "Magic," she said. "That's what they await, the re-emergence of magic. When the time comes they'll want it, and isn't that right? Isn't it proper that those who used magic to its full extent before should have it for themselves?"

"Of course," Nox said. "Yes."

Lenora glanced around at the bustling harbour-front, leaned in close, whispered in his ear. He smelled her breath—cool, stale, like a ruptured air pocket in a shifting glacier—and he could not help but draw back.

"They still have it, you know," she said. "Not true magic, but means. Methods. Knowledge. They know more than we can imagine. Now…here…they probably even know that we're together. They can see us. They'll smell us. And when I say this to you—when I tell you that the mages are your gods, and any god you betray will give you an eternity of pain—then they hear what I say. You hear, Mistress? You hear, Master?" Lenora stared into Nox's eyes as if looking way deeper than her own reflection. "Oh yes," she whispered. "They hear." And then she turned and walked away.

Nox watched her go. Faint from loss of blood, sick with terror, he waited until she was out of sight on the harbourside. Then he turned and started to make his way to the hospital barge. It was almost half a mile away along the breakwater. Every step of that journey, he imagined the mages watching.

Tim Lebbon

When he was twenty-eight, Nox fell in love.

She was another Krote, a warrior from a troop stationed at a remote village way along the coast. When they visited Newland to attend a training exercise run by the mages themselves, Lucie caught Nox's eye. Hours after first introducing himself he was screwing her behind a storage hut on the harbour-front, and hours after that he knew that this was something different. She did not seem to realise, but his devoted attention was for more than the physical, his comments to her over the next few days held far more substance than simple sex-talk. They screwed every night and fought every day, but when they returned to their barracks—bloodied, exhausted, confident as ever in their abilities to fight for the mages—Nox would always fall in step with Lucie. She would smile at him hungrily, and he would smile back, silent, unable to speak, painfully aware of her presence, her warmth, her smell. Her talk was of the day they had spent slaughtering slaves brought in from the north and given ice-swords to spar with; his own words sang her praise. Lucie heard nothing of it, or if she did, she smothered it with her sexual abandon.

Nox could not tell her what he felt. Love encouraged weakness and gave its victims over to mindlessness. Though not punishable, those who claimed love were often sent away to live in the northern mountains for a year or more. If they returned, they invariably found their way back to normality. If not, then their love was frozen into infinity along with their weak flesh.

One night, as she lay sleeping after sex, Nox laid his head beside Lucie's and whispered into her ear. "It can't always be like this," he said. "We can escape. You and I, we'll go away. There must be somewhere I can tell you the truth." She stirred and uttered a dreaming growl, and Nox turned onto his back and sought sleep.

Behind him, beneath the skins insulating them from the icy ground, a worm the size of a thumb squirmed its way northward. It had listened. It had heard. It had not understood, but knowledge was not its purpose, only delivery of what it had heard to the mages. The tone of voice it had been programmed to find had been here. The intent it was made to discover was evident in the man's voice, his words, the way he breathed and sweated and finally slept.

The worm's journey to the mages' redoubt took almost a year. That did not matter; a year was nothing. And once its message was delivered, its reward was Angel's teeth tearing it in half for the cool juice of its insides.

—⚇—

The hospital barge was far from refined. It was a large coastal sloop, stripped bare of its superstructure and covered by a simple timber and animal skin roof. It had glassless windows, a few doors, a couple of chimneys smoking lazily in the still afternoon air. Inside there was no pretension to comfort. Those that came here always left very soon after, either back on their feet again, or dragged to the end of the breakwater and given to the carrion creatures that lived in the cold sea. There was never a long stay; once wounded or taken ill, patients would either recover quickly to fight again, or they were no longer of use. There was as much treatment by the sword as by medicine.

Nox stepped onto the barge. He paused for a second, glanced down at his bleeding arm, felt the slight shifting of the boat beneath his feet. And here he was, once step closer to freedom.

Several medics glanced up as he went inside, but none of them rose to aid him. He was walking, his wound looked minor, and the pride of a warrior was precious. He found himself a bed—only a few were occupied—and sat down heavily. Closing his eyes, he could not decide whether his queasiness was due to the boat's movements, or his own blood loss.

"Cut yourself shaving?" a medic asked.

Nox glanced up at her and smiled. "Argument with a foxlion."

The woman raised her eyebrows, mildly impressed, and held his arm. "How long ago?"

"This morning."

"Should have stopped bleeding by now. You look pale. I'll have to flush the foxlion's poison from the wounds." She paused and looked Nox in the eye. "It'll hurt."

"I didn't expect anything less."

As the medic went to gather some equipment, Nox looked around at the few other patients. Most of them sat on their beds or lay propped up, conscious and alert, eager to leave as soon as possible. A few were prone, moaning softly in whatever sleep had taken them. One of them was dead. Blood pooled under their bed, and Nox could see a chipped sword glistening nearby. One more free meal for the sea creatures.

When the medic returned Nox felt a sudden stab of fear and doubt. He began to wonder whether his plan had held

Forever

any sanity after all, or whether the cold had finally driven him mad.

"Lay down," she said.

Nox did not move. "Are you sure?"

She smiled, but it held little humour. "Scared, Krote?"

Nox shook his head, lay down and held out his arm.

The medic was right. It hurt.

Later, at night, in the quiet, Nox kept himself awake. The medic had given him a chemicala powder to help him sleep and regain his strength, but he had retained it beneath his tongue and spat it out when she left. Dregs of it had found its way into his system. Shadows of sleep crowded in. But every few minutes he tensed his dressed arm, and the pain brought him back.

His wounds were flushed and had stopped bleeding, but the process had hurt more than putting them there in the first place.

The hospital barge was never completely quiet. There were a few snores from his fellow patients, and one of them moaned in her sleep, haunted by sleep demons. Nox was glad of this. He used a heavy snore as cover for sitting up. When a man cried out in his sleep, Nox stood from his cot. When the nightmaring woman muttered some ancient curse at whatever troubled her, he paced quickly to the windows and moved a curtain aside. The harbour was much quieter than during the day, but there was still movement here and there, torches flaring along the breakwater, shadows slipping through shadows. He had always known that there would be people around, but his plan was brazen enough to have a chance. Or so he thought. If he was wrong, then he would be dead by dawn. Floating in the icy seas. Fodder for the carrion creatures cruising its dark depths.

"Never seen the mages!" someone cried out, and Nox froze. Moonlight cast his shadow back into the barge. Anyone opening their eyes would see him silhouetted against the starlight, but there were no more words. It had sounded like the woman. Perhaps it was the mages that haunted her sleep.

Nox lifted himself slowly onto the window sill and stepped outside. The edge of the barge was just wide enough to walk around, but any missed footing would send him into the water. That would be the end of him. Night was a time for foxlions. How ironic it would be to fall victim to one now.

He worked his way to the end of the barge and back up onto the breakwater. At its very tip were moored some old fishing sloops. They had been there for years, and their ragged sails and abandoned appearance had planted the seed of his plan. He would steal one, sail it away from Newland and Dana'Man, never trying to hide. If anyone glanced out at the moonlit scene they would see a sailing boat heading confidently out to sea. They would assume that there was nothing wrong and go back to sleep. Or, they would raise the alarm and follow his stolen boat with a hail of arrows and bolts.

The more he thought about his plan, the more Nox realised how crazy he was. But in a way that gave him comfort, because it was that very craziness that would offer his greatest chance of success. No one had ever heard of a

Forever

Krote escaping the mages' island. No one had ever heard of anyone even *trying*. And the simple reason was that it was suicide. Even if they could escape, to truly be free of the mages' influence they would have to sail a thousand miles south to Noreela.

Standing at the end of the breakwater, Nox looked out at the dark sea that would be his home for the next few weeks. He planned to fish for food and gather rainwater to drink. A thousand miles...

No, he thought, *I can do it. It will work! It's so simple and foolish and impossible, it* has *to work*. He climbed down a rusted ladder onto the deck of one of the boats, untied its mooring ropes, used a paddle to shove it away from the breakwater, hoisted the sail, held the tiller and smiled as a breath of wind seemed to rise from nowhere, helping him on his way to freedom. *The breath of fate*.

And he was right. Fate breathed down his neck that night.

When he was thirty-five, Nox took part in a raid on a settlement to the north. The Krotes knew of the ice people, bands of rovers that wandered across the snow fields, killed birds for food, eking out a sparse existence. They were undeveloped, wild people, all but cultureless, spending every minute of their waking time embroiled in a battle of survival against the elements. The one talent they did possess was speed. It could have been due to their long legs, grown strong and thin over time to enable them to step through deep snow. Or maybe it was a gift borne of the need to flee the many predators that hunted them for food. Whatever the cause, it provided for excellent target practise for Krote crossbows.

The fight was ferocious. The surface of the glacier was left stained red with the blood of the ice people, redder than any blood the Krotes had ever seen, and the few that escaped became an enjoyable distraction for the next couple of hours. Nox and his companions followed the escapees through the snow, using refined skills of tracking and stalking that had been honed through many other such hunts. The ice people knew their territory well; they were adept at hiding; they could blend in with the snow-scape, so pale was their skin. But they were no match for the Krotes, and in truth it was simply sport.

Nox ran down one ice woman, finally bringing her legs from under her with a bolt to the back of the knee. He stood over her, panting, watching her blood seep into the snow and turn it a deep red. She stared up at him, rapid breaths condensing in the air and floating across the glacier like frozen screams. She spoke, but he did not know her language. He decided to slit her stomach open and let her insides out. A slow, cruel way to kill her. But she had led him on a long chase and now he was sore and tired, and his blood was up.

For a second as he bent down, the idea flashed across his mind that this was wrong.

He glanced at the woman's face and was amazed at the change there. She had gone from terrified to enraged, fearful to ferocious. Shock made him plunge his sword into her chest. She gasped, arched her back, and he pushed harder, twisting the handle and feeling ribs snap under the pressure.

She hissed blood. He did not know the words but their meaning was clear. He could see the hate in her eyes.

Forever

Nox withdrew the sword and brought it down onto her neck, severing her head. Then he stood and walked away.

The woman died. Her wraith rose up, colder than the freezing wastes that had been her home. And using a talent that the Krotes would never know, she looked into her killer's mind and saw his greatest, most secret wish.

And she knew how vengeance could be hers.

Leaving the bloody wreck of her body behind, the ice woman's wraith drifted south with a message for the mages.

—⚉—

They let him think he had escaped.

He spent that whole night at the tiller, sailing hard, aware of every boat length he put between himself and Dana'Man. His whole life was falling behind, and he felt nothing for it. No loss, no sadness, no sense of the version of himself he was leaving. Ahead, in the dark, the promise of something new loomed like the sun waiting to rise. The weight of all his bad deeds sailed with him, but they were lighter by the second. It was as if putting distance between himself and the mages was also diluting the evils he had performed at their behest.

And then as the sun peered over the horizon, he heard the screech of something diving down from above. Even before Nox had turned to look, the voice came down to slaughter all his hopes and dreams.

"Going somewhere?" Lenora shouted.

He thought to reach for his sword. But how could he fight this flying thing? The hawk was huge, tentacles trailing as it plummeted, wicked curved beak catching the first rays of sunlight. It would crush him.

The creature pulled up short and hovered above his head. The stink of its exhausts thrust down at him, billowing the boat's sails and forcing him to his knees, retching. When he looked up again he saw who else rode the beast's back…and hope left him forever, purged by the sight of the mage.

"Mistress Angel wants your help!" Lenora shouted down.

Nox could only stare, hands limp by his side, unable to tear his gaze away from this sorceress. Though bereft of magic for a century still she exuded malevolence, a sense of dread like sweat seeping from her pores. She was beautiful, but awful to behold. She looked down on him without expression. Lifeless. And he wished for all the world that she would speak, because her silence was most terrifying of all.

"Will you help?" Lenora said.

"You're toying," Nox said. "Just kill me and get it over with."

"*Kill* you?" Lenora said. "Of course not, Nox. What a waste!"

Nox could not begin to imagine the punishment he would receive.

He reached quickly for his sword. He would drag the keen blade across his own throat and gasp one last bloody laugh at this mage. Perhaps a century ago she would have been able to torture his departed soul, but now in a magic-less world dead was dead.

Goodbye, he thought.

Forever

The crossbow bolt passed clean through his palm. He dropped the sword and it fell into the ocean with hardly a splash.

"No," Angel said, her voice like a rumble in the ocean depths.

Lenora whistled and the hawk came down, its claws outstretched, and grabbed Nox from the boat. Its talons passed through his thigh and shoulder and he screamed, the mage's laughter a ghastly accompaniment.

"Mistress Angel *demands* your help!" Lenora shouted. The hawk rose swiftly, and Nox saw his own blood spattering the deck of the boat. Part of him may find freedom, at least.

—⚬—

The hawk rose high and flew fast, and Nox's petty attempt to flee was belittled by the short time it took them to reach Newland.

He hung from the creature's talons trying not to scream, weathering the pain, certain that there would be far worse to come. Pain is imaginary, he had been told. Control it as you control your imagination. But the feel of the thick talons scraping against his bones was real enough, and each change in direction brought a screech from his throat. Above him, out of sight on the hawk's back, Angel's Lieutenant laughed every time.

"Where are we going?" Nox asked. There was no answer, and he was not surprised. The mage would not deign talk to him unless she so desired. And when she did, it would doubtless be to tell him of some awful fate.

From high up, Nox saw that Newland was deserted. The usually bustling harbour had been left to the bobbing boats and scavenging sea birds, and the only movement in the barrack fields was the flutter of flags. *Where has everyone gone?* he thought. *And why?*

As if passing from above sea to land was a signal, one of the hawk's huge tentacles suddenly whipped around his waist. Its claws uncurled and Nox screamed as he was tugged from them. He struggled and tried to fall, but the tentacle held him tight, crushing his stomach and lifting him up, depositing him in the saddle on its back. The hawk let go, but Nox could not move. Before him, Lenora held the reins and guided the creature inland. And behind him, her breath hot on his neck, her presence like a hole that could swallow him up, Angel.

"I've known for years that you would flee," Angel whispered. Her voice was a shard of ice penetrating his skull. "My brother and I have been watching, waiting. We decided a long time ago that we'd make an example of you."

"Why?" Nox said, having to shout into the air disturbed by the hawk's flight. Angel's voice did not sound raised at all, and yet he heard her words clear and heavy.

"Because we wished it," Angel said. She rested her hand on his wounded shoulder and squeezed gently. "You have no friends, Nox. They've betrayed you. You have no comrades or lovers on your side. No one. You're quite unique. The others that try to escape we simply kill. Cut up. Eat. But time is moving on, things change. I want everyone to see what happens to you."

Nox pressed his hands flat against the saddle and pushed hard. He would tumble to the side and fall away, and for

Forever

every second of his descent he would relish those last few moments of freedom. But Angel's hand pressed him down, she whispered, "No," and Lenora whistled to the hawk to begin its descent.

"We're not warriors!" Nox shouted, directing his words at Lenora. To address the mage was too terrifying. "We're slaves! No better than the fodder we eat, the slaves we capture and kill. Lenora! What will this gain you?"

Lenora did not answer, but Angel did.

"You're right," she said. "The slaves we control with chemicala, you Krotes with promises and fear. You're all slaves to us."

Lenora laughed, her shoulders shook, and Nox looked down.

They were descending rapidly, and now he could see long columns of people marching up through the snow. There were thousands down there, all of Newland making its way into the mountains. A few Krote pennants waved shadows onto the snow. He wondered where his own troop would be, and whether any of them would care.

Nox suddenly felt his fear transmuting into something else. Not hope, nothing so limitless. But peace. He realised that Angel was helping him on his way. However terrible his manner of death, once gone he would be beyond the mages' reach.

"I'll still escape," he said, and Angel's hand left his shoulder.

"I'm sure you're right," she said, and Nox felt her smiling. "Even I can't see forever."

They landed on the glacier. It was a bright morning, no snow showers, and the cold air was sharp and clear. There were already a thousand Krotes and slaves there, huddled around hastily lit fires, cooking fish, drinking, already entering into something of a festival atmosphere. *And why not?* Nox thought. *They're here to see a killing, and killing is what they love.*

Lenora slipped down the side of the hawk. The assembled throng grew silent, watching her. She looked up at Nox and motioned him down.

"Don't make me come up there and get you," she said quietly.

Nox considered the weapons he carried. His sword was gone, but he still had throwing spikes, the slide-shock on his belt, maces strung along both legs. He could surely reach them before Lenora made it back onto the hawk, but Angel still sat behind him. And even if the mage did nothing to prevent him—he guessed she may enjoy the sport of seeing Lenora and him enter into combat—Lenora herself was more than his match.

At least it would be an honourable death.

He fell sideways, right hand reaching to his belt for a throwing spike, left held out to roll himself across the hard packed snow. He saw Lenora tense, and then smile, and then he felt a hand close around his ankle.

Angel stood on the hawk's back and held him high. He drew back his own hand, throwing spike ready.

He heard the familiar whistle before the slide-shock snapped off three of his fingers at the second knuckle. The

Forever

crowd cheered and Lenora grinned. Nox screamed, instantly ashamed at his pain.

"Here he is," Angel said. "The escapee! He didn't get far. Noreela is that way, Krote!" She swung him southward and jerked him back, blood from his fingers spattering a line across the glacier.

"We're all slaves!" Nox shouted, but the crowed cheered and jeered, and he wondered where he had ever found hope.

"My brother and I are slaves also," Angel said, and the shouting suddenly ceased. She dropped Nox to the ice and jumped down, feet landing either side of his head. He could see her mottled skin, smell her age, sense the power she still possessed. "Slaves to the magic that tore itself from us. Slaves to this place, our banishment. Slaves to revenge."

"Kill him!" someone shouted. Other voices rose in support. Nox turned and scanned the assembled crowd of Krotes for a familiar face, but they were all strangers to him now. He had left them less than a day before but already he no longer belonged. He had changed.

"Bless you," Angel said, as if talking to a thousand children. "Death is all you know." She reached down and gathered Nox to her chest, lifting him as easily as she would a baby.

Nox stared up at her face. Was she growing? Was he shrinking? He should be able to move, to struggle and fight. But each message he sent his limbs was translated into another pathetic whimper from his mouth. *Just let it end,* he thought. *Please, just kill me.* The mage glanced down, smiling as if hearing his thoughts.

"Lenora!" Angel shouted. "You know what to do."

Nox did not see, but he heard. The hawk shifted on the ice, clumsy out of the air. Its great feet crashed down, once, twice, three times. And then came a blast of heat, a gasp from the crowd, and clouds of steam formed an unnatural mist around them.

"All ready, Mistress."

"All ready," Angel echoed, looking down at Nox. "Betrayer," she whispered. She looked up again at the ever-growing crowd.

"This is a warning," she said, her voice carrying across the slope. "Anyone who tries to flee my brother and I will suffer a similar fate, or something worse. We may not have magic, but we still have knowledge. Ways and means. And chemicala. This is Nox! See him alive now! And see him live forever."

Angel dropped Nox to the ice and straddled his chest. Her long hair fell to either side of her face and there, hidden from the crowd, he saw her true madness for the first time. Her eyes glowed with something more than reflected sunlight. Her mouth hung open, tongue lolling, and her lips were twisted into a grotesque sneer. "Have this," she said, forcing a pellet of something into his mouth. "And this." She thrust a knife through his clothes and into his chest just above the heart. He whined and tried to jerk himself upward, urging the blade to penetrate further, but Angel withdrew the knife and probed inside his clothing, pressing something cold and hard into the wound.

She sat back and punched him in the face. His jaw slammed shut on the pellet and crushed it, releasing a foul-tasting fluid across his tongue.

"Put him in," Angel said, standing and stepping away.

Forever

Lenora approached, walking slowly. The crowd started to roar again, but their voices rose as if from miles away, starting low and deep and building relentlessly to a climax that never came. Looking up, Nox saw fresh snowflakes hanging in the air above him, just hanging.

What is this? he thought.

"I will see you again," Angel said. And her words sounded forever.

—⚜—

They buried him in the glacier.

Lenora had formed a cavern deep down, just large enough for Nox to lay out flat or stand up. The ice they piled in above him was melted with a blast of chemicala heat. The whole process seemed to take days. Lenora moved so slowly, and Nox never saw those snowflakes land.

His mind…that kept its speed.

Inside the glacier was not a silent place. It growled. It roared. Every few years, it moved. And when the sun hit it just right, on the last day of winter each year, its ancient ice glowed like unending fields of green.

Nox spent the first century trying to relive his dreams.

Old Light

In the beginning, I turned away.

I'm not sure why. I'm normally a helpful person, compassionate, and the sight of a man in such a state would usually urge me to aid him as much as I could. He was injured, though still alive; the twitch of an eyelid, a foot moving in circles as if dreaming a dance. Before I realised what I was doing I was back on the pavement, seven steps and a lifetime of guilt separating me from the prone figure.

Perhaps it was the shock of what I had seen. Walking along the canal the last thing I expected to come across was someone lying across the towpath, apparently bleeding to death. Maybe it was the sight of flies buzzing him. Or perhaps subconsciously I had already realised the danger. He exuded strangeness like the warmth of a dying breath. I must have picked up on that long before my morals kicked in.

Even then I did not return straight away. I looked around for help, but there was none to be had. The countryside was quiet, its solitude broken only by the bleating of new-born lambs and the mournful cries of a single buzzard circling high overhead. I wondered where its mate had gone, and whether it regarded this man as a possible source of carrion.

Standing at the top of the steps leading to the towpath, I was suddenly certain that the man would be gone. When I skirted the wild undergrowth and reached the level of the canal once more there would be nothing there; no body, no blood, no promise of pain. I would be left with the fact of my hallucination, but I would rather live with that than be marked by this stranger's blood and problems. And then there was that guilt again, flicking at my memories with its stale breath. I would much rather be without the guilt.

If he *had* been an hallucination, should I still feel remorseful for turning away? The thought troubled me, as if someone else were thinking it.

I went back down to the towpath. The man was very old. His forehead was badly gashed and bruised, and I saw the splash of blood on the rock he must have hit when he fell. But it was the weirdness of this fallen man that shuffled my thoughts, and fear was yet another consequence of my shock.

He was foreign, perhaps Eastern European, and his clothing set him aside. I had never seen clothing like that beyond a movie screen. His trousers were of sackcloth, rough and snagged, held up by a belt of rough animal skin. His shirt was colourful and bright, even though it was obviously aged and weathered. Cuts here, rips there, all of them added to the garment's mystique. I could see no bottle, but I was already certain that he was not a drunk. Nearby on the towpath a long, heavy coat lay like a slaughtered shadow, arms askew,

Old Light

the material so strange that I could not place it. Not cotton, not wool, it reminded me most of rough elbow skin.

The man coughed. His eyes sprang open and fixed right on me, as if he already knew I was there. He smiled.

I stepped back. There was so much blood on his face, and his smile looked fearsome. Something scurried in the bushes beside the towpath and I turned, ready to face whatever came out. Perhaps it was a wild animal drawn by the smell of blood; a rat, a fox. But it was only a bird startled by my movement.

The man was still smiling at me. Ridiculously I smiled back, having no idea what else to do. He was bleeding copiously from the head. It can't have been more than a few minutes since he had fallen.

"Here," he said, "take this." He sat up awkwardly, swaying. He looked so *old*. I thought of broken ribs or crushed hips, but there was little I could do about that right now. He held up a long object wrapped in an oily cloth, and beckoned me over with a tilt of his head.

I obeyed. It was that or turn and run, and I could not allow that a second time.

"Lie still," I said, "don't move, I'll go and get help."

"Hmph!" He tried to laugh, but it descended into more coughing. He looked up at the trees and down at the canal. "I'll be fine. My time's not just yet." His voice was heavily accented and distorted by pain, but still I understood every word.

"What happened?" I asked.

"I fell. I'm tired. I've been looking for weeks."

"I don't understand. Looking for what?"

"For you, Alex Norfan. Take it. You'll understand."

"I...I don't think I can."

"You must!" His vehemence brought on more coughing, and blood dropped from his nose onto the ground between his knees. "This is no simple trinket," he whispered, trying to remain calm.

"It's not mine," I said, unable to ask what I was really thinking: *Why was he looking for me?*

"It is, it is." Still he proffered the object.

"What is it?"

"The future," he said. "It's been mine for so long, and now you're the last of the line, so it's yours. It's from the old castle in the Carpathians...haunted, haunted by miracles from the past..." He closed his eyes. He looked so pale, so ready to die, and suddenly so familiar. The shape of his brow, the curve of his cheek, the hook nose. I put my hand to my own face, and wondered.

"But—"

"Alex Norfan? Orfanik?" the man said, and he must have seen the reaction that name inspired in me. "There are more things than you know," he continued. "You're a man open to mystery, yes? To exploration? And I came here for you, because this is yours by birthright."

I shook my head to dislodge the strangeness, but it only tangled it more. "I need to get you to a hospital."

"I've never been to one all my life, and I will not start now. It can do me no good. Now take this, curse you!"

I held out my hand and touched the thing he was offering. It was cold, even through the rag.

"I don't want it—"

"Don't you want to know...about when...you will die...?"

Old Light

"What?"

The man seemed to sink back into himself, as if shrivelling by the second. The flow of blood lessened and he lay back down as if to sleep.

"The future…" the man whispered, and I had to lean in close. "I saw the future in a beam of light. That tree! That bird! That smell and sound! Now…"

He died. One second he was there, the next he was nothing but a ruined heap of flesh, blood, bone. I stepped away. The canal fell silent but for the calling of the buzzard high in the sky. It had drifted away above the fields, as if the man's death had ended the bird's interest.

The corpse's arm was still raised. The weight of his offering should have dragged it to the ground. There was so much wrong here that I expected him to rise up at any moment, confound me some more. But he remained motionless, the arm raised, forbidding me to leave without at least looking at the object he held.

I snatched it away, and his arm sank slowly to the ground.

I should report this, I thought, *I should tell someone*. But there was more to this than normality could bear; the canal and the woods surrounding it were painted with a bizarre hue, as if the man's final exhalation had landed everywhere.

I had always known the presence of mystery. And now I would find it for sure.

Inside the oily rag lay a torch.

Tim Lebbon

I fled the scene of death and ran into the woods, clutching the torch to my chest with one hand. I had yet to switch it on.

Birds called out, ruffled by my crashing through the woods. I made no attempt to keep quiet.

I've been looking for weeks…for you, the dead man had said. I must have misheard him. I had only decided to walk here this morning, and even then I had almost changed my mind.

I dodged between trees, keeping to rough paths which dog-walkers had trodden into the woods over the years. I met no one. If I had, perhaps I would have said something about the body on the canal path. Or perhaps not. There was something so otherworldly about what had happened that I had already set it aside from earthly concerns.

I tripped and fell, gasping as the wind was knocked from me. Kneeling up, assessing my bruises and scrapes, I realised that I had dropped the torch. It had rolled, shedding the oily rag like a snake's skin, and fetched up beneath a bank of brambles. The thick carpet of pine needles pricked at my hands and knees as I forced my way beneath the bushes. I winced as thorns pricked my shoulders and scalp. The torch lay tantalisingly close, yet however hard I stretched I could not quite reach it. I had a choice: leave it for a while and try to find something with which to haul it out; or force my way into the thorny bush, and accept the pain that would entail.

I thought of the dead man, his bleeding head, his comments that I was open to mystery.

I pushed into the bush.

Old Light

The torch was cool in my hands, heavy, a weight in the world that should surely not exist. As I sat beneath the tree in my back garden, turning the item back and forth in my hands, I realised that the dead old man was right. There were more things…*always* more things, more than anyone could ever know.

Either the torch was a brilliant forgery, or it had been made hundreds of years ago. Its shell was beautifully wrought in iron, patterned with swirls of flowers and strange sigils which could have been letters, or pictures representing letters. Running my fingers over these designs I could almost feel time inlaid in them, cast into their patterns like air bubbles trapped in metal. They spoke of ages passed, and though there were no revelations here, the weight of the torch's age was obvious.

I opened the end. It unscrewed easily, as though it had been made yesterday. *Such craftsmanship*, I thought, *such care, none of that nowadays.* As I tilted the torch and looked inside, time whispered around me. It flowed through the tree, leaves kissing though there was no breeze. It ruffled the grass, shifted the air around my garden, as if to gain a better view of whatever I was about to see. The world had shrugged in defeat at something it sought to hide.

"Maybe it's all true." Silence was my only answer as nature withheld its secrets.

Inside the torch was a battery. It had the appearance of granite inlaid with large buttons of quartz. It was fixed, not replaceable, bound in by thin strips of twisted steel. If this was truly that old…

"It *can't* be true." But inside, I knew that I had been living my life as a lie. The dead man had sought me out, spoken that mysterious name, and given me this weird and wonderful creation for a reason. I knew the story of the Castle of the Carpathians, and my own alleged common ancestry with the fictional inventor. But now, sitting and holding this torch, readying myself to turn it on and see what it would reveal, I tried the name in my mouth.

"Orfanik."

It sounded so familiar.

I did not switch on the torch that evening. It rested by my bed as I tried to sleep, and in those dark hours strange dreams visited me, whether nightmares or oddities of my waking mind I could not tell. I saw flashes outside the uncurtained window, though the sky was bare of clouds. They forked across the glass again and again, and I began to believe that they were inside the room. I tried to close my eyes but still I saw them, blood-red wounds etched against my inner-eyelids.

I remembered my father telling me these tales when I was a teenager, handing me Verne's classic novel to read, and the weird feeling I had upon finishing it. "It's only a story," I said to him, and he smiled and nodded, then shook his head. "There's always doubt," he replied. His appearance changed to that of the dead man with his severe Slavic looks, and in my dream their faces were not dissimilar. The dead man spoke to me again, and though I could not hear the words I knew that he was angry at my doubt.

Old Light

You're a man open to mystery, yes? a voice said from the dark. I nodded in my sleep, shook myself awake, not sure whether the owner of the voice was actually there.

I reached for the torch to find out.

The beam of light that sprang out shocked me. I had not expected the old torch to work. My surprise set the beam quivering across the walls, furniture and reflecting from the window, and I rested my hand on my raised knee to keep the torch steady. There was something about the beam and what it revealed, as if this old battery made old light.

There was a spider on the wall, a huge wolf spider, its legs curled up to its body in death. I shifted the torch and sensed sudden movement in the dark, aiming it back at the spider again. Light passed across the window.

There was someone outside. Someone with a melting face.

I shouted and dropped the torch. It struck the floor and blinked off, leaving the bedroom in darkness. I closed my eyes for several terrifying seconds, letting them adjust to the dark again before opening them to stare at the window. I could see nothing, and somehow I reined in my fear long enough to go and close the curtains.

"Orfanik." I whispered that name again, the fictional character whom my father had often claimed to be real. "Orfanik, what have you made this time?"

I retrieved the torch and hid it beneath a pillow. Come daylight, I would see if it was still working. But not now.

Sleep eluded me as images of the melted face combined with my memories of the dying man. They were not the same, and yet surely they were linked.

At least my imagination was making me believe so.

Tim Lebbon

As dawn broke the darkness, I was still sitting on my bed, aware of the weight of the torch lying beside me. Daylight bled some of the fear, and my conviction that I had had a supernatural experience faded away. There was an explanation for what I had seen, I was convinced of that. Orfanik has supposedly been an inventor, not a conjuror, and whatever the torch had shown me had been through science, not super-science.

I opened the curtains quickly, jumping back as a huge spider scurried away behind them. Maybe it had just been asleep.

As the sun poured in I mused on the speed of light. Outside there were still a few stars fighting the dawn, and I wondered whether they were even still there. I was seeing them as they had been thousands, even millions of years ago. As a child the prospect of travelling faster than light, then looking back and seeing *myself*, had disturbed me greatly. It knocked me from the centre of things, which is where every child believes itself to be, and it was that more than my realisation of death that marked the point when I started growing up.

And now light was playing with me again.

I decided to return to the canal to find the dead man. Even as a corpse, he could have answers.

Old Light

The man was gone. I was not really surprised. What did surprise me was the total lack of evidence that he had ever been there. No blood soaked into the towpath, no impression in the grass, no barriers, tape or fences erected by police.

Here was yet another mystery. This weekend seemed rich with them.

I started walking along the towpath, the torch heavy in my pocket. I had yet to turn it on again, although the chance of it being broken seemed remote. It was old. If it had been made by Orfanik (and acceptance of my ancestry had come without my being able to identify the point at which doubt turned to belief), then it was hundreds of years old. Unlikely—hell, impossible!—but still there it was, hanging in my trousers and banging against my leg with each step.

I saw the future in a beam of light. The dying man's words rang inside my head, and I thought of the brief image of the face I had seen outside my bedroom window. I shook my head. Light glinted from the surface of the canal and blinded me for a few seconds, and when I looked at the woods the world had changed. Of course it had. It changes every instant.

I took out the torch, bent down and found a snail crawling along a twig.

I turned on the torch. The circle of yellow light was weak in the daylight, but it was still there. I lifted and lowered it, pleased that the light behaved as it should. Then I moved it over the snail.

Instantly the snail's body vanished leaving a hollowed, brittle shell behind. It was holed, probably by a bird.

I shifted the torch away and the live snail was still making its way along the twig. Back again, empty shell. Away, live snail.

I was seeing two times. The only question was, just how far apart were they? I could turn off the torch and wait to see when the snail would meet its end…but it may be days or months from now.

Amazed though I was, understanding still seemed to come easily to me. Perhaps it was the open mind handed down from my father, the belief in things we could not see, the acceptance of more things than we could ever know. Or maybe it was the face I had seen in my bedroom window, and the familiarity in its eyes.

I stood and walked away, pocketing the torch once again. Surely it must have its uses. I simply had to figure out what they were.

Back home in my sitting room, I sat in the leather rocker and looked around. All about me were hints to my heritage, yet I had never taken them seriously. A few trinkets my father had bequeathed me; a pocket watch from the last century that ran backward, a voodoo doll supposedly from Haiti, a crystal ball that could fly, or so it was said. Some of the pictures hanging on the walls showed scenes of technological genius from the past; the Wright Brothers on their first flight, Armstrong taking his first steps on the moon. The book-lined walls contained at least a hundred volumes on popular science, and many more on sciences not so well

Old Light

known. I was surrounded by the wonders of discovery and the vicarious pleasures in confounding expectations.

The torch showed time, and the man had wanted me to have it. He must have been a relative, perhaps a distant cousin from Eastern Europe, descended from Orfanik on some distant branch of my wild family tree.

I suddenly felt the need for company. I had become very aware of my own death, and knowing that the flick of a switch may reveal it to me—however far in the future it may be—made me feel very vulnerable.

Outside in the hallway I called Marlene. As I dialled I hoped that she would shed some light on the subject, and I found myself giggling at the literal image.

"Marlene," I said, "I think I'm going mad."

"*Going?*"

"Ha ha. I mean it." There was silence for a while, and I heard her drawing on her ever-present cigarette. She used the time to think.

"Alex, you sound strange," she said. "Seen a ghost?"

"Not exactly. Well…are there ghosts of the future, do you think? Can the dead haunt themselves?"

"Erm…" Another pull on her cigarette. She never had been able to understand the way my mind worked, and that had driven us apart. It was hardly surprising. I barely understood it myself.

"Honey, the last day has changed everything, and I need grounding, I need pulling back down."

"I'm painting for the next hour, but we could meet at Cicero's if you like?"

"That would be good. And Marlene…thanks." Marlene and I had been separated for almost six years. I adored her.

Tim Lebbon

—⚍—

Being outside made me feel better. I had brought the torch with me; perhaps that was a bad idea, but behind all the threat it still felt so precious. Leaving it behind would have felt like denying the point of the journey. I could *tell* Marlene about it, or I could *show* her. And there was a small sense of smugness at her anticipated reaction.

Cicero's was a great little café, and Marlene and I had continued meeting there ever since our break-up. It felt like neutral ground, somewhere we could discard our gripes at the door and sit in the pleasant, informal atmosphere with a latte and a slice of peach cake. After every one of these meetings I hated going outside on my own, feeling the familiar hurt descending again as I glanced back at where Marlene sat inside, waiting for me to leave. There was something calming about Cicero's. Nothing bad ever happened there.

Marlene was waiting in a window seat and she waved as I walked by. I raised the torch in greeting, and her eyes tracked it as I lowered it to my side once again. She looked more worried than interested.

The café was buzzing already, and I had to weave my way between occupied chairs to reach Marlene.

"Hey honey," I said, leaning down to kiss her cheek.

"Hi." She smiled as I sat down, but I could see her gaze drawn again and again to the torch in my pocket. "That it?"

I had not even mentioned the torch to her on the phone, and for a second her question threw me. "What?"

"The cause of all your troubles."

Old Light

I grabbed the coffee menu from the table and scanned the list, even though I had the same drink and cake every single time we came here together. I liked the regularity; it seemed to preserve something of our past, hold back the change.

"You look tired," she said, suddenly sounding truly concerned.

"I am."

"Been up late? Anyone I know?"

I snorted and shook my head.

"You spend too much time thinking about time."

I glanced up at her, surprised yet again at how perceptive she could be. "What do you mean?"

"Dwelling on the past…on us. Thinking about what the future may bring. You should live in the here and now. Every moment is an instant in your life that you can live without worry."

"So when did you become the great psychologist?"

"I'm a painter. I philosophise, I don't psychoanalyse."

"Very droll."

Marlene must have ordered for both of us. The waitress brought over our coffee and cake and we sat silently for a moment, sugaring, pouring cream, enjoying the familiar smells and processes.

"So are you going to tell me what that thing is?"

I took the torch from my pocket and laid it on the table. It looked so old set against the clean, crisp furniture of Cicero's. "What does it look like?"

"It's a torch," Marlene said. "A bit ostentatious, isn't it?"

"That's how they built things two hundred years ago."

She snorted. "Yeah, right."

I did not care about her disbelief. There was no need to persuade her as to the age of this thing, nor even its origins. Once I showed her what it could do, all such doubts would evaporate.

I took a sip of my coffee, looked around at the other people in the café. Hands waved, smiles were given, a dozen stories were being told, and everyone here was unaware of their future. I could shine their fates upon them, but would they really want to know? Would anyone, given the chance, truly wish to know the moment of their death? I doubted it. But being *able* to know would be a terrible temptation.

"What would you do if you knew you were going to die?" I said.

"I *do* know."

She'd seen! She'd seen the torch!

"Everyone dies," Marlene continued. "Most people just don't think about it that much. You're not ill, are you?"

"I don't think so," I said. "But with this, I could find out."

"I thought it was a torch."

I stirred my coffee unnecessarily, watching the bubbles spin on its surface. "You remember me telling you about my father's thoughts on our family heritage? The fact that he connected us with a character in a Jules Verne book?"

"Orfanik," Marlene said.

"Yes, the inventor. A mad genius. He made things that no one understood at the time, but reading the book now it's so easy to see what he was doing. I always thought that was the book's fall-down. It didn't age well."

"But you never believed your father."

Old Light

"Not really, no. But now..." I rolled the torch on the table, back and forth, trying to imagine the source of the power that lay inside.

"You're confusing me," Marlene said, and she hated that. Her confusion over my thoughts and interests is what essentially ended our life together. She did not have a mind receptive to mystery.

"What if you could see your future? What if you could see the moment you were going to die? Would you choose to see it?"

"No."

"Even if you could? Even if seeing might help you prevent it?"

"How could it?"

"I don't know."

I rolled the torch. It grumbled over the table.

"And you think this thing here can show you the future?"

"It shows the moment of your death. Orfanik made it, for whatever strange reasons he had. It found its way to me. And now I have the power—"

"Oh for Heaven's sake!"

"Marlene—"

She snatched up the torch and flicked it on. It slipped from her hands, hit the table and dropped to the floor. And in those couple of seconds, as the beam of light span across the café, I saw two briefly illuminated images of Marlene.

The torch hit the floor and went out.

"*No!*" I stood quickly, knocking over my chair. Heads turned, but Marlene was the only person I could see, the only pair of eyes I could face looking into. Ironic, as I had just seen them melted away by fire. "Oh, no!"

Something in my voice convinced her. Doubt was extinguished, her anger faded, her face paled, and for those few quiet seconds after the disturbance she wanted to know what I had seen. I could see it in her eyes. I shook my head, trying to dislodge the image that had stuck there like a subliminal message.

those flames that scream the cries...

Marlene gasped out loud, stood and fled the café. As the door swung shut behind her I thought, *I'm the one who should be running.* I watched her cross the street and disappear behind a building, waiting for a car to run her down and explode at any second. None came. Her image had been of no definable age. Perhaps we had years left yet, meeting at Cicero's and mourning a past that had not worked out.

Or perhaps I would never see her again.

I snatched up the torch. I had intended following Marlene, but as I left the café I turned in the opposite direction and ran.

—ɯ—

What use was a tool that would let someone see their own death? Why would someone strive to invent such a device? Where would Marlene encounter the fire that would kill her? Had my seeing Marlene's death brought it closer in any way? Had Orfanik used the torch himself? How had it left his possession and found its way through the centuries to

Old Light

me? Was I really related to a fictional character, or was this some cruel cosmic joke?

Sitting in the park, the answers to these questions—and many more besides—eluded me. I ascribed each question to a garden opposite my bench, and watched as bees went from one to another, unable to provide any answers. Time would take these flowers and make them mulch, and in time perhaps my fears and questions would fade as well. But for now—this exact moment, the one instant in life that held greatest importance—all I had were more questions. Soon, I would need to find a larger flower bed.

—⚋—

Guilt took me home and stood me in front of my bathroom mirror.

I held the torch, pointed it up at my face, fingered the button.

I looked into my eyes, seeing myself as no one else ever had.

And like a suicide seeking only attention, I could not go through with the act. If the torch had been a .45 I would have thrown it away then, but it was too precious to damage like that. I lowered it, continued staring into my own eyes, watching the tears form and flow.

I stayed that way for a long time. I cried because I wished my father had known the *truth*, rather than the *myth*. The tears were also for what I had seen of Marlene. I hated the selfishness of that, the thoughtlessness, but I was already grieving for her, even though I still had no idea of when she would meet her horrible death.

Tim Lebbon

In the end the torch slipped from my grasp and fate visited me again. It hit the floor, snapped on and bathed me with its strange light.

I saw through my tears.

Over the next few days I fell in love with Marlene all over again.

I eventually persuaded her to meet me at Cicero's and we sat there for hours, talking about everything except what had happened. I was never sure whether she truly believed that I had seen something, and I did my best to keep the haunting truth from my eyes. I think I succeeded. In all that time, I never saw the shadow of fear cross her face.

We met again a day later, and three times the following week, and the week after that we sat outside at a pavement table. This was a huge step for us, eschewing the neutrality of the café's interior, and it turned the meeting into a date. As I rose to leave Marlene stood up, closed in and kissed me on the lips. It did not surprise either of us, yet my heart paused for long seconds.

I walked away smiling and stepped carelessly into the street, knowing that no car would knock me down. That was not my way.

We take it one day at a time. The image of Marlene's death haunts me still, but there is an unspoken agreement that it will never be mentioned again. Mystery cannot come

Old Light

between us, as it did before. Love holds so much more power over me.

Especially knowing what I know.

Having seen my own old, weathered face wither and bubble in flames, at least I know that we will be together until the end.

Body

Love is...

Lyle had a tattoo of an eye between his shoulder blades. The tattooist had used the tines of a tarantula to prick it through his skin, deep down into the flesh, deep and painful so that it would never, ever fade or be damaged by scarring or sunburn. It was wide-open, all-seeing and all knowing, and it had the same emerald green iris of my own eyes, green with golden flakes. Lyle said the gold was like sheddings from the sun, but I had often thought it more likely to be a vitamin deficiency. In the camp we ate the best food in the land, prepared by the most experienced cooks and served with the finest wines. But luxury was our hosts' main objective, not healthy eating. After all, we were as good as gods.

The eye was green, and it was as big as my hand, and it only ever blinked when Lyle flexed his muscled shoulders hard enough. He never covered it up, even in the cold evenings when the desert heat dissipated to the clear skies and stars hung like frozen snowflakes over the landscape. It was only ever concealed when we made love. I would reach around his back and scratch at it with my nails, smother it with my palms, in a secret attempt to see whether I would feel it as well.

I could not, but I always tried.

Because Lyle said the eye tattoo was of me, and for me. He said that when we were separated at last, it would help him find me in the dark, help me see where he was when I searched. Through the long tunnels of pitch black, the arteries clogged with desperate bodies, the organs where slaughter and birth took place side by side, it would see. So Lyle said. Through the pain of death and the agony of rebirth, it would see.

I knew how much he loved me because they would never let him keep it. When his time came and the pampering and worship was over, the eye would be taken from his back with a hot knife or a boiling splash of iron. The wound would be cleaned, of course, because infection and death would only put rot into the system. But the pain would be exquisite.

Lyle knew this.

Love is blind.

—⁓—

"They're taking Brandon tomorrow." Lyle came into my tent and sat cross-legged on the rug, taking a pipe from his robe and lighting up. The tang of dope hazed the atmosphere and I breathed in deeply. "Did you hear me?"

Body

I nodded. For a second I'd been shocked, but then I always was when it was someone I knew well. "Yes. Brandon. Is he pleased?"

"Wouldn't you be?"

I smiled and waved a hand at him. "Don't play with me, Lyle. You know what I mean."

He puffed again on the pipe, letting out a spiralling cloud of smoke. I crawled across to him and pretended to bite it from the air, breathing in, feeling it tingle my nostrils and only wanting more.

Lyle was looking into my loose robe. "He's been offered the final day's prayers, the cleansing and purification by Jacobus, but he's chosen to leave the camp instead."

"Really? That's...strange."

"Brandon always was, a little."

I took the pipe from Lyle and drew deeply, enjoying his look of fake anger. Brandon would disappear from this world tomorrow. I'd grown up with him in the camp, enjoyed his company, been his friend. The only thing I wanted to do now was to get high.

"You're only jealous," I said. "You know what he thought of me."

"He wanted to screw you, same as everyone in this place. They all want to screw you. But none of them ever will."

"Why should I let them when I have you?" I could feel the dope working already, stretching my senses and sending smoky fingers down my backbone, relaxing bunched muscles and calming my mind. My heartbeat had doubled. I was sweating, and wet.

"Shall we go and watch?" he asked. We *always* watched, he knew that, but perhaps he was just playing along in the game. He could see the look in my eyes and he knew what it meant. Even as I reached out and wormed my hand beneath his robe, grabbing him, squeezing, still he played. "I'd like to say goodbye. Brandon will like it too."

I squeezed once, hard, angry that his attention seemed to have drifted. Then he pushed me over and was on me, in me within seconds, and we lost ourselves and left the camp as free souls the only way we knew how.

It was the same every night, every day. Our love was deep, our lovemaking desperate. And for those few minutes we forgot.

Love blinds.

We went to watch Brandon leave this world, just as Lyle said we would.

There were hundreds of Chosen weaving between the tents and heading for the camp gates. Many of them carried offerings, which they knew would never be allowed. Some of them looked grim, but most smiled, happy in the knowledge that they would be allowed to leave the camp today, at least for a while. Happy too that the future was being brought one soul closer. It's ironic that inside the fence was the nearest place to perfect any of us had ever experienced, yet we all craved time away. Perhaps it was simply a desire to see the truth of things in an attempt to make ourselves feel better.

Lyle and I walked hand in hand. In his other hand he carried a pot of honey. I'd told him that he'd never be able to hand it to Brandon, but he smiled and shook his head. "I

Body

never really believed I could. It's a gesture, it shows we care, and he'll see us all carrying these things."

"But it's such a waste!"

"You really believe any of us will go without because of this?" he asked, and I bit my tongue. I could see his point. These false offerings were just another part of our preparation, another luxury spared us at the expense of everyone else. And besides, Lyle intended it as a reference to us. I never needed reminding of our love, but I'm sure Lyle thought I did. When he licked me, he said I tasted of honey.

The routes between the tents had been baked hard so that the dust was kept to a minimum. The tents were all but permanent, with running water and air extractors worked by hand pumps, the slave pumpers hidden away in holes in the ground, and changed at night when they tired or died. Foodstuffs brought in were imported from across the world, and anything we wanted was given to us. Brandon had once asked for a fillet of fresh sea bass. The sea was a thousand miles in any direction. It took a week, but he got what he wanted, and then threw it away because it hadn't been properly cooked.

In the desert there was never perfection, because nature did not allow it. But we were given the best there was.

When we reached the gates we had to wait while the guards divided us into groups. One guard was assigned to every fifty Chosen. They kept their weapons meekly hidden away, holding their robes around their belts as if trying to hide hard-ons. I enjoyed staring at them, trying to see the weapons, making them uncomfortable. I knew that I was beautiful, and these men—rugged desert types, fighters, mercenaries, instilled with an almost supernatural awe of us Chosen—would find my gaze almost unbearable.

"We're really on the way now," Lyle said, the excitement evident in his voice. I was looking forward to our outing as well. We left the camp once or twice every moon to trail across the desert to the monolith, but each trip felt fresh and new, an adventure in itself. We saw things out there that we weren't allowed inside the camp. Not good things—those were never denied us—but bad things, the *truth* of things. Perhaps that's why we liked these journeys so much… because they told the truth.

And especially at the end, when Brandon was stripped of luxuries and comforts, honour and dignity, truth would be punching us in the face.

It was a walk of several miles to the monolith, but we could see it every day, lived in its shadow for a couple of hours each and every dusk. It didn't block out the horizon, it *was* the horizon. Black, stretching for miles to the north and south, higher at either end than in the middle, swallowing the light, crushing the desert, a constant reminder of why we were here and where we would eventually end up. Many Chosen called it simply *The Answer*. A reminder to the slaves as well, those tens of thousands of workers who were shipped in from around the globe to starve and die, or perhaps to be killed if their blood was required. It was a tomb or a folly, a city or a graveyard, one or the other or all of them depending upon what mood one was in whilst considering it. I had

Body

always seen it as an end of things, like a black hole against reality through which we would all eventually pass.

For every question...*The Answer*.

Lyle squeezed my hand tighter as we approached the slave village. Ahead of our huge entourage, slaves paved our route across the desert with white lily petals. Their cool moistness stuck them to our bare feet. It was respite from the hot sand, at least.

When the slaves drew level with the ramshackle village outskirts, they doubled their efforts. As they hit the ground the petals turned red from spilled blood, so more were piled on, and more. But the blood was tenacious. Lyle and I were halfway along the column, and by the time we reached the huts and hovels and wretched humanity, our route was paved red.

"Someone's had a bad day here," Lyle said, glancing around and trying to spot the bodies. "Look at all this wasted blood! Heads will roll for this."

"Already have." I nudged him and nodded further along the road. There were stakes in the ground along the path, each one topped with a head. Eyes and tongues had been eaten away by the desert wildlife, or perhaps stolen by still-living slaves. Tongues were meat, pickled eyes were charms. I thought of Lyle's tattoo and shivered, squeezing his hand for comfort.

"Don't be soft," he said, and I could hear similar whispers around us as other Chosen saw what we had seen. It was a sight we never really got used to. The slaves were worse than animals; rarely looked at, certainly not spoken to. Yet this mutilation was always distasteful.

Tim Lebbon

"I'm not," I said, trying to translate the hard squeeze into something else. "I'm just thinking about us." And then I was. Us, lying there in my tent with fine silk curtains shifting in the desert heat, sweat linking us, Lyle buried deep and joining us further, his tongue, his hands…his love, binding and blinding and safe.

"There's more ahead," he said. He lifted the pot of honey to his nose, breathed in deeply and looked at me from the corner of his eye, smiling. As always, he'd known exactly what was on my mind.

"Is it the blooding?" I asked. Seconds later cries came from the front of the procession, and I knew what we were about to see. "Come on!"

I pulled Lyle through the crowd, smiling and apologising as we nudged people out of the way. None of them became angry or aggressive. Some even groped a feel beneath my robe as we went by, and I knew that Lyle was probably receiving the same treatment. Sex was something that kept the Chosen the way we were, a luxury indulged in unfettered and unforbidden by any religion or law that might govern anyone else. Today, with Brandon going, everyone else knew that they were spared, for however short a time. As always after the building in, the camp would sing to the sounds of love and lust.

We forced our way nearer the front so that I could see the blooding. It was a basic, animal part of the ritual, but one that I relished and enjoyed. Sensual and gorgeous, it allowed the Chosen to have a say in his or her fate. If Brandon selected a good, healthy slave with whose blood to bathe himself, then it may well save his life.

The monolith watched us all, black and blank.

Body

And then I saw Brandon for the first time that day. He was naked, but adorned with lily petals where they had stuck to his sweating skin. He looked like a half-plucked bird, and I had to stifle a laugh.

"What's wrong?" Lyle hissed.

I shook my head, smiling, and he knew not to ask again. Some things, even here, were private.

Brandon was surrounded by several ceremonial guards. We only ever saw them during the processions to the monolith, although I guess they were always close by in case one or many of us had a sudden change of faith. None of us had ever been the subject of a guard's wrath. We'd only ever seen them strike out against slaves. But then the deaths were remote and meaningless, flashes of red in the summer sun, and we took little notice.

Standing before Brandon and the guards were seven slaves. They all wore a look of resignation, but that switched to fear as he walked the line, inspecting them before he selected his sacrifice for the day. He reached the last slave and turned, looking back at us Chosen and smiling broadly, raising a cheer when we realised he was playing, and a frown and shiver of fear from the slaves.

He caught my eye and his smile grew wider. His mouth moved and he spoke my name, but above the cheering and laughing I could not hear. I looked down at his body, some of it obscured by lily petals, the important parts clear and visible, and for the first time I wished I *had* screwed him. It was a retrospective wish, but even its thought sent a chill down my spine and made me grab Lyle's hand tighter, warding off the mental indiscretion as hard as I could.

Brandon turned back to the slaves, walked their line again and touched a young female on the shoulder. She was immediately shoved forward by her companions, eager to escape their own deaths for a short while longer. Brandon took the knife proffered by one of the ceremonial guards, pushed the woman to her knees, held back her head and slashed her throat. She gagged, coughed, put her hands up to catch her draining blood. He had to stab her three times in the chest before she was silent.

The crowed cheered.

Brandon collected some of the blood in a bowl handed to him by a second guard. It took a few seconds, he had to hold the body at various angles as the blood flowed, and then the slave's heart ceased its pumping and the gush faded to a dribble.

The crowd cheered again, and I joined in as Brandon drank some of the blood and poured the rest over his head. He shouted out, words I couldn't hear, and then rubbed the blood across his face, chest and genitals, standing then with his arms held wide so that it would dry quickly in the desert heat.

We proceeded on toward the monolith. Lyle still held my hand and I couldn't help but think of a time when he would not be there, or I would not, one of us chosen to be the one, cast to the front of the column and respected, loved and adored, and I was glad that it was Brandon today because that meant it wasn't either of us. Being Chosen was an honour above all honours, it was our raison d'etre. But for all that I still didn't want to die.

It was said that none of us would *ever* die, but I could not accept that as total truth. Through all the years I had been

Body

Chosen, I had kept a part of my own mind, secretly shoved away at the back where it could hide from indoctrination and 'teachings'. On those rare nights when I chose to be alone I'd stare up at the clear desert sky, trying to count stars and understand just what was happening to us here. And sometimes, when the dark was doing its best to suck all the heat and I wished for Lyle's body to keep me warm, I would know. Madness. This, all of this, was madness.

I could never question what we were told. Not even to Lyle.

The remaining six slaves were herded along by the ceremonial guards. They would be killed and their blood used to bathe the stones that would build Brandon in. Every stone that made up the monolith—each block seven by seven by seven, because that was how many years old the Emperor's daughter had been when she died—was blooded. They said it was to give life to the rock, and help the body live when the time came.

It stood before us, miles away but big enough and close enough to touch. We walked into its shadow, and its chill was like the purest paranoia. Somewhere deep in the heart of that thing, in chambers built before Lyle and I were even born, lay the remains of the Emperor's dead little girl.

It took another two hours to reach the monolith, and a further two hours for the Chosen to climb the narrow paths leading up its steep sides. On top, the sun blazed down once more. Hundred of slaves lined the route to Brandon's cell, heads bowed, hands holding out cups of cool pure water.

"I wonder if he's relishing the sun," I said.

"Of course he is," Lyle said. He was holding my hand again after the long climb. Our sweat fused us together.

"Maybe that's why he wanted to leave the camp for his final day."

"Where did he go?"

"It's said he visited the slave village." Lyle whispered this, glancing at me once to warn me not to react. "It's said he was in love with a slave girl."

I was stunned. So stunned that my eyes went wide and the sun dazzled me, casting ghost spots onto my vision. Even the phrase *slave girl* was something of a contradiction; we barely distinguished them as human, let alone attributing sex to them. And to fall in love with one…

I wondered if it had been the slave he'd slashed and killed for the blooding. It made sense, even if it was the sense of a madman. Blooded by his love. And the blood dried on his skin was all he would be allowed to carry in there with him.

"You're quiet," Lyle said, louder now. Everyone was chatting, no one would pay us any attention.

"I'm thinking of romance."

"I'll show you romance as soon as we're back at the camp," he said, and I didn't bother trying to explain. Lyle and I told each other everything, even our dreams, but this time I did not. Perhaps my own small rebellion had begun.

We reached Brandon's cell. It was a hollow in the monolith's top surface, its proportions seven by seven by seven, big enough for someone to stand and walk four paces either way, and that was that.

This was why we were chosen.

It had a hole in one corner through which Brandon's waste would pass, winding and dribbling down through the huge structure to the massive drains built generations ago.

Body

There was no water barrier in there, and even out in the open we could smell the rot of it.

This was why we were sought out as children and brought up in luxury.

In one wall of the cell, three holes as big as fists would disgorge fresh air, food and water. The air was pushed through by dozens of manual pumps located around the base of the edifice, each run by a gang of fifty slaves. Similarly the food and water chutes, the food mostly soup and other fluids, the water generally warm and dusty. The slaves running these were lucky because they were allowed to develop muscles. And they were well guarded.

This was why we *were*. This was our reason, our purpose of existence and the fate for every one of us.

Brandon stood at the edge of his cell and the ceremonial guards stood either side, glancing over his body for any signs of adornment or hidden belongings. They looked between his toes, under his tongue, in his anus, and declaring him clean they stepped back.

"I wish we could leave him with something," I said.

"Don't be stupid!" Lyle hissed, amazed, even though he himself had brought along the jar of honey.

Brandon was allowed nothing. A few people went to show him the gifts they had brought, and he eyed the gifts and thanked the people and looked back up at the sky as they took them away again. He was shaking, I could see the streaks of dried blood on his skin shifting tone as his muscles spasmed. He was trying desperately to control the fear.

In two opposing lower corners of his cell, dull grey slabs marked where one day Brandon's escape would be found.

Tim Lebbon

They would fall away and he would find another life, *make* another life, be part of a new beginning. One day.

There was chanting from the ceremonial guards, and the head priest Jacobus appeared from nowhere to give his blessing. It was supposed to be a celebration, but we had seen so many people built in that by now it was nothing new. Like waking up and making love and falling back to sleep, this was something we were all too familiar with.

Brandon was lowered into his cell by the guards. For a few moments his eyes went wide and I thought he was going to shout, panic, scream, shame himself and embarrass everyone else. Lyle held me close and we both stared, shifting slightly so that we could see through the crowd. Neither of us wanted to lose sight of him.

Jacobus chanted, his voice low and roasted by the sun.

The guards let go and we heard the sound of Brandon landing on his cell floor.

"See you all!" he shouted. He was supposed to remain silent, paying his respect to the old Emperor's dead daughter, but if he had something to say nobody could stop him now. "See you all sometime soon! Don't be too long, now! Stay in the sun too long and you go mad, you want to be in here with me, in here in the dark where everything is possible. Come on, don't be long! Go and ask the Emperor when we can finish!" The crowd was utterly silent. Only those right at the front would be able to see him now, and they had probably averted their eyes.

And then came the grinding of stone on stone, vibrating through our feet, as the first of the four blocks was pushed into place to seal him in. A guard slaughtered one of the slaves and cut off his head, wiping his gushing neck across the grey

Body

stone. Fifty slaves pushed, fifty more pulled on ropes, and the rock covered a quarter of the cell.

"There are people in here I can't wait to meet again," Brandon shouted, and while the second rock was blooded and heaved into place he told us who they were, why they were important to him and what he'd say when he met them once more. Some must be his enemy, he knew that, but it was simply the nature of things. "And if they are, I'll kill them," he said, and the second stone slid into place.

We were denying him the sun, light and fresh air. We were giving him only darkness. "It's wrong," I whispered, but Lyle elbowed me hard in the ribs. I looked at him, unable to decide whether it was fear or anger I saw in his eyes. He believed totally, he was utterly loyal, but I guessed that he must be aware of my deeper scepticism.

As the third block slid in Brandon began to weep. His voice was quieter now, dulled by the huge blocks above him, swallowed by the millions of similar rocks and cells below where we stood.

The fourth rock began its noisy journey. A slave screamed as she was stabbed, pressed against the stone and stabbed again, her violent death giving the stone more blood to soak up.

"Goodbye sky!" Brandon shouted. "Goodbye all!" And then the stone slid into the fourth corner of the square, and Brandon was built in.

There was silence for a while, broken only by the indifferent cries of birds floating in the warm air currents rising above the monolith. Lyle clasped the jar of honey to his mouth and inhaled, perhaps thinking of later. I thought only of Brandon. It may be totally silent in there, or perhaps he was shouting. Either way, he would not know when we left.

I guessed he was already mad. In my darkest, most secret moments, I thought we all were.

At some point the ailing Emperor would give the order to halt the building and open the valves. All the cells were linked by tunnels and chambers, and the thousands of Chosen built in over the decades, those who had survived, would at last have their new freedom. Inside. In the dark. Flowing like blood, fighting and mating like individual cells, congregating into central organs, breathing, drawing air from the outside. And in the Emperor's madness the monolith would be given life, become a life itself, rescuing his long-dead daughter from the ravages of the afterlife. Allowing her, at last, to take his place.

Yes. Perhaps we were all mad.

The walk back was quiet, subdued, and dark. The sun was sinking behind the monolith and the whole journey took place within its shadow. Lyle still held my hand, the honey jar clasped in his other hand, but he was quiet. He smiled, looked around, acting as if he didn't have a care in the world…but I knew that he was thinking.

We were *all* thinking. Musing upon Brandon's fate and that of the thousands before him. Our own, as well. Eventually we would all be in there waiting on the Emperor's word. And if he died before giving it, or changed his mind, or decided he loved his daughter more in memory than he ever could

Body

in some strange returned life…then maybe we'd be there forever.

I'd never thought like this, not really, but Brandon's eyes had shocked me. And Lyle's whisper that he'd been in love with a slave girl, perhaps even the one he'd blooded himself with…all these things drove slivers of shock into the solid wall of belief I'd built and nurtured over the years. And perhaps these splinters bore the sharpened edges of truth. I feared that, just as I feared my own inevitable fate. I feared the truth.

I was terrified that everything was wrong.

When we arrived back at the camp it was twilight, the heat dissipating to the clear, dark skies, the mercenary guards standing back and letting us in. They knew what was about to happen, they'd seen it so many times before. Some of them even still stayed behind to watch.

Lyle let go of my hand and drew me to him, kissing me and stroking the small of my back. He breathed into my ear, kissed my neck, but still I could not close my eyes and see past those strange thoughts. I watched as one couple dropped their robes and started making love there on the sand, just inside the camp entrance, the woman squatting over the man and offering us all a frank view of where they were joined. Others hurried off to their tents or dropped to the ground to do the same, in pairs or groups or, on occasion, simply on their own.

I closed my eyes and saw Brandon staring back.

"Come on," I said, pulling away from Lyle, grabbing his hand and heading for my tent.

"Why not here?" he asked.

I smiled at him and loved him, loved the way the dregs of sunlight lit his eyes, fell on his skin, darkened the tattoo on his back until it looked as though it were asleep. He was my rock, not that monstrosity back there taking up half the sky and filling our world. *Him.* "The things I want to do are for us alone," I said. "Open that honey. Put your tongue inside. Taste good?"

He dropped the jar and walked with me.

The cooling night was alive with the sounds of love and sex. The love was calm and caring, the sex loud and cathartic, an expression of life on this day when we'd all seen one of our own pass from this world and into another.

We reached my tent and Lyle was guiding me inside, hand inside my robe and hooked under my belt. His fingers were cool against my warm skin, as if—

I thought of corpses and the living dead, those who had been shut away inside the monolith for as long as I'd been alive, or longer still. Sitting in the dark, talking to themselves, freezing or boiling or going silently mad. The slaves were still made to pump the food and air and water, because there was no way of knowing how many were alive and how many dead. All alive, Jacobus would have us believe, all alive and awaiting the Emperor's word to bring the monolith to life, become its vital components. *All alive.* I thought not.

Lyle lowered me gently to the cushioned floor and parted the robes about my legs, kissing my thighs, licking and kissing higher. I gasped and arched my back, staring up at the ceiling of the tent. The material billowed for a moment as if the final breaths of the dead had set it moving. I heard a sigh outside, but it must have been someone else making love.

Body

Lyle knelt. We smiled and kissed and closed our eyes, and for a while we escaped the camp and our lives along with everyone else. I forgot about everything, narrowed my vision, concentrating only on what we were doing. Our familiarity made it passionate, each movement holding us together for a moment longer.

It was a necessary escape, as if to stay here was to admit complicity in Brandon's fate and face one's own. The guards stood around the edges of the camp, smirked, watching those who were rutting in the open. They grinned through the fence. Little did they know that, for the few dark hours of this night, none of us were really there.

—⁕—

There were eagles in the sky the day Lyle was chosen.

Years ago, they'd come down from the mountains far to the north, exploring and foraging and finding the monolith, huge enough to be called a mountain in its own right. And here they had stayed, riding the warm currents and picking off the desert creatures dwelling in the shadow of the monolith or the quarries further south. Sometimes when they flew low the guards would try to shoot them down, but they always missed. Everyone in the camp watched the eagles on occasion, but I wondered if any of them felt what I did: jealousy. I coveted the freedom these birds had, the *choice*, and once I even said it to Lyle.

"But we're as free as anyone," he said. "The only thing we can't do is move." In a way I knew that he was right, because we had *everything*. The Emperor's original order that we should have the best the land could give still stood.

But Lyle was right. We couldn't move. And we were all destined, eventually, to be shut away in another world.

So I watched the eagles and considered their freedom, trying to give myself their wings.

I knew that something was wrong as soon as Lyle came into my tent. He hugged and kissed me, and I reached down to his groin. He was limp and disinterested. There was sweat running between his shoulder blades as if the tattoo were crying.

"What is it?" I asked, but I knew. He would not meet my eyes, so I knew. Maybe by not looking at me he was already trying to let go.

He twirled the loose end of my belt around his finger, brushed my hip with his other hand and sighed. "I'm going tomorrow," he said. Then he looked me in the eye, and I was startled by what I saw. No sadness, no fear, only joy. "They've chosen me to go tomorrow!"

"But..." So much in one word. I could not think of anything else to say. *Don't you love me? We'll lose each other. You'll die.* It all should have been said but Lyle would not have understood. This was all wonderful to him.

I started crying instead, and he hugged me and kissed me on the forehead. Brushing my tears away with his thumbs, he looked again into my eyes. "What's wrong?"

"You're going."

"We'll be together again, you know that. When the time comes—"

"It's never going to come!" I hissed, tearing away from him. "That thing the size of a world will be there forever, full of dead people. And if the Emperor ever does deign to give

Body

the signal—if he can manage it before he dies—do you think all the doors and traps will work?"

Lyle stared at me open-mouthed. He was welling up, and the realisation that my disbelief had upset him so much made me feel like a murderer. I was dragging out his faith—his own faith that belonged to him and no one else, however much I loved him—and trying to slaughter it.

I had no right.

"Oh Lyle…" I said, shaking my head. "I love you so much. I just want to be with you." *I don't want to lose you*, I meant to say, but the two were so different.

"You'll never lose me," he said. He hugged me again, and I reached down and cupped him, squeezing, wondering why he was still unresponsive.

"No," he said. "No more. I have to pray. I have to cleanse myself. Please…I *will* see you again, tomorrow. I'd like very much if you walked behind me. But the last time we made love is the time we must both remember forever."

"Lyle—"

"I'd hate for us to make love when you're so sad and bitter," he said, and I knew that he was right. He turned and walked from the tent, and I stared into the tattoo, watching myself go.

Lyle spent his final day praying and preparing for his building in. I went to see him only once, but I was turned away from his tent by a ceremonial guard. Only Lyle could have given this command.

So I wandered the camp. There were a thousand Chosen living there, and I knew almost all of them by sight. I recognised faces and smiles and distant stares, acknowledged them when they spoke to me, ignored them when they did not. I looked into eyes and wondered what thoughts really went on behind them.

Could I be so different? If I could recognise the futility in what we were doing, as well as revel in the honour being that Chosen bestowed upon us, surely others could as well?

I thought of Lyle and our time together. It was in the past already, even though he had yet to go. He'd been my true love ever since we were children, growing up together in a nomadic commune in the western desert until a caravan of ceremonial guards had stumbled upon us one morning. A quick word to our parents and we were whisked away, without even a goodbye kiss. I could still remember the sight of my mother's smile bidding me farewell, the contented look in her eyes as she watched her nine-year-old daughter crying her way out of her life. I'd forgiven her, eventually—we were told to forgive, cleanse and forget our previous lives, and at first I had all but lived by that—but I'd never forgotten that sight. Me sad, my mother happy. It hadn't seemed right. It still did not.

Lyle had been with me ever since, and I'd been with him. Transported into a camp of children and adults, a place without the usual social and familial hierarchies, our love had blossomed quickly and been encouraged by everyone. Our love, our physicality, my ability to become pregnant stolen from me by a toxin in my food the first week we were there. At the time I hadn't known what had been done to me, but as

Body

the years went by and Lyle and I continued making love each and every day, I knew that I had been made barren.

Even back then I had wondered whether this was really the way for the Emperor's dream to be realised.

Neither of us had ever strayed. Casual sex was a way of life in the camp, group sex and homosexuality encouraged and enjoyed by a vast proportion of the population. We watched with interest but never joined in, because we were so perfect for each other. Neither of us could imagine anything better. *You should try everything*, one of the Chosen had once said to us, but we merely smiled and looked at each other and said, *we do*.

And now I was losing him.

Throughout that long afternoon of wandering, avoiding conversation, trying to steer around the edges of the camp where there were fewer people, I resolved to do whatever I could. I was resigned to losing Lyle, for the simple reason that he so wanted to go.

But I would ensure that I could still be with him.

I owed that to myself.

"I'm going to be happy," he said, standing before me as naked as I had ever seen him. He'd removed the necklace I'd given him when we were eighteen—I wanted to ask where it was, but I was certain he'd now consider it unimportant—and even his thumb-rings had been cut off. There were small wounds weeping blood where the cutters had caught his skin. I wanted to tend them and kiss them safe, but I didn't think he cared.

"I hope so," I whispered. I was so close to tears that I could barely talk. I didn't want him to see me crying, not yet.

"Of course I will." He reached out and clasped my upper arms, pulling me to him like a friend to a friend. I tried to turn my head and kiss him—smelt his skin, that faint spice that he exuded however much he washed—but he pulled away and smiled. "Now—"

"I don't want you to go!" I said, glancing around in case any of the guards had heard. They'd given us a minute alone inside Lyle's tent, but he'd be called soon. Naked, he'd walk across the desert and leave me. Forever. I never for an instant believed that we'd ever see each other again. "The Emperor is crazy, and we're mad for following him!"

Lyle's face dropped slightly—perhaps only I could have seen that, the change was so slight—and he turned away from me. "I love you," he said, and looking back he whispered his single, solitary statement of doubt. "But even now isn't the time for disbelief."

He left the tent, and we were never alone again.

Not exactly.

—⚋—

The procession followed the usual route. Lily petals rained down and stuck to our feet. I walked several paces behind Lyle and his escort of ceremonial guards. Every now and then I looked up from my feet and saw the eye tattoo staring back at me, and I felt as if I was in two places at once.

Lyle never looked back.

Body

There were hundreds of Chosen behind us being escorted by the bored mercenaries. Many of them carried gifts they would never be able to give Lyle, an offering as foolish as the tradition it honoured. I almost laughed out loud when I saw one man struggling under the weight of a healthy, fat goat. He'd be walking back with it, he knew that, but still he hauled it for miles across the baking desert. Being Chosen didn't necessitate a sudden drop in intelligence, did it? Did these people—and I realised that I was starting to distinguish myself from them now, a dangerous, foolish thing to do—ever think about what they were doing?

"Blooding," one of the guards said softly, but I was near enough to hear.

We'd come to the slave village and there were seven slaves lined along the road, wretched-looking creatures without a complete outfit of clothes between them, cursed by sores and sunburn and half-dead already. None of them drew away as Lyle walked the line, and none of them looked at him. That was forbidden. Right now he was as close to a deity as these untouchables would ever experience.

Lyle touched a female on the shoulder and she stepped forward, letting slip a high-pitched squeal of fear.

I edged forward until I was standing directly behind the guards. I was two steps away from Lyle, although he didn't seem to notice me at all. That hurt.

A guard handed Lyle the knife and he brought it up from waist height, slashing the woman from stomach to chin, stepping back as her insides tumbled out and she thrust her hands into the steaming mess, trying to hold it up from the sand, crying, screaming until he reversed his stroke and slit her throat. He dropped the knife and grabbed the woman by the hair, bringing her to his chest so that her leaking blood pumped down over his stomach and crotch.

For an insane few seconds I was jealous—we had never tried this, that was for sure, and I was certain I could see movement in Lyle's penis—but then I darted forward, snatched a handful of the woman's hot guts and slapped them across his back.

A guard hauled me away but I managed to hit Lyle one more time. The sickly mass made its mark. Lyle looked at me, and I think he knew what I was doing, he knew, I could see it in his eyes and—

—and he smiled.

I was sure then, even though I knew the truth, that everything was going to be alright. I let myself live the lie as the guards dragged me back and dropped me in the sand. I retained it as I stood and walked on with the Chosen, heading toward the giant monolith that was a tomb for thousands and hope for one. Even as we climbed the sides and headed across the top to the cell that had been prepared for Lyle, I wallowed in the illusion.

It was the only way I could stand there and watch him being buried alive.

He didn't moan or cry or rage. He was built in just as all the best of the Chosen were, and will be. He sat quietly, content in his fate, perhaps even believing that one day he'd be free inside this monstrous structure, free to live a new life and search me out.

He didn't look at me after I'd blooded him. The mess from the slave's innards had dried on his back, masking the tattoo and hiding it from the ceremonial guard's cursory

Body

search. I'd done it for me, but it saved Lyle a lot of pain as well. I hadn't even thought of that until then.

He stared down at his crossed legs as the four great blooded blocks were heaved in above him. Perhaps he had taken what he told himself was his last look at the sun, and one more would be just too unbearable.

He remained sitting like that as the light was taken from his world.

—⚊⚋—

I like to think it was me. I like to lie in my tent and imagine that Lyle had known what I was doing with the slave's blood, and after that he couldn't face seeing me again. Because his love was too strong, and he didn't want to shame himself, and really, truly, he knew it was all a lie.

The eagles are still there, but they are the offspring's offspring of those which had circled on the day of Lyle's entombment. I've gained thirty years and as many pounds, and a reputation as trouble amongst the other Chosen. They don't mistrust me, exactly, but they know I'm not like them. And they don't really avoid me. But sometimes days go by without me speaking with anyone. I don't mind. They let their beliefs buffer them against the truth. They go to the monolith and watch one of theirs built in, and they come back and screw through the night to escape the insanity of this. In reality they are only escaping the truth.

The Emperor died years ago without uttering the order to give life to the giant stone corpse. They're still building it higher and wider, and imprisoning more and more Chosen, simply because they don't know what else to do.

Tim Lebbon

I don't mind. I know that after thirty years Lyle is still alive. Because every night, when I close my eyes, I truly see the darkness.

And that is my escape.

The Evolutionary

The man should never have been there.

Daniel knew the woods well. He was familiar with the sounds and sights that prevailed when he was here on his own, and they were ever-present today. There was no one else to disturb his wandering and wondering, no one to spy on him or hide away, slinking between trees like a shadow looking for a home. He was alone. The man should never have been there. And yet, there he was.

He stood beside the old tree that Daniel had named Sparrow Oak. It was where Daniel had seen his first dead bird. That had been the previous year when he was ten, when his parents had at last allowed him to leave their garden and venture into the woods beyond. The sparrow's corpse had come as a shock. Though his parents' garden was alive with birds, Daniel had never seen one of them dead. He had never even thought about it until the sparrow, and then the reasons began to plague him; they rarely died, they lived to a hundred, they were *immortal*.

Or perhaps they came here to pass away in secret.

The man was a flicker at first, a haze in the woods that Daniel had to second-glance to see properly. And then when he did see him, Daniel knew that he had not been there before, not like this, not *solid*, the definite shape of a man standing in the shadow of a tree. A second before he had been only maybe, perhaps, possibly, an echo still considering being.

In his hands he held a dead bird.

"Hello, Daniel," the man said.

Daniel was not afraid. Surprised and startled, but not afraid. His parents had always warned him to stay away from strangers, and one rainy night when they were out his older sister Josie had told him what strangers *did* to small boys, smiling as she stoked his terror. But this man was not a stranger. Daniel had never seen him before now, but there was no doubt in the boy's mind that he was a friend.

"Hello," Daniel said. He left the path worn through the woods and approached the tree, pressing between a spray of ferns to the left and a wood ants' nest of pine needles to the right. The nest came up to his waist, and its surface was a constant blur of motion. At any other time he would have looked for a caterpillar or beetle to throw in, watch the ants swarm across it and pull it down into the darkness. But not now. The man had said hello, and in his voice there was a calling.

"Is that a sparrow?" Daniel asked.

The man smiled sadly, and though he *was* sad, the smile lit his face with something approaching joy. It was a strange blurring of expressions, and Daniel was confused.

The Evolutionary

"Alas, the common sparrow has its problems," the man said. "Its food sources destroyed by deforestation, its habitat ever-changing. But today isn't the sparrow's day. No, this is a siskin. See?" He lowered his hand to show Daniel.

The bird was splayed across the man's grimy palm, its wings spread, yellow streak on its head level with the man's thumb, its claws raised and clasping at the air. One side of its head had been flattened by an impact.

"What happened to it?"

"It flew into the tree," the man said. "Its eyesight isn't what it should be. Its nest is on the far side of these woods, in an old sycamore tree that grows right at the edge of the farmer's fields. That sycamore is dead. Its pores have sucked up so many pesticides and chemicals from the field that it gave up on life a decade ago. Yet little fellows like this still choose to nest there, giving the dead tree a semblance of life. And sometimes, those chemicals bleed through. This bird isn't quite blind, but will be in a few more months. Unless I fix it."

Daniel felt sadness at the bird's death, and confusion at the man's comments, talking as though the bird were still alive. It's head was flattened, skull crushed, brain turned to mush.

One of its wings twitched.

Daniel stepped back. "I thought it was dead!"

"Well, yes," the man said. "But this is a very special bird. An exceptional siskin. It has a future, and it should never have died. I'm here to see what I can do."

There was something not quite right about the man and his words, not quite *here*, as if he were acting in a film instead of standing in the woods with Daniel. "Can I watch?" Daniel asked.

The man smiled. "I was hoping you would. Now, sit down here at the base of the tree—"

"Sparrow Oak."

"Is that what you call it? I suppose you would. All birds die, Daniel. That was just the first dead one you saw."

Daniel wondered how the man knew his name and why he had named this tree. But only briefly. The bird and the man had grasped his interest, and such matters seemed unimportant.

They both sat at the foot of the tree—Daniel conscious that wood ants could be swarming over him in seconds, the man calm and quiet, holding the dead siskin before him—and the woods seemed to pause. Birds and animals and the breeze in the canopy waited to see what would happen next.

"A few days ago, this little siskin uncovered seed buried under the carpet of dead leaves on the forest floor. It used its claws. Small birds like this usually use their beaks to do something like that. This one found the seed whilst keeping its head up to watch for any dangers."

Daniel frowned. The dead bird twitched again. Perhaps it was the man moving his hand.

"It will teach its young how to do that," the man said.

He fell silent, and seconds later he started to touch the bird with the fingers of his free hand. Its claws first, then its small feathered body, and then its head, crushed and bent out of shape from where it had flown into the oak's trunk. His fingertips smoothed across the bird's body, pausing here and there and pressing down, shifting its feathers, changing the way light fell upon them and subtly altering their colour.

The Evolutionary

Daniel knelt up so that he could see better, leaned in until his head cast a shadow over the bird. The man did not seem to mind.

"But it's dead," Daniel said, as if in anticipation of what he was about to see.

The man did not reply. Instead, his fingers slipped inside the dead bird's skull.

Daniel felt the world tilt around him, dizziness threatening to spill him to the forest floor where the wood ants would overwhelm him. It felt as though reality had stumbled. But the man glanced up, and one look from him restored Daniel's balance.

"Watch," the man said. His fingers delved and twisted. He worked quickly and confidently, remoulding the brain, going deeper, fixing links and connections that had been torn away, mending thoughts and restoring instincts destroyed by death. Somehow Daniel knew exactly what he was doing, as if the man's efforts were charted in a book or on a TV programme. The brain reconfigured, the skull knitted together by a delicate touch, skin and feathers folded back into place, the bird rolled and sat on its clawed feet, stroked, whispered to in a language and tone that Daniel could never understand.

The siskin blinked.

A breeze gasped through the trees overhead, astounded.

"That bird was dead," Daniel said.

"That's why I'm here," the man said. "I have to look after the future."

The siskin sat on the man's hand and looked around, its head jerking this way and that, amazed at everything it saw. *And it should be*, Daniel thought. *It should be amazed. It's seen death, and now there's life in front of it again. What can that be like?*

"I don't understand," said Daniel.

The man sighed and stared off between trees. "None of you do." He threw the bird into the air and, having little choice, it flew away into the tree canopy, singing its surprise.

"Time for you to go home," the man said, smiling at the young boy.

"But I came here to play," Daniel said, thinking of everything he had wanted to do today; dam the stream, explore the basement of the demolished house in the woods, climb trees.

"You've come here to learn."

"What's your name?"

The man's smile slipped from his face. He averted his eyes, searching as though he would find a name pinned to a tree. "I had one once," he said, "but now it's long gone."

"But what do I call you?"

"You don't need to call me anything." And the nameless man stood and walked away without saying another word.

Daniel thought to follow, but suddenly his sister's gleeful description of what strangers did to little boys kicked home. So he sat there and watched the man pass away between the trees, listened as he pushed through the undergrowth, and finally he was seeing and hearing nothing but the woods. Birds sang, and maybe the siskin was one of them. *Its head was crushed*, Daniel thought. *It was* dead!

Suddenly the forest sights and sounds felt less friendly.

Daniel ran home, and every step brought the woods pressing in around him. The bird song sounded louder, trees felt closer together, leaves and mud stuck to his trainers to

The Evolutionary

slow him down, and when a startled bird took flight past his ear he lashed out, striking himself instead of the bird, his ear burning red as if the man in the woods was talking about him somewhere else.

He leapt the stream, vaulted a fence, and then he was running across a field toward the village, his house already in sight.

His parents were in the garden, trimming bushes and cutting the grass.

"There was a bird in the woods!" Daniel gushed as his dad halted the lawnmower, "and it was dead and its head was crushed and it was a siskin, but it flapped its wings and then took off again 'cos it used its claws to find food not its beak, and it'll teach that to its young!" He gasped for breath, and his smiling father ruffled his hair.

"Calm down, Dan. Catch your breath. Have you been looking for dead birds again?"

"No Dad, I wasn't. I was just walking and then I saw the man and—"

"Man?" his mother asked sharply. She held her secateurs open, ready to take the next snip. "What man?"

"There was a man in the woods, and he couldn't tell me his name. And he picked up the bird—"

"I've told you to never talk to strangers!" she scolded. "Daniel, what did he say to you?"

"Nothing, Mum. Just that the bird was dead but it was special, so he brought it back to life."

His parents glanced at each other, and his father sat on the stone steps. "Listen Dan, what was the man like? Did he ask you to go anywhere with him? Did you know him?"

"Dad!" Daniel said. "You know I wouldn't have gone anywhere. I'd have kicked him in the bollocks like you told me."

Daniel's mother uttered a short bark; a laugh or a gasp, Daniel could not tell. "Did your father really tell you that?"

His father smiled sheepishly. "Well, yeah. But that was supposed to be man's talk, wasn't it?" He reached out and grabbed his son.

Daniel laughed, trying to tear away from his father. The familiar smell of him was a comfort; the tang of aftershave, the staleness of coffee on his breath. Daniel was home, and he was glad.

"I don't want you going in those woods again for a while," his mother said.

"Aww, Mum!"

"I mean it! Unless you recognised this man from the village, we don't know where he's come from."

"I don't think he does either," Daniel said, realising the truth as he spoke it. *He's lost*, he thought. But he decided that would not sound good in front of Mum and Dad.

"So you and he had a good chat?"

"Well, I watched him fix the bird, then it flew away, then he left."

"And he didn't ask you anything? Didn't invite you anywhere?"

"No, Mum. I know all about pervs and stuff."

"Okay, Dan. Go in and wash, we're going to the pub for dinner."

"Yay!" Daniel ran inside, cleaned up, changed, read a comic book, watched some TV while his parents got ready,

The Evolutionary

and as they walked to the local pub the memory of the man and the siskin was as clear in his mind as ever.

—ᴍ—

Daniel's summer break from school was filled with new things, and he welcomed them all. He and his mother went bowling, his father took him to an archery range, and the four of them spent a weekend in Cornwall hunting through rock-pools for crabs, eating fudge and trying to prevent sea gulls from stealing their chips on the sea front. Dan recalled the man in the woods less and less, though there were a few occasions when he came to mind. Once, they found a dead crab washed up on the beach, a huge specimen almost as big as his head. Its shell had been holed and some of its insides eaten, and Dan thought, *I wonder if he could fix that?* The man's memory followed him across the beach for a few moments but was gradually eroded by the waves. Another time, when they were driving through the narrow Cornish lanes, Daniel heard a crunch beneath the car. His parents exchanged a brief glance and Josie said, "Gross!" *That was a rabbit*, Daniel thought, *squashed by the wheel. Beyond hope. Beyond even him.* They arrived at the outdoor water park, and with every slip down a slide the man's shadow was diluted more and more.

By the time Daniel returned to school the man was gone from his day, haunting only the occasional dream. And these were dreams where there was much more going on. "I wonder about diseases," he said to his mother one day, "and why we just can't take them out bit by bit."

"I'm sure the doctors have thought of that," his mother said, still reading her book in the back garden.

"But they try to stop it or kill it with drugs, instead of just taking it out and throwing it away."

She put down her book and sighed. "Well, sometimes they do. If you have a disease growing in you, they cut it out and burn it."

"Euch," Daniel said, thinking, *Well maybe they should teach people to take out* every *disease like that, whether its growing in you or not.* But he said no more, because his mother was reading again.

That night he dreamed of pulling a disease from his head and drowning it in the garden water butt. The disease was black and greasy, and it screamed.

It only took a few weeks for Daniel's mother to forget about his forest ban. He guessed his talk of a stranger had receded in her list of Important Things—adults seemed to be preoccupied all the time with new things that seemed to matter so much—and he chose the right moment to ask.

"Be back at five for dinner," she said, without even looking up from her newspaper.

Daniel ran before she could change her mind.

Approaching the edge of the forest was strange. It had grown up. He was not really afraid, but as memories of that time with the stranger and the dead siskin resurfaced, the trees and undergrowth seemed to take on a whole new sheen. A fir tree waved, beckoning him in. Brambles at the edge of the wood rustled secretively, though there was little breeze.

The Evolutionary

The darkness in there stared right back at him. It could have contained a million eyes.

He was not scared. But he *was* aware.

Passing between the trees seemed to draw the memories out and lighten them. The bird had not really been dead. The man without a name had meant no harm, he had simply been playing a joke on Daniel. But every bird Daniel saw could have been the resurrected siskin, and he scanned the forest floor for shapes uncovering seed with their claws.

He explored far that day, arriving home half an hour late, though his parents seemed not to mind. They ate dinner together, chatted, but nothing he said seemed to make sense to them. He and his sister bickered as usual, and his mum and dad had their own grown-up thoughts to contend with. After dinner, he returned to the woods.

He found a sick squirrel close to the stream. It was lying on its side, breathing fast, its eyes wild and terrified. He picked up a long stick and prodded at the rodent. It hissed but barely moved. Its front paws clawed at the air.

"What's wrong with you, then?" Daniel asked, looking around for the man. But he did not appear. Perhaps this was not a special squirrel.

Over the space of a few minutes Daniel crawled closer and closer to the creature, nudging it with the stick, frustrated by its lack of movement. It seemed to be dying before his eyes and he wondered about illness, what was killing it, and why now. Finally he flipped the squirrel over. There was no sign of any injury. It still panted, foaming slightly at the mouth now, its back legs shoving at the ground and kicking up a pile of dead leaves.

Why can't I just take it out? Daniel thought. *Open it up—just like that man—and take out its illness, and make it better? Why should it die just because it's here on its own? It's not fair.* He thought about sickness and things going awry. He thought about death and why it could not be prevented. It seemed so wrong that someone could catch a disease and die, so pointless, and buried deep within those concerns were forbidden images of his parents fading away in a hospital bed. His darkest nightmares, surfacing now because of this squirrel.

"That's not right!" he said. Nature should be perfect. Why allow its imperfections?

He took out his pocket knife, opened the largest blade, held the squirrel with his left hand and cut it open to see what had gone wrong.

Daniel gasped as the creature's blood pulsed over his skin. His idea of delving inside for the sickness suddenly seemed mad, a young child's bloody fascination, and he fell back onto his rump, crying. He wiped his hand on his shirt. The dying animal's blood was sticky and warm.

It hissed as it faded away.

And then he saw the man standing on the other side of the stream.

"Have you come to save the squirrel?" Daniel asked tearfully.

The man shook his head. "Why? It's just a dead squirrel. Death is essential for moving on."

"But the bird…you saved the bird!" Daniel was shaking now, shocked at what he had done. It had been dying anyway, but he had quickened its death.

The Evolutionary

"The bird was special and should not have died. I told you that."

"This squirrel isn't?"

"Not in the same way. It wasn't fit, so it didn't survive."

"That's not fair!" Daniel shouted.

"'Fair' is something for people," the man said, "and they're the least fair of all."

Daniel cried some more, taking some strange comfort in the tears. Perhaps because they prevented him from seeing the small grey corpse.

"I *travel*," the man said, and his voice was so filled with a child-like wonder that Daniel stopped crying instantly and looked up. The man held out his hand and smiled. "Will you travel with me?"

Don't go with strangers, his parents said.

They touch *you*, Josie said.

"Travel where?"

"Everywhere!"

Daniel held the man's hand, and in his grip there was only goodness.

They walked together, strange man and confused boy, and slowly they faded away from the forest. Daniel saw the familiar path changing, the geography of his memory struggling to keep up, and the man took them left into an area of evergreens, finding a path that had never been there before. They were remote from the forest. It existed around them but there was little interaction; no spider webs breaking across Daniel's face, no smell of freshly fallen pine needles, no spongy give underfoot. As they moved, time seemed to shift. It lapped against the shores of his consciousness, making itself felt and yet showing little. He had a staggering sense of time passing in huge waves; ten, a hundred, a thousand years with each breath. The trees remained the same, but with every step other aspects seemed to alter. He felt the forest flexing around him, shrugging time from its shoulders just out of sight. The man's hand clasped his own as if afraid to let him go. Daniel wondered what would happen if he did. He wriggled his fingers and the man squeezed even harder, glanced at him in alarm, shook his head.

"*You'd be lost*," he whispered, and it seemed so loud.

The forest settled down, and the man and boy became real again. Daniel's feet sank into the carpet of pine needles, the sun slanted through the tree canopy and speckled his skin, and birds chattered in a startled symphony at their sudden presence.

"Where are we?" Daniel asked. He knew every inch of the forest behind his house. He did not know this place.

"The forest," the man said. "Just not when you think."

"Then when?" Daniel asked.

Something was coming at them through the trees. A grey shadow, slinking from trunk to trunk, feigning covertness and yet destroying its effort with a long, low whine.

"A long time ago," the man said, "I came here to fix something. I'll do it again now, and you can see what it is I do. It's important you see this. Watch, Daniel. Take note."

"Do you want me to do it?" Daniel asked. *Is that what he wants*? he thought. *Is he teaching me? Is he—*

And then he saw the wolf. It emerged from behind a fallen tree, glanced at them and tried to slink away. But it was

The Evolutionary

injured. Something had cut it from behind its head, around its shoulder and down across its front left leg. The wound was open and raw. Blood soaked its pelt, black and dry, red and wet. Its eyes held a dozy sheen, like pain-induced cataracts.

"This one shouldn't die," the man said. "A human slashed at it with a sharpened stick, caught it with a lucky blow, and now it's looking for its own death in these woods. It will die, rot into the ground, add its essence to the trees and bushes and ferns, and it will be forgotten. Its cubs will be abandoned by its pack, and they will be picked off by eagles and bears. One of them will find out how to catch fish. Not soon, but later in its life. If this wolf dies now, that will never happen."

"But you can't change time," Daniel said. Every film he had ever seen, every science fiction book he had read, assured him of that fact. You can't change time, because...

The man looked down and touched Daniel on the back of the head. "Daniel, it's already been changed. I've just come back again to show you."

He knelt and held out his hand to the wolf. The injured animal lay down on its stomach, whining as the movement opened its wound some more. Daniel saw that the cut went deep; the white of bones, the dark purple of something inside that should never be seen. It growled as the man approached, but it seemed to have no energy to wrinkle its lips. By the time the man held his hand beneath its nose, the wolf was almost dead.

"It smells me," he said. "It knows I'm not here to harm it." Daniel saw the beast's nose twitch slightly. *Dry nose*, he thought, *must be really bad.*

"Come and watch."

Daniel moved closer and knelt beside the man.

He touched the wolf's head first, stroking the fur to calm the animal. It had started shaking, as if cold. Its eyes shimmered.

The man's hand went in deeper than the cut. The tendons in his wrist flexed, muscles danced, and as he drew his hand out the slash melded together, skin fused, fur closed over the wound. He put his hand in again, further down its neck toward its shoulder, and pulled down as if zipping up the injured animal. The blood was still there on the wolf's fur, incongruous now that the wound was gone.

When the man's hand plunged into the wolf's wounded shoulder it opened its eyes and howled.

Daniel fell back, terrified and exhilarated at the same time. *There's a wolf howling in the woods behind my house!* he thought. When he got home he would listen for its echo every night.

The man worked quickly, using his other hand to press the wolf's body on the outside. His fingers massaged the grey pelt in ways that could not have been random. He frowned in concentration. Sweat ran into his eyes and he shook his head to clear them, his hands and fingers never halting for an instant. His mouth twisted into a grimace and he cursed, a word Daniel had never heard, a language that seemed impossible from the man's mouth. It was as if he were talking animal.

The wolf growled and grumbled deep in its throat, then stood and pulled away. The man's hand left its body, fingers clawed like a dead spider, and its pelt fell closed. The animal staggered sideways for a few steps. It leaned against a tree and looked around, as if amazed that it was still here. The

The Evolutionary

blood on its pelt was almost all dry now, and the wolf sat like a dog and began to clean itself.

Daniel realised that the animal was beautiful. In his astonishment at seeing a wolf he had failed to appreciate its grace, its grandeur. And now, fixed and better, it stared at him with eyes yellowed by sunlight refracting through the tree canopy.

"That's it," the man said, sighing and sinking back onto his haunches. He seemed to be lessened somehow, and Daniel reached out to touch his arm.

"What's wrong?" he said, and he thought, *How will I get home if anything happens to him? Where is home? Where am I, really?*

"Tired," the man said, "I'm just tired. I'll sleep for a while, and then we need to travel again." He lay down on his side, asleep before his head touched the ground.

Daniel sat alone and watched the wolf disappear between the trees.

—⁂—

They travelled.

They remained in the forest but faded in and out of existence, passing through the years and settling here and there, places where the man had performed his work in the past. He had been here already, he told Daniel, but it was important for Daniel to see what he had done, and to understand. *Why?* Daniel asked. *It will all become clear*, the man replied.

Near a rocky outcropping that Daniel had never seen, where the stream burst from the ground as if forced by some pressure from below, they found a dying frog.

"Someone stepped on it," the man said, and when Daniel asked, *Who?* he shook his head, smiled. "We're a long time ago, and you'd barely recognise the people who live here right now. But even in its earliest days, humankind was interfering with nature."

Daniel was confused, but as he watched the man go to work again, fascination smothered his bewilderment. Fingers moved across the frog, searching for the injuries, finding them inside even though its skin was unbroken, forming no hole yet *going inside* the frog to touch its organs, meld its flesh, restart its heart and set it down again. With a slight nudge the frog launched itself into the stream and disappeared.

They travelled again, and this time Daniel saw signs of humanity. At first he thought there were fallen trees, but as he and the man hid behind a screen of ferns he realised that he was looking at an ancient settlement in the woods. Trees had been felled to form the backbones of several shelters, constructed from heavy branches covered with moss, mud and sheets of bracken. They blended so perfectly into the forest that they were all but invisible, but the people wandering around gave them away.

Daniel could hardly believe what he saw. These people wore animal furs, had long black hair, dark skin, stumpy limbs, and only one or two of them stood any taller than him. A woman sat with a baby suckling at each breast while she gutted a rabbit; a man squatted by the fire and worked at other animal corpses, spearing and resting them high above the flames on timber spits; two children tumbled and rolled

The Evolutionary

across the carpet of pine needles, naked yet hardy, one of them growling as if pretending to be a bear.

"This is like prehistoric times!" Daniel said.

The man smiled. "Not as long ago as you think, Daniel. No dinosaurs here. But yes, pre-history, in a time when humanity was thought to be at one with nature. But there has always been that destructive spark." Daniel looked up at the man and saw a glimmer of anger in his eyes, reflected from the fire.

"What are you?" Daniel asked. The questions surprised him, and seemed to jolt the man as well.

"That's a big question for a little boy," he said. "Come on. We have work to do over here." He pulled Daniel away and retreated into the forest, still hunkered down low to keep out of sight.

We *have work*, he had said. Daniel followed, and that question echoed through his mind: *What are you?* Though the man seemed to have no harm in him, its potential answers were terrifying.

Half an hour later they found the black bear. It was not as huge as Daniel had always imagined a bear to be, but it was twice as vicious. Its leg seemed to be buried in the ground and it lashed out as they approached, lethal-looking claws whistling at the air. It growled, dribbling bloody spittle, its whole fleshy body shaking with each lunge.

"Trapped," the man said.

"Where's its leg?"

"There, in the ground. They dig a small hole, set sharpened sticks in its base and catch anything from a rabbit to a bear. A rabbit would fall in and impale itself, the bear just gets its foot trapped."

"Will they eat the bear?"

"That's their intent. And its pelt will be highly prized. But not this one, not this time. This bear is special."

Daniel had already been expecting this. *Special*, he thought, looking at the bear. "So what can it do?"

"Nothing unusual," the man said, "but it's fit and healthy, larger than normal, and now is not its time to die. Its bloodline is needed in the future. It's young, and has yet to mate."

"But there are no bears in England now," Daniel said.

The man nodded and knelt next to Daniel, so that they could talk face to face. "Knowing the future doesn't change the many presents," he said. "If I disregarded this bear's predicament just because of what I know of its species' future, everything could change."

"What do you mean?"

The man shook his head. "Sometimes even I don't understand."

They travelled further, back and forth through the forest and through time. At one point during that walk Daniel thought, *This is it, this is where my house is at some time later than now*. There seemed to be no pattern to their journey. One time they arrived during a terrible storm, another time it was daylight and parts of the forest were aflame from a clumsy human's fire. Of all the animals dying from fire and smoke inhalation, the man chose a small butterfly to pick up from the ground, mend its scorched wings, slip into its minute head to reassemble shattered connections, carry it away from the fire and set it free. The butterfly fluttered into the sky and merged with the clouds of ash drifting through the trees.

The Evolutionary

"A butterfly flaps its wings..." the man said, and he smiled down at Daniel. "Every second of this journey, you've seen me making the future into what it should be."

Later, back in the forest that Daniel knew, he wondered what influence he himself had made on this time he called his own.

Though he had travelled far, he arrived home just an hour after leaving. His mother was dishing up dinner, chatting with his sister as she laid the table, and his father arrived home from work just as Daniel ran downstairs from getting changed.

The excitement of where he had been and what he had seen carried Daniel through the usual argumentative meal, and afterwards he ran upstairs to his bedroom. Sitting at the window, staring out over the fields to the forest, he wondered where the man was now, and what he was saving from death. Special, he had called all the creatures he saved. *Who's to say?* Daniel thought. *Might there be special people, too?*

A butterfly fluttered past his window, hanging in the air outside for a few seconds like a memory demanding recollection. Daniel stared, amazed. It was different from the butterfly the man had rescued—larger, its wings a deeper orange—and yet the boy saw it as a sign. Of what he was not yet sure, but he was plenty old enough to see the relevance in such coincidences. He opened his window and reached out to touch the butterfly. It danced further away, dipping and rising like ash on the breeze, and Daniel stretched some more. His arm burned with the effort of holding the windowsill, his feet lifted from the floor, and for a few seconds he was balanced on his stomach and hand, swaying there fifteen feet above the ground. His heart jumped and stuttered, and he was certain that the only factor affecting his fate—tumble back into his bedroom, or fall to the hard patio below—was whether or not the butterfly landed on his outstretched hand.

It fluttered closer to him, flew beneath his hand, and he tilted back into the room.

He slammed the window closed and gasped. *Was he here then?* he thought. *Did I actually fall in another now, and he came and changed it and now I'm back here again?*

Daniel was a boy who fought with problems until he had a solution, real or not. He was tenacious. He went to bed that night dwelling on what had happened. And when he woke up he knew how he could find out how special he really was.

On his way to school next morning Daniel saw a snail squashed into the pavement. He paused and let his friend walk on, kneeling beside the glistening remains, leaning in close enough to smell it.

"Dan?" his friend said. "What you doing?"

"Dead snail," Dan said. He had almost forgotten that Billy was there. Someone must have stepped on the snail recently, because its insides were still oozing out under their own pressure, catching the sun in bubbles of goo. He reached out and touched the remains. They were cool, wet, and he closed his eyes, waiting for the rush of whatever power he may feel at that moment, wishing it in and yet fearing it as

The Evolutionary

well. *What will it be like?* he thought. *Will I know what I'm doing. Does* he *really know?*

"Gross!" Billy said. He stepped back from Dan, uttering various expressions of disgust. "Dan, what the fuck you doing?" Fuck was a word the boys knew and used on occasion, and usually its shock brought them out of whatever they were up to. But Dan did not move. He barely even heard Billy.

"Come on," he whispered, prodding, poking, working his finger in beneath the crushed mass and trying to find the centre of things. "Come on snail, maybe you shouldn't die yet, maybe you'll go on to grow wings or something." But the snail remained crushed, his finger dripping with its innards. After a few more seconds he sat back, looked at his finger and gagged.

"Your head's messed up!" Billy said. "You going to taste it now?" He sounded appalled and fascinated.

Dan looked at his friend and shook his head. "Just thought I saw something," he said.

"What?"

Dan shrugged. "Pearl. Or something."

"That's oysters, you turd!"

"Well they have shells as well. Maybe…" Dan trailed off. He could not talk to Billy about what he had been trying to do. All the way to school his friend quizzed and mocked him, and eventually grew angry. But Dan remained silent on the subject. By the time their first break arrived Billy had forgotten the incident.

Not Dan, though. As he ran around he was wondering what he should try next. *That snail just wasn't special*, he thought. *Something will be. Eventually.*

But nothing ever was.

Over the next few weeks Dan realised how many dead things were lying around, if only you went looking for them. One Friday evening he found a mouse in his back garden behind a flower pot. It was still breathing, even though it had been holed by something; perhaps thrown there by his father when he had cut the grass. Its little grey sides shifted with its rapid breathing, its eyes were shiny and black, and when Dan picked it up by its tail a slick of something grey and wet exited the wound in its body.

He held it in one palm and stroked it with a finger, slipping his fingertip across the wound, trying to press inside, all the while thinking, *Get better, get better*. But the mouse did not get better. As he forced at the wound it stiffened, then died. It suddenly seemed heavier. The mouse was not special.

A week later Billy told him about a cat that had been run over on the other side of the village. It lay in a ditch, stiff and dead. Dan slipped away later that day and found the cat. He probed its cold, hard body, scraping aside blood-dried fur, but he found no way in. The cat remained dead, not special.

A blackbird, shot with an air rifle, already crawling with maggots. A woodlouse, poisoned by his mother's rose spray and curled into a ball. A spider, light and dry in a saucepan beneath the sink. He even found a rabbit hauling itself into a field, back legs crushed by a car.

None of them were special. Daniel tried, but all he received for his efforts were fingers both bloody and cold. He would nurse the dead or dying things and project his

The Evolutionary

thoughts, *Get well, get well.* He would search for the power he thought he must have, the same power as the man in the woods, and even though he found nothing he was convinced that there was something about *him*, something special that set *him* aside from his sister and Billy and his other friends. He believed this so deeply that eventually he began to feel it as well. It was deep down inside him, past dark places that he had never seen, and sometimes it itched. He began scratching at his stomach and back, and he closed his eyes and imagined the man's fingers and hands slipping inside the siskin, the wolf, the bear.

Daniel spent that Christmas holiday hearing about Jesus and how special He was, and he cried himself to sleep one night, wondering whether the man had watched Jesus' crucifixion with a tingle in his fingers that could never be answered.

I could try to kill myself. The man will come. He'll save me. He'll have to, and he'll let me know what I can do. He'll let me know what the itch is inside me and help me scratch it. I know there's something there, I can feel it, I can taste *it when I sit still long enough and don't eat or drink anything else. Mum and Dad don't even notice. Billy hasn't called me for days, he says I'm going weird. He says I should have a wank, but I'm afraid that'll lose the itch. I don't want to lose it. I never want to lose it. All I want is for it to grow bigger and clearer.*

I could try to kill myself.

He'll come...

I could try...

Daniel had seen films and read books where people killed themselves. Shotguns to the face, pills, jumping in front of cars, leaping from clifftops, lying across train tracks, slitting wrists in the bath...each image haunted and disturbed him, leaving a deep-felt sense of wrongness that he could not shake. He felt as if he had witnessed something not only sinful, but not of nature. The suicides shifted themselves out of reality. It was not only death, but the manner of death that mattered. The more he thought about it, the more Daniel believed that nothing the man could do—no touch, no muttered invocations—could ever save a suicide.

Still, the thought lingered for a while. *I could try, just try, not actually do it. I could pretend. And then he'll come, and tell me what I am and why I'm here.*

I could try...

But as time ran and fate frolicked, choice was taken from him.

—⚭—

The following spring, he and his family spent a weekend in a caravan on the Cornish coast. Daniel had shaken loose any ideas of trying to do himself harm, moving on and leaving that troubled boy behind. He was glad. Christmas had seemed to act as a point of change, and successive weeks and months had blurred the memory of the man, diluted the impact of those strange journeys. By the time buds appeared on trees and flowers pushed their way up out of cold soil, the man had become a dream. Sometimes Daniel could remember him, sometimes not. He thought of a wolf and a

The Evolutionary

frog and a butterfly, but he could not see them in his mind, could not picture whatever wounds should have killed them. Sometimes a dream will edge into reality, but more often the opposite will happen. Part of Daniel's life became a dream, and he was happy to sleep the sleep of the innocent and let it play itself out.

On their trip to Cornwall the family did a lot of walking, tracking the coastal path as far east as the little village of Polperro. It was lunchtime when they arrived, and the cafés and pubs were filled with tourists eager to stake their claim on table-space. Daniel and his family bought fish and chips and sat in the harbour, relishing the strong afternoon sun on their flushed cheeks. Seagulls buzzed them, darting in to snap up any scraps that fell to the stone breakwater. His sister smiled at him. His mother and father held hands and sat close together. It was the sort of day that goes by in a pleasant haze but lives in your memory as one of the best. And Daniel knew that. He was more than aware of growing up, and he knew that times like this would not happen for very much longer. He would soon be a teenager, and much as he looked forward to discovering his own place in the world, he was still young enough to mourn what would be lost. His mother kissed his forehead. His father took him down onto the beach and followed him into the narrow cave, and they both jumped back in shocked fright when they found a dead seagull with flies buzzing its open stomach. Daniel even held his sister's hand as they walked up through the town, heading for the bus stop to catch a bus back to their caravan site.

The bus did not stop. It ploughed straight into Daniel and his family, throwing his father and sister across the road into the front of a building, and his mother into the stream. Daniel was caught beneath the front wheels and scoured across the road, flesh and bone tearing and splintering, living long enough to feel the bus grind to a halt against a stone wall.

—⁂—

Why do you think you met me?

The voice came from far away, so quiet that it may have been a memory.

You always knew I'd be here if you needed me.

Pain, in rhythm with the voice, as if controlled by its shifting cadences.

And here I am, and here you are, and there's not long left until you know.

Daniel tried to open his eyes, but he was not sure that they were his anymore. None of his body felt like his. He could feel something happening—agony here, there, erupting at random points, flaring and then subsiding again—but feeling it did not mean that he belonged.

He had come back from a place where he had known nothing, been nothing, and now he was trying to accept something again. He did not know what that something was, but it felt important. It felt like life. Behind him the gravity of emptiness struggled to haul him back. He felt its endless weight, always there and always known, and it seemed to snatch away his thoughts as soon as they happened. He could recall nothing, and nothing fresh arrived. Back there, in the heavy void, lay everything he sought.

But there was a problem.

You can't go back, the voice said. Daniel felt pain blossoming, and he heard a sound. His soul was touched and

The Evolutionary

slapped, as if to wake it up. That sound again, a croak, and he recognised it. His voice, crying out in pain.

"Lie still," the other voice said, and Daniel heard rather than sensed it. "Time doesn't matter to you right now."

When Daniel opened his eyes, the pull of the emptiness suddenly faded and let him go.

A shape knelt by his side. The man from his dreams. He looked no different, although his face was washed of humour by the splashes of blood speckling his skin. His eyes shifted and met Daniel's, and he smiled.

"Trust me," the man said. "There's lots to do." He leaned forward, and Daniel felt something happening in his chest. At last, his itch was being scratched.

Other voices rose up, filled with shock and concern and something that could have been disgust. *What are you doing? Look at that. Is that his hand? Lucky to be alive, all of them...except the poor boy...no way he'll live...That man, is he a doctor? Ambulance on its way.*

Daniel opened his mouth, emptied himself of the scream that had been building, and then said, "Am I going to be left behind?"

"You'll never be on your own," the man said.

"My mum, dad, Josie?"

"Alive, but you're the special one."

Daniel tried turning his head but the man held it there somehow, pressing down inside so that it could not be moved, and Daniel felt another galaxy of pain fade away.

They're all *special,* he thought. *I can't live without them.*

"I've been waiting for this," the man said. "You're the special one now." That phrase again, as if it was a reason, an excuse, an answer, all rolled into one.

Daniel tried to shake his head to deny the truth, but he could not move. Perhaps the man had yet to reach his spine. "Why?" he asked instead, verbalising the endless question. So many people ask it, so few ever hear a reply. He suddenly realised that perhaps he would be one of the few.

"If I told you that," the man said, "it could never be."

And suddenly he was gone.

Faces appeared above Daniel, professional concern failing to hide the shock, and then his mother with blood in her eye and cuts on her cheek. Her tears speckled his face and he was glad to feel them.

A mask shut him off from the world, but only for a while. Daniel knew that he would be given back very soon. And then he would grow into a future that would be, in every way, extraordinary.

Nothing Heavenly

On the day I leave the world, I do not believe it is the End. There are no signs of chaos, no hints of Armageddon, nothing but the usual madness and loneliness in a world growing more accustomed to both. I taste only normality on the smoggy London air. I see a girl whipping a dog in the street, a man crying into a mobile phone, two boys swearing at an old man and an old woman cursing at something less obvious. These images leave me as soon as I walk away, because they are not unusual. Mad, lonely; I am neither, but before the day is through I will be forced to contemplate both.

I do not *believe* it is the End, but my beliefs are always shaky at best.

And I am wrong.

"Rosalie."

The voice comes from behind me, somewhere in the crowd waiting on the Underground platform. I turn, scan the faces and then stare back across the tracks at a poster advertising a new techno-thriller. Mine is not a common name, but not so uncommon either. Whoever is speaking can't mean me.

"Rosalie."

Same tone, same volume. I turn again. A couple of people catch my eye and look away in that embarrassed, aloof manner that only big city dwellers can muster. There are no smiles, no nods or winks.

A roar builds from the tunnel's throat as the train approaches. I look forward again, brace myself against the shove I always fear will come. There are news items every month about people being pushed in front of Underground trains, and just lately, it seems every week sees another cruel death or crippling. Pushing is becoming something of a sport.

"Rosalie!" the voice says again, harsher this time, and the gush of air forced along the tunnel sweeps my name away.

I frown, steady my feet and imagine falling forward into space, shiny metal, blackened stones and scampering rats ready to greet me seconds before the train wheels take off my legs and head. But then the train is there, loud and stinking and packed with commuters. It slows to a halt, the doors hiss open and I barge my way on board without waiting for anyone to disembark. Nobody complains. They won't, not down here where constant close proximity creates a private world for everyone. I can smell a woman's perfume, a man's

Nothing Heavenly

sweat, the hint of garlic breath, yet I am more isolated than if I were the only passenger in this carriage.

The train starts moving. There are no seats so I hang on to a strap, feeling the intimate swaying of coats and briefcases against my legs and hips. I stare at the Underground map above the seats beside me, because there are faces and eyes everywhere else.

"Rosalie."

I turn around, angry now, but nobody meets my gaze. I recognise one woman from the platform—dreadlocks, camouflage jacket, pierced eyebrow—but it is a man's voice muttering my name, definitely a man's. "Yes?" I ask no one, and no one answers. I shake my head and look down at my shoes.

I am being watched. I can sense it, and it's a peculiar feeling in this packed train. Nobody actually watches anyone down here—everyone maintains the disinterested tube stare—so feeling someone's attention upon me is disconcerting. I lift my head. The man sitting directly in front of me is staring at my breasts, but he seems miles away. I close my coat and his expression does not change. I look around, trying to make out who is watching me, and I can see no one.

"Come for a walk, Rosalie."

"I can hardly go for a walk," I say out loud, and a couple of people glance nervously away. I feel myself blush. There are many strange people to be found on the London Underground, but they're not usually me.

"I'll hold your hand," the voice says, and for the first time I am truly worried. No one is talking. Whichever way I turn the voice seems to come from everywhere, every side, as if it is inside my head. And that's really not something I'm comfortable considering just yet. Not yet, not so soon after my failure. It's a trick or a joke or some sick fuck playing with me, that's all.

"Did you hear that?" I ask the man standing beside me. He lifts his eyebrows, shrugs, looks away. "I heard it," I say, as if acknowledging it will make the voice real.

"It might be you," the voice says then, and for the first time there's some emotion that lifts it above a monotone. It takes a few seconds for me to place exactly what it is, and then the voice speaks again and I know: "Rosalie, it might be you!" Passion. There's passion in that voice, and I feel the small hairs on my arms prickling.

Nobody else seems to notice. A man reads a newspaper, a woman scratches her nose whilst staring back into yesterday, a couple sit and hold hands so tightly that their knuckles have turned white. The girl looks scared. She's staring at her reflected self in the window. I wonder whether she has heard the voice as well. I shift position slightly so that I can stare across at my own reflection, and that's when I see him, standing right by my shoulder and watching my image with something approaching wonder.

I gasp, turn, and he's not there.

"Now!" he says. Someone pulls my arms, tugging me along the crowded carriage. People shift out of my way, frowning at me but turning away again instantly. I look at the window and see the shape of the man, and then I catch sight of my own face and realise why the other passengers will not meet my gaze. Perhaps it's a trick of the light, or the dirt on the window, or splashes of soot on the walls rushing by outside, but my eyes are jet black.

"Let me go!" I shout.

Nothing Heavenly

"Now," the voice says. "Now, Rosalie!"

"Let me the fuck go!"

My arms are raised. There are indentations in my flesh where invisible hands are pulling me toward the doors. I cannot resist. I cannot hold back, however firmly I plant my feet. I look to the right and see the shape's shadow in the window.

Falling sideways, I shoulder into a standing man, hoping that he will hold me back. "Help me!" I scream at him. "Help me!" But his eyes go wide and he falls, his own hands held up to ward me off.

The sliding door buckles, punched again and again by an invisible force. The glass shatters, the metal creases, and then it smashes open. The thunderous clanking of metal on metal fills the carriage. I smell diesel and rot.

"No!" I scream.

"Stop her!" someone says, and I think it's the frightened-looking girl. But nobody moves to help. We're all strangers here, and for the first time I feel the centre of attention as I tumble away into the dark.

—⚡—

There are two creatures fighting in a darkened alley. One is taller and thinner than a human, its hands wide like shovels and its eyes glimmering yellow in the dusky light. The other is shorter, wider, its heavy shoulders seeming to distort every time it moves. It too has glowing eyes, but the colour is none that I have ever seen. It is a new colour. That disturbs me more than anything.

The tall thing hisses and leaps forward, its massive arms wrapping around the shorter creature and slapping the back of its head, gripping, twisting. The short one screams like a pig being gutted. Its head turns, its back ripples and something leathery hangs there, caught for an instant in the headlights of a passing car. Wings. It has wings.

It flaps, lifts, and the tall creature loses its grip.

There is something terrifying in this battle of unknown things. I can see the fight and smell the blood, but it is much more than that, something more elemental and significant that scares me. I have witnessed fights before—I once saw a man have his eye gouged out in a pub brawl—but nothing has prepared me for this. There is the sense that, with every punch landed or handful of flesh twisted, the elements are joining in. Darkness spars with light. A breeze flows along the alley, lifting litter to twist and joust in the night air. The ground cracks beneath the feet of the shorter combatant, pavement shifting, stone crumbling, and as it steps away I see something that looks like blood welling in its footprint. The liquid reflects pale yellow light from the tall thing's eyes, and then they merge into battle once more.

For the first time I notice several other shapes along the alley, leaning against walls or hidden in shadows that seem to lap at their edges. I am standing at the mouth of the alley—for the first time I have a real sense of location—and not ten steps away a body is steaming into the night. It is long, slender, and dead. Its yellow eyes have faded to black. Close by, half concealed by a wheeled dustbin, one of the shorter creatures is keening softly as its guts unfurl from a mortal wound in its stomach. Their purple coils are smoking,

Nothing Heavenly

not steaming, and I see flames flickering up and dying out amongst the slippery insides.

I open my mouth to speak, but then the two fighting creatures sense me, pull away from each other and stare. One of them gapes, the other begins to cry, and any remaining light suddenly seems to go from the world.

—⁂—

I sit up, gasping, winded by shock. I am naked, and the rough blanket coiled around my body is damp with sweat. I manage to draw in a breath to scream. Hold it. Look around.

"The sleeper awakes," a man says.

I scamper backward across the bed and lean against the wall. It is cold against my back but I like that, I welcome the feel of cool stone on my burning skin. *What* were *those things*?

"Who are you?"

"My name's Peter. Who are you?"

"You don't know?"

The man shakes his head. "I know your name, Rosalie, but I don't know who you are. That's why you're here: for me to find out."

I pull the blanket tightly around me, hugging my knees and looking around the room for my clothes.

"You'll get them back," Peter says.

"I want them now. You can't keep me here like this. I want to leave."

Peter is sitting in a chair, legs crossed, cigarette in one hand. With his free hand he smoothes his hair, flicks at a speck of ash on his immaculate suit. "You won't find your way anywhere," he says.

"Where am I?" I suddenly remember the train and the voice, and the door bursting open just before I fell through. After that, nothing. No sense of falling, no impact, no memory of walking or being dragged through the tunnels. Nothing, except for the dream of those fighting things.

"Somewhere safe," Peter says. "It's a dangerous world tonight."

"Just tonight?"

Peter nods. "More so than ever before. Angels and demons are entering into battle for the future of Humankind. Their fight will likely destroy most of the world, and the Second Coming is at hand."

I look at the man, watching for any hint of humour in his expression. I see none. "Right," I say. "Does this mean my date on Saturday is cancelled?"

Peter's face remains impassive. "Whoever it is, he'll probably be dead by then."

"Right." I nod and looks down at my bare feet. *Angels and demons*. I think of the dream, those things fighting and dying in a darkened alley. I swallow, cough, tasting only staleness in my mouth. He must be drugging me with something, but I have no idea what. I don't know about that sort of stuff. Maybe I should pay more attention to CSI. "I fell from a train," I say.

He shrugs, smokes, says nothing.

"So why aren't I injured?"

"I caught you," he says. "And now I need to ask you some questions, Rosalie. It's important you answer them properly."

Nothing Heavenly

"Why? One wrong answer and you rape me?" I tense, shocked at my outburst, but I do not let him see that. I have to be strong. I suddenly realise that I need to pee.

Peter stares at me for a few long seconds, looking only at my eyes. "No one is going to rape you," he says. He shakes his head. "Never think that."

"Well I wake up naked in a room with you looking at me, and—"

"Your clothes were messed up when you were brought here. You soiled yourself. I thought you might like them washed."

"So you stripped me?"

"Yes. And sent them away for cleaning."

"So you saw me naked?"

Peter nods. His expression does not change. "You're very beautiful. But I have no interest in raping you, Rosalie. Are you a virgin?"

"What sort of fucking question is that?"

"The first of many."

"Well it's none of your fucking business!" I am shaking now, and cold, sweat drying on my skin. I move away from the wall and try to wrap the towel around my back, but I cannot do so without letting go. And if I do that it could drop from my chest, and *whatever* this sick fuck says I don't trust him, not one bit, not even a smidgen of a bit, not—

I look around and suddenly realise where I am. I cannot call the room a dungeon—it is painted a clean bright white, the bed is comfortable, and there is a commode and washing area behind a screen in the corner—but the walls are bare, rough stone, the door is made of heavy iron, and the sense of weight around me is almost breathtaking. I can feel the pull of gravity heaving my flesh and lifting the hairs on my head, and when I swallow I suddenly feel very light, almost as if I am ready to float up off the bed. I am underground.

I remember the short creature in the alley, its leathery wings lifting it and its attacker from the ground, and I rub my back against the cold wall.

"What's the first evil thing you remember doing?" Peter asks. He leans forward in his seat, dropping his cigarette and grinding it out beneath his foot without ever looking away from my face. Smoke still seeps from his mouth, as if he is alight inside.

I blink, and wonder whether my eyes are still those deep dark pits I thought I saw on the train. And against every desire, against my better judgement, I remember.

The kitten was small and weak. The runt of the litter. My parents had taken it in from Mrs. Joyce at the post office, offering to look after it until a permanent home could be found. *It can't stay here forever*, my mother had said. *You father's allergic to cats. Why are we even having it, then?* I had asked, petulance turning my voice into a whine. *Because if we don't, Mr. Joyce will drown it*, my mother had said.

Drown it. I looked at the kitten cowering down in its cardboard box, clawing at its blanket as if trying to hide itself from my stare. I imagined holding its weak body in a water-filled bucket, feeling its pathetic struggles, sensing the final weak heartbeat as water drank the life from it and turned it into a hunk of rotting meat. *That's what we are,*

Nothing Heavenly

I had once heard father saying as he poured himself some more whiskey, *just rotting meat*.

I was six years old.

Can I take it for a walk? I asked my mother, but by then she was already on the phone. So I picked up the kitten and carried it into the garden.

It did not take me very long to fall in love. The cat was small but friendly, as if grateful at begin removed from a litter that would doubtless have bullied, or even killed it. I named it Suzy. Suzy lay in my lap as I sat on the garden swing. I kicked off and swung myself back and forth, into and out of the shadow of the house, trying to time my breathing with the sunlight on my skin. Sunlight, breathe in; shadow, breathe out. That way all my bad breath was kept in the dark beside the house. I looked down at Suzy and wondered whether she was doing the same.

The kitten was asleep. She seemed so contented, so cute, that I could not imagine drowning her, or killing her in any other way. Why destroy something just because it was weak? I'd heard my mother calling her the runt of the litter, but for me that was more reason to look after her. The others could look after themselves; Suzy needed help. I smiled down at Suzy, made clicking noises with my tongue, and when the kitten opened one lazy eye I looked up and saw a buzzard circling the garden.

Cats eat birds, I thought. That was strange. Cats were so cute and cuddly and so loved laying out by the fire, that I could not imagine Suzy ever coming home with blood and feathers around her mouth. *Cats eat birds*. I leaned back on the swing, hair trailing across the dusty ground, and stared up at the circling bird of prey. Suzy grumbled in my lap, purring silently. I stopped swinging and hung back, feeling the blood rush to my head, and I imagined my mother whispering in my ear: *Good girl, you're a good girl Rosie.* My name was Rosalie; I hated being called Rosie. It was like calling Jesus Je.

Rotting meat, I said. I smelled my arm, my hand, and they did not smell bad. But when I picked up Suzy and sniffed her head there was a mustiness there I did not understand. I put the kitten down on the grass, laying her out in the sun and tickling her behind the ear until she fell asleep. Then I went back to the swing.

By the time the buzzard came down and took Suzy away, I was swinging in total shadow.

I tell Peter about the kitten and he shakes his head. "More than that," he says. "There must have been something more than that. *Must* have! If not..." He stands quickly, his chair scraping back across the stone floor, and for a second I think he is coming for me. I tense and get ready to kick out at his crotch. But Peter turns and walks to the door. He opens it somehow—there is no latch visible, no lock—and turns around just as he's about to leave. "When I come back I'm going to ask you about the *last* evil thing you remember doing."

"Fuck you," I say.

Peter raises one corner of his mouth in a sad smile. "I still think it could be you," he says. Something flits past him beyond the door, something dark and short and inhuman. He seems not to notice, or if he does he's not surprised. He

Nothing Heavenly

leaves, and even though I do not hear any clicks or clanks I know that the door is locked.

—⁂—

The room is silent, the light remains on, the temperature is comfortable, and in one corner there is a tray with orange juice, biscuits and fruit. This does not feel like a prison.

Mark will miss me, I think. But he won't. I've only been out with him a few times, and the Saturday date has been arranged since last week. I doubt he'll call to confirm, and if he does and finds me out he won't be concerned. Maybe by Saturday he will. Maybe then he'll raise the alarm. But Saturday is four days away.

There's Mum, but I usually call her on Sundays. Sometimes I leave the city and go to visit her, but that happens less and less lately, and it seems the guiltier I become about that the less I feel inclined to visit. Too concerned at my own feelings. Too selfish.

Then there are my friends, all of whom call quite frequently, none of whom will be the slightest bit concerned when they find I'm not at home. They're a diverse gang, busy, and they have their own lives to lead. *Rosalie not in? I'll try again tomorrow*. Maybe they would or maybe they wouldn't. Either way it does nothing to help me now.

My phone has gone with the clothes, though I'm certain it wouldn't work down here.

I wonder where *down here* is, and why I think of it as *down*.

But there's something else playing on my mind, and though it's unreasonable still I want to encourage the thought:

Tim Lebbon

I'm not really scared. I've been kidnapped and imprisoned, I'm being kept here naked and cold, I saw something out there in the corridor, something that could have been one of those creatures from my dream…but I'm truly not that scared. Maybe it's shock. Maybe it's not really happening. Perhaps I'll wake up and find myself in a hospital bed or on a psychiatrist's couch, my mother bending over me and scolding me for not calling her if I was in trouble, because that's what mothers are for.

Or maybe none of this has really hit me yet.

"We're just rotting flesh," I mutter, and something beyond the walls whispers as if excited at my words.

―☙―

Angels and demons, Peter had said, and I wonder which ones are which. Like West Side Story remade by Guillermo del Toro, the two gangs of creatures are facing up to each other. On the left, five of the tall, large-handed things, faces split by bloody sneers, eyes glinting yellow. On the right, six of the short, muscular creatures. Both sides hiss and click in languages I cannot understand, though the tone is obvious. There is mockery here, and anger. The air feels slick with hate.

We are in some sort of hinterland behind a row of shops. Litter is drifted against walls, cartons and crates stacked in a small yard off to the left, and the buildings are vandalised and tattooed with crude graffiti. These are invectives of hate, scrawled by unsteady hands with paint meant to last forever. *Lucy is a bitch*, and *Robert can eat my ass*, and *If you make me cum back ergen I'll kill your baybee.* For some reason

Nothing Heavenly

they disturb me more than the things readying themselves for a fight.

I stand to one side, hidden from view beneath several sick-looking trees. It is almost dawn, and the sun is still asleep. Night holds on for its last few brave minutes. Birds sit above me in the branches—I can sense them there—but they utter no dawn chorus this morning. They, too, are watching.

One second I was in the room, the next here. I assume I am asleep and dreaming once again, though my senses are alight. The stench of violence, the sound of rage simmering in the air, and beneath my feet I'm sure I can feel the ground shaking. I pull back behind a tree trunk and see two names carved in the bark, *Jimmy lvs Jade*. I wonder where they are right now, and hope they're happy.

I think of Mark, my maybe-boyfriend, and realise I never knew him at all. I think of my poor mother, alone since my father died, filled with bitterness and regret, and a tear comes to my eye. But then the creatures launch at one another, and my grief loses its moment.

The fight is fast and brutal. The action moves so quickly that I can barely keep up. There is the sound of crunching bones and splitting flesh, wet splashes as things hit the broken tarmac, screeches and growls, claws on stone and teeth on bone, and the flapping of wings. The short things—those left standing—start to take off, but the tall creatures gang up and grab at their legs, pulling them back down.

A minute after the fight begins there are three of the tall creatures left standing. The others are dead, along with all of the short stocky things, their blood and insides spread across the ground. One wing still flaps feebly at the air, though its owner is gutted and its head is attached only by a few strands of vein. A thin red mist hangs over the scene, as if the blood splashed into the air has stained it. The survivors go from body to body slitting throats. They use long thin knives, slicing friend and foe alike.

One of the tall shapes opens its mouth and screams at the sky, shaking its head, thumping its chest with huge bloody hands, warbling long and loud. I cover my ears, close my eyes and gasp, and the screaming ceases.

Silence. I open my eyes and the three tall creatures are staring at me. Blood paints their naked bodies. Their eyes glow yellow in the rising sun, but they were yellow long before that, as if they hold the power of stars inside their heads.

"What are you?" I say, and the things turn and run. They are screaming, hissing and clicking, but I do not know their language. It could be fear or laughter.

—⚞—

Dawn turns into a blazing light bulb, and I am back in the subterranean room.

"Are you awake?" someone says, voice low and deep.

I sit up. The blanket falls from my chest and I grab it up, certain that I am being watched. It's the same feeling that I had on the train. I look around the room, stand, wrap the blanket around me and walk to the screened area. There's a sink back there with a mirror above it, and as the angle lessens and I come into view I look over my own shoulder. No one, nothing there.

"Where are you?" I say.

Nothing Heavenly

"In the cell next door. Look under your bed." I think it's a woman.

I kneel and peer beneath the bed. The light is bright and harsh enough to filter down here, reflected from the white-painted walls, and I make out the long, narrow grille running at skirting level. From the grille, the woman's voice.

"Ventilation," she says.

"Where are we?"

"Don't know."

"How long have you been here?" I lie down beside the bed and prop my head on one hand. I can see nothing through the grille—not even a shadow—but it seems only proper to talk at it rather than sit on the bed. It's contact, I suppose, nearness to someone else. I suddenly realise that Peter is not some*one*. He's a blank. A some*thing*. I wonder whether he's even human, but that thought must come from a part of my mind going mad. *I'm not mad*, I think. But at the same time I know that madness is the perfect fall-guy.

"Few days," the woman says. There's a lilt to her voice, an accent I can't quite place. "You're the second one they've had in that room."

"What happened to the first?"

"They took him out and killed him." The voice falls silent and I hold my breath. *Killed him*? How? Why? And why do I feel no real threat here, even now with this mysterious voice telling me an unbearable fact.

"You're lying," I say.

"No I'm not!" she hisses, and such outrage cannot be manufactured.

"What's your name?"

"Francine. I'm from Lyons. You?"

For a few seconds I keep quiet, wondering whether I should tell this stranger my name. *Names give you a face*, my father once said in one of those rare moments when insight smothered his sourness. At the moment I am faceless, but I have Francine's name, and therefore an advantage. Besides, what if she is one of them? What if Peter is sitting out there next to her, listening, eager to glean whatever information it is they want from me?

My fear is still a shallow thing at the back of my mind, like the memory of a dream fracturing to time.

"I'm Rosalie," I say. "Pleased to meet you."

"Huh. Wish I could say the same."

"So why are we here? What do they want? Have they…?"

"Nothing like that," Francine says. "They've asked me questions. About my past, and my ideas, and…very personal stuff. Like they're trying to understand me. It's been like having thirty dates in a few days, all with the same guy trying to get to know me."

"Peter?"

"Yes, him. And sometimes others. He's the best of them. The others aren't so human."

"He told me there are angels and demons," I say.

"He told me that too." Francine falls quiet but it is a loaded silence, primed with something both of us need to say.

"I've been having dreams," I say, not entirely sure whether that's accurate. *Dreams, really? Aren't they more like visions? Aren't I actually there when I* dream *these dreams?*

"Angels and demons," Francine says. "At first I thought they were drugging me. I stopped drinking and eating, and

Nothing Heavenly

still the dreams came. Always in Paris, always with…things. Fighting. Killing. Each other mostly, but one time two young lovers came in, just stumbled into the fight, and they died too. So I started eating and drinking again, and Peter keeps asking the questions, and I still have no idea what they want."

"He asked me about my first evil deed," I say, remembering Lucy the kitten and the buzzard I left her for. "It wasn't even that evil, not in the scheme of things. It was no real sin."

"He'll ask more and more," Francine says. "They're probably listening now. Sometimes I think there's someone in the room with me, though I can't see them."

"Who did they kill?" I say.

"His name was Dimitris. He was Greek. He didn't speak much French or English, so we hardly said anything to each other. Just the sound of his voice was a comfort, though. I heard him being questioned, but not for long, and then they took him out and I heard him screaming."

"Why? What did they do?"

"I don't know, but he screamed for a long time. An hour, maybe more. Then he stopped, and I haven't heard him since."

"When was this?"

"Yesterday. I asked Peter about it when he came to see me last night, but he just shook his head and carried on questioning me."

I sit up, stare at the wall above my bed, trying to absorb everything Francine has said and make some sense from it. But there's none to be made. We're having the same dreams, we're trapped in the same place, yet neither of us has any idea of what this is about. "Sins," I say.

"What?"

"Why's he asking about sins, evil deeds?" I think of Lucy and other things, worse sins. I wonder whether I'll ever be able to tell him. I don't like to think about it now, even so soon after. But it's always there, and if Peter keeps digging perhaps one day soon it'll be out in the open once again.

"It's almost as if he *wants* me to be evil," Francine says.

"Are you?"

The French woman is quiet for some time, so long that I begin to think she has fallen asleep. "No," she says then. "Not evil. No more than anyone else I know."

"I wonder if that's really an answer," I say, and this time Francine does not reply at all. I wait for a few minutes, sad at the loss of contact but also wise enough to know not to push it. She's been here longer than me. She's heard more, said more, and she probably knows more about who Peter is and what he wants, though perhaps she is unwilling to share her ideas as yet. "Tap if you want to talk," I say, and Francine says, "You too."

—⚏—

"So?" Peter says. "Have you thought about it?"

"The last evil thing I did was to dream about slitting your throat."

He nods, places a cigarette in his mouth and lights it with a match. He puts the match out on his tongue and places it in the breast pocket of his jacket. There is something very deliberate about it, but I cannot see the significance. Maybe he's just trying to confuse me.

"So you've met Francine?" he asks. I say nothing, and he takes that as assent. "She's a beautiful woman," he

Nothing Heavenly

continues. "Much like you. So much depth to her that I feel I've barely brushed the surface. I've only swept away the errant thoughts that have no meaning, and now its time to start mining. Digging in. Cutting her open to get at the truth inside."

"Why would you—"

"There are more ways to cut than with a knife," Peter says. He draws on his cigarette and exhales the smoke. It rises about his head, undisturbed. If the grille beneath the bed is for ventilation it seems not to be working.

"Can you tell me why I'm here?" I ask.

"No."

"Why?"

"Because I need you to realise for yourself."

"Realise what?"

He shakes his head and smiles, but says nothing.

"What about Dimitris?"

Peter shrugs. "A pretender. A mistake. After so long, I'm used to them." He stands and paces the room, running his hands along the walls. He reaches the screened area in the corner and peers in, as if interested in what I do in there. He is very slow, graceful, and his feet almost seem to float a finger-width above the floor. I find myself staring at the back of his jacket, looking for the tell-tale bump of wings.

"Why angels and demons?" I ask.

"You've dreamed of them again?"

"I wasn't asleep when I did."

He pauses, turns to look at me as though trying to make out whether I'm playing with him. Then he sits again, never looking away from my face. "Really?" he asks at last.

I shrug. The blanket is rough on my shoulders, itchy, and it's starting to smell. I sweat when I sleep. "Where are my clothes?"

"If I get them for you, will you agree to answer some questions?"

I stare at him, wondering whether bargaining is really the way to go. I'm not sure who would get the most out of that, and I have no idea how far it could get me. But I crave my clothes, their familiarity and closeness, and I see no harm in what he's asking. I nod, he stands and leaves the room, and Francine taps on the grille.

"It's the end of the world," she hisses, her voice fast and high, "and he's one of *them*, one of those *things*, angel or demon who cares, who fucking cares, and he's looking for something and the more you tell him the more he's going to see, the more he'll *know!*"

"Francine? You're not making sense, you've been here—"

"You'll see," she says, her voice slow and low again. She starts to giggle. I realise that she is mad. "You'll see!" Then she can say no more, because the giggles turn into a mad cackling that scares me more than anything my sleeping nightmares have yet presented.

—⚏—

Half an hour later the door opens again. I expect to see Peter coming in with my clothes, but what enters through is not even human. It looks human in many ways—it has arms and legs, a face with all the correct features in the right places, and it is dressed in a cheap suit—but it is too short

Nothing Heavenly

and wide, too grizzled, and when it looks at me its eyes shine with a colour I cannot know.

"No!" I try to squeeze myself back into the corner of the room, rucking up the bedding and holding the blanket to my face like a child protecting itself from the night. "*No!*" My fear is suddenly rich and full, fed by a realisation that I am somewhere very, very wrong, and that escape is not something I can even consider. I have given in before anything has really begun.

The thing exudes wrongness. It looks like a man but moves differently, as if uncomfortable in this flesh and skin it wears. Its shoulders keep shrugging, the jacket rising up, and the collar of its shirt has worn its neck red-raw. Its eyes are painful to observe. Its face hold no expression at all—it might as well be moulded from plastic—and as its mouth falls open I close my eyes, desperate to not hear what may come from there.

It sighs, and immediately the stink of its breath fills the room. I roll onto my side and pull the blanket over my head, realising how ridiculous this gesture is, yet unable to do anything else. I wish Mark were here with me, ready to hold me and fight this thing off, but he is as distant as ever, a blur in my memory. I think of my mother and how frightened she will be at my disappearance. And I realise that back in the world, she is the only person that would truly mourn me.

I hold my breath and sit up. The blanket falls from my face. The thing is still there, setting my clothes down on the chair, all of them washed and pressed and smelling of an autumn glade I will never see.

I glance at the door. It is still open.

The thing looks at me and I cry out again, burying my face in the blanket so that it does not see my scheming eyes. I peek and it is smoothing the clothes, being so gentle with them, working out the creases with its gnarled hands.

I stand and throw off the blanket. The thing looks at my nakedness and I dart for the door, grabbing its edge, pulling it open, pushing myself through and out into the corridor beyond. I have no idea where I will go or what I will do once outside—how difficult would it be to find a naked woman?—but I cannot stay in that room, not with that angel or demon or whatever the fuck—

It grabs me with both hands and hauls me back in. One hand covers my stomach, the other my breasts, crushing them flat and eliciting a scream of pain which I so want to keep inside. I hate to give it such satisfaction. But after it sets me on the bed it backs away, mouth dropping open and eyes closing as if from shock. It clicks and hisses and withdraws from the room, slamming the door closed behind it. No sounds of a key, but I know it is suddenly locked. It looks immovable.

What the hell just happened?

I dress quickly, feeling so much more complete now that I'm clothed, and as soon as I lace up my trainers the door opens once again.

Peter enters and sits, giving no indication that he knows of my escape bid. "I hope the clothes are okay," he says.

"Yes, fine." I smooth my jumper, enjoying the feel of woollen trousers against my legs. There's a security in clothing. Being naked is so vulnerable.

Peter looks me up and down and nods. "They look nice."

Nothing Heavenly

If he expects a thank you he can go whistle.

"So," he says. "Tell me."

"Tell you what? I don't have a fucking clue who you are or where I am or why, and you're killing people down here, and unless you tell me what the fuck—"

"We're not killing people," he says.

"The Greek guy, Dimitris…?"

Peter shrugs and takes out a cigarette. "Would you like one?"

"I don't smoke, they're bad for you."

He smiles, then laughs, a brief bark that he quickly reins in.

"Glad you think that was funny," I say.

He lights the cigarette. "It's the End of Times and you're worried about lung cancer."

"You tell me it's the End of Times, but I don't believe you. Things were fine yesterday when I left. People were going to work, people were living normally, and things were fine."

"Fine? Do you really think so? I'll tell you about fine, shall I Rosalie? I'll tell you what was fine with the world yesterday, and after you've had a think about what I've said, and realised just how right I am and how wrong you are, maybe then you can give me the answers I'm still waiting for." He takes a long pull on the cigarette and lets the smoke hang around his head. It gives the impression of blurring his features, and I sit back on the bed and let tears do the rest. They feel like a betrayal but I let them come anyway. I'm not even sure that Peter notices.

"Yesterday," he says, "thousands of people died of starvation all across Africa. Thousands more died of disease, many of them children so young they hadn't learnt to speak, other than to beg. The civilised nations of Earth paid vast amounts of money to maintain food mountains that will eventually rot, gave yet more money to finance oil and mineral exploration in Antarctica, and pledged to fund drug research to produce drugs available only to those who can afford them. Meanwhile in record centres too hidden and too deep for anyone to know about, the truth about a hundred disasters around the world lays buried…and men pay good money to keep them that way. There are still thinking heads on bloody necks that will roll if those records are ever revealed. Money changes hands, all of it watermarked with the blood of the innocent. And the sheep, the robots—people *like* you, Rosalie, though not you, and you'll realise why soon enough—they go to work. Then they go home. They turn on the TV and watch the inane shows put on for their entertainment, they drink alcohol to dull their senses, they screw and sleep and dream of better things without remembering them upon waking. And everything, Rosalie, is fine. Everything is good with the world."

Peter waves a hand through the cigarette smoke, as if to change its shape. He goes on. "Yesterday in Rio, sixteen children were gunned down by a gang of off-duty policemen, hired by the city to clean up its streets. These kids live in sewers and drainage pipes. They're orphans, and the only expense the city will spare them is a bullet. Tell *them* things are fine with the world." He falls silent, finishes his cigarette and lights a new one with the stub of the old.

"I don't know what you're talking about," I say. "I don't know why I'm here. But if you tell me, maybe I can help?"

Nothing Heavenly

"I hope you can," he says. "I hope you do. Because time is running out."

"Why do I dream of angels and demons?"

"You already told me it wasn't a dream," Peter says. "You observe. And one day soon, you'll have to pick a side and join in."

"I'm nothing," I say, and the admission shocks me. Am I really nothing?

Peter shakes his head. "No. It could be you're more than everything. Now that question…that answer…you owe me, Rosalie."

I sit on the bed and draw up my legs, looking down at the nails of my clasped hands. They are grubby. I should clean them. There's a rudimentary shower behind the screen, and I promise myself that as soon as Peter leaves I will wash. I will cleanse myself, and perhaps in that act I'll uncover more of what Peter is trying to discover.

Why me?

"Why can't you just tell me?" I say.

He shakes his head. "The answer."

I nod, close my eyes. "The last evil thing I remember doing," I say. "Though who am I to judge?"

I love coffee shops. They're places that always seem removed from their location by the diversity of the clientele. The shop might be in the centre of a busy town, but there could be travellers from China and students from France in there, shoppers from London and a writer forging their way into their first imaginary world. They're imaginary worlds in themselves, where everyone is grounded by one thing: good coffee.

I was in the newest coffee shop in Soho. It was not a chain shop—a Portuguese couple had bought an old porn parlour and converted it—so it had a very distinct feel. Bare timber floorboards, huge old beer barrels as tables, an upstairs with leather sofas and comfortable chairs, a basement with subdued lighting and intimate table arrangements. One wall of the ground floor was lined with books, and the owners encouraged people to sit and read, happy if they spent a whole afternoon there. That's what I liked the most about this place: they weren't eager to shuffle you out of the door as soon as you'd finished. It was almost as if they made friends with everyone who came in, and they hated seeing friends leave.

I was sampling a new Columbian brew, leafing my way through a tattered old paperback, but I could not concentrate. I was distracted. I'd met Mark the weekend before, in a bar in the West End. Nice guy. We had a few drinks and swapped phone numbers, and that scrap of paper had quickly become greased and grubby from the amount of times I looked at it. I'd tapped the numbers into my phone a hundred times…but I never got as far as pressing 'Call'. I don't know why. Scared? Not usually. It was almost as if I didn't *want* someone special in my life. As if I knew things were going to change.

But then he called me, and they did.

The second time we met we got on so well, like old friends. Same likes, same dislikes, interests which complemented each other perfectly. And he stayed over for the night. Best fuck ever.

Nothing Heavenly

I drank my coffee, flicked to the end of the book, dropped it on the table and looked around. The Portuguese couple were both working again today. It seemed that they were always here themselves, and that was why the place was such a success; they didn't leave the work to surly Saturday teenagers. I nodded at the wife and she smiled back, busy with empty cups and cake-crumbed plates.

I finished my coffee. Considered having another. Thought of Mark nuzzling down between my thighs. I looked up and sighed, and then I saw the money on the table in front of me. Two pound coins, glinting like yellow eyes in the table's surface, catching the sun from the wide front windows. The last person sitting at this table must have left them as a tip. I leaned forward, put down my cup and scooped up the coins. I looked around guiltily, and locked eyes with a little black girl sitting by the window. Her mother was chatting animatedly with another woman, and the girl had been left alone to drink her milkshake and read a book. She must have been eight years old. She had seen what I had done, and she refused to look away.

I felt my face burning with shame, but I could not drop the money back on the table. If I did that it would look like my tip, and in a way that would feel even worse. So I pocketed the two gold coins, stood, picked up my bag and left, feeling the little girl's eyes on me all the way.

Have a great day, the Portuguese man said as I opened the door. *You too*, I replied, not looking back. That was the last time I drank coffee there.

"That's really not very evil," Peter says.

I shake my head, surprised to find that there are tears in my eyes. "It wasn't very nice."

"Do you understand evil?"

"Does anyone?"

Peter raises his eyebrows and stands from the chair, pacing the room.

"Do you?" I ask.

"Oh, I'm well aware of evil in its myriad forms," Peter says quietly, as if imparting a secret.

A shiver runs down my spine. I look down at my folded hands and imagine the gold coins sitting there. I can't even recall spending them.

"There's more," he says. "Much more. Between the kitten and the theft there's so much more you're not telling me, and I have to know, I *need* to know. Time is running out."

"Time for me?" I ask. "Are you going to take me out and kill me, like you did to Dimitris?"

Peter shakes his head. "I hope it wouldn't do any good." He leaves quickly, shrugging off other questions I throw at him, and then I am alone in the room once more. For some reason, it still does not feel like a prison.

Francine taps at the grille beneath the bed but I lie back down, close my eyes, and after a few minutes I see that things are getting worse.

—⚘—

Angels and demons...

I am standing on the corner of a street leading into Trafalgar Square. People are running past me away from the

Nothing Heavenly

Square, terrified, screaming, though many of them looking more stunned than scared. What they are seeing has not yet hit home. For some, it never will.

A few people glance at me and their expressions do not change. I look into the bookshop window beside me to see whether I'm part of the horror, but my reflection is inscrutable.

The sun is up in the east, casting its fresh rays across a waking London. I've always thought that this is the only time of day when the city looks clean, as if the daylight bathing it is dirtied as the hours go by. It's rush hour. Millions are going to work—

—*the sheep, the robots…*

—but today is no normal day for them. Today, they are truly waking up.

A battle is beginning. The previous visions I'd had were of night-time skirmishes, taking place in an alley and behind a row of shops. Hidden away from human sight like the dirty things, or things still best left unknown by the world at large. *So long as the fights are hidden everything is fine*, I think. *Up to now, everything has always been fine.*

Here, the fight begins out in the open.

I see the tall ones first, and they seem to be prepared for battle. There are twenty of them marching into the Square from the opposite corner to me. They're naked but for belts and leather bracings that hold knives, spears and other, stranger apparatus of war and pain. I cannot tell their sex, or whether they even have any. Some of them have long hair tied up in braids, interwoven with things that look from this distance like snakes. They twist at the air and taste the morning sun. The creatures walk in a line abreast, hefting their weapons, clicking and hissing in that strange language that does not bear understanding. They cross the road and hack down a cyclist who has stopped to stare.

Demons, then. Tall and monstrous and so dismissive of the man bleeding across their feet. He screams, and one of them turns back, kneels on his throat and crushes his windpipe.

"Demons," I mutter.

But then I see the other things in the Square, rising from the fountains around the base of Nelson's column. They must have been waiting in ambush. These are the shorter, squatter creatures, humanoid and yet devoid of any shred of humanity in the way they walk and move, insect-like. Their leathery wings are gathered at their backs, but even at this distance I see some of them fluttering as if eager to be employed.

There are dozens of these short creatures, and each of them has a human clasped to its chest.

Some of the people are screaming. Several seem to have drowned whilst being hidden in the fountains, hanging now limp and lifeless in the things' grasps. They are as ignored as the screams and pitiful struggles of those still alive.

So *these* are the demons. They use human shields, alive or dead they do not care. But why use human shields against creatures that so obviously do not care for humanity?

The last of those fleeing the scene pass me by, and a man grabs out for my arm. "Come on, love," he says. "Get the fuck out of here!"

"I'm here to watch," I say.

"Those things…what are they?"

Nothing Heavenly

I shrug. "Much more than us," I say. I look at him, his eyes open wide and he runs away. His footsteps leave me standing so lonely in the shadow of the bookshop.

The angels and demons—or whatever they are—enter into battle in full sunlight.

Several of the short things suddenly spread their wings and lift off, circling Nelson's Column as they gain height, the living people in their grasp screaming and struggling even more. But the struggles do not last for long. At first I'm not sure what I'm seeing—it's a trick of the light, perhaps, or the sun reflecting from distant windows, dazzling and confusing my vision—but as the third trapped human bursts into flames, I realise the truth.

They're not prisoners. They're weapons.

The flying things are silent, consumed by the flames and yet seemingly immune to their touch. The screams of the people are terrible, hot and bubbly with an agony I cannot bear to consider. The first one drops from the sky and lands several paces ahead of the advancing line of tall creatures, bursting apart and erupting flames as stomach gases ignite. Two more burning people are dropped. The first hits the line and one of the creatures goes down beneath it, arms and legs thrashing, its own peculiar clicking scream soon cut short by the burning fat oozing into its mouth. The second hits some steps and rolls, comes to a stop…and rolls again. He or she is still alive. Ablaze, broken by the fall, this person still has the strength to crawl a few feet across concrete toward the fountains. But the flames of their agony are destined never to be extinguished, and they become still, smoking greasily into the morning air.

Tim Lebbon

Two more burning people are dropped, coming apart on the ground, kicked aside by the tall things that are now running across the square. Knives are drawn, other weapons slipped onto their arms, spinning and catching sunlight, throwing it my way.

Demons and angels begin fighting hand to hand, though still I am not sure which is which. The flying things swoop down and hack at the tall creatures' heads with their sharpened claws. The tall things fight back with knives and spinning metal discs. There are screams and clicks and hisses all across Trafalgar Square. Bodies hit the concrete, most of them terribly ruptured and leaking their innards under Nelson's glare. Those short things still carrying struggling humans set them on fire—I still can't see how they do it—and shove the burning people ahead of them, aiming for their enemy. The tall fighters step aside and lash out with knives, slashing into thick brown hides, opening them up, exposing red insides to golden sunlight. Eyes burn yellow. The sun steams blood from the ground. A red mist rises, drifting across the Square until it touches my face, cool and sweet and intimate.

This is so much more than a dream. There are details that give away the reality of the scene: a 'Sale' sign stuck to a store window with blu-tac; a used condom lying in a doorway like a dead snake; a police helicopter in the distance, hovering over some petty misdemeanour when the real tragedy is happening here, now, in front of me.

Is this really the End of Times? I think. I watch the battle with no idea of who is winning. The surviving stocky creatures take to the sky and rise up, several of them landing on top of Nelson's Column and calling back down at their

Nothing Heavenly

enemies, mocking and taunting. *Angels fly*, I think. *Do demons? I can't remember. I can't know.*

The remaining dozen tall things slit the throats of the fallen—friend and foe alike—and then they stand around the base of the Column, looking up. One of them bathes in a fountain pool, washing blood from its pale skin. Another climbs onto one of the giant lion statues, sitting astride its neck and clicking what could be laughter at its brethren.

I move out from the shadow of the shop, stand on the edge of the road. I have crossed here several times before, always dodging through the several lanes of traffic, dicing with death as London cabbies weave their way from fare to far and couriers on bikes let you know they own the road. Now, the road is silent. There is no traffic. Either it has been stopped by the fleeing crowds…

…or this is happening all across London.

The possibility hits me like a punch between the eyes.

It's the End of Days, Peter had said. And for some reason, I am allowed to see.

"No!" I shout, and pigeons take flight. The winged creatures, too, dropping from Nelson's Column, drifting down and entering into a final showdown with their tall enemies. "*No!*" I shout again, running across the road, unsure why I'm doing this but knowing only that it feels right.

This time when they turn to look at me the fighting things do not look amazed or scared. They do not turn and flee or step back, mouths falling open. Instead, they forget their own battles and face up to me instead.

The Square is incredibly quiet. I can hear the crackle of flames from the dead people, and the intermittent *scrape,*

scrape of claws as something not quite dead drags itself from one place to another.

And then a growl.

A hiss, a click, and I feel hands shaking my shoulders.

—ɷ—

Peter steps back quickly as I come around. I sit up on the bed, still fully dressed, and Francine is tapping frantically at the grille.

"She's back!" Peter calls, and the tapping stops instantly.

He seems scared. His brow is furrowed, and his pupils are so dilated that his eyes appear black. I could fall into them, and I wonder what the people fleeing the Square saw in mine.

"Terrible dream," I say.

"It's moving on apace."

"I could smell it, taste it. I…" I put my hand up to my face and it comes away sticky with drying blood. It is not mine. It stinks, as though already beginning to rot.

"The fight is spreading quickly," Peter says. "Soon it'll turn. Now it's just angel against demon, but soon humanity will have a part to play. And that's when the real killing begins." He seems more concerned with me than what he's saying. He leans left and right, as if looking for wounds on my face, and I dart forward, reaching out for his lapels. He gasps and stumbles back, only preventing himself from falling by grabbing hold of the chair.

"Who am I?" I ask.

"Wh-what?"

Nothing Heavenly

"Who am I, that you keep me down here? Why me? Why Francine and Dimitris and whoever else you have prisoner?"

Confused, startled, perhaps he lets on more than he should. But perhaps not. I know already that he is wily and sly. "We can't know which of you it is, or even which is which, or…" He drifts off, smoothing back his hair and adjusting his tie.

"Had you rattled there, Pete."

He smiles. "You think so?"

I'm not sure but I nod.

He nods back. "Now perhaps some more questions. Time is short. There's only a few of you left."

"Not just me and Francine?"

"Of course not. Why, do you feel special?"

"Not right now. But if it turns out I am…maybe you'll be the first I come visit." That really does shake him. He actually turns pale, and for a few seconds I feel sorry for him. But then I remember Francine telling me about Dimitris, how long he'd screamed, and this bastard suddenly deserves everything he may get.

"You have no idea," he whispers.

"So give me a clue."

He sighs, looks down at his hands as if asking them for help. Then he looks up, and his lips are moving as he mutters something into the air.

"What?" I say. "Praying? Asking God for help in these End Times?"

Peter looks at me. "You've seen it, Rosalie. They're not dreams, they're real. You know exactly what's happening right now, and you need to accept it. You need to embrace it. And I have to find out quickly what I need to know."

"My mother," I say, closing my eyes and hoping she can be spared whatever horrors really are happening up there. *'Up there'?* I think. *Are you sure it's not 'Down there'? Are you really sure you even have an idea of where you are?*

"Did you ever wonder whether they were your real parents?" Peter asks.

I had, and I say so.

"Did you ever wonder why your father was so bitter with the world?"

"Yes," I say. *We're just rotting flesh…*

"You might be an angel, Rosalie," Peter says. "It's down to me to discover just how far you've fallen."

"I was adopted," Francine says. "My parents never told me but I always knew."

"How?"

"It was the way they looked at me. They never looked like that at anything they truly owned."

I am lying beneath the bed, pillow beneath my head. I'm still thinking about what Peter said. *You might be an angel, Rosalie…*

I'm no angel. I've done some bad things—stuff Peter doesn't know about, and which I can barely think about without going mad—and surely if he were talking literally then I would be *good*? But I remember those creatures going at each other in Trafalgar Square, and I wonder just how much the definition of 'good' can change between worlds.

Nothing Heavenly

"It's all coming to an end, isn't it?" I say.

"I don't know," Francine says. "I don't dream any more."

"You don't?"

Francine falls silent, and I lie here and listen to her breathing through the grille.

"I've never been a believer," I say after a while. "I don't believe in God or Satan, even though Peter tells me I'm seeing angels and demons at war. I always wondered how my intelligent friends could really put so much faith in something so nebulous and unlikely. It *amazed* me that they could believe in something like that. And I always wondered why, if there really was a God, there couldn't be proof."

"Proof denies faith," Francine mutters.

"And that's another bullshit get-out clause! Religion's full of them! Peter tells me about children slaughtered in Rio, and if I asked him how God could allow that he'd say *God moves in mysterious ways*, or *That's Satan's work*. Don't you ever think that if God really is there, if He showed us proof it would change the world forever? If everyone knew for sure that there was an afterlife—if they took Christ into their heart—then the world would be a better place? Wouldn't it?"

"Maybe that's too easy," Francine says.

"Yeah, too fucking easy. Why *shouldn't* it be easy? Why shouldn't God want us to have an easy time of life, instead of making it torturous and painful? Instead, He lets us kill each other in wars, poison the planet, rape and murder little children…so long as we have faith. Put a machine-gun in my hand and a crucifix in my mouth, and I'm doing God's work. Well fuck that. Fuck it!"

"Rosalie..."

I pause, willing my anger down. "I'm sorry, Francine. You're a believer aren't you?"

"I'm scared. I heard Dimitris...I'm scared, Rosalie." She's sobbing now, and I can smell her tears through the grille.

"Whose side is he on, do you think?" I say.

"Peter? I still don't know."

I think of the things I've seen fighting in the streets of London, and I don't know either. "Are there others?" I say. "Peter told me there were others."

"I'm not sure. I think so. I hear voices sometimes in the night. Outside the door."

"I saw outside the door," I say.

"What's there?"

"Nothing. An empty corridor. Other doors." *Yet this still doesn't feel like a prison*, I think. I close my eyes and feel the weight of the world all around me. They took me from the train, hauled me off while it was still roaring through the tunnels, and somehow while I was out of it they dragged me here. I must have been knocked unconscious...but I have no bruises, no cuts or scrapes. There's no sign at all that I fell from an Underground train travelling at forty miles per hour. And that thing holding me, calling me...?

"I think maybe we're in Hell," I say. And then the screaming begins. It's muffled by distance, dulled by the thick walls, yet I can feel the agony causing it.

"Francine!" I say quickly, fearing she had been dragged out while I was lying there thinking.

"One of the others," she says quietly. "This may go on for a long time."

Nothing Heavenly

We can't talk through the screams. They are spaced a couple of minutes apart to begin with, short, sharp cries that seem to penetrate my bones and cool my blood. I remain beneath the bed, comforted by the proximity of someone I have never seen, and I keep glancing at the door, expecting it to open and that short, inhuman thing to walk in. *A demon, I think, if I'm truly in Hell that's a demon. But what do they want of me?*

I cannot make out whether the screamer is male or female. Each silence is loaded with the potential for more screams, and each scream comes as a sudden shock. My heart is racing, sweat trickles down my sides. I want to press my hands to my ears but I am afraid of what I will miss; if I do that, I will be even more cut off from the world than I am now. I may not hear someone entering the room. I may not hear Francine tapping on the grille for me. And if they come to take her away as well, I will not know. Already, she is a friend.

The intermittent screams go on for what seems like hours, though I guess it's maybe fifteen minutes. Then they suddenly increase in frequency, the space between them narrowing from minutes to seconds, and there's a new panic in their tone that makes me want to add my own scream.

"Rosalie," Francine moans, and I tell her I'm there, and that's really all I can do.

The noise goes on. Five minutes, maybe ten, and I finally try pressing my fingers into my ears, but it's as if the sound is carried through walls and floor, transmitted through the stony heart of this place, and it enters my body through heels and shoulder-blades, travels through my bones, and my fingers force the sound harder and heavier into my ears. I take them away and the screaming is worse. I scramble from under the bed, trying to ignore Francine's whimpering, and pull the blankets and pillows down to me, wrapping them around my head. But somehow muffling the scream makes it even worse, less human, and I realise that I must hear.

I sit on the cold floor in the centre of that brightly painted room, and listen to someone die. The final scream is cut off halfway through. There are no more. The silence is terrible. It stinks of death, feels slick on my skin like the misting blood of the battling angels and demons, and I put my hand to my face, actually expecting to feel blood there but finding none.

Francine taps hesitantly at the grille, then louder, more insistent. I slip under the bed.

"I'm here," I say, and she begins to cry. "Was Dimitris like that?" I ask.

"Not so long. Not so bad." Her voice sounds wet and clogged. The grief and fear is real, and I finally find complete trust for her. She is not one of them, whoever they may be.

"Maybe they'll come for us now, while we're scared," I say. "While we're weak."

"I think I'm next," she says.

"No!" I say, but I have nothing to support my denial.

"Tomorrow," she says. "I got here the day after Dimitris, I got that much out of him at least. Tomorrow you'll hear me die."

"No," I say again, but I hate the weakness of my voice. I close my eyes and try to picture my mother, but she is a blur of memories and images that cannot seem to coalesce into a single whole. She is the smell of toast in the mornings, the feel of soft flesh and a steady hand stroking my hair,

Nothing Heavenly

the sound of metal tapping against glass as she stirs cake mixture, and the soothing song as darkness scares me awake in my childhood bed. "Mother," I whisper, but my voice sounds wrong. "Mum," I say. But the word does not suit the images and sensations, and I wonder again at what Peter had said about my real parents.

I hear a soft snore coming through the grille, vow not to sleep, and then I am in the midst of war once more.

It looks like late afternoon; the light has that tired quality, the air warm, the sky ready to welcome in night once again. But night is here already in the shape of Armageddon. And the battle is raging.

I am in a London park, floating on a lake in a tourist's rowing boat. The water is strangely placid, and ducks and seagulls bob on its surface seemingly unconcerned at the chaos surrounding them. I wish I could close my eyes and become just as calm, but I am seeing the End of Times all around me, I cannot tear away, and I fear that the fight is about to be brought to me.

There are hundreds of demons spread across the park. I think of them all like that now—the short ones and the tall ones—because neither kind seems particularly angelic to me. They are fighting each other, the shorter ones using fire, the taller things utilising the strange weapons I saw during the Trafalgar Square battle. Bodies lie here and there on the dry grass, leaking red and turning the soil into mud. There are corpses of people scattered around as well, those obviously caught up in the fight and unable to escape. Even from this distance I can make out the dreadful mutilation. Their limbs have been parted from their bodies, heads crushed, flesh scorched and blackened into dust.

And then I see the living people. Several of them are being held prisoner by the short demons, their clothes and hair bursting into flames as I watch, and burning and screaming they are shoved forward into the throng. The tall things bat them aside or fall beneath them, and the humans' screams mix with those of demons as their flesh burns and melts into one.

But there is also another group, huddled in the shelter of some large trees; a mother and father, and three children hanging onto their legs, terrified. I can see the look of hopelessness on the father's face, and I feel his pain. I want to shout to him, tell him to bring his family to the water and wade out to the boat, but I still my voice. I do not want to bring attention to them.

The demons battle and rage and kill. There seems to be no pattern to the fight, no front line; this is a free-for-all. Something screams and dies, something else cries out in victory. A horde of the short demons flies in overhead, passing above the lake and falling onto the blood-soaked ground to join in the battle. They hack with long claws, kick with horned toes, bite and punch and butt with their ridged heads. If they manage to get one of the tall things down onto the ground, there is no hope of it standing again. Whereas the tall demons usually seem to fight alone, the shorter ones seem happy to work in small groups, concentrating on one target until it is brought down and taken apart.

There is no sign of any mercy at work here. Nothing Heavenly. There is only wrath and loathing, the air thick

Nothing Heavenly

with venom. The red mist rises again, as if all the spilled blood is evaporating and thickening in the dry atmosphere. It drifts across the lake and leaves a sheen on the water's surface. Fish splash up to taste this new experience, and they immediately die and float belly-up. Ducks try to take off but the blood holds them like oil, sticking their feathers together, clotting in their eyes, pulling them down to be drowned.

The mist reaches me and I hold my breath, but I cannot do so for long. Fear has already left me breathless. I breathe in and close my eyes, but other than a sour taste at the back of my throat I notice little difference.

The man and one of his children are looking across at me. He half raises a hand, and I wave back. The gesture feels foolish, but it also seems to give him resolve. He talks to his wife, gestures across at me, pushes his family down behind a tree and then steps out toward the lake.

One of the flying things swoops down and knocks him to the ground. His wife rises, then sits down again, arms around her children. She is hiding their eyes, but she cannot turn away.

The man stands again and, running low, heads for the water. The flying thing has turned and it powers down again. The man punches out at it but it sinks claws into his back and shoulders, lifts him up, sets him alight and drops him toward a tall demon running from the trees. I hear him scream all the way down. The tall creature steps aside, lets the burning man hit the ground, then stamps down on his skull to silence him forever. It runs on.

I look at the woman hiding beneath the trees. She stares back at me, her eyes hidden by tears, and she too raises a hand to wave.

"Stay there!" I shout, but the noise of the battle has suddenly risen into a roar. More and more demons seem to be running and flying in from every direction, and when some of them turn to me I look around in a panic, searching for an oar, wondering how fast I can paddle or how deep I can swim.

The woman is standing, the children hanging onto her skirts like large crabs.

"Stay!" I shout, holding my hand palm-out. She waves and nods, stepping toward the lake.

To my right, some of the tall things have started striding out through the water toward me. The short demons jump on their heads and try to push them under, and there is an eruption of blood-stained water as a brief, furious fight takes place. The remaining tall demons then continue to push through the water at me, going lower, heads submerging until there is only a bubbly disturbance in the lake's pink surface.

"Stay there!" I shout at the woman, and I step from the boat. My foot touches the water and does not sink in. The woman emerges from the trees, falls beneath a tall demon, screams as it burrows into her chest and rips out her already burning heart.

I lock eyes with the youngest of the children, and I want to cry when they start to scream.

I step from the boat, and I wake up dry.

—⚘—

Peter is in my room. I have no idea how long he's been watching me.

Nothing Heavenly

"Is it bad out there?" he says.

"It's just a dream. A waking dream." I am panting, trying not to remember.

He looks at my face, leaning left and right again as if looking for an injury.

I sniff, smell the rot, put my hand to my face, bring it away, see the blood already turning sticky and black. "I must have coughed it up," I say.

"If you did you must be dying. Do you feel like you're dying?"

"I think I'm already dead. I'm dead, I don't really care, and now I'm in Hell." He begins to shake his head, but I cut him off. "It's Hell, and you're here to torture me for what I did. I'll have those visions forever, and now you're going to ask me about another evil deed I did when I was alive. Well, I've got plenty to tell you, Peter. Not enough for eternity, true…but they'll last us a good while yet. And I'll be interested to see what comes next."

He frowns, and for the first time I realise how dishevelled he has suddenly become. Gone is the smart suit, sharp lines and slick hair. He's rough around the edges. Not a mess, not totally, but he hasn't combed his hair in a while, and the suit looks as though it needs dry-cleaning and pressing. And his face has changed too; the confident grin has slipped, and in its place there's a frown that seems to be deepening by the minute.

"We don't even have a while," he mutters. "Not long left. Not long at all. Bad news, everything I hear is bad news."

"Are you losing?" I ask.

He looks at me, and his face is as open and vulnerable as I've ever seen it. I almost feel sorry for him. "You need to find yourself," he says. "Tell me what I want to know, look inside, find the truth, because if you don't—and if it's not you—then next time, maybe you won't come back."

Maybe you won't come back. I think of those tall demons walking through the lake toward my boat, and wonder what would have happened had I remained there.

I have no idea what sends me into those visions or pulls me back, but I have no desire to trust to luck.

"So why not just tell me what it is you want to know?" I ask.

"I *told* you!" He almost loses his temper, and that gives me a brief flush of satisfaction. "I told you Rosalie, you have to discover yourself. If I'm forced to do it for you, I don't know what the implications may be. I've been *instructed*. I've been *ordered*. Please Rosalie, search inside yourself."

"For what?"

Peter looks away. "To find how far you've fallen," he says, "and whether you've hit bottom yet."

I close my eyes and look inside, but I no longer know myself. There's fear, but it's distant again, like a forgotten pain. There's desire, but I no longer know what for. There's concern for my mother, but I no longer understand who she really is. Just a woman who raised me? I shake my head, and the movement stirs my visions and images into a confusing stew. If I don't even know what I'm looking for; how can I be expected to find it?

"It's almost too late," he says again, standing and reaching for the door. He pauses, looks back at me, uncertainty twisting his features.

"What?" I say.

Nothing Heavenly

"I'm certain it's you," he whispers. "So certain that I really don't need to do this. But it's necessary, and I'm sorry."

He opens the door, slams it shut behind him, and I know what is about to happen.

I slip under the bed and tap on the grille.

"Rosalie?" Francine says.

"Francine…" But I do not know what to say.

"Rosalie?"

I hear the door to her cell swing open.

"Oh no" she says. "Not yet. Not yet! Rosalie, I can't, I can't do this, help me!"

"Don't try to be a hero," I whisper through the grille, but the sounds of struggling and Francine's screams swallow my words. Her door slams and her screams fade. "Die quickly," I say. But I'm thinking only of myself.

—∞—

Francine does not die quickly.

Her screams begin, and they go on. And on. Spaced a few minutes apart at first, each successive cry comes sooner. Whoever is torturing her has experience now, and their timing is perfect. It takes almost an hour for the screams to become continuous.

I hear my name in there, and as much as I try to cover my ears, her voice is just as loud. Perhaps my imagination has taken over, charting the course of Francine's torture and death, filling in all the blanks that I cannot hear. It is unbearable. I look inside myself, searching for whatever it is Peter is so sure resides there, but I find nothing but the terror and pain I feel for Francine. I had never even seen her, but she is my friend.

I bury my head in the bedclothes, but still I hear.

Peter is doing this for me. Wherever she is now—tied in a chair, strung from the ceiling, pinned to the ground—Francine is being tortured for my benefit, to affect me. *I'm sorry*, he said as he left the room, and he knew what had to be done.

But nothing has changed, and nothing is changing. I feel no different. I haven't sprouted wings or horns, there's no halo above my head and I can't play the fucking harp, so *what the Hell is he trying to do*?

I scream, trying to drown Francine's agonised cries, but it does no good. Beneath my voice I hear her, and I can almost sense her agony. Almost. A time will soon come, I'm sure, when I understand what she is feeling.

I wish I could sleep, drift away and miss Francine's inevitable death. But the room holds me tight. It denies me that escape. The stark light keeps me awake, the white walls inviting me to picture a whole slew of tortures as if projected from my eyes.

Francine dies more than an hour after they took her away. I cry for the first time and then slip into sleep, cursing my inability to do so before.

There's still no change. I'm still Rosalie. I wonder how angry Peter will be when he returns.

—⚉—

I dream of my mother waving me away from her house that last time I saw her. There is something in her eyes which

Nothing Heavenly

I had always believed was sadness at my departure, but now in the light of memory I think there's much more there. It's sadness not just because she misses me, but because she knows that I am something she never truly had: a daughter. I'm not of her blood, her flesh, her soul. I turn away from the rearview mirror, unaccountably relieved that I am on my way back to London. The tear in my mother's eye glints at me all the way home.

I wish I could go to her now, hold her and tell her that she *does* have a daughter, that love is stronger than mere flesh and blood, and that she gave me more of her soul than she had any right to give.

But I wake alone in that room, and I know that I will never see my mother again.

—⚊—

"It may already be too late," Peter says. He's watching me as I wake up. I'm still crying from the dream, and fresh tears come when I remember Francine screaming my name.

"Good," I say. "Whoever you are, you deserve to lose."

Peter shakes his head, holding it in his hands in the universal gesture of hopelessness. "You still have no idea," he says. It's a statement, but I answer anyway.

"No. Not a clue. Other than you kidnap people from life and torture them in death."

"You're not dead," he says.

"Francine is."

"That doesn't matter."

"Bastard. You're a heartless *bastard!* You kill someone like her and tell me—"

"Francine wasn't someone, she was an imposter, a demon, sent to confuse and buy time so that…" He looks up at me and shakes his head again. "Do you not know that you're an angel?"

"I'm Rosalie," I say, "and I don't believe a word you say."

He looks at me for a long time, leaning this way and that to check both sides of my face, my neck, trying to see my back. He turns away then, staring at the wall as if divining some truth in its pure whiteness. "Then there's only one way," he says. "It'll likely fail. And if it does, all is lost."

"You're going to kill me now?" I ask. I'm not scared. Even after hearing Francine's cries, imagining what the hell they'd been doing to her, I am calm at my approaching fate.

"I hope not," he says. He is still staring at the wall, as if addressing someone other than me. "If we do, then we've got everything wrong. All the writings, all the prophecies, every little detail and nuance of each uttered and written word down through history: all wrong." He shakes his head. "I suppose it's possible that we've been duped…but how unfair!"

"Peter," I say. He turns to me. "I'm not scared. I never really have been, even when that thing was in here with me. I'll give you that much, at least."

He smiles, and his eyes seems to light up. "Then that's a *good* sign," he says. He leaves the room quickly, and from outside I can hear a low, deep *shush*, like the distant sea on a stormy day.

Nothing Heavenly

That sound continues for the next hour, washing against the shores of my perception.

I stand behind the small screen, strip and wash my whole body. There's no towel so I pull the sheet from the bed to use that instead. I'm quite sure I'll not be lying there again. As my hands smooth water and soap across the scars on my chest, I wonder whether I should have told Peter about them at the beginning of all this. Perhaps then things would have been different. Maybe Francine would still be alive, and maybe somehow I'd be back with my mother even now. Because I still think of her as my mother, whatever Peter told me and whatever my heart has always said. She changed my diapers, rocked me through the night when I was sick, saw me off to school, cleaned my clothes and cooked me dinner and read me books. She was there for me when my first boyfriend left me, and when I left my second. She had, I realise, been the cornerstone of my life, the solid rock about which my precarious attempts at living had swung back and forth, left and right.

I wonder what she knows about me.

Dressing, I feel eyes upon me. There's no voyeuristic intention, only curiosity. I look around the room, move to the mirror, and as I approach it a shadow passes quickly across its surface. The room is suddenly empty. I think of the thing on the train, and wonder how often that shape has been here since the first time that door was locked behind me.

I lie down beneath the bed and tap the grille, searching for Francine's ghost. I find none. *She was an impostor, a demon*, Peter said, but I suspect that there is much more yet to understand. Perhaps even he cannot know the full truth of things.

Am I becoming more accepting of what is happening? I've washed and dressed for my execution, my mind is calm and contemplative. I touch my chest through the blouse, the rough scars there, and I close my eyes and wish things could have been different.

Still, that sound. It permeates the room from all directions, radiating from the walls and breaking around me. I am like a rock in a stream. The sound is a sigh, never-ending and deep, and my eyes snap open. The sound continues, unaware of me. I'm relieved.

I pace the room, running my hands along the walls, feeling the smooth cool rock beneath. The weight of whatever surrounds this room still draws at me, pulling in every direction at once, and I wonder if it would eventually tear me apart. But there's no chance of that happening, as I know for sure that I will be away from here in a few heartbeats.

As if linked to that realisation the door opens. Peter steps in, and for a brief moment I see utter panic steal his face. His eyes melt open, his mouth droops, but then he sees me from the corner of his eye, standing at the junction of two walls. I smile at him, but he cannot muster a smile in return.

"Are you ready?" he says.

"Do I have any choice?"

"I hope so," he says. He walks from the room and I follow.

The corridor outside is grey and rough, nothing like the painted walls of my cell. There are other doors here, all of them closed, the rooms beyond silent at last. Many doors.

Nothing Heavenly

The corridor curves around and becomes lighter, and I realise that we are slowly climbing and approaching daylight.

And then the opening to outside is revealed, and all coherent thought leaves me for a while.

—⚜—

"You're made for something special," my mother once said to me. It was a time when my father had gotten drunk and stumbled off to bed, muttering about the unfairness of the world and how grim his life was. My mother's answer was always to point at me, but he would glance over, grumble some more and walk away. Still I loved him.

"I don't feel that," I said. I was sixteen years old.

"You will," my mother said. She hugged me, and I felt the coolness of her tears dropping onto my head. She seemed to cry a lot. I always thought it was my father that made her do that, but as I grew older I realised that it was me.

—⚜—

I have never seen so far. Any view I have ever observed always curves away to the horizon eventually, stealing itself around the corner of the world. Here there is no horizon, there is no corner, and I can see forever.

And forever is filled with demons. It is an ocean of living things. They stand shoulder to shoulder, a heaving, flickering mass of the short creatures from my visions. Close by I can see them in detail; their wings tucked in, faces aimed up, vicious mouths open and uttering the soft hiss that I heard in my cell. Their eyes hold many mysteries in their unknown colour. Further away, individuals blur into a grey mass. It moves, throbs like a naked brain, and across the vast plains steam rises from the assembled masses. Here and there fires seem to be burning, gushing greasy black smoke at the deep blue sky. I do not wish to see what is feeding these fires.

None of the demons are flying. Perhaps they reserve that only for war.

The hiss is slow, deep, never-ending. I wonder if I am simply hearing their breathing. There are millions of the things out there, covering the landscape and mimicking its gentle contours.

The distance draws away then, and I see what is close by.

Peter and I are standing on a narrow ledge in the face of a cliff. There is nothing on it but dead trees. I guess we are maybe a hundred feet above the plain. I edge closer to the sheer drop, look down into the faces of a thousand demons staring up. Their eyes open wide, and some of them reach up as if to grab me, their clawed fists opening wide.

I try to comprehend what I am seeing, but I cannot. The blue sky is smeared here and there with pinkish clouds that might be made of blood; I don't know why. To the left and right the cliff stretches out, rising higher in places, and here and there its uppermost edge seems to be cloaked in snow; I cannot understand. There are many other ledges like ours, some near and some far away, and they all bear the same dead trees. And it is the sight of one of these trees on a faraway ledge that breaks through my shock, and I begin to realise the truth.

The tree is moving.

Nothing Heavenly

I close my eyes and step back, seeking the safety of the tunnel leading to the cells. Peter is standing behind me. He places his hands on my shoulders, soft yet insistent. My eyes are still closed. Without sight I could be almost anywhere, and I imagine myself standing on the seashore in Cornwall. I had been there for a week with my mother just after my father died, staying in Polperro and trying to drown out grief by spending hours at a time watching the sea. We would sit on cliff-top benches and watch, listen, smell, taste the salt air and relish the wildness that place evoked. Its sense of timelessness—the eternal heartbeat of nature compared to our brief, unimportant lives—had comforted us then. Now, I no longer find reassurance of any sort in that idea.

But those trees…

I open my eyes and stare up at the crucifix to my left, and even from behind I know it is Francine hanging there. She is dead. Her bare skin is streaked with blood and gore, and her insides hang lower than her nailed ankles. To my left there are three more, to my right four, all of them bearing corpses in varying states of decay. One of these corpses must be Dimitris.

I feel sick. The smell hits me, and I cannot believe I didn't notice it before.

"What is this?" I say. "Where am I?" I thought I knew, but now nothing seems certain any more.

"Take it easy," Peter says. He's holding me up, hands beneath my armpits. I can smell his breath over my shoulder and it is neutral, not the scent of anything alive.

"You can't do that to me!" I say. I begin to sob, and Peter edges me forward toward the single empty cross.

"We've been lost for so long," he says.

I look left and right, up and down at the other ledges, the thousands of crosses all bearing human fruit. Most of it is rotting. The movement I saw on the distant ledge was some sort of flying thing, its black wings flapping as it nestled on the head of a corpse. I'm too far away to see what it is doing, and I'm thankful for that.

"This is Hell," I mutter, and behind me I sense Peter shaking his head.

"Nowhere near. We've been lost, Rosalie, and we've been searching for our only hope. You're the very last one of all the possibilities we discovered. Perhaps that's cruel fate, or maybe there's a message in there, but there is no more hope after you. Your visions are alive and true, and soon we'll know only defeat."

"But those things," I say, pointing down at the hissing masses. "Those things…millions of them…all ready to fight!"

"They need a leader. They need their Messiah."

I can hardly breathe. My chest is tight, the scars there burning as if renewed, and the sin behind them scorches the insides of my skull.

"You think I'm the daughter of God?"

"God is mad. I think you may be an angel, the daughter of Humankind, its Saviour. But we have to know for sure."

He steps back and four of the short demons take his place. They grab me, their wings unfurl and they lift me up, and our flight is smooth and soft. *Angels*, I think. I look at their fearsome faces and leathery wings, and even the truth seems far away. I struggle but it is hopeless. I am weak from fear, drained by shock. The only sound from the angels is the flap of their wings. I turn and look into one of their faces and

Nothing Heavenly

its eyes are wide, incomprehensible, deep pits of wonder. "I'm no angel," I whisper, but the thing's only answer is a soft hiss.

They manoeuvre me before the final empty cross and drift back, holding me splayed against the rough wood. I notice that there are pale green shoots on the cross-bar, wrinkled leaves and black flowers almost too sick to be called alive. The cross is a living thing. They all are. They have been growing here in preparation for this moment, and I wonder how my blood may feed its denuded, dried trunk. Glancing over at Francine's cross—I can view her from the side now, see the ruin of her face, chest and stomach—I notice that her blood has simply run down the timber to the stone ledge. There it has pooled and turned black. The cross is as dead as Francine.

Peter appears before me, and in his hand he carries a heavy mallet and three iron pins. They are thick, and at least eight inches long. He looks up at me. "If you are what I hope you to be, forgive me," he says.

"If I'm not?" I say.

"Then we're all dead." He shrugs off his rumpled jacket and sweat-soaked shirt, and the wings that spread out from his back are like nothing I have seen before. They are thin and membranous, veined and opaque like a dragonfly's wings, graceful. I see the obvious satisfaction as his discomfort is relieved. He flaps his wings and rises easily before me. His chest is criss-crossed with thick white scars, and for a crazy few seconds I think he is someone just like me. But these are the marks of battle. I can see the proud evidence of cuts and burns, and my own scars throb in shameful sympathy.

Tim Lebbon

The short angels suddenly pull back hard, forcing my arms against the cross-bar, my hands splayed and wrists bared to Peter's approach.

"No," I say. Peter cannot look me in the eye. "Peter, no!" I surprise myself and begin to cry.

He places the tip of the first spike against my left wrist, raises the hammer and looks me in the eye. "Don't die."

—⚭—

Maybe the pain drives me out. Or perhaps it is a vision involving the death and agony of others that succeeds in insulating me against my own.

I am above London. My body is not there—that is somewhere far different from here, being nailed to a living cross—but my consciousness drifts over the burning city of old. I can smell the flames, the tang of fear, the stench of cooking flesh. I can hear the screams and calls from the streets below. I taste the mist of blood on the air. And I can see what London has become. It is a battleground now, a burning, belching mess of fire and smoke.

The Thames is a mucky silver line below me, spotted here and there with floating bodies and those still struggling in vain against impending death. Several tourist boats float out of control down the river, decks spotted red with the mess of dead humans. Further up the river I see a burning slick spreading from one bank to the other. The London Eye has tumbled and lies in the water, a large river cruiser trapped beneath its heavy steel structure. There are splashes and explosions, and downriver a battle seems to be underway, tall demons and the shorter, winged angels exchanging fire

Nothing Heavenly

from one bank to the other. The demons throw weapons of some sort—knives, lances, exploding things—while the angels still seem to be relying on human fodder for their fiery attacks. Many burning people fall short and steam out in the water, floating downriver as blackened masses for the things of the sea to feed upon.

Don't die, a voice says, and I am suddenly somewhere else. St Paul's Cathedral is in ruins. Its great dome, survivor of the Second World War, has a huge hole in one side. I can see a dozen angels hunkered down on the dome's internal walkways, while demons climb the façade outside and prepare to attack. I want to shout a warning but cannot. My voice is somewhere else, and it's probably already screaming. Flames erupt from the dome and things cry out as they die.

Don't die, the voice says again.

I am down in the streets now, in the thick of it, a disembodied consciousness drifting out of control. I pass by a demon's head just as it is enveloped in flame. The heat shoves me away, straight toward a line of angels. The humans they are holding struggle for freedom even as they are set alight. The angels shove them forward and steer them—screaming, burning, melting—toward the demons around me. I pass right through a halo of flame and spin off along the street, ricocheting from a wall and entering the open door of a public house. Inside there are three men gathered at the bar, drinking pints of beer and smoking like it's going out of fashion. They are chatting, though I cannot quite hear their words. They seem resigned. One of them slips behind the bar and refills their glasses, adding a ten pound note to a small pile next to the till. One of his friends looks around at the sound of an ear-piercing scream from outside, but the other two merely stare into their glasses. He strokes the condensation from the outside of his glass and downs his real ale in one long swig. He smacks his lips and lights another cigarette.

I drift through the pub, passing the empty restaurant at its rear. Into the back alley, past a man sleeping in a pile of rubbish bags, past two dogs fucking in the twitching shadow of a burning building, and then I am back out in the street. Here I find some people fighting back, and much as I admire their bravery I cannot help thinking they would do better to join the men in the pub. Enjoy themselves, while they still can. Drink to happy memories.

They are desperate. Several men are carrying shotguns, and they go against a gang of the lanky demons with gusto. One demon takes a double-barrel to the face, shakes its head and runs at the shooter, grabbing him and caving in his head with his own shotgun. More gunshots, more running, and the inevitable screams echo after me as I drift further along the street.

Higher, and I see the landscape of fire that London has become.

Lower, and I feel the pain of this grand city's inhabitants as they run through the streets, cower in doorways or shops, die.

Lower still and I am in the Underground. There are thousands of people down here, lining the platforms or trooping into the tunnels. But there is no hiding from Armageddon. Even as the visions start to fade out, and pain begins to kick in, I hear the hisses and clicks of angels and demons fighting on the downward escalator.

Hell finding its own level.

Nothing Heavenly

—❦—

"Don't die," Peter says. I open my eyes and he slides a thin blade in between my ribs.

The pain surprises me. Away in the vision I was sheltered from physical sensations, experiencing only the sensory input from that Hellish London. Now, looking down at my body, I realise that quite a time must have passed. My flesh is pouting in several places where the knife has been thrust in. A curl of intestine is bulging from my stomach. My clothes have been sliced away from me, and I am naked and bloody under the gaze of a million angels.

"Don't die," Peter says again, withdrawing the blade and closing his eyes at the gush of blood that follows.

I groan, my flesh cooling as more blood pumps from my wounds. That stab was close to my heart, and he must have ruptured a major artery. The blood is thick and dark. Peter steps back and watches, eyes wide. Perhaps he expects me to cure myself. Maybe he's waiting for the lips of those cuts to stitch together, healing from the inside out as I will myself well again. But I am surely not who he believes. I can't be. Not knowing what I know, and having lived such a sinful life.

My head droops and I see those old scars between my breasts, and they seem to be weeping blood. But that's no surprise; they were always so fresh.

The pain roars in fully then, welcoming me back from my brief sojourn with gusto. My wrists are on fire, my shoulders and arms seemingly melting with the tension, my crossed legs shaking as the flesh of my ankles rips, the bones snap. My own weight is killing me. I find it hard to breathe and suddenly facing death for real, I wonder what possessed me.

Did I really mean to do that? I think. Those old wounds on my chest seem to welcome the new blood.

"Don't die," Peter says. He steps forward and pushes the blade into my throat.

I want to scream, but metal blocks the way. I try to twist away, withdraw from the pain, but he has me pinned there like the rarest butterfly. And even there—in agony, facing death—I shift my bare back against the tree to make sure there is nothing wrong.

"*Please* don't die," he says, and there's a note of desperation in his voice now. He sees the blood, recognises my pain, and perhaps he finally knows the truth in my eyes.

He whips the blade from my throat and goes at my chest and stomach, again and again, forever beseeching me not to die.

"One more evil," I say, and I fade away to the sound of angels hissing and Peter sobbing wretched tears of failure.

—⚋—

My father left, and my mother cried, and I realised that I knew neither of them.

I was an empty vessel, drained of interest and expectation and anything approaching hope. My last boyfriend had left me after taking out his frustration on my face. My nose was broken. I left it like that, slightly twisted, hoping it would heal into a permanent testimony to my wasted life. Ambition

Nothing Heavenly

was dead in the water, and self respect had drowned in the years of failed relationships and bad dreams.

Bad dreams. They came thick and fast, and though I often woke up screaming I never could recall them in full. There were hints of immense spaces, a woman pinned to a tree on a hill, the hill itself ripping open and exposing its guts to view. Other than that the nightmares were a mystery, but they left me with the feeling of incessant dread. Wandering through the day, I caught glimpsed reflections of shadows following me. I hated shop windows and passing cars because of what they threw back. I was lost. I was empty, once so filled with potential and now drained, useless, ready to die.

To die. A vague concept became an idea, and the idea became an obsession.

The dreams always accompanied me up out of sleep, and as I drifted off eighteen hours later it was images of my own death that welcomed me back down. The images were mostly as gentle as death can be; drowning in a country lake, or dying in my sleep, my heart giving out to those awful nightmares at last.

I mentioned suicide to a friend, and she told me it was a sin, and I laughed. I was an atheist. And I was a hollow spot on the world. The only true sin was keeping myself alive and taking up space.

It was easier than I thought. I had feared that the preparations would scare me off, that the act of closing my front door, climbing the stairs and sitting on my bed—all for the last time—would flick some switch inside. But the only change as I looked at the splash of pills nestled in my palm was a stronger desire to go through with this.

Tim Lebbon

I swallowed the pills and drank half a bottle of whiskey. I slept. I woke with a hangover, and an idea that something awful had been watching me sleep.

I ate more pills and drank more Scotch, but this time I could not drift away. My eyes remained wide open, and I sensed the shadows of my nightmares waiting for me in the dark. I saw them every time I blinked.

There was a razor in the bathroom, and I stamped on it to retrieve the blade. Slitting my wrists did not hurt; the alcohol had dulled my senses. Blood sprayed the pale yellow tiles and blossomed in the full bath. I sat on the lowered toilet seat and sliced again, splitting veins and watching the blood flow. It soon stopped. I grew faint, confused, and banged my head as I fell from the toilet.

When I woke up later my wounds had closed, leaving only thin white scars behind. My hangover was immense, so that every step I took down toward the kitchen pulsed like an explosion in my head. Each explosion revealed a nightmare waiting for me; that woman on the hill, and the hill opening itself to view.

In the kitchen I grabbed a carving knife and fell on it. I was desperate by now, my resolve still amazingly strong, and I felt the knife go in. And again. And again.

When I woke up the sun was shining, and the phone was ringing.

I never tried to kill myself again. I was too scared.

—⁂—

There is nothing, and I wonder if this is death.

Nothing Heavenly

I have never imagined such emptiness. All I am is thought. I feel no pain from the wounds Peter has inflicted upon me. I hear nothing from the countless angels assembled before the cliff face, and I cannot taste the blood-mist on my skin. I smell nothing, and when I open my eyes there is only a blank before me. Not even darkness. It is as if I exist as pure potential, and all I have is a mind with which to realise it.

I'm dead at last, I think, but then I remember Peter's refrain: *don't die, don't die*. If I am dead then all hope is lost. The demons will win, and whoever they fight for will have the Earth. Satan? Fighting against God? I cannot believe that. I have never believed it, and yet what I have been through should have battered that disbelief from my skull. *God is mad*, Peter had said.

God help me, I think, and nothing changes. I recall another of those phrases from the Bible, another get-out clause that I always believed aided those with faith in fighting off the sneering doubt of those without: *God helps those that help themselves*.

There is a twinge of something that could be pain.

I think of my mother crying those tears of betrayal after father left, and I feel a deep sense of shame at what I did so soon after. I tried to kill myself, just when my mother needed me most. She may not be my flesh and blood, but she is always my calm port in a storm. How selfish of me. How awful. I'm glad I did not succeed.

I couldn't die, I think. *However hard I tried, I couldn't die.* For several years after my suicide attempt I tried to rationalise the fact of my survival. It had been a call for help, I thought, not a concerted attempt to die. But however hard I tried to believe that, I remembered all those pills, that razor, that knife.

The scars on my chest were always there to counter any such doubts.

Another niggle somewhere at the heart of me; pain, struggling to come through. I welcome it in and it grows rapidly, a burning bright light against the emptiness. For an instant as that agony drives the darkness back, I see the massive nightmare shapes flailing against it. Too fast to make them out properly, too quick for me to make sense of form, I know only that they are gone for good, fooled by my sudden waking.

I open my eyes and the light is so bright. There is a roar, like the largest wave breaking against the highest cliff, and from closer by a gasp that I hear above all else.

"The Angel Rosalie!"

My eyes become accustomed to the light and I see Peter kneeling before me. I have come down off the cross, somehow, and I'm standing on my own feet. As I catch Peter's eye he averts his gaze.

"Peter?" I say. My throat is hoarse and sore, as though I have not spoken for two thousand years.

"My Angel," he says.

I look down at my body. The wounds are still there but they are closed, pink and fresh yet no longer spewing blood. I run my hands over my neck, my chest, my stomach, and I cannot tell the difference between new wounds and old.

"I sinned," I say. "Peter, I tried to kill myself."

He looks up at me, never quite meeting my eyes. "That only makes you more human," he says. "The daughter of Humanity." Peter stands and faces the assembled angels,

Nothing Heavenly

raises his hands and shouts. His voice carries forever, heading for the horizon that still shows no curve. *"The Angel Rosalie!"*

The sea before me roars. And then the waves begin.

London is on fire, and the demons think they have won. I sense the murder and rape and unbridled slaughter going on below, and I wish I could have accepted the truth sooner. But I also realise that the process of believing was an important one. It has made me stronger. It has made me as strong as I can be.

I sense the demons looking up as one. I feel their gaze upon me as I swoop down on Heavenly wings. And behind me, united by their Saviour at last, a million angels hiss their song of war.